For Christine

The Stepping-Stones

Best wishes

Barbara J Rane

Barbara Rane

Paragon Press Publishing, 27 Greenhead Road, Huddersfield, West Yorkshire HD1 4EN
an imprint of Vista House Ltd.

e-mail: info@paragonpress-publishing.com

Website: www.vistahouse.co.uk

Paperback ISBN 1-84199-100-7

In memory of my parents
Hilda and Nicholas Harland
With love and gratitude
And grateful thanks for a
Thousand happy memories

"Children's children are a crown to the aged, and parents are the
pride of their children."

Proverbs 17:6

Chapter 1

Silence.

Frederick Thackeray gazed down at his wife's pale face, still damp from the exertion of expelling their child from her womb. He was aware only of the scene enacting itself in front of him. Everything else slipped away, including the assault of wind-born rain on the bedroom window. Nothing ever again could compare with this moment; the last few minutes had succeeded in turning his entire world upside down. Nothing would ever be the same again, he realised.

Twenty minutes earlier Faith Thackeray had given life to her child; and ten minutes later had given up her own. Traumatised and unable to take it in, Frederick stood as though sculpted beside the still form of his wife on the bed, his statuette figure forgetful of the need to breathe.

Call himself a doctor! The man was a fool. The idiot didn't know what he was talking about. Faith was exhausted. That was all – nothing else. She was exhausted and probably asleep. Yes – that was it, asleep. It was a mistake – a stupid one at that – a dreadful, dreadful mistake. Faith would open her eyes in a moment.... she would.... if they would only wait....

Please God – don't do this – not this! Let her breathe and open her eyes!

Frederick shot an irritated glance at the skeletal hand fidgeting at his elbow, his glazed eyes struggling to take in the elderly features of its owner. Ellie Rodley, his stooped little neighbour, had assisted with the birth and now strove to coax him past the bed, blood-soaked and the pillows damp with the sweat of childbearing.

Surprised he was still upright let alone able to walk, Frederick allowed the old woman to lead him to the bedroom door from where his eyes were drawn like magnets to the porcelain face on the pillow. The facts registered, his face contorted and futilely he searched Faith's face for movement. But she was gone. He had a sudden impulse to go to her, scoop her into his arms, but that would invoke a memory impossible to expunge from his mind. He did not want that; he did not want to remember Faith as an inert object in his arms. Frederick turned away and finally giving in allowed himself to be guided from the room.

The doctor emerged from the bedroom to find him slumped in the paint-chipped wicker chair on the landing. He placed the infant in his arms and watched as the vulnerable person succumbed to pain-filled weeping when the tiny bundle stirred in his arms and the silence splintered with the shock of newborn crying.

The sight of grieving tears splashing the child's face evoked comment though the doctor felt the need to concentrate on his own breathing before seeking the eye contact that was not awarded him. "She's a fine child Frederick. That's a lusty cry you're hearing." He stood a pace behind, discretely wiping his hands on a blood-soiled towel. No amount of experience made one immune to this, the worst possible outcome. He had known the Thackerays a long time, a devoted couple, he always joking, she just as quick though rarely getting the better of him. All they needed to complete their happiness was a child Faith told him one morning in the surgery. He remembered sharing her joy on the confirmation of her pregnancy.

Retracing his steps to attend to the body he wondered how the husband would cope on his own and saw the same question etched in the lined face of the neighbour.

Abandoning everything else, Ellie Rodley saw to the baby's needs for the next few days whilst her once lively neighbour took up occupancy of the chair adjacent a framed photograph of Faith; his face unshaven, his hair unkempt and eyes refusing to see anything beyond his own private thoughts. It grieved her to witness the fine-looking man so changed.

On the third day Ellie was preparing to bathe the child when, after showing little interest, without a word Frederick took the naked child from her. Callused hands went hesitantly to explore the downy head of hair resting in the crook of his freckled arm. Then, as though defying sorrow, a narrow smile slid to his face. Tiny, exquisitely formed fingers had grasped his thumb; the tenacious grip truly remarkable given the size of their owner. Consumed with emotion he drew the baby closer, and sobbing uncontrollably, promised to give her the world.

The world? With a measure of relief Ellie retreated to the scullery shadows.

Six weeks later, Frederick christened his daughter Hope, the name signifying a following on from Faith and his own personal wish for their child, and for the next five years he worked hard to give Hope the world – or at least the best he was able to provide.

Ellie delayed speaking to Frederick. She adored the bubbly five-year-old but her husband's declining health demanded her time.

This blow was only tempered when Frederick's sister persuaded him to move in with her and her husband in the village where she and Frederick had grown up. The cottage was small. It would be a squeeze but they would be welcome, wrote Isabel.

Mowlem held innumerable memories and the thought of Hope's growing up in the countryside was appealing. Furthermore it would be good for her to gain a mother figure in Isabel.

Mowlem – a beautiful village with a river running through it. Very little had changed in the last hundred years and one might imagine there had been a time-slip. The elderly still remembered children gathering after school by the dairy gate clutching large enamel jugs, waiting for the cows to be brought up from the fields. Those same tenants of the Tudor-style, tied cottages recalled gas mantle lighting and baths in front of bright log fires. Today's villagers too had employment on the estate, or were connected in some other way to Tarnville, the stone-built house standing in vast acreage, a landmark in the area and the home of Sir Charles Lurdmayne, the local landowner.

In his youth Frederick had taken his easel and tubes of colour to the riverside to paint. Such peaceful, tranquil moments borrowed from what now seemed an immeasurably long time ago.

Frederick's search for employment proved difficult. He found nothing in the immediate vicinity but eventually acquired work at the far side of Stillingford, separated from Mowlem by the river and gentle hills, selling crockery and other household items from a handcart. Working away meant having only the weekends with his daughter. But two weeks later when Hope climbed on to his lap he buried his face in her hair, instantly detecting change. Hair that had

7

once felt gritty and smelled lightly of city soot now shone with sunlight and bore the subtle fragrance of meadow flowers. His child was thriving under Isabel's care.

He had not seen his 29 year-old sister since Faith's funeral. Her appearance shocked him. Her life had not been easy; nevertheless he was disturbed by what he saw.

Little shape showed beneath the faded print dress draping her skinny frame, and once-glossy hair already showed tracings of fading colour verging on grey. The girl had not lingered and the emergence of an older woman had already taken place. Isabel now had ownership of her grandmother's hands, reddened and rough with toil: scrawny, coarse, unattractive hands, the fingernails flecked with bruising and torn from daily drudgery. When her husband switched from working the land to managing the dairy his hours had changed, enforcing Isabel's need to cope alone with the smallholding, tending the vegetables and few livestock of pigs, rabbits and hens. Frederick would have helped but the holding provided little money as it was and certainly insufficient to sustain a further wage.

His youngster cuddled closer and Frederick wished he knew what life held in store for her – an echo of Isabel's lot? Never! If only for Faith's memory he must protect her from that. In that instance he determined that Hope's fresh youthfulness should not be snatched away only to be remembered down the years in sad, lonely moments. His arms tightened protectively round his child. He had been right to bring her here though must guard against her slipping unnoticed into village-life toil, poverty and possible obscurity. If he allowed that he would have failed Faith and it would have been better if Isabel had not taken them in – better if she had turned them away.

Burdened by responsibility his insides lurched for the child in his arms and the cruel drama of circumstance that had delivered such insecurity. He relaxed his hold to gaze into the bright green eyes smiling at him. He would give his daughter a dream. Happiness was a right, not a privilege. Everyone should have a dream. Otherwise what was life about?

From that tiny seed grew Frederick's dream for Hope.

It was Saturday. Straight after breakfast Frederick led Hope the short distance to the river. Her discoveries gave him enjoyment beyond measure and actively encouraged her hunger for knowledge, prompting her curiosity, all the while smiling at her urgency. He was as enthusiastic as Hope when she paused to marvel at the hundreds of tiny lace curtains, enhanced by beads of pale, clinging mist, draped neatly along the hedgerows. Whilst she did not appreciate the intensity of the labours involved in fashioning the exquisite crocheted doilies – more intricate even than those her Aunt Isabel worked – Hope was loath to disturb their occupants; creatures she preferred not to think about. A cousin had recently thrown her into squirms of hysteria with an appearance in her bathtub.

Even at this tender age it was clear to Frederick that Hope had her mother's sparkling disposition as well as Faith's colouring and beauty.

Hope glanced around, aware of the quietness disturbed only now and then by short bursts of birdsong deep within the hedgerow. The silent wrap of the fields felt strangely comforting as she followed in her father's measured footsteps, all the time carefully avoiding the spiders' gauzy webs. Her young legs strode over rain-soaked tumbles of undergrowth with mischievous tentacles that reached to deposit icy droplets to run unpleasantly down her legs. But it did not matter – she was with her Dad.

The river was swollen, its banks torn by autumnal rains. Aided by his daughter, Frederick searched the embankment for large stones. Satisfied, he chose a site carefully.

"Now mind you don't come too close or you'll get wet. I'm going to put these five stones in the river to make stepping-stones. One for each of your birthdays, and I'll place another in the river every time you have another birthday. They'll be your stepping-stones because they're magic."

"How magic are they?" Hope squirmed with delight at the idea.

"They're right magic, and when they're all in place you'll be able to walk across the river and into your wonderful future." Overtaken by his thoughts he completed his task in silence.

Throughout the activities Hope danced about on chubby legs. "My own future," she squealed, following the direction of his gaze to the far embankment where Tarnville rose majestically to predominate the scene. "How many birthdays will it take to get into my future?"

Unrolling his trouser legs Frederick considered the span of water. "I reckon 18 should just about do it."

Hope could hardly wait for him to put his shoes and socks back on so she could go to tell her aunt about her magic stones.

Chapter 2

The late afternoon sun escaped briefly behind a cloud. Hope was sitting on the riverbank beside the stepping-stones and shivered with the disappearance of the warm mid-summer rays. This was her spot, the place where she could often be found and without fail every Friday when her father was due. They had met in the same spot every week for as long as she could remember. Theirs was always a joyful reunion and the expectancy of his homecoming tingled the air.

From habit she counted the stepping-stones, one representing each of her birthdays. She counted 16. Another would be added next week and the last stone would be put in place next year in readiness for that promised symbolic walk across the river into her future. A tangible display of her father's love and aspirations, the stones would always remain dear to her.

In her younger years her father made up stories about her stepping-stones and each Friday there would be a new one for when he tucked her into bed. Sometimes pixies and fairies played a role but in an attempt to make her mother known to her, he frequently incorporated a fond mention of Faith. Because she longed to be picked up in his strong, muscular arms, Hope had waited on the riverbank every Friday for the most important person in her life.

She studied the hill for the familiar bob of his sand-coloured head then suddenly saw him and at once her arms began circling above her head whilst straining to catch the sound of his baritone voice. He enjoyed singing, particularly if he had stopped off at The Fleece before making the trek home. Today though she could hear nothing save the call of a distant bird to its mate and the soothing sound of the diamond-bright water lapping against the stepping-stones in its path. It was not until he drew nearer that Hope saw he was labouring to carry a heavy object.

"Evening darling!" Frederick spluttered five minutes later, struggling across the wooden bridge further upstream.

She was astonished to see he clutched an Imperial typewriter.

Promising to buy her a machine one day, he had encouraged her to keep a daily account of her life in the village, which he looked forward to reading each weekend. Through those notes he learned how one of the missing piglets had been found curled up in the dog-basket with Hattie Middler's elderly border collie and how his daughter cried when the other was found drowned in a ditch two days later. He read how much she enjoyed the barley-sugar sticks left beside her bed early one Monday and reading on he accompanied her to pick bluebells beneath an azure sky when the air was filled with the strong, pungent scent of fresh, green living things.

All the important and tiny inconsequential things that go to make memories, good and bad, were recorded there. Those simple essays helped him share the days he was away.

Hope remembered his promise and could not take her eyes off the gleaming black machine. "I wondered why you weren't singing. Now I can see why – not enough puff!"

Frederick grinned. "It's for your birthday. I know it's a bit early like – but didn't want another'un to snap it up." He spotted the machine in a shop window last week. When he passed yesterday someone else was admiring it and without further hesitation he strode inside and laid his money on the counter. It had left him short but it was worth it to see his daughter's delight.

That night Hope worked on her notes. Typewriting was more difficult than she had imagined. The letters were all over the place but by morning she knew enough to impress her father. Frederick had another surprise. He took her across the village to talk to her Head Teacher about having typewriting lessons after school.

Hope proved to be a keen student. Within a short space of time Josephine Bradley had to admit that she had taken Hope as far as she felt able in the field of typewriting – not one of her specialised areas, she had been quick to point out. Hope might care to pursue a proper, structured secretarial training at evening classes in Braefield, she suggested. Frederick mirrored his daughter's eagerness and saw the suggestion as the start of their dream: Hope's escape route from the submergence beneath village-life toil.

When shown her first shorthand outlines Frederick's head bobbed with satisfaction. Shorthand – *Pitman's New Era* – it sounded just grand. He was so proud, and for several wordless moments was reduced to tapping the pad filled with her first attempts and grinning foolishly with disproportionate gratification.

"Shorthand - well, I never," he managed eventually, overwhelmed. "If only your mother could see this. She always said, 'Make the most of every opportunity.' You're certainly doing that. You'll get a good job in the city one day. That'll show them."

It was not that he belittled the efforts of others; he simply suffered the same parental view as every parent before him. There was no doubt in Frederick's mind that his daughter was unique and the world had been created just for her.

"Dad! I never want to leave home and work in the city. I love it here and I like my job." On leaving school Josephine Bradley had engaged her to work in the school office, an arrangement that worked well for them both. "I'll crack this shorthand – you wait and see."

"Aye – I've no doubt you will." He laughed. "I don't doubt that for a minute."

Catching the humour twinkling in his eyes she tossed her head back and chuckled. "Perhaps Mrs Bradley will make me School Secretary – or something."

Hope never ceased to amaze him. He admired everything about her. He was immensely proud. Slender and poised, she had grown into a strikingly attractive young woman. Abundant blonde hair, which turned to a remarkable pale red during the winter months, moved with her every movement making its own magnificent display down her back not dissimilar to pale, shimmering candle flames. But it was her eyes one most appreciated. They were green like the promise of spring and brimming over with expression as her mother's had.

His daughter would soon be 18 – how the years had flown. He still thought of her as his child but with Isabel's careful prompting he had begun to realise the child was almost a woman and soon young men would pursue her in courtship.

He pretended not to notice the heads that turned when she walked into Chapel each Sunday, but the pride shining openly in his ruddy features betrayed him. Courting, marriage – he wondered how he would feel when the time arrived and he was not the only man in her life.

Chapter 3

Hope removed the last batch of baking from the black-leaded range and wiped her hands. She had baked alongside her aunt all afternoon for her birthday picnic tomorrow.

Isabel watched her niece drift over to the parlour window. "Never mind pet. Y'Dad won't expect you on an evening like this. You'd be soaked in minutes of setting off." Sensitive to the sudden drop in temperature she rubbed her bare arms as a sudden crack of thunder shook the few china pieces displayed on the dresser. "It's more like November than June. If he's any sense he'll not make the journey this evening but leave it till tomorrow."

Hope could not disagree but of all the Fridays for there to be a storm it had to be this one; the evening they planned to ease the last stone into position for tomorrow's river crossing.

Necks twisted towards the door when it flew open moments later but it was Bert coughing deeply who lurched unsteadily into the room, a small flurry of white plaster floating to the floor from where the doorknob had struck the wall.

"It's a filthy evening out there and no mistake. Owt good for dinner?" His words were slurred by whisky, which did not go unnoticed by his wife.

His arrival brought a cessation to Isabel's relaxed mood and she began scraping together pastry trimmings from beneath the table. "Rabbit and leek pie. Won't be long – by the time you've had your swill it'll be about ready." Her forehead struck the sharp corner of the table.

"Buns, tarts...." Bert prodded the wire trays. "Don't want none of this 'ere rubbish."

"No – Bert. The fancies are for the picnic tomorrow – that's if this ever lets up." Rubbing her head some more, Isabel glanced past her niece at the weather outside.

"Aye – it's the lass's s-s-s-special d-day tomorrow in't it?" The slurring of Bert's words confirmed his wife's suspicions. Moments later he staggered from the room.

The others exchanged a knowing look that said, he's been drinking, watch what you say or he'll turn it into an argument. Isabel

14

winked and Hope knew what that meant too, before long he'll fall asleep in the chair and then we can relax and chat.

Both now thought about their cosy fireside chats when they talked about everything and nothing though there were some things that were never mentioned. Hope would never tell of the latest talk about Bert's association with a married woman from the dairy. She wondered whether her aunt had any suspicion but apart from the odd protracted silence she gave no indication.

As for the things Isabel chose to keep to herself – she had been overjoyed when Bert finally agreed that her brother and his child could move in. She had not been blessed with children and the prospect of a child in the house brought the promise of brightness to her otherwise dreary days. Indeed, Hope's presence had gone a long way towards banishing the chill from her lonely existence.

Almost from her arrival the child reminder her of someone – Isabel Thackeray – that fun-loving girl who had taken a wrong turning in life to become Isabel Patterson whose cancerous marriage had seeped beneath her skin to invade her very being. She had had such expectations of life then but where were her dreams now? Like her mother had said before her, We're born, we live, we die. Isabel's concurrence displeased her.

She made no excuses for Bert these days. He drank too much, slept all evening – often remaining in the chair all night – which suited her just fine. And she suspected he had other women – and that suited her just fine as well. She could not understand his mutation from the person she had married, to the bitter drunk who now shared her life. It was as though it were of no concern to him whether she existed or not. What had happened? When had it started? She sighed not caring to know the answers.

But there was always her brother's child, a reflection of Freddie – and of course dear Freddie himself every weekend. They made up for a lot. They had made her life worth living again. Though Freddie did not miss much; he frequently threw her a look whilst knowing she would change the subject if probed. But Freddie was not daft; she was damned sure he knew what was going on. She only hoped the child was not as observant as the father. These things were clutched to Isabel's heart, never to be admitted or spoken of.

The evening passed slowly. As usual Bert fell asleep immediately after his meal, and despite Isabel's assurances Hope regularly gravitated back to the window in the expectation of glimpsing her father.

Shortly after ten, when the fire had burned to a low, crimson glow and there seemed little point in adding more logs to crackle it back to life, Hope accepted her aunt had been right. Her father would not be coming tonight. After clearing away the supper dishes she typed a brief entry in her journal and turned in for the night. Tiredness soon overtook her and despite the storm she was asleep moments after slipping between the cool, worn sheets.

The storm, less savage, still rumbled overhead when Hope rose the next morning but not even that could dampen her spirits. Today was her 18th – the day their dream could begin.

But as the morning wore on the weather worsened, the picnic was cancelled, and there was still no sign of Frederick.

"Bell, I'm worried," Hope said at last.

"Don't worry y'head lass. 'Spect he was tired and had a lie in – I know him. He'll be here soon." The sound of a footfall outside drew their attention towards the door and a bathe of relief washed gentleness to Isabel's voice. "There – now what did I tell you?"

Hope ran to fling the door wide but found herself looking into the sad, watery-blue gaze of Revered Timothy Horrocks. The Reverend's attempt at a smile was half-hearted. He went to stand in isolation in the middle of the spotlessly clean though otherwise shabby parlour that smelled pleasantly of lavender polish. Instantly he became enthralled with the threadbare carpet square and began scrutinising it though not to the detail of detecting the frayed corner discreetly concealed beneath the one easy chair, Bert's chair.

The instant clamour of her aunt's arms should have prepared Hope but it did not. Timothy Horrocks had begun speaking, saying words she did not want to hear – words she could not bear to hear.

Isabel's embrace tightened though provided no comfort. Disbelief accompanied senses too complicated and intricately woven for Hope to gain understanding. Overtaken by despair Hope – her name now incongruous – no longer felt any confidence in her expectations of life.

The Reverend waited for the news to sink in. Isabel's bony shoulders shuddered beneath her grief but Hope's grasp of understanding was slow in coming. One moment she had been laughing, the next transfixed, motionless and unable to comprehend.

Thoughts were spinning out of control in her head. It was her 18th. None of this should be happening. It was like being trapped inside a nightmare. Finally she dragged her eyes from the empty expression in her aunt's face to look at Reverend Horrocks.

He continued gently, "My dear – I'm sorry to be the bearer of such tragic news. Your father was a fine man. He'll be greatly missed by us all."

The word *w-a-s* danced in the air making Hope giddy. She wanted to scream *I S....* my father *I-S* a fine man.... not *W-A-S*. But his use of the past tense brought home the magnitude of his message. Her father was dead.

It seemed that Frederick Thackeray had slipped when placing the last stone in the riverbed, struck his head and drowned.

Reverend Horrocks referred to it as a tragic accident. He had no way of knowing the effect it would have on the rest of Hope's life nor the direction it was already steering her towards.

Isabel saw the Reverend to the door. Before leaving he pressed a small parcel into her hand, explaining. "This was on the body. It appears to be for Hope – presumably a birthday present."

It was several days before Hope could face opening the package. When she did she found a large piece of amber shaped, aptly she thought, like a large golden teardrop. Held captive deep within the fossil resin was a small winged insect, exquisitely preserved forever, like her grief.

Bert shot a glance at his wife. "How does she seem?"

"Don't know.... a bit too early to tell. She's hurting." Isabel forced a smile. Though no longer close to her husband she was grateful for this show of concern. "We'll know better once we're over the funeral."

Barely containing her own grief Isabel strove to support her brother's child during the long days leading up to the Inquest and the funeral, when Hope seemed to shrink deep inside herself, only speaking in monosyllables in response to direct questions.

The simple chapel service took place on a Friday two weeks later. Hope was almost hysterical and at one point looked as though she would be unable to attend. The circumstances surrounding her father's death had taken their toll but having his funeral take place on a Friday – the day when of long-standing she would normally expect to be reunited with him – was a pain almost beyond endurance. One of the hardest elements was writing the message to accompany her flowers. She could think of no appropriate words but then penned, "Thank you for a thousand happy memories", her mind too burdened to remember a single one.

Encouraged by her aunt's embrace Hope was eventually led from the sanctuary of Ivy Cottage to say farewell to her father.

Seeing her niece beside the coffin outside the Chapel dragged a sob to Isabel's throat and the great bulbous tears she had fought to suppress welled up to slide down her face. Through the swim of tears she watched a figure rest a hand on the coffin before returning to clutch the amber drop at her throat. Hope would never be the same again.

Life without her father was inconceivable. He had portrayed everything stable, permanent and secure and Hope would always hate Fridays in future.

She functioned as though on automatic pilot, rising early, working late, often not leaving the school office until evening. She refused to meet with friends other than Amy Reid and Gregory Archer from her school days. She routinely helped Isabel every evening before retiring to lay awake for hours on her bed willing sleep to take her away for a few hours' respite.

One evening she found herself staring at the group of oil paintings on her bedroom wall. Her father had painted the larger two; she had painted the others. The largest and to her mind the most beautiful, was of her mother, painted shortly after her marriage. Faith was sitting near where the stepping-stones were placed later, and rising majestically from the riverbank behind her was Tarnville. A bouquet of wild flowers lay across her lap. The other large picture was of herself at the age of five. Her father had painted her in the same spot with the first five stepping-stones visible in the riverbed. In this Hope held a posy of wild flowers and field grasses. She remembered posing for the picture. When her father struggled to capture the texture and movement of her hair he explained he wanted to paint the wind in her hair. She smiled remembering her question. She asked what colour he was going to paint the wind. With the luxury of this memory, the first she had allowed herself since her father's death, tumbled others one after another – a whole parade of memories, all pungent and heady like favourite fragrances freed from confinement – an entire lifetime of memories, perfect and pure.

Months had passed but the healing process had finally begun and when her aunt became involved in planning the May Day celebrations Hope allowed herself to be drawn towards taking charge of some of the arrangements.

Like the preparations for Christmas, the hive of activity commenced weeks in advance. May Day was always a special occasion. It was a holiday.

Helpers congregated in the Chapel hall for band rehearsals and to make costumes and decorations, and exchange gossip. The chatter ceased abruptly one evening when a little dog accidentally stumbled into the wall-to-wall noise. It yapped excitedly before throwing back its muzzle to emit a howl and add its own contribution to the noise. The ensuing laughter halted with the unexpected appearance of Reverend Timothy Horrocks. Hope had seen that look on his face before and felt as though her heart would explode, though on this occasion his eyes did not seek her out.

The Reverend said the event should be cancelled; this was not a suggestion. Richard Lurdmayne, the only son of Sir Charles, had died unexpectedly at Tarnville that afternoon, something to do with his heart, he informed the people. In the circumstances it would be wrong for celebrations to go ahead.

The whole village had been on a switchback of excitement for weeks, and suddenly all evidence of May Day was put away – out of mind and out of respect for the death of Richard Lurdmayne. The sudden loss of the heir to Tarnville permeated quickly to hang heavily over all their lives.

None felt they had really known or indeed understood or even liked Richard Lurdmayne. Demonstrating no sense of commitment towards anything other than his own pleasure, he had not given a damn about his ancestral home. He had breeding certainly but no character – unlike the old gentleman. Nevertheless, the passing of Sir Charles's son affected everyone and Hope more than most. The news brought the resurrection of her own suffering and she re-entered the same painful grieving endured in the beginning.

Seated in her spot on the riverbank a week later Hope happened to glance across at Tarnville. Someone, a man, was at one of the tall ground-floor windows. At first he did not move or give any indication that he had seen her but then Sir Charles Lurdmayne raised an arm.

They had never actually spoken but she knew him well from St Mary's Church. She and her family attended St Mary's every Sunday morning and Brunswick Methodist Chapel in the evening; the latter was generally followed by a social of some sort in the hall. Sir Charles and his son had always occupied St Mary's centre front pew whilst she and her family squashed together in a pew five or six rows behind.

Why should he greet her? Perhaps he had been merely stretching. Just then a shaft of sunlight exploded on the diamond-shaped panes and prevented further scrutiny but she knew what would be written in his expression.

The ashes of her own grieving fanned, Hope felt an inexplicable compulsion to visit Tarnville to offer her condolences to Sir Charles Lurdmayne.

Chapter 4

Hope had no awareness of the young man until almost colliding with him on the bridge. Soft brown eyes smiled at her from a handsome face as she returned his nod and continued across the bridge. He was a stranger. If she had seen him before she would have remembered if only for his eyes, and clothing as unfamiliar to her as neon lighting and tarmacadam roads. Clearly he was not from hereabouts dressed in beige sweater, well-pressed slacks and snugly-fitting shoes of smooth leather – not boots cracked and crazed by working the land, made overly big by wet and wear. Everything about him labelled him a stranger – a *Townie*.

The young man turned to watch Hope clamber up the daisy-speckled bank across the river but her attention was not on him but on the figure at Tarnville's window as she cut across the stone-flagged path, overgrown in places with cushions of spongy moss. Soon a profusion of wild flowers would appear as if by magic to cram colour between the same flagstones. The young man watched a flurry of pale blossom escape a spreading broom to eddy dizzily in her wake. He had not failed to appreciate the green eyes that sprang wide on seeing him. He would like to have had a plausible excuse to call her back or retrace his own steps – anything to be able to study for a few moments longer the face belonging to the greenest eyes he had ever seen. She could not be much more than 16 or 17, making him around ten years older. Admonishing himself he turned away but not before filing a memory – *like an orchid amongst the daisies*.

The light breeze played with Hope's loose hair whilst she waited for her knock on the door to be answered. She leaned against a column in Tarnville's portico and looked about her from this vantage point.

Familiar landmarks took on an irregularity from this angle. The village assumed a storybook quality, whilst the school became like a doll's house, and her stepping-stones, marching proudly across the river, took centre stage linking the picture together. From here she could see far upriver and round the bend to the great grassy mound that forty years previous had been black clinker, oppressive and often unstable and a constant reminder of tomorrow's toil. Over the years nature had advanced to soften its ugly lines in a green intermingled embrace before boldly marching on unbridled to paint her own intricate clash of colour over the re-claimed canvas. The transformation complete it had become a place of gentleness and peace with no hint of what had gone before – the mine – the infancy of the Tarnville Estate.

Hope shut her eyes and tried to imagine the landscape as it had been then, when men wearing the same shabby garments and grimy mask stomped wearily through ice-glazed puddles on their long trek home. In this parallel likeness she thrust her hands deeper into her pockets in a bid to cheat the raw wind blowing in gusts across the river. An equal in the blackened group she shuffled along, shunning the damp cling of winter darkness. Now and then a man would cough and spit loudly in an attempt to clear coal dust from stinging lungs. Picking up the staccato rhythm of their clogs she hummed along to the pulsating song that would announce their homecoming to the womenfolk.

The sound of the metal-studded door being opened extinguished the illusion and Hope found herself again bathed in bright sunlight. The Housekeeper peered at her. Sarah Kaye had arrived at Tarnville as a young kitchen maid before Sir Charles's wife, now deceased, had arrived as a bride. Her dainty-framed appearance gave no indication of the rigid discipline she demanded from Tarnville's modest staff.

Something in the woman's scrutiny made Hope wish it had not occurred to her to come to pay her respects, but after stumbling through an explanation for her presence Sarah's expression softened into a smile.

"Come along in dear," she bade. "Sir Charles will be pleased to see you. Come along.... come along," the tiny woman urged as though afraid she might take flight. "A bit of young company will do him good. With a bit of luck you might cheer him where the rest have failed. He's low you see.... so low. Can't properly take it in. What with his daughter and that fellow.... her Ladyship.... and now his son...."

Sarah's disjointed sentences were like tiny seedlings urgently nudging the earth's surface to find sunshine. Steadfastly loyal it was not her custom to enter into discourse connected with her employment but these had been a difficult few days and her thoughts became words, albeit untidy fragments.

Hope caught the gist but much eluded her; she had certainly heard no mention of a daughter. But nothing missed her notice whilst waiting in the drawing room. Dark wood panelling met her on entry but here rich walnut and mahogany played for supremacy over the splendid marble fireplace and furnishings. An immense glaze of windows strove to draw fanciful topiary and even the very grounds themselves also into the décor. Freshly cut flowers were tastefully arranged in crystal vases, and highly polished silver candlesticks sparkled in the sunlight streaming through the windows. The quality, style and antiques had been purposely woven together to create the sum of their parts, a very pleasing, comfortable room. She could not help reflecting on the treasures and furnishings to be found in the cottages, almost tacky by comparison.

Within moments Hope detected a subdued elegance; elegance that was no longer shared or enjoyed. But for the presence of flowers one might believe the room rarely occupied. The faded brocade fabrics hinted at deeper hues and she imagined the depths of their folds rarely had cause to muffle the sound of laughter.

A landscape above the fireplace caught her eye. She was about to examine it when Sarah reappeared to take her to the library where she learned Sir Charles Lurdmayne was waiting for her.

Charles was still at the window when his young visitor entered his favourite room. He had watched her growing up over the years and knew her well by sight. She looked no different from when he had seen her strolling along the riverbank. She advanced towards him, her procession of footsteps on the polished floor the only sound in the room. An outdoor glow illuminated her skin whereas his own complexion, the colour of ageing ivory, told of aching joints that curbed outdoor pursuits.

His hand outstretched in welcome, Charles returned the warm smile he was entranced to see in her face. "Please, do come in and sit yourself down." He was embarrassed by the tremor of his hand in hers.

"I'm Hope Thackeray."

"Frederick Thackeray's daughter. Yes, I know. I was sorry to hear of your sad loss my dear. It seems we've both lost those important to us."

Charles sensed her curiosity at his knowledge. "I often saw you meeting up on a Friday afternoon by the river." He did not admit how often or that he had rarely allowed anything to prevent his witnessing the reunion. The weekly meeting had evoked strong, painful emotions but like playing with a smarting sore he had been unable to prevent himself. Seeing Frederick Thackeray swing this girl into the fondest of parental embraces had lifted his spirits to dizzy heights whilst at the same time reducing him to despair, not unlike the sorrow he felt now, and a perpetual reminder of happier times lost to him many years ago.

"It was because of my own loss that I came to offer my condolences. I'm not brave enough to say I know how you feel. It's impossible to know exactly how another person is feeling, but having lost my father only recently I know something of what you're going through. At the moment none of it will seem real."

Moved by the profound understanding of one so young Charles was unable to speak but managed a nod.

"The hurt never really goes away but over a period of time acceptance becomes inescapable."

He inclined his head in partial agreement. "Eventually – though I know from experience how some losses never seem to lessen." He became thoughtful, permitting other sorrows to crowd in on him.

In the ensuing silence Hope quietly settled back into the comfortable winged chair, appreciative fingers exploring the feel of leather.

As though sensitive to her unease Charles spluttered an apology. Then, feeling a need to explain if not voice his emotions, he too leaned back in his chair causing the burgundy leather to creak slightly. Straying beyond the boundary of hurt that was at the same time strangely comforting he began to speak of his son, permitting Hope to witness his son's last moments as he lay dying in his arms.

"I couldn't make out everything but he mentioned feeling angry with life – I took that to mean since Christina left. A distance had grown up between us but I never stopped loving him but suppose I never showed it. That's something I'll have to learn to live with. I'm guilty of creating the feelings he described. I regret that. I should have stepped back to consider how losing his sister and then only a year later his mother.... how those things were also affecting him." Charles pushed a smile into his craggy face and looked at his young visitor. "I loved him so much and showed it so little after my wife died. Margaret died almost a year after Christina left. I should have shown Richard how much I cared about him but I left it too late. I'll never forgive myself for that."

These bittersweet memories were interrupted with the arrival of an impressive tea trolley bearing a beautifully embellished silver teapot, china cups that Hope could almost see through, and a feast of sandwiches and sliced cake; enough for a gathering of half a dozen or more. "I thought you might enjoy your chat over some tea." The early trolley was Sarah's attempt to keep the Master's young visitor with him a little longer.

After gingerly replacing the teapot Hope picked up the conversation. "You mentioned a daughter.... Christina? I didn't know you had a daughter. I'm sorry," she said, seeing something in his eyes. "I didn't mean to pry. It's just that I've never heard her mentioned."

The furrow in his brow deepened as though striving to draw something from the shadows of the past. He was surprised she had not heard about Christina, especially the scandal; he assumed at the time the episode to be the talking point of the whole village.

He exhaled lengthily. "It was a long time ago." Realising how long, he added, "Before you were born. Like any father I wanted only the best for my children and when it came to Christina's choice of husband I was unable to approve her choice. It was in this very room that she told me she'd fallen in love with the handyman I'd engaged for the summer to do some bits and pieces around the Estate. I wanted more for her than that. I wanted her to have a future...."

"A future....?" Hope grinned at him. "I understand. My father had such plans for me too," she said, swiftly escorting him to one of the most cherished days of her childhood, and promptly provided him with an explanation for the presence of the stepping-stones in the riverbed below his window.

"Charming," Charles said gently when she finished. "What a lovely idea – stepping-stones to take you into your future." He had witnessed several of the birthday rituals, often wondering why only one stone was added.

With embarrassment she confessed, "When my father told me the stepping-stones would lead me across the river and into my future.... with a five-year-old's understanding I looked across at Tarnville, believing Tarnville to be my future!" She laughed. "And for a long time after that made up stories about Tarnville. Imagine...." Her words halted at the sight of bemusement in his face. "You know the sort of thing.... fairy princesses and knights in shining armour." Charles's new-found ease slipped away when he saw the fun suddenly go out of her face as she concluded, "But then my father died.... and the magic ended and real life came crashing in."

A sting sprang up behind his eyelids. He nodded understanding, then saw hurt shining in the corners of her eyes and became almost envious of the man who had been the subject of such passion.

He offered, "Your father and I were alike. We both wanted the best for our children." Then, as though seeing something he glanced towards the centre of the room. The memory of his daughter stared back at him, angry and defiant. Aware of his reverie he explained, "Christina stood there, in the middle of this room. Not much older than you are now. She said if our surname had been anything but Lurdmayne things would have been different and her mother and I would have blessed their union. We didn't and the next thing we knew she'd run off with the fellow. That was over 20 years ago. And that was the last we ever heard of her. It broke her mother's heart. Margaret had a stroke shortly after. She lasted not quite a year and then I lost her too...." Weariness took hold. He no longer had the power to remember.

Hope leaned across to rest a hand on his. No words were necessary.

Charles rallied and purposely lightened his voice. "In fact I would probably have found fault with anyone who asked for my daughter's hand. Years before that, when she was only a child, jokingly I told her I doubted if there were a man alive I would consider good enough. Christina had been giving an exceptional performance of temper. No doubt I smiled with amusement, enjoying the explosion. My daughter – my pride and joy. I was prejudiced of course but who wouldn't be?

My duckling – or rather cygnet – had grown to become the swan, surprising even I who watched enthralled from the wings. But now there's only me to remember and trust that one day...."

A clock somewhere deep within the house chimed the hour announcing the afternoon gone. Hope apologised for staying so long.

"Not at all my dear. It's been a pleasure having you here."

He'd enjoyed her company more than he had anyone's for a long time. "I feel better for your visit and hope I can persuade you to come again." She had been like a breath of fresh air seeping through his thick fog of sadness.

The same radiant smile that had lit up her face from time to time shone once more. "I should like that very much. Thank you. I look forward to coming again. This is the first time I've felt able to talk about my father since he died. You've made it possible to enjoy the wealth of memories he left me."

He returned her smile, feeling younger than he had for years. He confided, "I think we've helped each other and I'm grateful you came. If nothing else we've identified that if time appears to have run out for the individual then surely those of us who remain gain the right to live on through those whose lives have touched and changed us." He continued on a brighter note, "I was surprised when Sarah told me I had another visitor." Detecting a question he explained, "I had another caller a while earlier; a young business man enquiring whether Tarnville might be for sale – always on the look out, he said, for suitable hotel premises."

"Sell Tarnville! You wouldn't do that would you?" Horror stole the smile from her face.

Charles shook his head. "Tarnville belongs to someone else...." If she ever comes back. Instantly he cut off this thought. "When I heard I had another visitor I expected it to be in connection with May Day, to discuss the facilities that can be made available."

"May Day? Sir Charles, we've cancelled it – out of respect."

His eyes widened. "I should've realised." He studied the polished floor. He knew how important these occasions were and how much the villagers looked forward to them. "Cancelled? No! It must go ahead – in fact I want it to go ahead. Like we've just been saying – life goes on – it's for the living. There's been far too much misery at

Tarnville. Believe me – I'd like nothing more than to see people enjoying themselves. When you get back you must tell them it's my specific wish that the event go ahead as usual, and they are to let me know what help they need from here."

Hope burst into Ivy Cottage, almost knocking her aunt off her feet.

"My but you're bubbling right over pet."

"Oh Bell I am! You'll never guess where I've been. I've had afternoon tea at the big house with Sir Charles Lurdmayne!"

"You've been to Tarnville?"

"Yes, and that's not all...." She paused to make sure she had her aunt's full attention, "May Day's to go ahead – Sir Charles says so!"

Isabel insisted on making a fresh pot of tea before hearing all about Hope's afternoon. At the conclusion she was convinced she knew as much about Tarnville's private rooms as she did the kitchens, where for many years she had assisted Sarah Kaye with the various functions for which the House was renowned. "Well I never – my niece has had afternoon tea with the old gentleman!" she chortled, her eyes going to the squat brown teapot on the hearth.

"And I'm going again. He made me promise."

"Well – wait till I tell Bert." Then, turning from the girl, she glanced upwards to smile at the memory of her brother.

When Hope finally drifted off to sleep she dreamed of maypole dancing on Tarnville's sweeping lawns, picnicking in the woods and a handsome stranger with soft brown eyes beckoning to her from the bridge.

In Leeds a young man tossed and turned in his hotel bed trying to sleep, but the room felt airless and stuffy. The thermostat had stuck again and he made a mental note to mention it in the morning. When he eventually slipped into unconsciousness he found himself struggling to climb a daisy-strewn riverbank in an attempt to catch up with a young girl with emerald green eyes and hair the colour of pale, ripe corn. But try as he did she eluded his grasp, always remaining just beyond his reach.

Chapter 5

The bright maypole ribbons snagged a second time, with Katie-Jane the culprit. Moments earlier when William Bates tripped over his own feet bringing down two more children Mrs Bradley leapt smartly amongst them, deftly reclaiming three lost ribbons and directing the offenders smoothly back into sequence. Now it was her granddaughter who, as a result of waving to her grandfather, had lost concentration and skipped merrily off in the wrong direction.

"Katie, the other way – the other way!" Josephine Bradley rolled her eyes at her assistant who like herself stood at the side watchful for possible tangles and ready to prompt the children. "I've come to the conclusion that a good rehearsal doesn't necessarily mean a good performance." A slant of humour rounded Josephine's lips. She had correctly judged that the occasional tangle and a child out of step only added to the performance. They were children after all and the audience proud family and friends. The tiny ones had only to put in a fleeting appearance in their costumes to bring the audience to rapturous applause.

"You look charming my dear. That colour suits you, really compliments your eyes." The Headmistress glanced admiringly at Hope whose eyes looked even greener today, if that were possible.

Warmed by her employer's comment Hope smoothed her hands appreciatively over soft, green muslin. Her aunt had surprised her with the dress only the other evening.

Like others able to handle a sewing needle Isabel had been commandeered into helping with the May Day costumes, and seeing her labouring over her sewing basket night after night Hope had felt unable to request a dress. The purchase of a new dress was out of the question for after her father's death she insisted on tipping up her wage, though she was already thinking along the lines of seeking better-paid employment.

Resigned to wearing her faded taffeta skirt teamed with a pretty blouse Hope had been overjoyed to find the pale-green garment laid out in gauzy splendour on her bed. It was the most beautiful dress she had ever seen, let alone owned. Urgent fingers had explored the sweetheart neckline, snugly fitting waistline and the full skirt that finished at mid-calf; each line so different from the tapered skirts and tailored shirts she wore to the school office.

A satisfied sigh escaped Josephine Bradley when the Maypole dancing concluded with no further unscheduled knots or twists in the ribbons. Hope excused herself and went to investigate the other activities taking place in Tarnville's grounds.

She had not gone far when she noticed Sir Charles beckoning to her from the far side of the lawn. His Estate Manager, Joseph Fearnley, a stooped man who looked significantly older than his 53 years, accompanied him.

Joseph watched as signs of strain disappear from Charles's face. He followed his line of vision to the girl who had brought about a discernible change in his employer. The Housekeeper had been the first to notice; he had merely laughed though soon acknowledged that Sarah had been right.

The unlikely friendship between the teenager and the old gentleman had surprised the entire household. None expected the girl's visits to continue but true to her word Hope had called regularly at Tarnville. She had even brought a change to *his* role. With her ceaseless questions and fascination in Estate matters Charles's demeanour had altered from that of indifference to one of renewed interest. After a long interlude of distraction his employer's interest in the day-to-day running of the Estate had been rekindled, and if the girl were responsible he welcomed her to the fold. Like Charles, Joseph smiled warmly at Hope's approach.

The young woman walking towards them was unaware of appreciative eyes trained on her, though she responded with a smile when seven-year-old Katie-Jane exclaimed admiration.

"You look ever so lovely Miss Thackeray. You're 'vu lu' for 'very lovely'," she added, keen to reveal developing spelling skills.

"And you're 'vu kicking-cu' for 'very kind'!"

The seven-year-old collapsed into squirms of delighted giggles before galloping off to twirl dizzily at the end of her mother's arm.

Charles slid his head to one side. Miss Thackeray? Yes – he supposed a child would see Hope as an adult whereas to him she would always remain the child waiting patiently beside the stepping-stones for Frederick Thackeray.

Hope bounded up the slope with the lissom sprint of one not yet fully emerged from the chrysalis of childhood to flaunt adult plumage. But unlike her companions Charles had never witnessed displays of irrational behaviour or the motiveless mood swings brought about by the complexities of teenage tribulations. Her time for taking initiative and responsibility had been thrust upon her with Frederick's death. Left to navigate her own future she had matured over night though still displayed a purity of heart. Innocence is a state to be appreciated and protected he found himself acknowledging.

Spectacular corn-coloured, waist-length hair billowed out behind Hope in a brilliant display. The long tresses glinted in the sunlight and wafted gently in the warm afternoon breeze to form an ambrosial frame for her lovely face; a golden crown of undulating light.

It was a lovely face, mused Charles, reflecting on the contrast between this child and his daughter Christina. They were like negatives of each other; one dark the other fair, though strangely similar and both strikingly beautiful, determined young women.

Charles snapped himself from his reverie. "We were about to get a cup of tea. Will you join us?"

Hope had plans to picnic with her family and neighbours in the woodland flanking the lawns though not until later. Smiling she took his arm and allowed him to escort her to the terrace where refreshments were being served.

The rockery, a feature of the gardens, adjoined the terrace. There an extravagant explosion of aubrietia had crept into every nook and cranny to throw a mantle of rich purple and mauve along its length. Stunning clumps of sunshine-coloured irises had pushed through the fluid tumble of purple to intensify the excitement of early springtime colour, but more pleasing to Charles's eye was Hope's expression of appreciation.

"It's startling, isn't it? I know it's there and yet it still has an effect on me."

Hope turned to display the wonderment in her face.

Several villagers nudged each other and exchanged whispers when they noticed Hope in the company of the old gentleman. The observation evoked an element of surprise but nothing more – except for Bert who had formed his own opinion.

His expression immobile, Bert surveyed his niece over the top of his pint. "Getting above 'erself, that un." He coughed and spat a mouthful of phlegm into the aubrietia.

His wife, incensed by his action, watched from their perch on the low stonewalling but her interpretation was different. "He lost his wife and both of his children. She lost her father. They're gaining support from each other." She spoke with the knowledge gained from lengthy conversations by the fireside late at night.

A short time later Hope was busy passing round a tray of sandwiches to friends sprawled on rugs at the edge of the wood. A single cloud in an otherwise clear blue canopy strayed in front of the sun, instantly adding to the coolness already hanging over the gathering. Bert's mood was reflected in the silent faces of the others. Isabel, her expression one of anxiety, was mindful of the atmosphere. She put it down to a clash of beer and whisky though had the good sense not to say so.

Hope was more enlightened. She had witnessed the smiles exchanged between Bert and the woman from the dairy, following which she had been unable to prevent her eyes from trailing the woman whose painted lips were so red Hope was surprised no one attempted to post a letter in her mouth.

It was a strained hour and when Gregory Archer invited Hope to accompany him on a tour of Tarnville's grounds she welcomed the escape, though wondered about leaving Isabel, but her aunt was already apart, preoccupied in light animated chatter with others from the sewing circle.

After the crowning of the new May Queen; winning a goldfish in a leaky plastic bag; watching the Morris Dancing and chatting with mutual friends – Hope sank down on to the cool grass with Gregory.

She stretched out. The warm sun felt good on her face and her mind strayed to an earlier May Day when her companion had been someone else very dear to her. She won a goldfish that day too. She squeezed her eyes shut to hold fast the memory of her father.

Gregory studied the face that held a permanent place within his dreams. They had been friends since kindergarten but that was all it was; instinctively he knew Hope was not yet ready for courtship and was happy to give her the space she needed.

He had loved her from the first moment he saw her. Her father brought her to school one Monday morning. Upon his departure a brilliance of tears slid into her eyes and Gregory had gone to her side to become her champion. That was the way he still felt about her. He wanted to protect Hope from whatever life threw at her, especially now with her father gone. Since that tragedy a change had come over her. Displays of pleasure and humour were now infrequent and when present they were controlled and less spontaneous. Gone was the girl he had fallen in love with. Occupying her space was a young woman in many ways more vulnerable than the pretty child Frederick had dropped off at school that Monday morning years ago.

Two people advancing towards the woods caught Gregory's attention. The man staggering up the incline was Bert Patterson; the woman giggling beside him was the woman he knew Bert was seeing. He glanced back at his companion dozing beside him but Hope's eyes remained shut.

Gregory looked towards Isabel supposedly conversing with friends. Her manner gave nothing away yet he was certain she had seen her husband disappear into the trees with Annie Wilks. There would be raised voices in Hope's home before the day was out. The explosion of anger would erase the delights of the day, which would now dissolve to nothingness.

Hope had been watching Gregory. "Penny for them. Thinking about college? She assumed his frown was due to his imminent start at farming college.

"Yer…..a bit," he managed, grateful for the explanation innocently provided. He moved a strand of shiny hair from her face. His hand lingered and he had to pull it away. He was going to miss her. Would she miss him?

"I bet you'll have a whale of a time. You're lucky...."

"Lucky?"

She kept her eyes on his as she nodded. "Yes. It's lovely here – the village and everything." Unaware that she did so she slanted her eyes in the direction of the stepping-stones, which were not visible from this side of the house. "It's the most beautiful place on earth – but I'm beginning to want more than my little job at the school or a humdrum marriage overrun with children, and for the whole pattern to repeat itself down the generations like a habit." She was even growing wearisome of the village events with the attendance of the same individuals.

"Like a habit! Is that how you see....?" Gregory looked crestfallen.

"Yes – in a way I suppose I do. You're lucky. You've got the chance to make more of yourself." She held out her hand for him to pull her up then glanced about her, breathing deeply. "Where do you think we'll all be a few years from now?" Her arms swept wide to indicate the inclusion of friends.

Gregory's eyes clouded over then he bravely said, "Who knows? What do you think?"

"Well, let me see...." She pursed her lips and became thoughtful. "You'll be qualified, of course. Be running someone's farm – or even your own – and perhaps.... married with a...."

Gregory perked up. "You see me married? Who to?" He held his breath.

"Perhaps.... Amy?" Not wishing to appear obvious, she watched for a reaction. Her curly-haired friend was dotty about him and Hope was certain they were perfect for each other. During her time of grieving Gregory and Amy remained steadfastly close, each doing their best to help her through the long days that eventually laboured into months. They sensed when she wanted to be quiet, listened when she eventually found cognitive thought and helped her rediscover laughter whilst all the time easing her from bizarre feelings of guilt. She cared about them both and was keen to sow this particular seed of thought.

"Amy!"

"She likes you a lot Greg. She's a lovely person and lovely on the inside too." His height and broad shoulders belied Gregory's shyness but perhaps with a little push she could open his eyes to his biggest admirer. Even though he had always been like a big brother she dare not glance sideways to read his expression for fear she had overstepped the boundary of their friendship.

Reluctantly, Gregory escorted Hope home. Pondering whether to take her back to his people he hesitated at the gate. But even if he did take her home he would have to bring her back eventually. Perhaps he should tell her about her uncle and Annie Wilks, but Hope was already expressing thanks from her doorstep; she had had a wonderful afternoon. The following hours would put a different slant on that and he waited at the gate until she went in.

Once inside, Hope suspended her goldfish in its plastic bag from the doorknob. She was about to search for a suitable container when her uncle lurched through the door almost on top of her. The smile slid from her face when she detected drunkenness. She stepped away. How could he let himself get into such a state and it not yet evening? She questioned how Isabel coped with this man – her husband – but already realised it was a poor example of marriage and certainly not the quality of union she would be prepared to settle for.

"B-Bell not back?" Bert's eyes widened in an attempt to improve his vision. Hope shook her head. "Back soon I expect. She's probably taken some of the costumes back to the hall." Out of the corner of her eye she watched him stagger further into the room to collide with the dresser where Isabel displayed her few treasures. Hope immediately went to steady it, at the same time aware of blurred vision sweeping over her.

Bert blinked at the image that relied on memory. His hold purposely tight, he caught her roughly by the arm and dragged her to him. When she struggled and turned her face from whisky fumes, he snorted, "Bit above us now aren't you – little Miss Lady Muck – now you've gate-crashed into posh world belongin' big 'ouse? All la-di-dah and fancy knickers!"

His hold tightened. She could not breath. He was too close. Saliva seeped from between his lips. Too close – he was too close. He began fumbling with his belt buckle. Aghast she reached in frenzy round his bulk to beat clenched fists on his back, all the time struggling to escape his hold. A stride away was the door and freedom, but his wet mouth was all over her face and hands were already trespassing beneath green muslin to explore the area of warm flesh above her stockings.

"Get off! You're drunk. Your only interest in life is the contents of a whisky bottle." Ricocheting through her head were the angry words shouted by her father when Bert had spoken unkindly to his sister, "You're a bad tempered bugger when you've had a drink!"

With a surge of energy Bert forced her backwards until she was against the door. "Lemme tell y'summat. You're nowt special. Y'count for nowt – just like the rest o'us." He began tearing at the delicate fabric of the dress Isabel had secretly laboured over each evening after she had gone to bed.

"I've never hated you as much as I hate you right this minute!"

More words would have followed but her breath was snatched away when the next tear of muslin exposed her nakedness and callused palms groped at her unyielding form.

Bert pressed his whisky-smelling mouth over hers again in an eager attempt to part her lips with a foul-smelling tongue. She bit his face, sharp with beard stubble but he snatched his head away spitting rage at her before lunging at her with renewed determination. Her arms ached with the effort of forcing him from her but the burden of his weight finally took her gasping to the floor. She fought to roll away but a cruel wrench of her hair pulled her back.

All remaining air was crushed from her when he threw himself on top. In that moment her weeping became hysteria; her screams became shrieks but the sound that reached her hearing was but slight, like that of a fallen animal.

He had won – she had lost – but then Bert relaxed his hold to fumble with his clothing. In that split second she mustered the strength and energy of the same creature that seconds ago had whimpered pathetically in her ears. With the heel of her hand she struck an effective blow to Bert's face. Attuned to survival she strove to free a leg and bring her knee up sharply. Bert gasped and bowed his back. In spite of her predicament she was shocked by the severity of pain she inflicted. Sensing this her only chance she reached for the edge of the carpet square and dragged herself free from the writhing mass, where genitals had become important.

Legs that moments earlier had failed to support her now propelled her from him. She longed to flee the cottage but it would have been a further affront to be seen with her clothes hanging from her, and instead she darted to the stairs.

Even before her foot was on the second tread she knew it was a wrong decision and afforded entrapment rather than escape. Her feet fled the stairs. Terrified and gasping for breath she hurled herself across the narrow landing into her bedroom where she rammed the bedside chair beneath the doorknob. Her father had found the seat at an auction when she was young; he would have been horrified to know that years later his daughter would rely on it for protection. She leaned her weight into the pathetic barricade but the chair was old and its frame creaked even at her touch. Frantic, she scanned the room for something else but there was nothing. She was lost and she slumped weeping beside the chair that would shortly splinter to uselessness.

Sorrowful thoughts of Isabel came to plague her but concern for her aunt dissolved upon hearing the backdoor slam. Had Bell come home? Had Bert gone out? Her ears strained to pick out any trace of sound that might provide the answer but there was nothing.

She went to the window to peer round the blue gingham curtains just in time to glimpse Bert pitching through the gateway. Overtaken by involuntary shaking she flung herself on to her bed to sob tearlessly.

After a while she got to her feet and went to the dressing table. The mirror, crazed with age, revealed a barely recognisable image. The face was aflame from bristle burns. The eyes looked dead, and hair that normally shone with sunlight, hung limp and tangled about her face.

Crying afresh she swept the dishevelled mess behind her. She eased the chair from behind the door and ventured hesitantly on to the landing, all the time reminding herself that Bert had gone out, though that knowledge did not prevent her from straining her ears as she made for the bathroom.

Ten minutes later, tingling from her efforts to cleanse herself in cold water, she went downstairs. The area by the backdoor looked the same as it had always done. There was no indication of the horror that had just taken place. The urge to run far away and put distance between herself and Ivy Cottage was strong, but then thinking again about Isabel, she took her handkerchief to wipe away what she took to be a smear of blood on the shabby square of linoleum.

It was not blood. There on the floor, its scales dull and motionless, lay the goldfish she won on the hoopla stall. The leaky plastic bag had been knocked to the floor during the struggle. Apparently she had not been the only one to experience trauma – though she had not lost her life – but the way she felt she might just as well have done. She disposed of the fish outside then returned just long enough to straighten the peg rug before fleeing the empty cottage.

Chapter 6

Fine rain floated in the air when Hope fled from Ivy Cottage. Trauma written in her pale face and keen to shrink from view, she made for the narrow dirt track that led to the river. Her pace only slowed when she reached the sanctuary of her stepping-stones. As she flung herself down she longed for the comfort of her father's arms and the sound of his voice, and tears hot as embers swelled behind her eyelids. She was barely aware of the change in the weather. Neither was she conscious of the concerned face at the window across the river, or of the younger, more handsome face beyond.

Charles paused in conversation. Yes, eventually he would have to decide what to do with Tarnville. The years were passing – but sell Tarnville? He glanced back at the man who had arrived again unannounced, though did not speak but returned his attention to the scene below his library window; the person slumped, sobbing on the opposite bank.

He had watched Hope's approach. There had been an agitation about her that made him believe her pursued but a glance along the path revealed no one. Compared with earlier she looked almost boyish. Her dress had been discarded in favour of jeans. Charles's eyes remained on Hope whilst turning over in his mind the proposition that had been put to him a second time.

He had to agree that Tarnville would make a splendid hotel, but it was not just a wonderful structure in a picturesque setting. Tarnville was more than that; it was a home, which had been in his family since the early-1800s. A lengthy sigh escaped him. It was always going to be the home of those who followed – Richard, now gone, but Christina....?

His attention refocused on the figure on the far bank whose shoulders heaved beneath racking sobs. The cause of Hope's sadness eluded him. Many times he had seen her similarly distressed following Frederick's death, always in the same spot, but he remained baffled as to what had happened to extinguish her earlier happiness.

He turned back to the young man whose face looked up expectantly. "Mr. Colendon – I regret Tarnville is not for sale. Now if you will excuse me there's something I must attend to."

It had been his intention to go to comfort Hope, albeit his involvement might add the additional burden of embarrassment to her state of mind. For that reason he was pleased to see that Gregory Archer had joined her. Appeased, Charles left the window and went to the bureau where more from interest than conviction he took up the papers his caller had left and began to examine the details again.

Gregory had been unable to settle after leaving Hope and elected to take Mrs Middler's young border collie for a walk. Spotting Hope by the river brought an instant swell of pleasure, until he saw her dishevelled appearance.

When he sank down beside her he could not help noticing her face was blotched and her eyes swollen, and how she shrank from him. Bobby, little more than a puppy, flopped quietly on her other side to study the movement of his feathery tail skimming the grass. Gregory felt the urge to encircle Hope in his arms but detected the presence of a barrier around her person.

"Come on flower, keep your pecker up. Whatever it is don't let it spoil the day. It's been brilliant and all because of you. It might never have happened if you hadn't gone to see Sir Charles." He was aware of how unnatural his voice sounded and found himself wishing he had not seen Bert take Annie Wilks into the woods. He toyed with confessing he knew the reason for her misery but instead asked, "Would it help to talk about it?" It had been a slow process but opening up after her father's death had helped her in the past.

Hope drew her knees tighter to her chest. "No! Sorry. It's too…..it's personal."

Nodding understanding he slipped a comforting arm around her.

"Don't touch me!"

The sudden, almost venomous spit took him by surprise, the words burning like red-hot fragments of brittle bark spluttering from an otherwise cosy log fire. His arm fell away instantly. "Hey! Hope it's me. We've always been able to talk about things. I hate to see you like this – all upset like."

Locked in anguish she eventually strung some words together. "It's okay. I'm all right. I've just had a shock that's all. Yes – that's what it was, a horrible shock." She uncurled her legs. Bobby looked up sympathetically before resting his soft muzzle in her lap to doze, his round puppy tummy rising and falling in the gentle rhythm of sleep. The regular movement was a welcome distraction from the real life that was pressing in on her.

In spite of her wretchedness it was during those moments of refuge that she faced up to the idea that had floated in and out of her mind since her father's death. She would find employment far away from the only home she remembered, and put as much distance as possible between her and Bert. Sadly that meant wrenching herself from this place, which was filled with memories of her father like a box filled to overflowing with priceless treasures. But perhaps she could come back sometime, secretly, to walk along the riverbank.... and remember.

Another decision was being reached in the library at the other side of the river. After watching Hope for several minutes Charles took up his pen and began to write to his lawyer.

But for the sudden change in the weather that brought her and her companion hurriedly to their feet Hope might have remained trapped in tangled thoughts for her future; a future overwhelmingly different from the one that had been planned for her. The wind carrying slanting rain cut angrily across the river, tearing the surface that slapped briskly against the large stones protruding from the riverbed. A delighted Bobby began turning giddy cartwheels at the end of his lead, his burst of excitement more to do with the presence of a ginger biscuit in Gregory's pocket, than any change in the weather.

"Steady fella.... you'll hang yourself!" Gregory untangled the puppy's legs. "It's a pity I can't just take his batteries out!" He threw Hope a lop-sided grin and was immediately struck with disappointment when her face remained unchanged.

Nearing Ivy Cottage Hope's pace lagged. It was obvious she didn't want to go inside so he suggested her accompanying him to return Bobby.

Hattie Middler welcomed them warmly, straight away insisting they join her in a hot drink in front of the fire that blazed in the grate irrespective of the temperature outside. Gregory might have waived this aside but for the calming effect the invitation had on his companion. He returned the smile in the elderly features beaming up at him.

Hattie had been widowed for as long as Gregory could remember, and was now one of the oldest inhabitants of the village. Not being employed on the Estate he believed her continuing occupancy of the cottage an arrangement resulting from her deceased husband's employment as Head Groom at Tarnville. Richard Lurdmayne had learned practically everything he knew about horses from Charlie Middler and following the old groom's death Richard had kept in regular touch with his widow. The majority of the villagers had been merely sorry when Richard died. Hattie had been devastated and shortly thereafter a new phrase had been added to her brief repertoire. "He's gone too now" had been added to "it'll be dark early tonight; what day is it – is it Sunday?" and the most repetitive, "are you warm enough?"

Gregory knew little about her early years other than she had worked as a Nanny. Something had happened – the child became ill, or died, or something – and the story went that she never quite got over it. Like so many others, Gregory remained fond of the old lady who years ago prepared great quantities of treacle toffee and gingerbread men for the local children. Her popularity continued and she had a regular string of visitors with whom to share a pot of tea. Gregory frequently brought a curve to Hope's lips when he told her how he invariably came away knowing far less than when he arrived. He could tell that today would be no different; all the signs were there.

The confused little woman's fireside lent a distance to the reality known to be waiting impatiently outside. He was grateful for this temporary harbour that allowed Hope to sink back into plump patchwork cushions that brightened the two-seater settee of otherwise indeterminable colour.

All too soon they dragged marbled shins from the fireside and took their leave, promising to call again soon. Gregory noticed Hope had fallen to silence and supposed her deep in thought and perhaps searching for an excuse not to return home. If that were the case the decision was taken from her with the unexpected appearance of her aunt and Amy Reid in the narrow lane.

Isabel smiled brightly as she joined them at Hattie's gate. "Hello you two – enjoyed the day? Hattie okay?" Not waiting for a reply she went on, "Sorting out the costumes took a while. I 'spect you're hungry, and I know someone else who will be – Bert's always impatient for his dinner. You walking back with me?"

Going to her aunt Hope forced a smile into her tight, pale face, which did not reach her eyes Gregory noticed. That recent tears had been shed was in ready evidence and he felt himself shrink beneath Isabel's questioningly look.

Had he been aware of it, the change in the early evening breeze would have felt pleasant on his inflamed cheeks as he stood in the middle of the lane watching Hope walk away. Isabel's words continued to reverberate in his head. It seemed the exchange between Isabel and her husband had not yet taken place. Then what had been the cause of Hope's extreme distress?

He watched the two figures until they disappeared round the bend. Amy slipped an arm comfortably through his but did not press him towards conversation. The only sound came from the treetops high above where a colony of rooks jostled noisily for predominance and the highest branch on which to roost.

The evening meal was an ordeal. The torture stole Hope's appetite and her eyes remained purposely lowered from her uncle who ate noisily directly opposite. Soon after the meal she feigned a headache and retired to her bedroom. Isabel was not convinced but had a more pressing matter; she needed to speak to that husband of hers and it would be best if Hope were not present.

In Hope's bedroom soft green muslin protruded from the pillowcase where she had pushed the remnants of her dress. The torn garment was withdrawn and stowed more carefully at the back of the deep drawer beneath the wardrobe until she could dispose of it properly.

That night she hardly slept but all night long relived her ordeal whilst sobbing gently into her pillow. Quite deliberately she chased away the memories with plans for her future, some ridiculous, others feasible, until the busy cocktail of abstract notions saturated her mind and she rose to perch on her bed in an anguish of weeping.

The next day proved endless. Hope laboured through her duties at the school. She felt strangely detached and unable to add to the excited chatter of the others in the Staff Room who remained charged by the previous day's event.

That evening she settled by the fire with her aunt who took up her basket of mending. There in the basket was the shirt Bert had been wearing the day before. It gave Hope a start. Her breath caught at the sight of the long frayed tear, a heartless reminder of her struggle. She glanced up to see Bert smirking from the comfort of his chair.

Noticing his expression Isabel admonished her husband. "Honestly Bert! I don't know how you managed to do that – your best shirt an'all. I can sew but I can't perform miracles." She examined it more closely. "You'll have to use it for work." She forced more friendliness to her tone than she felt and she began to stitch. She was still smarting from their exchange of words the night before. Determined not to display her hurt, Isabel smiled kindly at the one person left in the world she really loved. Her niece was unable to muster a smile and merely gazed blankly back at her.

During those first days Hope went about her daily activities routinely, at the same time carefully avoiding Bert. She exercised great pains to ensure that they were never alone and insisted on accompanying her aunt on her early-evening deliveries of fresh pastries and bread, newly laid eggs, and vegetables with a dusting of fertile soil on them. During Isabel's preoccupation at her oven Hope searched the job vacancies in the back pages of the Evening Post.

As the days came and went Hope almost doubted her own sanity. Her uncle had reverted to displaying the same indifference she had previously tolerated but now welcomed though his inattention did nothing to encourage a lowering of her guard. Her endeavours to ensure that she was never alone with him became well practised.

Consequently she was fearful when one evening she realised her aunt had set out without her.

She rushed to finish at the kitchen sink but when she felt the violation of fingers inside her waistband she had to swallow down the bitter taste that entered her mouth.

She spun round to confront Bert. "Don't even think about it! If you so much as breath on me I'll...." But hands were already exploring a breast and tugging at her clothing. Somehow she managed to drag herself into the parlour. "Get off! You have no right."

He began clawing at her slim-fitting skirt, wrenching it upwards. Annoyance showed in his face when it did not yield to his endeavours. The whisky he had consumed since getting in from work was taking effect and he swayed unsteadily. Hope seized the opportunity to break free and push him from her. Unselectively she grabbed one of the pieces from the display lovingly arranged by Isabel on the dresser but before the ornament could be brought down Bert lost his footing and went down, severely gouging his face on the rough plaster wall.

The expected string of curses did not assail her as she ran to the safety of her room. This time, with the strength that comes only from raw emotion, she dragged the heavy timber-framed bed to the door.

The overpowering silence that followed was at variance with the comforting quietness she frequently sought by the river. There was no tranquillity here, no soothing birdsong only an insidious silence pulsating in her ears. She guessed Bert's alcohol intake had taken him into his usual drunken stupor and that he now slept where he had fallen. She considered steeling downstairs to seek the key to the front door but feared movement might snatch him back to consciousness.

Rain had fallen incessantly for days and a wet, staccato rhythm clattered against the window. The sound would have proved a relief from the deafening silence but for the fact it reminded her of another stormy night when there had been a knock on the door and everything meaningful had been snatched from her.

At the sound of the first rumbles of thunder Hope was relieved to hear the return of her aunt. But she would not go to her; she would not go downstairs.

She strained to catch an exchange between Isabel and Bert but heard none. The only audible sound was evidence that the storm was building. Isabel knew her terror of thunderstorms. Anticipating that Isabel might check on her she eased the bed from the door as quietly as possible. Before long Isabel's light footsteps could be heard on the narrow staircase that creaked gently beneath her slight frame.

"You in bed pet?"

Hope nodded towards the wrap of love reaching out to her from beyond the closed door. "Yes." She hoped she sounded as though she had been pulled from sleep.

"I'll not disturb you then. See you in the morning. Good night, God bless." Tiptoeing on, Isabel murmured, "Sleep on my pet. Likewise that fool downstairs and may he return to his senses – though please God not to my bed."

Throughout the night Hope drifted in and out of sleep. At one point she was beside her stepping-stones with her eyes trained on the hill where presently her father would appear. It was a comforting interval and when she was transported back to wakefulness she was disappointed and fought hard to return to the river to await her father….. it was Friday. She succeeded in slipping back but almost immediately the storm entered her dream and the previously sparkling water suddenly changed to a dark confluence of muddy water. It splashed up the embankment to soil the hem of her lovely green dress, and a sudden wash of fear swept over her.

The echo of the water lapping over the stepping-stones pursued her throughout the night and when she awoke the same sense of disquiet persisted.

A scream broke into her recollections of the dream that had brought her to within a hair's breadth of catching a glimpse of her father. Almost dropping her hairbrush the shrill sound plummeted her smartly back to reality. That scream, though terrible in itself, was nothing compared with the stretched whimper that was to follow when she and her aunt made a terrible discovery.

Isabel appeared in the bedroom doorway, her mouth open, her face drained of what little colour might have been present in her lean features. "It's happened before but never like this!" She read confusion in her niece's face whilst she sought support from the doorframe. Hope's startled expression initiated further explanation. "The river – it's burst its banks. It's half way up the stairs!"

The enormity of the statement only registered when Hope threw open the curtains. The river had indeed burst its banks and as with the first magical fall of snow the landscape had been changed almost beyond recognition. The exact position of the meandering lane that led towards the village could only be vaguely determined beneath the watery landscape. Boundary hedges were dwarfed with only their tops displayed above the surge of water transporting all manner of debris dragged up in its wake.

Hope left the window and sped past her aunt to behold a scene that pulled her up sharply. The river had entered the cottage and was lapping against the third rise of the staircase. Items of furnishings floated in the narrow hallway below. The cork doormat, the half-empty coal scuttle and even one of Bert's boots bobbed up and down in the water. Looking more closely Hope saw that it was both of his boots, but then made another discovery. Her mouth dropped open to expel a silent scream that travelled the extent of her person and in that same moment the air was filled with a long stretched sound from beside her.

Like her niece, Isabel had realised that the boots were not empty. Lying face down in the dark, cold water was the body of Bert.

For what seemed an age the two women stood at the top of the stairs clinging together and trying to absorb the horror of their discovery. Hope broke the embrace to go to stand trembling at the head of the stairs whilst Isabel, looking older in that instant than she might in 20 years time, threw thin arms around herself and squeezed her eyes shut refusing to accept the knowledge being thrust at her. Hope descended the steps until she was only inches from Bert. Gingerly she reached to take his hand. Smooth save for the corrugated effect the water had brought to the underside of the fingers, the hand looked younger though it was cold and did not feel at all like flesh. She allowed it to slip back into the water.

"He is – dead?" The intonation made the hesitant statement a question.

Hope nodded before looking up at the woman overcome by grieving hysteria at the head of the stairs. It was imperative to get help but Hope resisted the impulse to wade beyond Bert's body to the door. To do so would be dangerous; the river was in a cruel mood. So near the main riverbed the angry confluence would likely sweep her off her feet. She went to rejoin her aunt.

"Bell – I'm so sorry." Hope laid a hand for a long moment on Isabel's shoulder then suggested trying to attract attention from a bedroom window.

Four hours later, Gregory Archer and his father took the two women carefully through the front bedroom window and transported them to safety. Built on a gradient Tarnville stood proud of the flood. Similarly the school and village hall had escaped the onslaught. A small, self-appointed rescue team spent the rest of the day transporting villagers to one or other of the three relatively safe havens. Hope and her aunt were amongst those taken to Tarnville.

Sir Charles Lurdmayne issued instructions to his Estate Manager and Housekeeper who promptly gave directions to the rest of the staff. Most of the ground floor and the west wing were made ready for Tarnville to receive its guests.

The enormous piles of bedding that began to appear in the long corridor amazed Charles. Great quantities of grey woollen Forces' blankets were piled at various points in the corridor connecting the two wings. The heavy, coarse blankets – an inheritance from those billeted there during the war – were drawn from the back of airing cupboards on the upper floors.

The hive of activity permeated quickly through the house, its energy having its beginnings in the two connecting basement kitchens where hot drinks and nourishing soup flowed and where foodstuffs had already been pulled from freezers. Well accustomed to preparing elegant dinner parties Sarah had never deserted what she referred to as wholesome home cooking, and knowing what hungry people liked she was determined that no one would go hungry during their stay at Tarnville.

It had been a long time since the house had seen so much activity. The slight figure of Sarah appeared every now and then, her calm manner giving no indication that the influx of bedraggled refugees was anything but normal.

Chapter 7

Vacant faces gazed out from Tarnville's leaded windows throughout that day. Few had viewed their homes from inside the house, and even Hope, a regular visitor, was held captive by the watery scene beyond the glazing.

There was no evidence of the floodwater receding and Sarah Kaye had sleeping arrangements in hand for more than 40 guests. The numbers had swelled quickly during the first few hours but as the day wore on the rescue boats arrived less frequently and then to bring fresh provisions and clothing. There had been a stir of excitement when a heavily pregnant cat and a bedraggled kid were unloaded. A temporary bed was provided in a quiet corner of the main hall for the former and because the nanny had perished at her tethering one of the Estate workers undertook the role of surrogate mother to the goat.

Despite the drama a camaraderie spirit settled on the community bedding down on Tarnville's polished floors though Hope did not form part of it. Her attention remained tied to her aunt who had been silent since their arrival.

Shortly after Hope and her aunt arrived at Tarnville, Gregory and another went back to retrieve Bert's body and take it to the Chapel, which proved difficult. Manipulating Bert Patterson's bulk into the flat-bottomed boat required skill and the journey took them against the current into the perilous obstacle course of drifting vegetation and partially submerged debris that crashed mercilessly into their leaky planking.

Bert was not the only casualty; Bobby was feared drowned. When his elderly owner was lifted into a boat – enquiring of everyone what day it was and whether it was Sunday – the puppy struggled from her arms and jumped overboard. Despite attempts to coax it back it had been swept away whimpering pathetically.

The early embrace of evening was already closing in by the time Gregory returned to Tarnville. Lighting in cottage windows was conspicuously absent. A shroud of eerie gloom hung over the village and for once, despite her lack of awareness, Hattie was right when she announced that it would be dark early.

Gregory had spent the entire day ferrying people to safety but despite his exhaustion and sore shoulders he went immediately to find Hope who had not been far from his thoughts all day.

The hours spent at the oars fighting the current had focused rather than deflected his mind. Bert's passing would bring changes, not least the increased rent of Ivy Cottage; with no Estate employee living there the rent would no longer be subsidised. He doubted Hope's wage and Isabel's meagre income from the smallholding would be enough to live on and secure their tenancy. He had explored all angles but the most obvious, and the one with most merit, came to him during his last trip when he and others had struggled to persuade a group of seemingly suicidal sheep to the safety of high ground. It meant he would be unable to take up his place at college, but that was suddenly of low priority and he could not wait to speak to Hope. He found her with her aunt in the dining room leading off from the great hall.

In days gone by music would have filled the hall whilst glittering couples taking a break from dancing would drift to the adjoining room where long voile curtains caught by evening summer breezes formed a pleasing backdrop to lavish buffet tables.

Gregory strode across the room. "Here you are. I've been looking for you." Evidence of his day's activities dripped to form a pool on the floor.

"You're saturated – just look at you. You look done in."

He pressed her back into her seat, waiving aside any suggestion that he should change. He was too exhausted even to think about it or indeed guess at which location his possessions eventually ended up; he and his meagre bundle became separated sometime during the morning. Suddenly aware of his fatigue he slumped to the floor by Hope's feet.

Although the subject was not voiced his nod told Hope that Bert's body had been removed from Ivy Cottage.

Isabel was offered food and drinks from the trays that arrived periodically from the kitchens where over the years she had assisted during large functions. Her dry eyes and reluctance to eat anything troubled the others.

As a consequence of the turmoil it was not until later that Charles learned of Bert Patterson's death but on hearing the news he acted quickly. Sarah Kaye was asked to prepare his daughter's bedroom where he suggested Hope and Isabel might gain privacy for their grief. The room had remained virtually untouched since Christina's disappearance two decades ago but if the Housekeeper was surprised by the instruction nothing showed in her face.

Gregory accepted that for the moment his thoughts must remain unspoken and he escorted the women to the bedroom.

After bidding them goodnight he left by a side door to stroll on the high ground surrounding Tarnville. He sought fresh air and solitude to think and appreciate the future. If someone had told him yesterday that it would be Hope's uncle – or more precisely his death – that would provide the key to the future he would not have believed them. He brushed away the sensation of guilt that threatened the pleasing picture that had begun to fill his mind.

It was a long time before Isabel finally succumbed to a sleep of forgetfulness but when Hope was satisfied she had detected the regular rhythm of sleep she slipped quietly from the bed to go to the window seat where she moved a china-faced doll that had been left there.

Her tired eyes swept the large room whose floor-length drapes concealed glazing that spanned almost an entire wall. In keeping with the others the room had a lofty ceiling with embellished moulding. It was impossible to define hues – a pastel shade certainly – pink or possibly mauve, which only daylight would confirm. Presently her eyes became more focused in the gentle wash of moonlight illuminating the carved fireplace where Hope imagined a fire would have been lit for Christina on cold winter evenings. She took up the china-faced doll again. The light filtering through the windows was pale but she was able to make out some of the detail of the dark-coloured velvet dress with matching cloak edged in what felt like fur, and the delicate necklace of small beads.

As though at once charmed she caught the atmosphere of the room and glimpsed a time when Charles had been happy and before sadness had creased his eyes. She saw a pretty child playing with a china-faced doll and years later, as a young woman, at the dressing table brushing long, dark hair.

The dressing table beckoned and glancing furtively at the sleeping form behind her, Hope advanced to explore a cut-glass tray containing hairbrushes and an arrangement of decorative perfume bottles, their contents long since evaporated. She glanced into the mirror almost expecting to see the dark-haired beauty Charles remembered and still sought, but her own reflection stared back, a glint of reproach in the eyes. She chastised herself; daydreaming was a luxury she could not afford. The present closed in on her, firm and unyielding and insistent upon recognition. She returned to the window seat where she must have dozed, for in the next moment she was being nudged awake by Sarah Kaye. Hope's eyes swept protectively to the mound in the bed and motioned that her aunt should not be disturbed.

Sarah's face creased. "Poor love. Let her sleep as long as she's able. I'll bring fresh tea once she's awake." Reverting back to role she checked that Hope had everything she required on the breakfast tray. She hesitated. "It doesn't seem right, you in your night clothes and everything, but that young man of yours is wanting a word."

"Gregory?"

Sarah nodded. "He's outside the door."

Hope found Gregory lolling against the dark wood panelling. There was a noticeable heightening of colour in his face as he apologised for seeking her out so early. He was in one of the parties setting out shortly to check for any missing persons and to secure homes, he explained. "I don't know when I'm likely to be back and I wanted to see you before I left. I would've spoken to you last night but there were too many folk milling around. And we can't really talk here." He jerked his head, signalling that she should follow.

In a borrowed nightdress and robe much too large, she padded after him down the staircase to the floor below.

At the door Gregory stood aside for her to enter. It was a room that Hope knew well. He pressed her gently into one of the dark-red leather chairs then went to the window as though seeking inspiration from the devastation outside.

"Hope...." He turned back to her, a gentle expression in his handsome features. "I'm not sure how the two of you will be fixed now with the cottage."

He did not need to elaborate; she understood. "The same thought occurred to me last night." Already anticipating a financial shortfall she had totted up her wage and what she thought Isabel probably made selling home produce. She was mindful that it had been Bert's employment on the Estate that qualified them for a subsidy in the rent. But Bert was dead and that would bring changes. "Once things get back to normal.... if you know what I mean," she added, suddenly embarrassed by the inadequacy of her words, "I intend asking Sir Charles to allow Bell to remain in the cottage. If he agrees, and I think he may because something similar must have happened when Hattie's husband died, I aim to get a job in the city. Earning more I'll be able to help Bell out." She noticed his sudden intake of breath and finished, "It's the very least I can do. She's been the only mother I've had and you can't begin to imagine the amount of caring she's bestowed on me, especially since my father died."

Gregory peeled himself from the windowsill and for a moment looked like he had as a child when he had made up his mind about something. "I've decided not to go to college," he said simply, his chin lifting. "I'm going to take a job locally, hopefully here on the Estate if there's a position. I'm going to have a word with Joseph Fearnley. But Hope.... that's only part of it." He came to lay his hands gently on her shoulders. "I want to look after you.... you and Bell. Hope – I want to marry you."

The words were just free of his lips when the first tears since the discovery of Bert's body began to slide down Hope's face. When she made no response he took her hand gently between his.

"I'll make you very happy. I'll take proper care of you. And you'll have the best I can give you. Hope.... I love you."

Her thoughts went immediately to Amy. Poor Amy!

With familiar skill he slid a smile into his voice. "I think I've loved you ever since your first day at school when, with all the chivalry of someone 20 years my senior, I offered you my seat but Helen Braithwaite's fat backside beat you to it!"

She remembered the incident, not least her warm glow. She remembered as though it were yesterday. But those recollections belonged to another time – a lifetime ago. They had grown up. But seeing the nervous glint of moisture above his lip she restrained her refusal.

He stooped to return a hand to her shoulder. "Don't say anything …..not now," he urged. "Think about it. Please do that." He straightened up, his face pained. "I shouldn't have asked you like this, with your uncle just gone." He raked a nervous hand through his hair. "I should've had more sense. It's not the time. It's too soon. I wasn't thinking. Forgive me?" He placed a finger against her lips to halt the formation of any words. "Just think about it – that's all I ask."

For a stretched moment Hope looked into eyes that searched hers for an indication of her answer. Then he left the room without another word.

There had been desperation in his eyes and she regretted that she was the cause. With another emotion added to those already troubling her she went to lean against the windowsill, her eyes going instinctively to the location where her stepping-stones lay hidden beneath the confluence of brown, silted water. Even the comfort of her father's caring was denied her. He was gone forever – but not his dreams; the stepping-stones would continue down the years to act as a reminder of those aspirations. He had been fearful of her slipping unnoticed into eventual obscurity and one of his dearest desires slid into her mind lively, promising and real: "You'll get a good job in the city one day."

Looking at the precise spot where she knew her stepping-stones lay she sighed. "I'd trade all my tomorrows if I could return to one of my yesterdays with you Dad," her voice choking on sadness.

She went slowly from the room and as she closed the door she sensed she was drawing to a close an entire chapter in her life.

With quietness resumed a reluctant witness to the scene, concealed by the high back of a winged chair at the far end of the library, rose stiffly to return a book to its rightful place on the shelf before returning to the familiar seat to think.

Isabel was dressed when Hope returned to the bedroom. Whether because of her uncle's death, Gregory's proposal, or a consequence of the flood, or a combination of all that – and everything else – she went to her aunt's waiting arms unable to check the flow of tears.

The surge of emotion stirred Isabel from the apathetic being she had become and her arms tightened around the slender young woman she loved with passion. "We'll be all right, you and me. You'll see." Isabel brushed away the tears that had mingled with her own.

They went to the window in the hope of seeing a drop in the water level but none was evident. Familiar landmarks half-submerged in baptism broke the surface of the waterline like a series of remote islands.

An urgent shout took their attention to the terrace below, where Amy was leaping about and waving. Retracing his steps Gregory came into view. Amy spoke urgently to him about something to which he appeared to be agreeing and she reached up to kiss him.

Isabel's head tilted. "I wouldn't be surprised if those two settled down together." There had been a time when she was optimistic that Gregory and Hope might strike up a meaningful courtship, but Hope had not displayed any real interest, or indeed in any who had taken her out. It was even rare for her to have more than one dance with anyone at the Chapel socials. Her thoughts ran on as she wondered whether Mowlem could offer whatever it was her niece seemed to need – or perhaps more accurately – demand from life, for it had long been evident that Hope would not be satisfied with a retiring village-life role. Always poised on tiptoe, appreciative of life, her niece was bursting with vitality and had an excitement about her unlike anyone else she knew. The child had grown and was already pressing gently against the confines of her cosy, village-life existence.

The day stretched endlessly before them and they pondered how to occupy themselves. Not wishing to disrupt Charles's household any more than was necessary they took themselves down to the main hall where friends were quick to offer words of comfort to their newly bereaved neighbours.

After breakfast Isabel noticed the little cat, swollen and lumpy with kittens, brought in yesterday. The pangs of birth were upon her and the she had begun circling, pausing only to knead the floor with frenzied paws and to sniff the chosen area.

"Apparently she was rescued just in time." Without fuss Isabel removed her cardigan and placed it and the cat beneath a chair. After a further prolonged period of investigative sniffing and more circling the she eventually presented three perfect tortoiseshell kittens and once detached settled down to cleaning them.

Purposefully Isabel took Hattie's arm and encouraged her to lead a few children at a time to peek beneath the chair where the new family had residence. The new mother washed each tricoloured ball of fluff almost to shrinkage, unaware of the void she filled as Hattie stroked her, whispering the name of Bobby.

"Life goes on," Isabel murmured thoughtfully.

"Yes."

The husky voice at her side startled her. Charles nodded before turning his attention to Isabel. "Are you all right Mrs Patterson? Is there anything I or any of my people can do for you?" Genuine concern lay heavily in his voice.

Isabel shook her head. He had done more than enough in providing a room. Those first hours of solitude had helped, she told him; she would not have wanted to remain with the others whose chatter ceased abruptly upon her approach. He emphasised the room was hers for as long as she required it. Similar assurances had been given to the others.

Charles glanced around the hall filled with his tenants. "Each of them wondering what they will find on their return," he said half to himself. "Their only certainty that there will be no upturn in fortunes in the foreseeable future." He shook his head. "I marvel at their spirit. Until Joe reports back I can't begin to imagine the suffering that will be endured when the cleaning up process begins. But whatever can be done will be done," he finished on a definite note.

His mood changed. He glanced about him. "I'd like a word with your niece, or more precisely a favour, and should be grateful if you'd mention I was looking for her. Tell her I'll be in the library."

On her way to the library Hope resolved to pick up the reins and take control, though chose not for the moment to disclose to Isabel her plan to leave Mowlem. Whilst she had a strong feeling of belonging to the village, which would always represent home, she felt an even stronger need to move away. Yet inexplicably she knew Mowlem with her stepping-stones and the pulsating echo of the river would always draw her back. Neither would she mention Gregory's proposal. Unlikely to understand or appreciate the drive deep within her – an inheritance undoubtedly derived from her father's encouragement – her aunt might advocate the nurturing of a union with Gregory. She would see it as security; something she feared Isabel had had little of in her own marriage.

She was certain that Amy was the one for Gregory. With that analysis came the knowledge of which she was already aware and her chin went up in the manner she had displayed since an infant; she did not love Gregory enough to marry him – and she loved Amy too much to hurt her.

Hope reached the library and knocked on the door. She peered in to see someone she had not seen before. A tall, broad-shouldered gentleman with the ownership of a friendly face and thinning sandy-coloured hair returned her smile. Charles stepped from his guest to meet her somewhat formally in the middle of the floor.

"My dear, this is Kevin Lester, a family friend." Charles turned to his guest. He introduced Hope as the young lady he had been telling him about.

Kevin Lester, she learned, had been staying at Tarnville when the flood struck. Her curiosity as to why that should result in her being summoned to the library and she become the subject of conversation, showed in her eyes as she mumbled something about being happy to meet him.

"Hope, I've been meaning to mention that I'm going away for a while," began Charles. "Probably for a couple of months. I'm going to Greece, the island of Corfu." The overt surprise in her expression drew further explanation. "Margaret and I spent many happy times on one or other of the islands. I've suddenly felt the urge to do it again." He laughed lightly. "Though I don't like to admit it, I'm getting on. That's what's probably encouraged the need to search out past memories. We once thought about living out there...." He swallowed down the emotion in his voice. "I'm leaving at the end of the month."

The irony of the news startled her. Only a matter of hours ago she had decided to tell him of her own plans to leave Mowlem, and to seek the favour of her aunt being allowed to remain at Ivy Cottage.

Charles motioned with a flip of his hand that Kevin should take up the detail. Kevin explained that as he was stranded by the flood Charles had suggested setting up a temporary work base at Tarnville, and Hope had been recommended as having suitable secretarial skills.

The envelope that Gregory retrieved from the Post Mistress on Amy Reid's behalf contained long-awaited news. It was her acceptance as a student nurse at Meridian College of Nursing. Equally pleasing was the fact that Meridian was not far from Farrington Agricultural College where Gregory was due to take up his place next month.

Conversely, the news that met Gregory's return to Tarnville was not what he had been hoping for. Despondency overwhelmed him and he made no attempt to hide his irritation when Hope steered him towards a quiet corner not to give him an answer to his proposal but to tell him about her day – in fanatical detail.

As well as a family friend, Kevin Lester was Sir Charles's lawyer, she told Gregory. She had spent the day taking copious shorthand notes that she subsequently transcribed with the aid of a portable computer. Despite an initial fit of panic as to whether her speeds and only recently acquired computer skills would be adequate, she settled into the assignment that had unexpectedly presented itself. After belabouring the joys of computers as opposed to her antiquated typewriter, which despite its shortcomings would be treasured always, Charles's imminent departure for Corfu was explained at great length.

"And some of the paperwork related to that. Also – and this is the best bit – Sir Charles is placing an advertisement in the local and national newspapers in an attempt to find his long-lost daughter. He wants to hand Tarnville over to her before he gets round to settling in Greece for good. Fancy that.... after all these years...."

"Yer – fancy."

The reason for Gregory's disinterest dawned on her suddenly. It was unforgivable to have gone on at such length, and to merely switch subject matters would be an added affront. She thought for a moment then suggested a walk on the terrace.

When Hope finished speaking, Gregory's eyes had never looked sadder. She did not wish to add to his despondency by telling him that she had made up her mind to leave Mowlem.

The next hurdle, even before looking for another secretarial position, was to rekindle her dear friend's interest in taking up his place at college, which had been his goal for as long as she could remember.

Chapter 8

It was more than a week before the cleaning up operation was able to begin in earnest. Starting at one end of the village co-ordinated teams under the direction of Joseph Fearnley began to free blocked drains and clear offending brown silt and debris from homes. It was five days more before the tenants began filtering back to their homes and Tarnville returned to normal.

Immediately upon their return Isabel and Hope went to view the empty cages that ran along the back of Ivy Cottage. One of Joseph's men had already broken the news that the rabbits had drowned. Nevertheless the absence of inquisitive faces at the mesh dragged lumps to their throats, as did the chain coiled at the foot of the post in next-door's yard where the nanny had been tethered. The hens were gone; strayed rather than drowned, they imagined, though two of the *old ladies* clucked forlornly from the top of the rabbit hutches.

They worked hard to get the cottage back to some semblance of order. A great deal had been badly soiled and Hope was relieved the journals containing the record of her life, and her father's paints and easel had escaped damage. Piles of ruined furnishings and treasures began to appear outside dwellings and Ivy Cottage was no exception. For the next few days Hope and her aunt worked together in double harness, mopping and scrubbing, and taking themselves beyond all previous boundaries of tiredness. Eventually their toil reaped rewards and the little dwelling was coaxed back to something habitable, though glaring evidence of the flood remained. Despite vigorous endeavours an ugly, greasy reminder remained high above the skirting boards, and the insidious smell of damp was everywhere. The odour clung thickly to everything. Isabel declared the stench reminded her of slimy weed dredged from duck ponds, and she swore it would remain forever.

The activity helped to deflect attention from the Inquest into Bert's death, which was to be held in Braefield. Though it had been explained as a formality, Hope was deeply anguished during the preceding days. When she effected an escape it was but for a few moments, for recent events were repeatedly reported in the newspaper beneath such headlines as "Flood, Sweat and Tears".

Despite her misgivings the proceedings were concluded in under an hour, though those long drawn out minutes seemed like an eternity. Since her aunt's retrieval of a broken ornament from the parlour floor Hope had come to wonder whether she had inflicted a blow to Bert's head as she intended during those abhorrent moments that continued to haunt her. She could no longer be sure, but if she had....

Plagued by uncertainty, and worrying that something might be detectable of the shame connected with the period prior to Bert's death, her fingers had gripped the edges of her hard wooden seat during the entire address of the Medical Examiner, but his summing up brought a measure of relief. It came as no surprise that the stomach contents confirmed Bert Patterson had been drinking heavily preceding death. The conclusion was that he had fallen into a deep sleep, drowning where he lay. In offering an explanation for the deep wheals on Bert's face the expert told the Inquiry that in all probability they had been caused by the movement of the water buffeting the body against the rough plaster wall.

Mentally and physically drained, Isabel and Hope accepted Joseph Fearnley's offer of a lift back to Mowlem. Back home, worn out and wearisome they settled with a pot of tea beside the fire that had burned constantly in an effort to dry out the property. Both women looked towards the one easy chair where Bert, intoxicated, had slouched most evenings. The chair yawned emptily at them, an air of reproach in its gape. It was as though similar thoughts entered their minds at once.

"He told me he was leaving me." Isabel's voice was toneless. "He had said it before. I suppose he meant it, he just couldn't be bothered to get round to doing anything about it." She stared at the armchair, now no longer the focal point of torment. "He left me in the end though."

This was the first time Isabel had indicated her marriage had not been easy. Hope reached for her hand. "Bell.....he tried to rape me.... here in this room." The words had come from nowhere and in embarrassment Hope returned her stare to the drunken form slumped awkwardly in the chair, his mouth agape, before the image dissolved a moment later.

Isabel's eyes shot open. She shuddered. "I always felt that there was something.... but I had no idea he...." Her face crumpled with the

61

pain accompanying her comprehension. "Bert was capable of many things – but that? Awh love – I feel crushed at the very thought."

"It's over, done with. We need never mention it again," Hope whispered, fervently hoping that one day she might be freed from the abhorrent memory.

The day of the funeral passed off quietly, almost unmarked. What few floral tributes there were had been sent more out of respect for the widow than the deceased. There were embarrassingly few mourners and despite everything Hope found herself feeling sorry for the man who had made such a small impression on those around him that few felt the need to show their respects on his passing.

As though fate had purposely turned the page, the next day brought promises of change. Hope returned from work to find her aunt practically twitching with the news that secured their tenancy of Ivy Cottage. Joseph Fearnley had invited her to join him in the Estate office to help with all the work generated by the flood. Though it had been Bert's responsibility to keep the books for the dairy, Joseph had long been aware that it had been his wife who ended up doing them. Isabel's neat, accurate hand had been a welcome change from earlier inaccurate entries scrawled by her husband.

The news had put a hitherto unseen sparkle in the woman Hope loved like a mother. In her elation Isabel had almost forgotten the envelope in her hand. Hastily excusing her preoccupation she held out the long, white envelope that was addressed to her niece.

Puzzled, Hope took it from her. The postmark more resembled a smudge of rouge glaring unflatteringly from an elderly pale face, and gave no clue as to the sender.

Bemused, bright colour flooded her cheeks as she reread the letter. She handed it to Isabel who adopted the same stunned look.

To one it was the answer to her prayers. To the other it was what she had dreaded whilst at the same time appreciating it was only what Frederick had planned for his daughter years before.

Isabel had been aware of Hope's strive towards improving herself, particularly her career prospects. Taking herself off to night school she had gained her last two secretarial diplomas with distinction, and computer skills had quickly followed. The urgency dated back to around the time of Frederick's death. Whether an attempt to bathe the hurt by filling the void with other things she was unsure but knew she could no longer hold on to Frederick's lovingly created essence of free spirit. Like a limp posy of faded wild flowers clutched tightly in a child's hand, the natural bloom would go out of Hope if she were restrained and freedom denied in which to chase her dreams and paint her own canvas in life.

"Kevin Lester QC." Hope grinned as she reread the name typed beneath the flowing signature. "Heck! Sir Charles's lawyer is a Queen's Counsel – and he wants me to work for him!"

"Temporarily," put in Isabel. "Only while his secretary is on maternity leave."

"Granted – but once I'm there I'll have the opportunity of gaining recognition and hopefully acquiring something permanent."

Had Hope been aware of the size of the organisation she was being invited to join she might have been knocked off balance, but for the moment all she appreciated was that she had finally secured a job in the city. She saw the same shadow of sadness creep into her aunt's eyes as it did when she explained her post at the school didn't pay enough and that something inside her wanted more.

She flung her arms round Isabel. "I'll always come back Bell. Mowlem will always be my home." She pulled back to look wistfully at her aunt but could not prevent the brightness that bubbled back into her voice. "Both of us with such terrific news! I don't doubt that Sir Charles had some input." Hope laughed, and then glanced at her watch. "I think I'll just slip over to see him – and he can tell me about his forthcoming trip."

She struggled back into boots, the only form of footwear possible since the flood. "He's a really lovely person. I've grown quite fond of him. In some ways he reminds me of my father." Smiling she withdrew a happy memory from her memory bank. There was a way that Charles looked at her before giving in to laughter, almost indefinable but it was there. And there was the way his eyes grew wide with anticipation when she embarked on telling him something that he detected was important to her. "I think the villagers have come to know him better over these last few months, especially during recent events." A picture of what had seemed like the entire neighbourhood bedding down on the polished floors at Tarnville came to mind. "They no longer see him as that remote personage from the House."

"That's true enough. I delighted in an echo of just that with the Post Mistress only this morning. I told her you played a part in that, marching over there as bold as brass to offer condolences on his son's death. Any separation barriers lowered noticeably after that."

Hope shunned the compliment and changed the subject. "Wouldn't it be wonderful if his advertisement has brought some success in tracking down his daughter? Then all three of us would have something to celebrate!"

"You should consider the offer carefully," Isabel said quickly. "I mean – for a start it would mean y'getting digs in Leeds. Have you thought about that?" Her smile collapsed. "Oh Hope...." She chastised herself for the uncertainty in her voice. "I'll not beg you to stay. I've seen the same expectation I only vaguely remember from my own youth," when life had laid itself before her, and before she married Bert Patterson. "It was meant to be. There was always something about you that set you apart."

Isabel had seen that beneath Hope's gentle demeanour lurked the spirited determination her father had carefully nurtured. Deep down she had always known that Hope was destined for something better – something more significant – and would follow her own destiny.

After the flood an air of change tinged with uncertainty fell upon the close-knit community of Mowlem. John and Annie Wilks moved away. After a flurry of scarlet gossip and conjecture most agreed that Annie was no better than she should be. The subject of the imminent departure of the three inseparable friends, Gregory, Hope and Amy, was constantly raised. Doubtless more young folk would follow. Only a generation ago the youth had emerged from the village school to be absorbed into various roles of employment on the Estate. But the passing years had brought an imbalance of numbers and consequent lack of employment. The young expected more.

Nevertheless not everything was negative; Bobby had been reunited with his owner. Peter Summerville who owned Broad Gates Farm three miles down river had plucked the young dog from the turbulent floodwater. When he enquired as to the owner it was Isabel who had had the pleasure of escorting him to Hattie's cottage.

That unexpected shaft of happiness passed and thoughts turned once more to Tarnville. At the forefront of everyone's mind was the recent departure of Sir Charles Lurdmayne for what was likely to be a lengthy absence. The news had an unsettling effect and despite Joseph Fearnley's reassurances that the Estate would remain intact, the entire neighbourhood speculated how the occurrence might affect them.

After Charles's departure, Amy left to follow a career in nursing. Then it was Gregory's turn to go and take up his place at Farrington Agricultural College, though not before calling at Ivy Cottage.

Like old times Hope and her friend chatted by the fireside before wishing each other much success and happiness. It was not until the last moments of Gregory's visit that mention was made of his proposal of marriage. Before slipping out into the night he took Hope's arm. He pulled back instantly when he caught the familiar fragrance of her person. It was a warm, pleasant smell that had nothing to do with perfume or soap. "You were right, we have always been like brother and sister." He raised his hands to indicate the remark warranted no response. "*We* – simply weren't meant to be, but that doesn't change the fact that I'll always be there for you Hope – always – I mean that."

After closing the door gently behind him, unbidden tears crept into Hope's eyes. In Gregory she had a rare gift – a true friend.

Before attending to the last-minute packing for her own departure the following day, she found herself reflecting on the question she had put to Gregory on May Day and wondered again where they all would be in a few years' time.

When she was to remember that moment some years later she was pleased she had not known then what was in store for them, for she was certain if it were in the scheme of things to be able to see into the future many would not dare to continue on their choice of path.

Chapter 9

Though not as picturesque as Mowlem, the view from Hope's window was nonetheless pleasing and an immense improvement on that of her previous flat. That flat had had a small window set into the ceiling, which made it necessary to stand on a chair in order to see out of it. It had not been worth the effort for when she did the view comprised of nothing but row upon row of terraced houses; a blackened legacy from the days when there had been two railway stations in close proximity, both emitting choking black smoke, and factories spitting out filth. Added to that it had been situated near the University and therefore far from peaceful, and a jarring contrast to the quietness of Mowlem previously taken for granted.

Hope had put up with the noise for one sleepless week then, foregoing the month's rent paid in advance, moved to a flat in Eastkirk, some 20-minutes' bus ride from her place of work. She considered herself fortunate in securing her next safe haven, not least because her landlady, Daphne Carr, welcomed her into her home as though she were a valued member of her family.

The advertisement had not even been placed in the shop window before Angela, one of the secretaries at Lester Associates, brought the accommodation to Hope's attention. The rent was more than she wanted to pay but after viewing the room she had no hesitation in changing her address.

The room was a good size, bigger than her bedroom back home and situated at the back of the semi-detached house it looked out over a long garden made private by tall, privet hedges. The lawn needed mowing and the neglected borders, victims of nature's assiduous encroachment, resembled the relaxed countryside Hope missed and the naturalness went some way to providing a balm of comfort.

Hope was at the gate-legged table eating a hastily prepared sandwich. Her mind was on her aunt. She had been surprised how much she missed her. Isabel's regular news-filled letters were torn open the moment they arrived but it would be better once the telephone was installed at the cottage; a device they had never felt the need of before. Soon they would be able to chat to their hearts' contentment – like they had beside the fire so long ago whilst Bert slept soundly only a matter of feet away.

The familiar music announcing the commencement of the BBC news drew Hope from daydream. She needed to hurry if she were to be ready for when David arrived.

David Stratton, a conveyancer in Lester's Property & Estates Department, had pursued Hope relentlessly since her arrival at the firm three months ago. It had been remarks in a letter from Isabel and a few short lines from Gregory that had encouraged her to accept David's invitation to join him with others on an evening out. Isabel had expressed concern that she seemed to be throwing herself into her role of Personal Assistant to the exclusion of everything else. Isabel's pointed remarks persuaded her to take stock of her new life and appreciate the need to play a little.

The remaining half of her sandwich was consigned to the bin and she went to wash and change into something suitable for the evening. She had never been ten-pin-bowling, and after rejecting several outfits she opted for what she considered a fairly safe option, a pair of jeans teamed with a cotton shirt. Jeans and trainers seemed to be the compulsory uniform away from the workplace.

Shortly before midnight Hope stepped from David's car. She wrapped her arms around herself in an attempt to ward off the crisp, late-January night air as she ran to Daphne's front doorstep to wave goodbye to the happy group squashed into David's old Ford.

During the evening she had seen her work colleagues in a different light – all except Marty, which was short for Martinella, the name by which her colleague chose to be known in favour of Mary Ann, which appeared on her Birth Certificate. Marty had remained her usual difficult self, lapsing into silence much of the time.

Right from her first day at Lester Associates Hope had detected something about the overly thin young woman with whom she shared an office. Within hours of her arrival three different members had taken her on one side to warn her to keep an eye on Marty. Determined not to prejudge a colleague Hope strove to kindle a friendship but soon discovered a disturbing side to her roommate.

A month after joining the firm Hope's attention had been caught by one of the protracted sighs for which Marty was famous. From across the office, her arms folded against the human race, Marty muttered that she could be a Personal Assistant – she did all that kind of stuff now anyway. Hope took this to be a reaction to the newly engraved nameplate being attached to the door. Her designation of Personal Assistant to the Chairman, Kevin Lester, as opposed to Marty's title of Secretary had not been well received. When Kevin's previous PA decided not to return after her baby's birth Hope's post was made permanent; this was followed by a lot of shuffling of papers and banging of cabinet drawers at the other side of the office.

When a number of disturbing incidents followed, not least the rearranging of Hope's pending file whereby she almost missed picking up a client's deadline and the vital financial papers appertaining to a large merger, Hope grasped what others had been trying to tell her. Very soon the habit of checking everything whilst constantly watching her back became second nature. The practice stood her in good stead; it gained her an eye for detail, which went towards aiding her career. It was a frequent source of amusement to Hope as she maintained her position of a jump ahead of the girl who, well practised in avoiding detection, was hell-bend on tripping her up.

Occasionally Marty did get through Hope's carefully applied veneer. "The woman's a maniac!" she exclaimed to Angela one lunchtime.

As she prepared for bed Hope recalled their conversation, appreciating that it was easier to smile about it now, three months later.

"The woman? I take it you mean the one known to us with questionable social skills; who should be put on tablets; is several sheets short of a toilet roll and closely resembles the human version of a cod liver oil sandwich! The one who has no less than six GCEs – mentioned with boring monotony at every possible opportunity.... am I getting close?"

Angela had listened sympathetically whilst Hope spoke about her first week of sharing an office with Marty, who would insist on referring to her previous experience as having done a bit of typing for a village school. Whilst the comment amused Hope, its repetition began to jangle the nerve endings a bit, but detecting Marty was on an ego trip she had not bothered to put her right. Even in those early days she sensed the hothead was on a self-destruction course.

Angela had continued, "Six GCEs – and I bet you've never mentioned your even grander number of RSAs – several with Distinction – or that other little thing – that you were the fastest recorded typist in the county for two consecutive years? Maybe you should. Working in Personnel I'm well aware of your qualifications, and your other qualities, not least your modesty, which is something Marty can't compete with. Her ladyship could do with being pulled down a peg or two – or a hundred and two!"

Hope had picked up the conversation. "I swear she lays awake all night plotting what she can do next. I only hope she never turns to politics. Instead of kissing babies she'd issue a proclamation to sacrifice the first-born!" She had just witnessed one of Marty's many blatant lies.

Angela agreed. "She gives evolution a bad name!"

"And her mood swings are unbelievable." Hope had begun to dislike her roommate, a new experience for her – not counting her even greater hatred for another – but the memory of Bert had been quickly pushed from mind. "I think I've just about got the measure of her stupidity and then she goes and does something else to amaze me!"

Angela took up the cry. "She opens her mouth before she knows what's coming out, singing snatches of other people's songs but slightly out of tune, and goes around with a face like a smacked bum!" She grinned at her adoption of Hope's expression, one of many she in turn had borrowed from Gregory. Angela pulled a face from across the table then exploded into laughter, easing the moment and bringing shared support to a recognised problem.

The telltale signs were usually apparent on Marty's arrival at the office. Within the time it took Marty to remove her coat and hang it on the coat stand Hope prided herself on being able to assess the type of day she was in for. More often than not Marty's demeanour hinted at sulkiness – the likes of which that should have been left behind in the school play yard – and this punctuated by deep weeping and wailing and attention seeking.

"You know she's anorexic? I reckon that's a lot to do with it. Doesn't eat enough!" The bubbly blonde grinned and took a hearty bite from her sandwich.

Hope liked Angela. She did not package her comments in frills. Something similar had crossed her mind, but anorexia – she was not sure about that.

Now, departing from those recollections, Hope turned her thoughts to the evening she had just spent at the bowling alley. It had been her suggestion to include Marty. The others had thrown up their arms in horror but she assured them that including Marty was the best way to encourage a change in her, but as the evening wore on she knew she would not be so generous again.

Notwithstanding Marty's unsociable behaviour, Hope had thoroughly enjoyed the evening and took a few minutes to make an entry in her diary notes to exclaim the joys of ten-pin bowling.

No specific record relating to David Stratton was made, though many would be written in the months to follow, and many would fall short of this evening.

Before finally turning in for the night Hope took up the letter she had been writing to Isabel and added the postscript, "I miss the taste of your home-made bread, but I miss you much more!" But for the fact that Isabel might worry she was not eating properly she might have elaborated further. She decided not to mention her first trip to a supermarket where she purchased bread as dull as sawdust compared with the crisp cobs pulled from her aunt's oven, and spotlessly clean vegetables that shone like plastic and tasted of nothing.

That night Hope slept soundly until the shrill ring of her alarm clock wrenched her from slumber to drop her abruptly into the misty, early hours of the next day.

Chapter 10

The next day a rail strike and a blanket of fog brought the city to a standstill and prevented Hope from going home for the weekend. Instead she had to make do with a telephone call. Shortly after replacing the receiver the telephone rang again. Believing Isabel had forgotten something she was surprised to hear a male voice.

"Hi, my name's Dave. Sorry to disturb you – I'm from Stratton Enterprises. We're currently doing some work in your area and looking for people interested in having a good time. Would this be of interest to you?" David Stratton had guessed she would be grounded in Leeds. "If you don't take up the option you may regret it for the rest of your life."

The pause in his sales pitch repartee was filled instantly with Hope's laughter. This was fast becoming the effect David had on her. His light banter, some might say flippant, helped to lighten the effects of her roommate's moods. Just the other day he had described the drama queen as being only marginally more interesting than Formica, then becoming more serious, advised her not to make an enemy of her. Confident she was well acquainted with all Marty's tricks, Hope shrugged the warning aside. She had reliable insurance in place. From comments Kevin Lester made it was evident that senior management was abreast of the *Martinella* situation.

That was the start of their relationship. David and Hope spent almost every moment of that weekend in each other's company, often in each other's arms, only parting to sleep. The parting was not David's idea though went along with it good-humouredly.

Early on he had identified that Hope was different, and not just because of her stunning looks. There was something, as yet unfathomable, that always seemed to hold her back. Knowing he would not have tolerated these abrupt switches to coolness from anyone else brought the realisation that Hope Thackeray held his interest more than any of her predecessors – and there had been a long parade of them. With Hope's entry into his life David conceded the days were gone when he had amused himself by seeing how many women he could juggle at any one time.

Six months later, David was still enjoying admiring glances cast in the direction of the beauty on his arm.

"Happy sweetheart?"

Feigning more ease then she actually felt, Hope smiled, her body moving in unison with David's on the dance floor. The invitation to Gregory and Amy's engagement party in Mowlem's village hall was precisely the news she had hoped for. Moreover the occasion awarded the opportunity to introduce David to her friends, and particularly Isabel who had been keen to meet the recipient of the lengthy telephone calls she made from the cottage each weekend.

Hope's first feelings of unrest presented themselves upon her arrival home with David. After an exchange of news with Isabel – still singing the praises of working in the Estate office – Hope suggested taking David down to the river. He agreed somewhat reluctantly and Hope sensed that had the width of the path permitted, he would have elected to take the car.

Mowlem was vital to her; an enduring link with her father it would always hold a special place in her heart. Determined that David should enjoy his induction, Hope pointed out things along the way: the gnarled oak tree she had climbed expertly before falling equally spectacularly badly grazing elbows and knees; the particular hedgerow where hedgehogs could always be found with the arrival of dusk; and the shrubbery used for dens. At the sight of her stepping-stones she broke into a run, whilst behind her David picked his way more carefully, commenting that he had stepped in something.

At the edge of the river Hope breathed deeply, filling her lungs with sweet-smelling air. The river was lazy, its surface elaborately decorated with a myriad of flashing diamonds; a different animal from the untamed flow of not so long ago. The torn banks had mended themselves over the ensuing months and save for a tree slumped like a drunk further upriver no hint remained of the flood the year before.

"I just love it here. It's the most beautiful place in the world! It holds so many memories." She turned to share her joy but David's attention had already transferred to the impressive stone structure on the opposite bank. "Tarnville," she explained. "Beautiful isn't she?"

"She? You make it sound like a living entity." The note of sarcasm wavered when he noticed how her eyes soften as they swept the breadth of the house.

Perceiving his lack of understanding she told him about her elderly friend who lived there, swiftly following that with an engaging account for the presence of 18 stones in the riverbed. Laughing with the rebound of the memory she admitted that with a child's comprehension she had taken her father's comments literally. But even before she finished speaking his attention had wandered to something else, and she suffered disappointment. She glanced back at Tarnville, but the delicate thread was lost and the treasured memory gone.

That evening David insisted on taking the car to the village hall. Isabel was amused: all of ten minutes' walk away, folk would either think them barmy or gentry; she did not know which was worse.

During the drive Hope detected a subtle change in her aunt. She marvelled she had not noticed it before. Isabel looked younger and had put on a little weight, which suited her and there was a happiness about her eyes that had not been there before; apparently working at Tarnville agreed with her.

The party was well underway when they arrived. Amy was the first to notice them and she pulled Gregory through a gap in a group making a brave attempt at line dancing. Hope caught the bathe of happiness in Gregory's eyes as he beamed at Amy, who had become joyfully articulate. His entire manner confirmed what Hope wanted to know.

Despite warm introductions Hope sensed David preferred to keep a distance. Fearing others might detect this unexpected aloofness she steered him towards the buffet table where they made their selection whilst watching Isabel waltzing with one of the local farmers. The David she knew and had come to love resurfaced and she might have believed herself guilty of misjudging him had it not been for what followed.

Hope cringed at Isabel's look of disapproval when David was heard to say he had never been so bored and fancied finding a pub where he could get drunk. Hope did not trust herself to keep her feelings hidden and coaxed him on to the dance floor where a smile sat awkwardly in her face for the remainder of the evening.

The next day was Sunday. Hope accompanied her aunt to chapel; David had indicated a preference to losing himself between the thumbed pages of yesterday's news.

It had been Hope's intention to find an opportunity to tell Isabel of their desire to marry, but the moment was never right, and that afternoon, having made no mention of their plans, Hope and David returned to the city.

It dawned on Hope that that was the first time she had been home and had not called on Hattie or Sir Charles. She hoped neither had been offended.

As it happened Hattie, who still did not know what day it was, had had her hands full keeping Bobby away from Spice, the smallest of the kittens born at Tarnville during the flood, which had found its way into her care. Newly operated on to prevent any little surprises Spice felt sorry for herself and spat furiously at Bobby who still had more energy than sense. Charles had anticipated a visit but comforted himself with a mental picture of his young friend catching up with friends of her own age.

Despite working full-time there was always an appetising aroma escaping Daphne's kitchen to welcome Hope each evening. Daphne planned it that way. Like Isabel before her, Daphne Carr's life had changed with Hope's arrival into her home. Her teenage son Billy, with a mental age of ten, plus her job working with the mentally handicapped, more than filled her days but Hope had unknowingly reintroduced elements into her life that had been missing for some time. Conversations had taken on a spontaneity that had almost been forgotten and no longer had to be held within a tight boundary of measured understanding; Hope had brought something intense and complex back into her life. Daphne's only regret was that Hope had not entered her life sooner.

"Something smells good!" declared Hope, instantly reminded of her aunt's kitchen.

"Your favourite, it'll be ready by the time you and Billy get yourselves to the table," commented Daphne, cherishing the little kiss blown to her. Right from the start she insisted that Hope should dine at her table, explaining it was as easy to cook for three as it was for two.

And Billy with an unexplained fascination with horses had made up his mind that coming from the country Hope probably knew more about horses than anyone else. He had been thrilled with the large calendar Hope retrieved from Kevin Lester's waste bin at the turn of the year and spent the entire evening admiring the pictures of the huge *Tetley Brewery* horses at work and at rest.

Similarly Hope appreciated her home with Daphne, whose affection for her was evident in everything she did, Instead of the lodger she was made to feel like the daughter of the house.

The large dish of cauliflower cheese on the table looked too good to eat. "As usual Daphne – you've excelled yourself!" Hope looked at Billy who exclaimed agreement.

"Someone should."

Hope wondered if Daphne's remark were directed at David. Loving them both she was attuned to their moods and frequently picked up on the strain that appeared to exist between them. After dinner when Billy left to pursue some activity in the garden, Hope turned to Daphne.

"Daphne.... I've something to tell you." She fidgeted with the hem of the tablecloth. "David has asked me to marry him." The pause that followed was a shade too long and Hope smiled to encourage a response.

"Marriage!" Daphne looked more as though she had been told of an air disaster than a forthcoming marriage. "Congratulations.... I'm very pleased for you – both of you," she managed eventually, her voice dry and toneless. "David's.... a very lucky young man."

Hope watched the face that did not match the brightness of this affirmation. "You are pleased for me.... aren't you?" She reflected she had felt the need to ask the same of her aunt in Mowlem only the day before.

"Of course – yes, of course." Daphne left her place at the table to go to drape her arms round Hope and to press a kiss to her silky crown. "Does Isabel know yet?"

When Isabel had come through for a weekend the two of them shared concerns about David Stratton. He was much too brash for their liking and as Isabel pointed out, sizing him up in her own discerning fashion, he seemed to enjoy his drink too much, and they both agreed he was much too cocky.

When Hope married David Stratton six weeks later, Isabel was disappointed by the choice of ceremony and unable to refrain from telling Hope that her father would not have wanted a Register Office marriage for her. Hope knew she was right but David had no living relatives other than a cousin and an aged aunt. He had not wanted any of the usual trappings, and in the end she had agreed to a civil wedding.

Had she not been so distracted, Hope might have picked up on Isabel and Daphne's disquiet who, though resigned to the marriage, were nevertheless reluctant participants.

The prospect of a physical relationship was the cause of her preoccupation, a subject she felt unable to discuss with anyone. Despite David's persistent coaxing they had not become lovers. More than once he had displayed something approaching annoyance that his powers of persuasion had not succeeded in overcoming whatever it was that held her back – and which she feared would continue into marriage. But upon marriage she found her anxiety without substance as their coming together was natural and tender and within a short space of time she came to enjoy the skills of his lovemaking.

They made their marital home in David's flat in the nearby district of Halden. It was nice enough though could not boast of being as prettily situated as the home Hope had shared with Daphne and Billy, but the flat was brought to life with a few new acquisitions. A new carpet was purchased for the main room with co-ordinating curtains, a new bed, and a low sideboard that caught Hope's eye in the local second-hand shop, plus a small refrigerator. She would have preferred the combined refrigerator and freezer she had admired in the Co-op but their savings had not stretched that far. But situated above a row of shops the flat was ideally situated for amenities and was not far from the park.

Hope found herself missing things, not least the stimulation of her taste buds the moment she stepped through the door, but mostly she missed her extended family and the evening chats around the dinner table. Bred to appreciate the value of loved ones, Hope shared her time between David, Isabel and Daphne.

The months passed pleasantly enough whilst they saved hard for a deposit on a house. In secret Isabel had put to one side all the money Hope sent and shortly before the wedding had surprised them with a cheque to boost their savings.

Soon after marriage David applied for a better-paid job nearer home and was working hard, often working late, which trespassed on their time together and his attendance at the gym. Then Hope would take the opportunity to go to Daphne's after work, with David offering to organise himself with a take-away.

"DON'T YOU THINK you're doing too much?" Hope had just finished telling Daphne about undertaking some evening work, typing for a literary agency. "I should've thought that with working, running a home and looking after a husband, you had more than enough on your plate without taking on more."

"Actually, I quite enjoy it. It's only copy typing, which I find relaxing and some of the material is really very good." She admitted the extra money came in handy.

Relaxing in Daphne's sitting room Hope opened her bag. "Actually, typing other people's scripts inspired me to try my own hand at writing." With a soft blush she handed Daphne half a dozen typed pages. "I've had a go at writing a short story. I thought you might like to keep it to read sometime and let me know what you think – though I'd appreciate it if you didn't let anyone else see or take a copy of it." She giggled, adding, "David would be more than a little amused at the mere thought of anyone in their right mind wanting a copy!"

The story was important. That much was apparent from Hope's face and so was something else. Seemingly her husband had done little if anything to provide encouragement, and once again Daphne felt annoyed with David Stratton. "Like to read it? I certainly would.

In fact I'm going to read it right now. Pop the kettle on Billy love, let's have a cuppa."

During those minutes Daphne was whisked away to witness an incident with an unexpected conclusion. Eventually lifting her head she asked, "Where did you get the idea? It's beautiful." Sensing her eyes were moist she confessed, "It's very moving and extremely clever how you managed to turn the tale around like that. I'm not just telling you what I think you want to hear. It really is very good. Tell me, is it based on anyone?"

Hope shook her head then turned to Billy who was tugging at her sleeve.

He pointed to the pages in her hand, "When you lived with us you used to type lots of stuff like that for those folders."

His mother nodded. "I miss that period when I regularly drifted off to sleep with the sound of your typewriter in the next room. And Billy's right – there must be a wealth of material there to work with. Not only do you paint well," Daphne glanced up at the oil painting of Mowlem above the mantle-piece, "but you can write too. You should keep it up."

Hope felt elated by the encouragement; a complete contrast to the feeling David had left her with. When she asked him to read her work he took all evening to get round to it and when he did he broke off twice, once to pour a drink and then to go to the toilet with the newspaper. The stilted verdict had not been worth the wait though, and did little to encourage her to seek entry into the field of writing.

When Hope arrived back at the flat she was surprised to find it in darkness and David not yet home. It was getting late when she eventually heard his key in the lock.

One look at him confirmed her suspicions. Eyes with the inability to focus betrayed an evening of heavy drinking and once more she wondered whether David were happy in his new job. She greeted him warmly whilst patting cushions back to tidiness. There was no response. She tried again. "Have you had anything to eat or can I fix you something?"

"Eaten?" He shrugged. "S'pose so. Can't remember. And what the bloody hell does it matter anyway?" His reasoning gone he muttered,

"Yeah, I 'spect I have." Then, belching from the region of his boots, "Been to see y'friend with the loopy kid?"

The ugliness of his words jarred her senses. "That's horrible David! Don't refer to Billy in that way. Daphne and Billy are two of my dearest friends."

"Yeah, yeah – if you say so, but I tell you the kid's a nutter, a schizo. He gives me the willies." He lurched off in the general direction of the kitchen.

From the clatter of pots it was evident he was getting something to eat, but new experiences – which were uncomfortable echoes of old ones – had taught her he could be argumentative after a drinking session and was better left alone. It had been such a pleasant evening; a quarrel now would only spoil it.

In bed that night, with David laid like a dead thing beside her, she thought back to something Gregory whispered during his engagement party. He asked if she were happy and without awaiting a reply told her to be sure to follow her own dreams. At the time she had not understood what he meant.

Chapter 11

"Bring it straight to the Board Room when it comes through." Kevin Lester swivelled his head from Hope to scowl at the fax machine beside her desk as though doing so might encourage it to spew out the document he had been awaiting since the close of business yesterday.

The day ahead would be demanding. It was not yet 08:30 but all the signs were there: Kevin's taut expression, the furrowed brow of Marty's boss and the buzz that lingered in the Administration Department after their work on the agenda for the Special Board meeting. Various changes had been made and every time Hope issued an instruction to slide an item down for discussion under Any Other Business she had been met with the same chorus of groans.

A prickle of anticipation accompanied the knowledge that some of Lester's biggest clients, a hotel conglomerate, would be on the premises for the proposed merger with another multinational hotel chain. At the conclusion of the meeting members of the Press would be invited into the Board Room, not for precise detail of the merger itself, but to be given a taster. They were expected to push hard for more once they learned of the massive investment in the pipeline that would transform a derelict area in the city of Dalekirk. A glimpse would be given of an artist's impression showing two hotels, some 350 luxury apartments as well as shopping malls, car parking, a range of bars and restaurants, a cinema, nightclub and casino.

Edric Colendon, the Acquisitions & Mergers Director from the parent company, would then lead the discussion towards the appreciation of the development's potential of becoming a main focal point in Dalekirk. Likely to attract Blue Chip company interest it would generate further substantial investment opportunities and job creation in an area sorely in need of it. His allotted role in the proceedings was to gain as much good press and free advertising for the project as was humanly possible.

Now, everything was in place save the missing fax. Hope's input had necessitated her staying late at the office over a period of weeks, a fact that had inflamed her husband. She thought about this now as she nodded to her employer, assuring him that the all-important document would be brought to him the second it was pulled from the fax machine.

Hope's late arrivals home had been met by a string of complaints made more bitter by the quantity of red wine David was in the habit of consuming. His attitude struck her as unreasonable; after all she had had to put up with his late arrivals home.

Only the other evening there had been a real dingdong over the lateness of their evening meal and Hope snapped that it should not have been beyond him to do something towards it. That resulted in David's fork being hurled across the room accompanied by the comment that he did not intend keeping a dog and barking himself; then adding more injury, he scraped his meal into the bin. Soon afterwards he stormed from the flat throwing a further hurtful remark over his shoulder about her having an insignificant position at Lester's, and even if she did not want to admit it, she did not run the place.

He did not return until after work the following day. His mood was less volatile but evidence of further drinking had deterred Hope from tackling him, though she did wonder where he had spent the night.

Now it was Hope's turn to scowl at the fax machine, glad the demands of the day would keep her mind off the difficulties in her marriage.

When the machine burst into life a short while later, she was relieved to see it was the financial details the Board required in order to advise their clients. Page after page spilled into the tray. When a bleep announced completion Marty was already on her feet. She snatched up the document and made for the door on spindly legs.

"It's okay. I've something for Simon. I'll take it in for you," a note of superiority in her voice.

The smugness! Hope was convinced the action had been planned. Marty liked nothing better than to find an excuse to go into a meeting and be noticed. It was Hope's belief that she would even resort to slowing the production of a report just so she could take it in once a meeting had been convened, thereby providing a platform for her grand entrance.

Marty reappeared moments later, her face almost matching her bright red hair. "Kevin wants you."

Hope knew better than to seek elaboration. She smoothed her hands over her hair, which she wore swept up for the office. Armed with her shorthand pad and a clutch of sharp pencils – always ready to make a note of any instruction – Hope made her way to the Board Room.

She refrained from glancing at the sea of faces that met her entry via the sliding doors but walked towards the Chairman at the head of the inlaid table that was of such magnificence it had necessitated its creator being brought over from Italy to reassemble its sections when the office had been relocated some years back.

Kevin Lester glanced warmly at his assistant. "Gentlemen, for those of you who have not yet met my PA, this is Mrs Hope Stratton." He motioned for the Company Secretary to bring a chair.

Once she had taken her place beside the Chairman a lively discussion ensued relating to the figures contained in the fax and Kevin took the opportunity to whisper that at the conclusion he would dictate the Board's response. Insight slipped into place as Hope imagined the scene of earlier. Her colleague had never got to grips with shorthand and when she delivered the fax Marty would have been asked to summon her to take the dictation.

The Chairman pulled the meeting to order and, save for the round sound of a pencil doodling on a blotter, the lofty Board Room switched to silence as Kevin Lester began to dictate the Directors' response to the proposal. Once or twice a Member or guest interrupted to add or change something and Hope glanced at the Chairman for affirmation or otherwise.

Hope found taking dictation from Kevin almost pleasurable. His voice was clear, his words came from positive thought, and unlike many he never paced the floor taking his voice with him. Despite all this Hope was uneasy. Without the need to look she knew all eyes were keenly trained towards the head of the table, but she detected something else. She had the queerest feeling that somebody was studying her – albeit that was quite ridiculous. Nonetheless she was left in no doubt that someone at the left-hand side of the table watched her intently but taking shorthand at speed allowed little room for analysis.

Any opportunity to return to the Board Room for possible enlightenment was removed when Kevin came to her desk to collect the finished letter a short while later. A sense of something vaguely familiar lingered and set Hope wishing she had a plausible reason for returning to the room. Whose eyes had studied her so intently? Had she merely imagined it?

The day drew on. Papers were filed away to prepare desks for the next project, which would be disappointing in substance following the merger.

Marty looked up from her desk. "It's my birthday next week, my 21st. I'm throwing a party and I'd like you and David to come. I'm inviting some of the others." She looked brightly at Hope who surprised herself by saying they would be delighted to come.

David could not stand Marty! But it was the girl's 21st and Hope doubted many of the others would accept. Additionally she felt sorry for Marty. Kevin's rejection of her dictation skills would have been a bitter pill to swallow. She was a proud, puffed-up little entity and in truth Hope had expected to be exposed to a lot of huffy nonsense as a result. The day had been heavy enough without any of that; an invitation to a party was infinitely better.

Only a handful accepted Marty's invitation. The more brave were very sorry but had prior arrangements. Hope did not expect to gain David's agreement so was taken aback when he offered no resistance. He must have had a good day, better than hers, but having a so-called *insignificant position* at Lester's she did not enlighten him.

They found the address from Marty's typed directions. David had to knock hard on the paint-chipped door to make their arrival heard above the bass music thumping within. Presently the door flew open and David stumbled forward, colliding with the young woman at the door. One of the shoulder straps of her tight-fitting red dress became displaced and apologies were given – a little too effusively for Hope's liking.

"Hi there you two! You've met my cousin." Marty and the young woman exchanged smiles.

"I'm Fanny.... to my friends," the contents of the tight-fitting red dress gushed at David.

Hope studied the woman and decided she was attractive in an overstated way. The words tarty and exhibitionist, plus one or two others, came to mind.

"And my friends can call me anything they like." Aware of the need to adjust the hang of his trousers David stamped his foot.

Hope looked from one to the other and back to her skinny redheaded colleague; clearly she was not going to be introduced. Just then she caught sight of Angela's blonde head in the room beyond. She took her husband's arm and steered him towards safer ground. Angela was pleased to see familiar faces and introduced her boyfriend Alex who was on a 48 hours' pass from his RAF base.

"You've been forgiven then?" whispered Angela.

Hope looked puzzled.

"The incident in the Board Room. You know.... Doodah's inability to take shorthand. I thought she might peg you out to dry after that – not invite you to her party!"

Hope felt obliged to explain how she believed Marty had orchestrated an appearance in the Board Room only to find her skills did not match the occasion, but David looked disinterested from the moment she started. She followed his gaze, then briefly considered her choice of outfit, a honey-coloured tailored trouser suit, which she knew suited her colouring – though apparently not well enough to compete with the little red dress behind her.

Sensitive to the moment, Angela drew the others to the middle of the room to dance. David's attention returned to his wife and when the tempo slowed, his arms found their way round her waist.

"I've been a bit distant lately haven't I?" He looked into the large green eyes that still amazed him. Hope's hair moved gently against his hand. He liked it when she wore it loose. It made her look sexy – which she was – when he remembered it. "I've been having some trouble with Harrison. He's been as awkward as hell lately."

His boss! She had been right then. It was the job that was getting him down. Relief settled in. His job – it was nothing to do with anything she had done. Her spirits lifted. She was relieved that David was finally talking about it.

"There's no flaming pleasing him. The guy's unreal I tell you – not normal."

She was not troubled with the whole story – that Peter Harrison had given him his second verbal warning for turning up for work still drunk from the night before. David deftly skirted round those finer details whilst Hope clung fiercely to the one point of significance – that it was not she who was responsible for his moodiness.

His unexplained moods had surfaced early on in their marriage and having learned lessons from her aunt's marriage Hope resolved to tackle head on any discord that arose in her own. A heated argument had occurred only the other week as a direct consequence of David's frame of mind with the familiar label of "I'm not speaking today – and I'm not going to tell you why." This was her life too she told him. She also deserved consideration. The challenge surprised both of them but in its wake she received a seemingly genuine apology.

But now, enjoying his nearness, Hope melted into her husband's arms. How pleased she was that Marty had invited them to her party and how odd that it had been she who had provided the magic that would bring her marriage back on course.

Later, when Hope brought their coats from upstairs she did not at once spot David in the crowded room but then she saw him. He was leaning over Marty's cousin, allowing the wall to take his weight. Hope adopted a confident stride and walked towards him. She was determined that nothing, not even the contents of a little red dress, was going to deter her from the campaign to rescue her marriage.

David was less than brisk in pulling away from the red dress but on the pavement later his arm went round his wife and she forgave him even that momentary lapse. Whatever problems they had they were not insurmountable. She could build again – all she had to do was find the right bricks.

Chapter 12

David found his wife on her hands and knees sorting out the washing when he entered the kitchen the following morning. He knew that under the guise of her activity Hope watched to ascertain whether his mood of the previous evening had followed him into the new day.

He recalled being in a foul mood by the time they arrived home from Marty's party – booze did that sometimes – and prior to turning in, spending the best part of an hour getting things off his chest, which included a verbal assault on her friends when once again he had referred to Billy as *that loopy kid*.

To pre-empt a return to the subject he threw her one of his boyish grins, instantly disarming her. Extending his arms tentatively, he adopted the stance of a youngster anticipating reprimand.

"I was out of line last night wasn't I? You know I wouldn't hurt you for the world." He watched her expression soften and was not surprised when she slid into his arms. He kissed her then, banishing any last trace of reproach.

He purposely produced one of his more buoyant moods. Maybe it was a shade too buoyant, for in the next breath she was suggesting they spend the weekend in Mowlem. Over the 18 months they had been married he had managed to reduce the frequency of their visits. He couldn't stand the place. There wasn't a half decent pub for miles.

He wrinkled his nose. "You know I'm not into all that country stuff. Anyway I'm probably working Saturday."

"More overtime? Your place must be really busy. There's little wonder you're always so tired."

He could almost hear the cogs turning in her brain. Skilfully, he played his trump card before she started whingeing on about his so-called tiredness being the culprit for a dropping off of their fun in the sack. "Why don't you go? Take Daphne and Billy with you. You keep saying you'll take them one day."

He watched her whilst she weighed this up. Quite deliberately he had risen above his usual style of patter when referring to Dozy-Daph and Loopy-Loo. He had been sounding off about them again last night. Bad move. It hadn't gone down at all well – though the details were somewhat fuzzy.

As expected, Hope's face lit up as images presented themselves of showing her friends round the village, and taking Billy to see the horses at Tarnville.

Moving in on cue he said, "I could run you to the station after work on Friday if you like," his voice purposely pleasant, deliberately persuasive.

For the remainder of that day it tormented Hope that she found the idea of visiting Mowlem without her husband so appealing, but without him she would be able to relax without her having to think about his needs, and forever checking he was sufficiently occupied.

Isabel experienced parallel emotions, and eagerly awaited her niece. She could understand why Hope visited less often but when she did there was evidence of change. At first she thought she imagined it but found herself watching helplessly as Hope's natural exuberance diffused. Even the way Hope sat in a chair had altered. No longer did she recline but sat stiffly on the edge of her seat as though ready to spring up, her hands fidgeting, and her eyes always shifting towards that husband of hers, as though checking what he was doing – or more likely thinking. Gone were the days when they had shared peaceful moments like those when Bert lolled sleeping in his chair and they stared into the flames of a dying fire, thinking about nothing, talking about everything and planning so much.

When Hope and her two highly-charged companions arrived at Braefield railway station on Friday evening she was surprised to find Isabel waiting on the platform. Clearly pleased to see them Isabel embraced each in turn, then with an easy movement slipped an arm round Billy to give him an extra hug. Peter Summerville, the owner of Broad Gates Farm, was waiting in his car outside, she told them.

Hope thanked Peter who assured her it was no trouble. Isabel smiled up at the lean, kindly man with light brown hair and neatly styled moustache and beard, her gratitude readily identifiable – as was something else. In that moment Hope identified the reason for the subtle changes in her aunt. The brightness in her eyes; her ease of laughter; the flattering way she now did her hair; and even the slight increase in weight that had returned her youthful shape; Hope realised were not entirely due to working in the Estate office but were just as likely to be due to the attention of this caring person whose eyes creased pleasantly at something Isabel was saying – a private moment shared.

During the drive Hope examined these thoughts recalling it had been Peter Summerville who pulled Hattie's puppy from the floodwaters and Isabel who accompanied him to return the dog. Such a lot had happened in the short time she had been away. She had missed such a lot! Pleased for her aunt she felt like singing and knew she had a stupid grin on her face when they finally tumbled down from Peter's new 4x4 vehicle outside Ivy Cottage.

Peter took his leave soon after helping with the luggage. Hope watched with interest as Isabel saw him to the door. The way his hand slid discretely from the doorknob to rest momentarily on Isabel's hand confirmed her suspicions. The pleasure she felt on witnessing the tiny gesture was of such magnitude it deserved a place in her box of treasured memories.

That evening it started to drizzle and the happy group opted to stay in and chat around the fire. In unison Daphne and Hope enthused about the luxury of a real fire, each considering Daphne's utilitarian gas appliance back in Leeds. The comment inspired Isabel towards instructing Billy in the art of making proper toast in front of a fire with a toasting fork.

Later, enjoying buttered toast expertly made by Billy from wholemeal bread pulled from Isabel's oven earlier in the day, Daphne threw Isabel a look of gratitude. She had taken to her from their very first meeting. Unlike many, Isabel made a point of including Billy in conversations and was careful to avoid his exclusion. Few made the same effort and there had been times when the ignorance of others tore at her heart as she watched her son floundering on the edge of significance, striving to make sense of what was being said.

The next morning the sound of disharmonic whistling and water splashing full pelt into the kitchen sink signalled that Billy was up. Not wanting to waste any of the weekend Hope slipped out of bed and into her robe. Half an hour later she and Billy, giggling together like a couple of school children, carried breakfast trays upstairs to surprise Daphne and Isabel.

With Billy's attitude towards simple pleasures, secrets and discoveries, Hope delighted in his company and was rarely aware of his difficulties. She saw him more as a growing child who was still learning, than as a young adult with a disability. This was most evident when she took him down the path that led to the river.

The enthusiasm Billy expressed at everything he saw was like an echo of the discoveries she made the first time her father had taken her to the river and she had been five years old. The hundreds of gossamer-thread cobwebs bejewelled with tiny beads of moisture amazed him. He had seen spiders' webs before, in the garage rafters, webs with dust clinging to them – dingy, ugly creations compared with this delicate lacework that festooned the hedgerows and held him spellbound.

Last night's shower had brought a freshness to everything. Hope loved the countryside after a fall of rain when the inestimable shades of green were transformed into hues more vibrant than any clashing pigment on an artist's pallet. Everything smelled wonderful, fresh and invigorating. Her father used to say that one could smell the scent of life after a downpour. She could identify with that.

Tangled undergrowth encroached upon their path. It weighed heavy with moisture though did not detract from Billy's enjoyment as he strode out. Hope thought how carefully David would have picked his way along the same route and just as quickly was annoyed at herself for having made the comparison. Guilt ridden she pushed away these negative thoughts to refocus on her young companion.

The story of how the stepping-stones came to be placed in the riverbed so captured Billy's interest that Hope feared he might elect to use them. She was not ready for that. She held her breath for several moments whilst Billy contemplated the boulders. Eventually he skirted them with a kind of reverence and headed for the bridge. Hope's shoulders relaxed and she went to catch him up and match his stride.

She would never forget the look on Billy's face the first time he saw the Tarnville horses, particularly Tarkenta, Sir Charles's grey,

Richard Lurdmayne's mount, Illusion, and her two-year-old foal Mirage. Not long ago one or other of the Lurdmayne gentlemen had been a regular sight galloping around the surrounding countryside.

His mouth open, all Billy could do was nod his head in response to the questions Hope put to him. Isabel had alerted Joseph Fearnley to his visit and smock and boots of the correct size were waiting for Billy so he could spend the morning with Joseph in the stables.

Altogether there were five thoroughbreds and at the other end of the scale two English Shires, Bill and Ben, each with an impressive shoulder height. The magnificent long hair on their feet that reached all the way to their fetlocks was being shampooed and intricate work was being carried out on their manes with the introduction of interwoven silks.

Joseph told Billy how these two beloved creatures, with such tremendous pulling power, were in the midst of preparation for the ploughing competition in Farnham the following day. The gentle giants had gained a First for the last three consecutive years, and Joseph could already feel tomorrow's award in his hand.

With her charge happily occupied, Hope went in search of Charles. At Sarah's direction she went straight to the library. Peering round the door her eyes went straight to the leather chair moulded to his form at the far end of the room.

"Well, well – what a welcome sight for these old eyes!" Charles chortled; his smile mirrored the one that peered round the door. Delighted, he rose to his feet and gestured with an arthritic hand in such a way as to indicate that every moment Hope remained by the door was a moment lost to them.

The person walking towards him was no longer the tantalising child who had waited patiently beside the river for Frederick Thackeray every Friday afternoon. The transition from child to woman had taken place in so short a time he had almost missed it. But the thickly-lashed eyes were the same, though Charles detected something was missing. The happiness that used to dwell there was not so readily definable. Even so they remained arresting and, like the rest of her, were totally captivating.

Their greeting was warm and over coffee brought to them by Sarah, Charles enquired whether she still enjoyed her work at Lester's. He drew satisfaction from her spontaneous affirmation.

Presently he commented, "I take it your guest is happy in Joseph's company?"

"Indeed he is. It's kind of you to allow Billy to see the stables. He's talked about nothing else since I spoke of your invitation. It's truly very kind of you. He's in ecstasy – I left him shampooing Ben's feet."

Charles nodded, visualising the scene. Through things Isabel had said to his Estate Manager, he had learned of Billy's interest in horses. He had learned other things too; things that worried him as they would Frederick Thackeray if he had still been alive.

"Kind? Nonsense! Horses are no different from us. They enjoy a visit. I don't ride as much since Richard's death and they've come to depend on Joseph and his team for exercise." Regardless of that he made a point of visiting the stables twice a day to whisper into pricked, velvet ears. Wonderful creatures, soft muzzles, gentle eyes; he well understood Billy's infatuation.

"They respond to kindness and affection in much the same way that we do. Like us they need to be wanted...." He had not meant to say that. It was clumsy of him. If he had come right out and asked whether her marriage was happy his meaning could not have been clearer.

The comments Joseph had made following Isabel's remarks were still fresh in his mind. A silence followed during which he could not bring himself to look at Hope for fear he might detect disenchantment. He wrenched himself from his chair to go to the Queen Anne bureau behind him. In his anguish he almost dislodged the white marble elephant, smooth and ice-cool to the touch, a gift to his wife one anniversary. After some unnecessary rummaging he returned to his seat with an envelope of photographs.

Ignoring the photographs he asked, "Did Kevin tell you about the person who responded to my advertisement?"

Even though she was his Attorney's assistant and therefore worked on various Tarnville projects, many as a direct consequence of the flood two years ago, Hope did not want him to think himself a mere topic of conversation. She nodded, "It was mentioned when you forwarded the letter. It must have been dreadful for you. I fail to understand how anybody could be so cruel – deliberately building up your hopes like that."

What surprised his young friend did not surprise Charles. Kevin had prepared him for possible bogus responses to the advertisement seeking his daughter's whereabouts. In fact he had been surprised there had not been more. "Someone somewhere must know where she is.... even if she's living abroad." His emphatic words led him back to the envelope in his hand and he told her he was returning to Corfu.

"You must like it out there."

Indeed he did and he spent the rest of the morning telling her all about a particular locality he had found that so far had eluded the majority of tourists. Photographs were drawn from the envelope and Hope could well understand his next disclosure.

The estate agent with whom he had registered his interest had sent particulars of a property that he intended viewing. She would learn this from the paperwork that would from necessity cross her desk, and he preferred her to hear it first from him, though for the moment he did not divulge that if he went ahead with the purchase it would be more than just a holiday base – but it was necessary to find Christina before he could allow himself to think along those lines.

When Hope and Billy arrived back at the cottage Daphne was placing a batch of bread on a cooling tray. She had persuaded Isabel to give her some tips on bread making and was already declaring that she would never buy soggy supermarket rubbish again. Isabel was smiling but Hope knew the happiness splashed across her face heralded more than the mere joys of bread making. Intrigued, she looked enquiringly at her.

"Do you fancy the village social this evening?" Isabel's hands went to perch on slender hips. "I think you will when I tell you that Amy and Greg are over for the weekend. They made me promise we'd go along."

Later, before going to change, Hope rang home. The telephone seemed to ring an interminably long time before it was finally snatched up and she heard her husband's voice.

"Yeah?"

"David, it's me. Everything all right?" He sounded breathless and snappy, as though the telephone had disturbed him.

"Hope....? Yeah, everything's fine. You okay? What're you finding to do down there?" he asked, already knowing the answer – ambling down damp dreary country lanes – looking at some big stones in a river – attending a boring shindig in the village hall – an endless weekend of sheer excitement and fun – shame he'd missed it!

"Oh, this and that, you know the sort of thing. Greg and Amy are over for the weekend. We're meeting up tonight. It'll be good hearing how they're getting on."

Yeah – flipping great – sorry I'm not there, he thought sourly but managed, "Good. You'll enjoy that. By the way, what time does your train get in on Sunday evening?"

"That's my main reason for ringing, darling." She ran the weekend's agenda through her mind. "We should arrive back at 7:10 – unless we catch the later train but in any event there's no need to meet us. We'll get a taxi. You get yourself down to that gym of yours. You've hardly had a chance recently. I know you miss it. We don't want you getting flabby." She laughed, anticipating some light response. There was none.

"The gym – yeah that'd be nice. I might just do that – if you're sure."

"Of course I am. Allowing for the taxi journey I'll be home around 7:30 at the earliest, or 8:30 if we catch the later train. I'll see you on Sunday night and then we can...." but a click in her ear told her he had already hung up. She frowned momentarily at the silent receiver in her hand before replacing it in its cradle.

In those same moments David smiled lengthily over his shoulder at the person wrapped in a bath towel standing behind him.

Isabel stood framed in Hope's bedroom doorway. She looked attractive in a new frock of a tiny print fabric that followed her slender shape to perfection. Her hair, worn in a new short style, shone with health.

She considered her niece though it was her state of mind rather than her state of dress that concerned her. She was relieved to notice that calmness had replaced whatever it was she had glimpsed shortly after the telephone call to David. Everything seemed to be back to normal.

She went to assist with Hope's zipper. "I've been meaning to tell you something pet...." Even before her aunt continued, Hope knew it would be about Peter Summerville. "I've been seeing someone. Peter has taken me out a few times – dinner, the pictures in Braefield – that sort of thing. He's coming with us tonight. He's picking us up. You don't mind do you?"

"Mind? Of course not. I'm very pleased. He's a really nice man. You deserve some happiness." She had already guessed that the tall, good-looking farmer was now part of Isabel's life.

It was like old times again with a pleasing mix of both young and old coming together for an evening in the village hall. Popular with the villagers, the trio attracted interest, and group after group advanced to enquire after the well-being of the young friends. Welcoming arms embraced first one then another. This almost forgotten caring caught at Hope's very being and she felt a need to slip away to catch her breath, to remember and appreciate.

Gregory found her outside. Detecting that tears were near the surface he went to fold his arms round her. "You've got a face like a smacked bum." The early trace of a smile soften frown lines.

"A bit of a headache, nothing to make a fuss about," she replied.

He watched her crumple and a swim of tears flood her eyes. "Easy now, let it go." Without pressing for an explanation he swayed with her in his arms, drinking in the remembered fragrance. Amy appeared just long enough for Gregory to incline his head. She read his unspoken message and went back inside.

Hope took a faltering breath. "I'm so frightened, Greg. Frightened I'm not what he wants."

"David?"

Filled with embarrassment she attempted a laugh that sounded forced even to her own ears. "From different backgrounds you see. Me, brought up with the cows. I've tried, I really have and I purposely don't come back here as often as I'd like. But I love this place. I need to keep coming back." A feeling of belonging to the area was so strong that sometimes she felt as though some strange magnetic force insistently drew her back. "The surrounding countryside is like a backdrop to my life, and the river a repeating echo binding it all together. But David hates it here."

"I wondered, when I heard he wasn't with you."

"Whenever he comes I feel awkward. He.... he doesn't look at the countryside when I bring him. He looks at it with his eyes wide shut if you know what I mean."

Gregory nodded. "I have to admit we've sensed his boredom. Amy believes he'll grow to appreciate the place, if only for your sake.

Hope noticed he did not voice sharing that optimism.

"Give him time. He'll probably grow to love the place just as much as the rest of us – once he's learned to identify with village life," he lied. "You have to remember he's a *Townie* – a completely different species to us. He just needs educating to our ways."

He was right. It was early days. She did not know why she had allowed herself to become so upset and she apologised for giving in to weeping. Amy reappeared and Hope beckoned for her to join them.

"Amy, I'm sorry – I felt a need to borrow your fiancé's shoulder."

"They're broad and accommodating and there's nothing wrong in opening up about things. You know what I always say – better out than in!" Amy took Hope's hand. "Seriously, whatever it is our shoulders are never far away. If you've got a problem, we've got a problem – just you remember that."

With that the three friends returned to the hubbub of activity in the hall. Amy's eyes looked enquiringly at Gregory who mouthed that he would explain later.

Everyone was worn out and longed for bed when they arrived back at Ivy Cottage, save Isabel, who could be heard singing softly to herself as she went around the cottage putting the clocks forward an hour for the start of British Summertime the next day.

Chapter 13

The taxi dropped Daphne and Billy in Eastkirk and minutes later pulled up outside the flat in Halden with Hope ruminating on something Gregory once said; cultivate your dreams and grow on them, he had told her. Those words, so typical of his background, had encouraged her to think long and hard about her marriage during the train journey; a marriage that she now acknowledged fell short of her dreams. A picture of her father's face came into her mind, which disappeared just as quickly when the handbrake was applied with a jolt.

Hope paid the driver who took the opportunity to study his passenger. Without the need of the mirror he admired her openly now as he lifted her case to the pavement but his scrutiny went unnoticed.

There was nothing wrong with her marriage that some real effort could not put right. For a start they could go out more, get a change of scenery and see people like they used to. In the early days they had socialised a lot, often into the early hours, and had rarely felt the need of sleep.

Filled with positive thoughts Hope went to her door located in the narrow ginnel between the shops. It did not immediately dawn on her why the door was locked but then realised she had not reminded David to change the clocks to British Summer Time. An hour behind, he would still at the gym.

With amusement twitching the corners of her mouth she let herself in. If she hurried she could prepare supper before he returned home. Furthermore a meal by the fire might encourage conversation, which would be an improvement on the monologue of late. On this positive thought she ran up the steep staircase to put her things away. Given the lead David would surely follow. Focused on what was important she felt more sure about her marriage than she had for months.

She was still smiling when she switched on the bedroom light and, but for her revived optimism, she might have suffered annoyance to discover the bed unmade and David's clothes precisely where he had dropped them. A sigh escaped her as she stooped to retrieve the clothes from the floor. But in the next moment all happiness drained away as the bed suddenly became a living tangle of thrusting, naked limbs.

David! The single word that screamed in her head was oddly silent. No words formed on her open lips whilst she watched her husband struggle furiously to untangle his naked body from the glistening naked form of the woman in the bed beneath him. Words failed her and she strove to breathe. She staggered backwards through the doorway and groped her way back downstairs.

Almost immediately David was beside her in the sitting room, his torso glistening and his hair saturated with sweat. He was wearing the first article he could lay his hands on, a pair of boxer shorts. He reached towards her, but repelled by his betrayal and the stink of drink on his breath Hope pulled away.

"Hope – I can explain...."

"No – you can't David. You can't explain this!" she interjected, reclaiming ownership of her voice.

"We should talk...."

"I've nothing to say to you. Not now – not ever!" She watched the magnitude of his actions register and that this time boyish grins and light banter would be wasted on her. And yet he slanted his head and attempted a cajoling smile.

Her arms fumbled their way back into the coat she had discarded moments earlier. Just then David's female companion sauntered into the room dressed in something glittery that looked out of place in the brightly lit room and encouraged the thought that she had missed her way to a party. Hope watched in undisguised disgust as the woman sidled up to David.

Hope wondered whether anything like this had ever happened to her before: the husband caught in the act by a wife who had returned early. If it had there would have been lots of swearing and shouting – unlike now. Perhaps she had had to duck the fella's clothes being hurled out the bedroom window into the street below.

From the back it was impossible to tell what was going through her head. Maybe she wasn't thinking anything at all and it was only her own sanity that was under attack.

The young woman shrugged indifferently; seemingly it was not her problem. She continued to face David. When he did not take the initiative he was prompted. "Payment for services rendered....?" The shoulders lifted again. "I think we agreed the sum of....?" the voice matter-of-fact, which made it worst. It was as though she were indifferent to the bombshell her presence had brought to their lives.

Instantly averting his eyes from his wife, David went to the sideboard where for the first time Hope noticed that the clock showed a difference of two hours. He had remembered to change the clock, though had put it back an hour instead of putting it forward! His error explained a lot. David took a handful of notes from the *Terry's All Gold* chocolate box where she kept the proceeds from her evening typing job. He counted the notes into the extended hand.

Hope watched the hurried procedure. She said nothing. There was no need. Everything she could possibly say was etched in neon on her face. And David read every single word.

There was a moment's intense quietness, not unlike the pause at the conclusion of a stage production when the world stood still to absorb the drama. Hope half expected in the next instance to be deafened by an explosion of applause from an unseen audience and catch a glimpse of the Producer in the wings.

As though Fate had a hateful need to amplify the happening further, the woman turned and Hope looked into the face of Fanny, Marty's so-called cousin.

Daphne wondered who could be knocking with such urgency at her door. Tired, she was in no mood for visitors and especially not Jim. He was a good soul but she had heard every one of the stories about his beloved Liz and she was now into the repeats. She adjusted her dressing gown and went to peer through the glazed panel in the door. When she saw it was not her neighbour but Hope slumped against her door Daphne fumbled urgently with the lock, and in the next moment Hope fell sobbing into her arms.

"My little love – whatever's the matter? What on earth's happened to get you like this?" Daphne's face pleated with concern as she looked into the saddest eyes she had ever seen.

Hope tried to smile but it was a weak effort. Longing to shut out the world she squeezed her eyes shut but bulbous tears strained through her lashes to betray her emotion. "May I stay with you?" was all she said.

"Stay....? Of course you can – you know that." Daphne felt a smart behind her own eyelids. Eventually she whispered, "You needn't say another word, unless you want to. And you know I'll do whatever I can to help." Hope's face contorted horribly with an attempt to suppress further tears. "Hush my love, hush. You're safe now." Silent sobs pulsated through the slender form in Daphne's arms and she shushed the girl some more whilst she offered what she trusted were appropriate words of comfort.

Eventually Hope ran out of tears. She took a faltering breath. "I've left David...." She added the precisely measured words, "It's.... finished."

The announcement removed any likelihood of Daphne's retiring to bed. Now she was wide-awake, a hundred questions flooded her mind, though knew this was not the time to ask any of them. "Shhh.... shhh love. Things will look better tomorrow. They always do."

Her eyes downcast, Hope shook her head. "It's over. There'll be no forgiving or forgetting." Her tone was resolute. "What a fool I've been, and how naïve! All those occasions when David told me he was working late!"

Watching the formation of fresh tears Daphne sensed she was witnessing a turning point that would change Hope's life forever and she fervently hoped it would be for the better. Something akin to maternal impetus overwhelmed her. There was nothing she would not do for the person sobbing in her arms. Hope had come home! Then came the strangest feeling: inexplicably Daphne sensed that their lives would always remain linked together.

Though she had no way of knowing it, Hope had stepped on to the first of her stepping-stones.

Hope entered Daphne's kitchen the next morning with eyes that held no resemblance to the bright, inquisitive gems that normally peered out from her face. Billy had already left for the Centre where his mother worked and he spent his days, in his pocket a hastily scribbled note of apology for the Principal.

"I'd no idea it was that time." Hope had tossed and turned for most of the night until, finally exhausted, she had drifted into a deep sleep from which she had only just awoken. Slightly peeved that Daphne had not called her, Hope frowned at her watch.

As though reading her mind, Daphne set her shoulders. "You're not going anywhere today except back to bed. That's the best place for you."

Before Hope could utter a word of protest a bout of nausea seized her and propelled to the bathroom. When she emerged she looked as pale and as drained as she felt and she no longer had the strength to resist and at Daphne's say-so went meekly back to bed.

While Hope slept, Daphne took the opportunity to speak to Kevin Lester and her own employer, Miss Wilkinson, at Manstonleigh Day Centre.

As Daphne knew it would, with a telephone in her hand Phyllis Wilkinson's normal style of speaking disintegrated into stilted phrases from which one might imagine her late for a meeting. But she did not seem to mind her Administrator's unscheduled leave though expressed a wish to be kept informed of when she would be back.

After displaying caring skills and a keen interest in fund raising, Daphne Carr had been invited to join Manstonleigh's staff shortly after Billy's enrolment some seven years ago. Commencing as an Auxiliary Carer, undergoing an intensive training programme and working hard, she had risen through the ranks until being made Chief Administrator three years ago. She enjoyed her role though had never lost sight of her beginnings and could often be found in one of the activity rooms where she assisted colleagues in their care of the mentally handicapped.

Daphne remained anxious throughout the day following Hope's unexpected arrival. Should David make contact, and she be expected to field awkward questions, acquaintance with some of the facts would be helpful, but as it stood she knew nothing. However David made no contact. Oddly this annoyed her. Whilst she did not want to hear from him – she had never liked him anyway, too cocky by half – nevertheless she could not understand how he could bear to let Hope go.

Once the evening meal was over, and Billy had left the table to watch television, Hope described to Daphne the hideous scene she had stumbled upon the previous evening; she left nothing out.

"All I ever worked for.... and all my father's dreams disappeared out the window last night." That wonderful person had wanted so much for her. "I'm almost glad he's not here to see this." Miserable, a sense of failure swamped her. It would have broken her father's heart to see her the casualty of a broken marriage. "I feel used and empty." That did not even begin to describe her feelings. First Bert, then David and there had been a couple of unpleasant incidents with dates. "Men!"

"They have only one thing in mind, and the only upright thing about them is in their pants!" volunteered Daphne with a half smile.

"Men!" Hope said again. "I'll never trust another as long as I live!"

"You and so many of us dear," Daphne said, and then commented more helpfully, "It's certainly going to be a drastic change but try to look at it as a new chapter in your life and celebrate your freedom. Don't look back with regret. Look towards the future and invest your emotions in other things. Otherwise you'll remain stuck in your memories and continue to ruminate on them and they'll hold you back." Daphne spoke with feeling and looked as though she would go on. but she said no more.

Hope was thinking about where she had come from and where she was going, though she was not entirely sure about the direction of the latter. Her entire world had been turned upside down.

Had she really known David? She doubted that she had. She questioned when the marriage had started to fall apart and what had been missing from their relationship or worse, from her. Or perhaps it had been a deficiency in his makeup, possibly stemming from his childhood, which she knew had not been happy. At the age of seven he had returned from school one day to find his infirm mother dead on the floor, and he had never known his father. The lack of detail on his Birth Certificate completed the story – or otherwise – whichever way one chose to look at it. He had no one apart from the elderly relative who reluctantly took him in because she feared what others might think if she didn't. Though he had seldom spoken of it Hope picked up on his abhorrence of their hand-to-mouth existence from his mention of the misery in the elderly face. Identifying his bitterness Hope had once likened him to a hawthorn hedge, prickly and unyielding except when he lowered his guard long enough for her to reach the person inside.

Hope heaved a sigh, and then looked straight at Daphne. "Isn't it strange how things turn out?" Involuntarily her mind had wandered to the incident etched forever in her memory, the day she resolved to move from Mowlem. "If I hadn't left home and come to Leeds I'd never have heard of David Stratton. And if Billy hadn't had a liking for horses I might never have suggested taking you both to Mowlem.... and if it hadn't been for the introduction of British Summer Time I might not have found David out."

"If.... if.... I don't suppose there's a person living who hasn't said, what if.... or if only.... But you should remember something: it's yesterday's experiences that make us what we are today. If we don't experience the black how can we possibly begin to appreciate the white?" Daphne drew the girl to her. "Be patient with yourself. Remarkable as it may seem now, you'll be stronger and a better person as a result of all this."

"I might need reminding of that from time to time." Hope attempted a smile.

Daphne pushed a stray tress from Hope's eyes. "I suppose life's a bit too fast and complicated for us to understand sometimes and, like a record, we need to play it again to grasp appreciation."

The next day, when they were sure David had left for work, Hope and her extended family cleared the flat of her possessions. Jack, a retired neighbour, lent a hand.

When it was over and they were back in the safety of Daphne's home, Hope expressed relief that the removal had gone smoothly. All the time they were filling every square inch of Jack's car she had been afraid that David might appear, his curiosity having been aroused by a passing friend or prying neighbour.

Clothing and soft furnishings had been absorbed into Daphne's home with larger items stowed in the garage.

Hope went over their day. "I didn't believe your friend last night when he said he could move all my stuff with just the aid of his car."

Jack had made trip after trip between Halden and Eastkirk, his old Vauxhall crammed with Hope's possessions and the occasional large item secured to the roof with rope. The sideboard was one of these and it was to Jack's immense relief when he unloaded it at the other end without attracting police interest.

"He never stopped. The strength of that man...." Hope managed a laugh as they said in unison, "Hands like shovels!" the same comment Jack had made about himself several times that morning.

The day would have been more torturous had it not been for Jack's droll humour. Hope giggled at his suggestion that if she ever planned to do it again she should make a point of not tacking down her carpets so thoroughly and to defrost the fridge beforehand. As it was they had had to leave the fridge but apart from that they managed to retrieve everything else that she could legitimately claim as being hers.

Billy had been following the conversation and made a bid to join in. "His hands are big".

"They sure are," agreed Hope. "Just like yours. Give me five!" She raised her hand for Billy to slap. He laughed and slapped his hand smartly to hers. "And you helped a lot as well Billy. We couldn't have done it without you."

"I done a good job didn't I?"

"You certainly did!"

A great deal had gone over the lad's head but his appointment as their lookout had put a temporary lid on any questions.

Billy continued to beam. "You've come back home."

His mother threw Hope a look. "Yes – I think that just about sums it up."

Chapter 14

It had been sunny all day though now there was a chill in the air and Hope's suit jacket billowed in the late-afternoon breeze whilst she waited at Tarnville's door. Rather than cart her luggage with her she had left it at the railway station for collection later, and caught a bus. A telephone call would have secured a lift but she wanted the solitude, and the stroll from the bus had been a gift. The explosion of spring was everywhere. An elaborately orchestrated trill of birdsong had accompanied her every step and even now the rousing symphony of precision continued. There had been no need for the coat slung casually over her arm but now shrugged it round her shoulders.

A regular visitor to the house, it was difficult to appreciate her nervousness on her first visit when, not yet 19, she had stood taut with tension in this same spot to offer condolences to Sir Charles whom she now had the privilege of knowing as a friend.

A great deal had happened in the ensuing three years. She had twice been subjected to an attempt of rape; her uncle had been drowned in waters from the river she loved, the same river that had claimed her father's life; and she had turned down an unexpected proposal of marriage from a dear friend. But she had moved on to secure what her father would have considered to be a good job in the city, then crowning all that, at the age of 20 she married a man whom she now realised she had never really known, and walked out on him just 18 months later. Notwithstanding all of that she had found a friend in the old gentleman from the big house, and a smile of satisfaction replaced her former frown.

The metal-studded door laboured opened and Hope looked into the flushed features of Sarah Kaye who beamed back believing the smile was for her. The housekeeper welcomed her warmly.

Both her landlady and employer had persuaded Hope to spend a few days with her aunt. With the passage of four weeks Daphne considered it high time Isabel was told about the split with David, whilst Kevin Lester sought to lessen the sadness in his assistant's eyes.

Although her aunt had never really cared for David, Hope did not relish the interview. When she rang to arrange her visit Isabel had turned all giddy, and instructed her not to bother with the Estate office but to go straight to the main house where she was assisting Sarah who was getting over flu. Then, as though an afterthought, she said she had some news, which she preferred to convey in person. Intuitively Hope knew from the thrill in her voice that she was to learn of her marriage to Peter; at the precise point when she was preparing to announce the ending of hers. The irony struck her forcibly.

When Hope repeated the conversation Daphne had drawn the same conclusion though unlike Hope she reaped a sense of relief, albeit recognising it selfish. If Isabel were getting married it seemed unlikely that Hope would want to live with the newly-weds. Daphne had made herself miserable with the thought that Hope might move back to Mowlem. She could not bear the idea of losing the young woman who had become so important to her that it pained her when she saw her cry, which happened often. Even Billy filled up when he saw her like that.

"So you have a few days off from Kevin and all his little problems," concluded Charles, knowing full well his Attorney's problems did not remotely fall within the description of *little*. Like the rest of the nation he had been drawn to the recent media coverage of one of Lester's current cases. Kevin Lester himself would not normally take on a divorce action but this was a big case and apparently messy, involving a pop star, custody of offspring of varying parentage, coupled with the confusing factor that the initial marriage ceremony was now in doubt as to its validity.

Charles's attempt at humour did not gain a smile. During the last hour he had detected something that had not been there the last time he saw Hope. Today the green eyes had been slow to flatter her enlivened smiles and bore traces of sadness – or loneliness – or was it fear he read there? He could tell that something troubled her. During a routine telephone conversation Kevin had intimated this brief holiday would benefit his assistant. He had added that she was in need of a break from things, though would not elucidate further except to say that Hope could do with a proper holiday and not just a four-day break.

Having secured a property in Corfu, Charles was planning a return trip. It would be nice if Hope could accompany him, he mused, smiling at the thought and the prospect of setting tongues wagging.

Though not on the same scale as Tarnville, Villa Marchriard – the title derived from the combined names of his wife, daughter and son – was sufficiently large for Hope to be apart if she wanted. It was absurd, of course. Nevertheless she had come to mean so much to him that the idea wafted around in his mind now, daring his tongue to break convention and speak the words of invitation.

Disappointed with himself he turned his attention to other matters. "I have a surprise for you but first I should call my Housekeeper." Stifling his mirth Charles went to the bell-pull whilst Hope looked back, intrigued by his suggestion that Sarah Kaye had something to tell her.

A few minutes later the library door swung open and Hope turned to smile at Sarah, but framed in the doorway was the taller figure of her aunt. About to go to embrace her, Charles motioned that she should remain seated.

"My new Housekeeper," explained Charles. Sarah Kaye hovered outside in the corridor. "Isabel, Sarah – come in." He turned to his guest. "Sarah has decided to retire." He looked fondly at the tiny woman who had been in his employ for more years than he cared to remember. "She's leaving me to go to live with her sister in Stillingford – to prune roses – and that sort of thing she tells me." His young companion fell silent, her eyes probed his, and he nodded agreement. "Yes, that's right. Your aunt has agreed to take up the post of Housekeeper and for her sins to keep me in check."

Pleasure instantly showed in Hope's face with her appreciation that probably for the first time in her life her aunt would have some proper security. She looked into Isabel's face and saw at once a level of happiness she had never seen before.

Charles's next words went some way towards counterbalancing the realisation that her aunt's appointment would from necessity be residential, with the consequence that the cottage lease would lapse and she would no longer have a home in Mowlem. "My dear, as your aunt will be taking up residence here I want you to feel free to come to stay whenever you wish. That includes your husband – no invitations or any of that sort of nonsense." His young friend flinched for some reason he did not understand but that was forgotten when a most rewarding expression crept into her face.

Isabel beamed and Sarah dabbed her eyes as they watched the girl go comfortably to Charles, his arms drawing her even closer when she reached to kiss his cheek.

The gentle gesture reminded Charles of those he had cherished years ago before his cheeks became crazed with the advancement of the years that brought him nearer to his 80th than his 70th year. His embrace tightened with the revival of the memory.

There was a long moment of comfortable silence that spilled over with smiles. Presently Charles suggested that his *new Housekeeper* might like to show Hope her room.

Sarah Kaye had a good-sized corner suite in the west wing that would pass to her successor after the agreed overlap but until then rooms had been prepared for Isabel and Hope further along the corridor. Charles had purposely chosen the west wing. Whilst the other side of the house overlooked the sculptured grounds, woodland and main driveway, he felt that Hope would prefer the less formal view of the river and her stepping-stones.

He sighed, "I told Kevin four days wasn't nearly long enough." A couple of weeks away with him would do her far more good....

As they ascended the majestic staircase Isabel slid an arm round Hope. She remained convinced that her good fortune was an extension of her employer's affection for her niece.

"It was a blessing when you and y'dad came to Ivy Cottage."

She had never had a moment's trouble with Freddie's child. The whole neighbourhood liked her. Everywhere she went people asked after her niece. Not jealous like, nothing like that. She could tell that folk were genuine when they asked how Hope was getting on in the city. And she enjoyed telling them, though not boastful mind, she was always careful not to come over that way, though it was impossible to conceal her pride.

"Pet," she continued, "I'm so happy! My whole life changed for the better with your arrival. And now look at me – Housekeeper no less. I told you I had a surprise. It takes a bit of getting used to doesn't it? Thanks to your concern for Sir Charles at the time of his bereavement and the closeness you now share, we've both landed on our feet. You at Lester Associates and now me here at Tarnville! Who'd have believed it – me here! Don't pinch me, I'm afraid I might wake up!" Laughter escaped her smiling lips. She patted Hope's hand, "If y'dad could see us now he'd laugh his socks off! Aye – he would right enough, and he'd be that proud of you. Everything you touch seems to turn out well."

Hope's expression changed and did not match the spirited laugh engineered for her aunt.

That evening, in Sarah's quarters, Hope barely ate anything, but distractedly moved the food around her plate. However the following morning saw no such curb on her appetite.

Isabel entered the bedroom to find her breakfasting in bed from the tray that Clarice, the rosy-faced maid fresh from the village school, had brought to her room.

"My! I saw that tray and didn't think you'd get through it all."

"Correct me if I'm wrong but this is yours, isn't it? I'd know your marmalade anywhere. I'd ask for more but don't want to risk busting the scales!"

Isabel made great quantities of preserves but her marmalade had always been one of her best sellers. Hope licked the last sticky traces from her fingers and grinned like the child Isabel remembered so well.

"Craving marmalade of all things – you know what they say about cravings...." Chuckling to herself, Isabel removed the tray and in her preoccupation did not see the smile vanish from Hope's face.

Pregnant? Impossible! But now that she thought about it there had been occasions when she felt queasy. She had put it down to all the upset, as she had the fact that her period was late. Oh! Just how late was it? With everything that had been going on she had lost track, but fancied it was eight or nine weeks since her last bleed.

Horrified, Hope drew her legs up beneath the bedcovers. It couldn't be – it mustn't be! How would she manage? The latter thought was instantly pushed from her mind. She was *not* pregnant. Anyway – she'd know if she was – but then she remembered an item in the news a while back when a woman had gone into labour without her even knowing that she was pregnant. Hope froze.

Oblivious to the turmoil in the mind of the one behind her, Isabel chattered on from the other end of the room, "I declare those birds know when you're home. I swear their song is sweeter."

Later, still agitated, though making a concentrated effort to dispel her fears, Hope made her way along the wood-panelled corridor towards the main staircase. The day stretched luxuriously before her. No trill of telephones to break her concentration, or a paper trail of deadlines to follow up – and no disconcerting sighs from her prickly roommate.

Hope had every intention of enjoying her escape from a world governed by the clock, deadlines and the constant pursuit of increased profits – *volume, times gross margin percentage, minus overheads*. With no specific plans she intended taking each day as it came, and to savour every minute. After all, she was following instructions. Take a break, forget about things, pamper yourself a little, Kevin had told her. And Tarnville was just the place to do that.

Isabel expected to be tied up for most of the day with trades' people in connection with May Day, which meant she could please herself. How different it would be for Isabel this year. No doubt it would feel a little strange her co-ordinating the event from Tarnville; her aunt would surely miss the chaos in the village hall, the preparations and the sewing circle chat.

At the head of the carved staircase Hope glanced down at her jeans. Whilst they blended into the city scene, here they clashed with the sweeping gowns she imagined had descended the stairs over the years in response to a resounding dinner gong. Goose bumps assailed her arms with the knowledge that she trod in Christina Lurdmayne's footsteps. What style of dress had she made her own – strictly formal or rarely formal? A peek into the long wardrobes remembered from her occupancy of Christina's room during the flood would provide the answer but despite her host's emphatic words that she should make herself at home, peeking amongst his daughter's personal effects did not fall even loosely within a parallel extension of *making oneself at home*. She sensed Christina's presence everywhere – or perhaps it was

109

fancy born from the knowledge that her father sought their reconciliation.

Practically detecting the rustle of crisp taffeta round her ankles, Hope descended the staircase, her denim momentarily forgotten. Moments later she left the house. She breathed deeply, her lungs appreciative of the sweet-smelling air. The birds were singing as they always did in Mowlem, unlike the starlings and pigeons, dingy in colour, that she fed on Daphne's lawn.

Mowlem, Mowlem – she loved every square inch! The seasons were more marked in the country and she loved each one from the lush intermingle of a thousand shades of green right through to when naked sycamores and elms broke a pale, wintry horizon with elaborate silhouette designs. She tried once to explain to David how she felt about the place. Each time she returned it was as though her entire world changed and she was transported into another where she found peace and quiet and the renewed security of her father's love. When he made no comment she knew he had grasped no feel of any part of it.

This intrusion of thought served no purpose but to annoy her; the frequency in which memories of David came into her mind wearied her. She had heard nothing from him. The lack of contact remained a source of surprise and every time the telephone rang she still expected to hear David's voice.

She resolved that David should not be allowed another thought. She lengthened her stride and was soon at the river. The sight of her stepping-stones filled her with revitalised joy, a purpose for living, and treasured memories of her early years, though today she did not linger but strode on towards the bridge. One day she would use the stepping-stones, but not yet.

Curious faces peered out from beneath lace curtains but when the stranger in their midst was identified as Isabel Patterson's lass, warm smiles replaced the inquisitive expressions. Several exchanges of conversation were made as Hope wended her way through the village to take short-cuts down familiar snickets known only to residents.

Hope was toying with the idea of paying Hattie Middler a visit when she heard a shout.

Amy darted up to join her. After a quick exchange of news, primarily about Amy's recent nursing examinations, they were still chatting together when they knocked on the old lady's door and Hattie drew them to her as she had when they were young and the occasion of a grazed knee had brought them wailing to her door for a sticking plaster and a slice of cake, knowing full well it would be the latter that would bring forgetfulness to the injury. As expected there was an offer of tea from the pot that from habit brewed on the table.

Until the old lady's repertoire commenced, Hope had forgotten how confused Hattie had become and for the first time found it faintly irritating.

"It'll be dark early tonight."

Glancing out at the bright spring day her visitors exchanged understanding looks.

"What day is it?"

She was informed that it was Saturday.

"And there's me thinking it's Sunday. I wonder where I got that from. Anyroad it makes no difference. Every day's the same but I'd best not start singing any hymns!"

The girls gave synchronised nods when asked if they were warm enough, whilst each knew that Hattie would ask the same questions several times more before they took their leave.

"He's gone too now.... "

Hattie was off again and entering that obscure loop of confusion known only to her. In an attempt to break the cycle Amy went to kneel beside her. Hope looked on as Amy's nursing training surfaced and she cupped her hand over an arm dappled with brown age spots.

"Hattie, I bumped into Hope just a few moments ago. Neither of us knew the other was over for the weekend. David couldn't make it," she continued, employing Hope's words. "Neither could Greg – too busy swatting for exams. Hattie.... I've got some news." Amy's glance included Hope. "Greg and I are pulling our wedding forward to later this year. Probably the back end, we'll have to see how we go." Her face radiant, Amy explained they were saving hard.

Hope offered her congratulations but then looked wistfully beyond her ex-school friend who made a mental note to ask what was troubling her.

111

After devouring a chunk of sticky parkin the size of a doorstop, and answering the same questions many times more, the friends took their leave and stepped out into the bright sunshine.

"Poor dear Hattie, she's getting worse." Amy had counted one repetition well into double figures. "But she seems happy enough and apparently gets a lot of callers." Amy kept her eyes focused in front. "You were a bit quiet in there. Something wrong? You are pleased about the wedding....?"

Hope exhaled then replied, "Yes to both questions. There is something wrong, and I'm delighted that you two are finally getting your act together. I always knew you were right for each other."

"Then what....?" began Amy.

Hope stopped walking. "I've left David." A sigh from the region of her soul accompanied the statement. "It happened a month ago...."

"Oh I'm sorry!" Amy shuffled her feet uncomfortably as she searched Hope's eyes. "I feel dreadful now. Me going on like that in there." Her glance swept back at Hattie's cottage, then towards Tarnville, only partially visible from this side of the village. "How's Bell taken it?" She watched Hope grimace. "You've not told her have you? Oh – Hope! How would you feel if she heard it from someone else?"

"*I know – I know!*" Then more gently, "Sorry – I didn't mean to snap. That's why I'm here.... to tell her." You've no idea how bothered I've been that she might ring the flat and get a distortion of the story from David." To prevent this she had made a point of ringing Isabel daily, and sometimes more than once.

She gave an account of what had awaited her return to the flat, before concluding, "And there's something else, but please keep it to yourself. There's a chance I may be pregnant."

Immediately Amy's arms went round her just like they had many times after Frederick's death. "And you've kept all of this to yourself?" Amy regarded her with sensitivity, and then spoke authoritatively. "First things first. You must speak to Bell and then get a pregnancy testing kit, better still make an appointment to see your doctor. Honestly you'll feel much better once you've spoken to Bell. That's the spirit," said Amy, encouraged by the beginnings of a smile. "See – you're feeling better already."

Amy was right. The declaration had opened a safety valve; she no longer felt so alone. Nodding now, Hope gave the assurance that she would speak to Isabel at the earliest opportunity, though refused to mention the possibility of her being pregnant. Neither would she agree to go to Braefield to buy one of those testing kits. She declared the whole of Mowlem would know about it even before she arrived back to do the test.

Amy deftly extracted a promise that she would make an appointment to see her doctor, and gained permission to tell Gregory about the breakdown of her marriage – and the possibility of having to place an order for a large quantity of white knitting wool.

There in the little disserted lane they hugged each other, each vowing to keep in regular contact, and Hope made her way back to Tarnville to speak to Isabel, where for the first time in her life she walked past the stepping-stones without even noticing them.

Chapter 15

With the short break ended Hope knew it would not be long before Amy rang to check the outcome of her doctor's appointment. But it was not a doctor she needed – it was time. Everything would sort itself out in time. Besides, the thought of being pregnant was bizarre and too unreal to grasp. Totally rejecting the idea Hope returned to work determined to forget the failed marriage hanging over her and the vague possibility of life developing inside her.

It had been a pleasant few days. Nevertheless it felt good to be back. Equally pleasing, the far side of the office had been cleared in its entirety. Kevin had informed her of his intention before she went on leave. Marty's introduction of Fanny to Hope's husband had destroyed his respect for Marty and it would not be long, he told Hope through lips that scarcely moved, before the organisation and *that girl* parted company. Meanwhile there was no need to suffer her moods, he said, and Marty had been despatched to another floor. The exile was a fiercely proud, puffed-up little entity and Hope was certain she would not take kindly to banishment. Nonetheless Marty and all her trappings, including her Kevin Costner calendar, had been removed, and the newly vacated area yawned a wide welcome to its sole inhabitant.

Exercising care with the cabling and wires Hope inched her desk to a more balanced position over by the window, then she gathered up the large plants and grouped them together to form a natural screen beside the low seating used by guests. She nodded approval. Almost perfect, all it lacked was birdsong, a little water and some stepping-stones. Then it really would be perfect!

She settled at her desk and unlocked her drawer where she knew she would find papers left to give her a feel of what had been going on in her absence.

As he entered, Kevin Lester noticed the bloom in his assistant's cheeks. It was the same freshness he had admired on making her acquaintance at Tarnville. He noticed she was wading through the documents he had left for her. Annotations had been made on some whilst others had already been consigned to the filing and pending trays. He wondered about her but she was not the type to welcome demonstrations of concern, and swept her straight back into her role of looking after his needs, and like the professional she was, Hope leapt straight back into harness.

After the usual pleasantries he was reminded that his dinner engagement on Friday was black tie; given a quick run through of the day's diary notes; informed that some artwork was not yet to hand; and everything relevant was placed in his hands; as always Hope detecting his needs even before he did. Extremely competent and with an innate talent for organisation and detail, whatever it took to be a first-class PA, Hope had in good measure.

He turned from her then to pass through into his office, knowing that once he was out of earshot she would telephone his wife to inform her that Friday's dinner was a formal affair and to check he had not forgotten to mention he would need his dinner jacket and dress shirt. Between these two women he managed to get from A to B properly dressed, punctually and with all the right papers.

By the time the post was brought to her desk Hope was fully briefed and confident that everything, save the artwork, was to hand for Kevin's meeting in York to finalise the hotel merger. It was to be more of a celebration than a meeting. Following the exchange of contracts that Kevin had carefully nursed to fruition, avoiding more than one pitfall that could have resulted in a less successful conclusion, there was to be a champagne luncheon with the Press in attendance. After the photo-call the Media was expected to push for more information relating to the massive investment in the pipeline to transform the outskirts of Dalekirk. At that point the artwork and a model would be produced.

Before chasing the absent artwork Hope slipped through to Kevin's office to check she was not duplicating something he had done.

People were often surprised by Kevin's office. Whilst it was obvious from the presence of cabinets and the grand desk that it was an area where a great deal of business and decision-making took place, it also enjoyed a sense of comfort, enhanced by the restful green and ivory décor and the addition of comfortable cream leather settees in the L-shaped area beyond the desk. Despite a heavy presence of rich mahogany in the expansive antique desk, bookcases and long table used for informal management meetings, the room had an unpretentious feel about it. Hope's introduction of floor-length curtains, the soft leather settees and a low coffee table aided this. Kevin had initially opposed the low table; considering it too informal. Yet on its arrival he found himself gravitating towards this area of his suite at the close of most days when due to the lateness of the hour he felt able to relax with a glass of Scotch, and quietly thumb his way through documents in a more leisurely frame of mind away from the demands attracted to the business desk.

"I've just been speaking to them on my private line," Kevin responded to Hope's question. "There was no need to break you off when it was just as easy for me to dial the number." He stood up and began clearing his desk. "The artist's impression will arrive here no later than 11:30. When it comes I want you to take it across the Square to Kwik-Print." Disliking the increasing use of bastard spellings he almost growled at the name. "I want two copies. Ring George Strattis or his son.... "

"Samuel," supplied Hope.

"And alert them to the fact it's coming. Tell them it's urgent and you'll wait. Give one copy to Edward. He knows what to do with it." The Company Secretary was arranging for it to be hung in the Board Room. "And bring the original plus the other copy to the hotel. I'll send Crawford and the car back for you. He can run you home afterwards." Kevin tapped the remaining papers smartly on the desk to straighten them before placing them in the cabinet to which only they held keys. Hope took the opportunity to play back a summary of his instructions, a style he liked. They had never yet been at cross-purposes.

"These are the best sort of days Hope." He grinned like a juvenile opening excellent examination results. "I'll save you a well-earned glass of champagne."

After delivering the artwork and indeed joining Kevin in a glass of champagne, Hope took the lift back down to the hotel foyer, still littered with the same cameras and cables she passed on arrival. Her initial thoughts had been that the Press had misunderstood her instruction and congregated in the wrong place but then recognised them as a film crew shooting a shampoo advertisement. Several large posters for Sally Lox merchandise had provided the clue. The activities appeared to be linked to a re-launching exercise following revamped packaging.

Now, with her errand complete and officially finished for the day, Hope allowed herself to linger there, to watch. Earlier she had seen three willowy models, a redhead, a blonde – with hair colour too solid to be genuine – and a brunette, but now saw only two; the suspect blonde was no longer present. The brunette was being dabbed with face powder whilst the other twirled within the gale obligingly created by the floor-standing fan placed just out of shot to swirl her auburn hair high above her head. Several exclamations of "That's nice! Excellent! Again! Give me more.... still more!" and the inevitable, "Hold it!" echoed through the hotel foyer.

Hope was mesmerised by the activity. She drifted to a pillar where she watched for several minutes, the models who looked more like sculptures than breathing entities. Just then the blonde model reappeared. A young man with crisply-spiked bleached hair and the woman in charge of the powder-puff came forward to help the ashen-faced model negotiate the revolving doors. After watching her disappear into the street on unsteady legs Hope returned her attention to the activities in the foyer only to notice that one of the men was studying her intently. The undisguised attention made her uncomfortable. Her discomfiture increased when she glanced back to find him still studying her only now through a box arrangement formed with the aid of his thumbs and index fingers.

Any enjoyment derived from the diversion became short-lived and she made a move to leave but as she did, the tortoiseshell slide was snatched from her hair. Instantly her voluminous pale mane spilled spectacularly over her shoulders and down her back. In annoyance Hope whipped round to confront her assailant, at the same time aware of a commotion all around her.

Before she could spit out her anger, the person responsible held up his hands in feigned submission. "It's all right.... calm down."

"It's not all right! How dare you!"

"No – you're right." The hands lowered slowly. "But you see – if I hadn't taken you by surprise we wouldn't have got the shot." The man spread his arms wide, the gesture matched his smile, which was not returned. For several seconds he watched whilst she regained composure and her manner changed. The next moment was calmer than the last; she was no longer poised ready to strike, though maintained astute eye contact. He jerked his head towards a camera behind her. "It was a good shot Sweetie," he almost cooed.

Hope was about to inform him that she was nobody's *Sweetie* when a balding, rotund little man emerged from behind the camera. Nodding enthusiastically he raised a hand to the others who were noticeably silent, then forming a circle with his thumb and index finger glanced across the foyer.

Harry Nichols was in charge of the proceedings. With something resembling a salute he acknowledged the universal sign of excellence and went to join his operative and save him from being floored by the girl he apparently had upset.

For the moment ignoring Hope, Harry peered into the camera mechanism to examine the rushes. His head bounced several times before re-emerging to slant a smile of satisfaction at the assailant.

"It's good. Very good in fact. It works. I like it!" He stepped towards the subject of the frames. He extended his hand. "We – I owe you an apology. Perhaps you would care to take a seat...." With a broad imperious sweep of his arm he indicated a seating arrangement in the far corner. "I should like to explain."

Taking advantage of her momentary bemusement he guided Hope to the seating and before she could protest he snapped his fingers, motioning for a crewmember to bring coffee.

Harry took his place on the settee directly opposite the young woman perched at the edge of her seat. Huge startled eyes stared back whilst he engaged in noting every detail. Her demonstration of restraint might have amused him had his entire attention not been trained on the hair framing her face. She was host to the most amazing head of hair he had seen in his entire career of photographing the best. Harry felt he had just died and gone to *Page Three Heaven*. He lived alone and had never felt the need of a woman's knickers and stockings festooned across his bathroom but looking at this exemplary personage he could be persuaded to change his mind, though the gold band on her finger told him her underwear was already draped across someone else's bathroom.

Gently and without further pause he steered her through these awkward moments. "No – I'm not going to apologise...." he began, labouring the enunciation of his words. "I'm going to offer you a job!" He waited but her lips remained motionless. He was disappointed not to hear more from the extraordinary individual who had appeared out of the blue to save the day. The questionable blonde the agency sent had not pleased him. He had made no effort to conceal it and the poor girl feigned illness rather than suffer the indignity of being thrown off set. Marlene would be hearing from him. His requirements had been clear. She knew this was an important shoot. She should have contacted him if she had a problem in meeting his requests.

He studied his subject openly, appreciatively. As a one-off he might have been tempted to run with it and not bother to approach her but he had an eye for these things and he knew he had spotted something in this one, as would S-L's Marketing Director when he got a look at her. That magnificent head of hair made her perfect for the campaign. As for the body – that was worth an absolute fortune! Harry knew about these things.

Treading carefully Harry began again. "I want to use the footage we just shot. I'll make it worth your while.... say...."

There was a sudden barked cough behind them. "Is everything all right Mrs Stratton?"

Harry observed the girl barely concealed her reaction to the appearance of the middle-aged man and bit her lip. The quite deliberate widening of her eyes was also noted.

"I appear to have been offered a job.... photographic modelling."

"The money's good.... say £250 for these takes," put in Harry, purposely refusing to look in the man's direction. For someone with no experience he was deliberately going in high. He needed to ensure he caught her interest right from the start. "Obviously there'll be more for other shoots." Once more Harry clicked his fingers to attract the attention of another. "Pass my briefcase Pete." He turned back to the little gem on the sofa. "As it happens I believe I have a contract with me. We can go some way towards tying up a few loose ends here and now – subject to their man's nod – but he'll listen to me. What d'you say?"

Harry waited for her to become putty in his hands at the suggestion that he held the key to her future as a photographic model. It always worked.

"Contract....?" the voice as big as the person towering above Harry from behind the settee. Kevin's broad hand and expanse of shirt cuff reached over Harry's shoulder to take the document being handed to Harry.

Unable to ignore him any longer, Harry turned in his seat to flash annoyance at the man who looked more than a little formidable. "And you are....?" Furthermore he looked vaguely familiar.

"I'm Mrs Stratton's.... lawyer." The lawyer took the opportunity to exchange a look with his client. "Mrs Stratton signs nothing without it goes through me first." After a cursory glance he returned the single-page document.

Harry had a vague awareness of things having moved on apace and of innuendoes of which he knew nothing about, but before he could muster his thoughts the man had advanced upstage to parry adroitly from behind his legal shield of protection whilst *Page Three* slanted her head away, to suppress a smile.

"Her lawyer.... I see.... " said Harry, not entirely sure that he did. He glanced back at the girl for confirmation but it was the man's turn again.

"Your offer was.... £250?"

"Well.... let's say.... £300. That's good money for a few minutes' work."

"£300....?" the settlement figure was emphasised as before.

"Ok.... £350 – but that's my final offer. Take it or leave it."

Without Harry's knowing quite how he had done it, the bloody man had positioned himself like a lioness between her cub and a hyena. *Page Three* remained silent.

"You'll excuse us – Mr....?"

"Nichols – Harry Nichols." Harry inclined his head then watched the lawyer steer his beautiful client – his potential find – into a quiet corner from which they emerged moments later, the girl's face giving nothing away.

"£350 for today's photo-call, plus another £100 to compensate for the manner in which the whole thing took place, and that's my client's final offer – take it or leave it."

Beaten, Harry's head eventually nodded. He had expected to get the girl's services for half that. Appreciating at last that the geezer in the impeccable suit meant business he addressed his further remarks directly to him. "And other work – would Mrs Stratton be interested in doing further shoots for Sally Lox?" He was aware of *Page Three* sliding in from her place in the wings.

"I already have a career but if you supply details of any tasteful work you have in mind I'll consider it so long as it doesn't interfere with other commitments."

Tasteful? The word dangled itself provocatively in front of Harry who promptly waved goodbye to any *Page Three* ideas he might have had.

The lawyer took centre stage again, if indeed he had ever left it. He placed his business card on the table in front of Harry. "Send your proposals to Mrs Hope Stratton at this address and I'll be pleased to run my eye over the paperwork. Meanwhile.... a cheque for £450 will be in order for today."

A cheque book was hastily located in one of the pockets of the briefcase and a cheque written and passed across.

Moments after watching the lawyer and his client disappear through the revolving doors it came to Harry where he had seen the man before and a low whistle escaped him. That female had more class than he had already credited her with. Her Lawyer chum was the bloke he had seen on television all last week speaking on camera – though giving nothing away – regarding his client, Craig Ireland, the lead singer from Shambles. He had photographed the group years back, before Ireland joined them and they adopted the name of the famous street in the city where they originated. Harry examined the business card in his hand. He read the name aloud – "Kevin Lester QC". The name said it all. If he wanted the services of Hope Stratton he would have to play a straight game.

Kevin slid into the seat beside Hope in the rear of the Mercedes. Hope started to chuckle. "That was better than a game of Monopoly.

121

At one point I thought I was going to have to throw a six to avoid going to jail!" Then becoming serious she thanked him for stepping in. "I'd have settled for a great deal less than £450."

"I know you would. That's why you need a good lawyer. It's a good job you've got one!" That was the only flaw in this jewel, her inability to appreciate herself as others did. He wondered what perception she held that was so out of tune with the rest of them.

Recounting every detail, Hope did a good job of entertaining Daphne and Billy over dinner.

"You can tell a good tale," said Daphne at the finish. Still chuckling she spluttered, "And if you're going to be the next *Shrimp* in the glossies my girl you won't be able to go on eating like you did tonight." She clasped her hands, "Love – don't look so horrified. It was a joke! You know I like to see someone with a good appetite. It makes cooking worthwhile."

That was the second time attention had been drawn to her increased appetite. Was it a sign that she was getting back to normal, or could it be due to something else?

Hope's expression became a mask, whilst Billy pondered what shrimps had to do with the story.

Chapter 16

Success in gaining a doctor's appointment at such short notice threw Hope off balance. Part of her wanted to ring back to say she was recovered and did not need a doctor after all, but then swallowing hard took herself off to produce the urine sample she knew would be required.

It was mid-morning before Hope arrived at the office. The group huddled round the oval reception desk might have gone unnoticed had it not been for a shout.

"Congratulations!"

Intense green eyes shot towards the voice. With some difficulty Hope struggled towards comprehension, but then she noticed the newspaper the group craned necks to see. The young man would be referring to the merger coverage. She breathed more easily and nodded acknowledgement.

Others tossed strikingly similar remarks to her as she made her way to her office. Seemingly everyone was in good spirits as a result of the deal finalised yesterday. But her mind was not on the hotel merger; it was back in the doctor's surgery and still striving to come to terms with other congratulatory words.

When Hope entered her office the coffee was already perking, the morning papers had been arranged on her desk, and the person responsible was practically wearing a hole in the carpet with her pacing.

"Angela?"

Angela broke her stride and bounded across the room to Hope. "At last! I've been watching for your arrival. I want to be the first to hear all about it!"

Hope slipped her coat from her shoulders and focused her mind. "There's not a great deal to tell. It all went smoothly. Kevin seemed pleased." She nodded towards the newspapers. "What's the picture like?"

"Not the merger! I couldn't give a damn about that. I mean your little escapade. How did that come about?" Angela shook her head. "Tch! You're clearly on another wavelength this morning. This –

dopey!" She stabbed the newspapers with her finger. "You left here yesterday as Kevin Lester's Personal Assistant only to arrive back this morning as the new Sally Lox Girl! How did that happen? It's been driving me crazy waiting for you to get in. By the way, you're late." Angela's eyes swept to the clock, a mild note of sarcasm flattening the bubble in her tone.

For the moment ignoring the jibe, Hope asked how she knew about her run-in with the Sally Lox Corporation.

"Wow you're slow today. Everyone knows about it. It's all in here." The finger repeated the stabbing action at the papers on the desk.

Hope selected one of the nationals. Beneath a headline of "Pounds, Shillens and Sense" was a picture of Gordon Etherington, the retiring Chairman, with his hand grasped by Samuel Shillens, the Chairman of the newly formed hotel chain. Then her mouth dropped into a gape, for from the opposite page under the headline of "Here Today and Hair Tomorrow" her own face stared back at her. Hope lowered herself into her chair.

Her eyes darted over text that informed readers that she, the new Sally Lox Girl, had been plucked from the street. The feeling of exposure brought on a flush of embarrassment. It was so public. Everyone who knew her, even the dear people of Mowlem, would learn about yesterday's incident, which had already been dismissed as being no more significant than a story to amuse friends.

"Stop gaping. You look like something battered that goes with chips!" Angela teased. She leaned closer. "Well....?"

But before Hope could say anything the trill of the telephone claimed her attention. Shrugging pleasantly she reached past her friend.

"I'd like to speak to.... Sally Lox." Hope frowned at the receiver until recognition dawned. "Greg....?"

"Got it in one!"

"I take it you've seen it too?"

"Yep, but like I've told the guys here, you're much better in the flesh. And talking about flesh – I never thought I'd see the day when a friend of mine would appear on Page Three!"

Gregory was right. Her picture was on page three, though not in that particular tabloid. For a split second Hope revisited the scene of earlier; the expressions of those pouring over a newspaper in the entrance lobby now made sense. Once again she gaped hopelessly at Angela. "Greg's ribbing me because my picture's on Page Three!"

Gregory caught her comment. "It's the first time I've been able to boast about knowing a *Page Three Girl*. The lads here are well impressed! Say, Hope – d'you expect to be over for the weekend?"

"That's the plan. Will you be there?"

"Yep. Now that I'm seriously looking for a position I rang Joe Fearnley to see whether Tarnville had anything. Nothing doing but he suggested I try Anthony Wilcox over at Longdyke Farm and I've got an interview there on Saturday morning. So keep your fingers crossed. Wilcox is mainly cereals and a lot of rhubarb but his sizeable herd services Tarnville's dairy. Securing a place with him would give me the best of both worlds. Look love, I have to go. I'm due at a lecture."

"Right then. See you at the weekend. By the way, we're at Tarnville now. Did Amy tell you about Bell's new post?"

Gregory's tone changed to one of caring. Amy had told him *everything*, he said.

Hope's earlier distraction returned as she put down the phone.

In contrast, lively and still visibly intrigued by the newspaper coverage, Angela continued to stand her ground. It was evident that little work would be done in Personnel until she heard everything about what had taken place yesterday. Yielding, Hope inclined her head towards the freshly perked coffee.

They took their coffee to the low seating used by visitors, where Hope finally divulged how she came to have a sizeable cheque in her purse.

"Wow! I can't believe it."

"And there's something else you won't believe. I know I can't."

Angela's eyes widen in the anticipation of a sequel.

"Angela.... I'm pregnant."

"No! Are you certain?" but Angela could see the answer in Hope's face, which left nothing to supposition. "Does David....? No – of course he doesn't." She reminded herself of the whole David-Fanny saga. "Do you.... do you intend keeping it?"

The question shocked Hope, though she could not imagine why, for she had been asking herself exactly the same question. "I don't know," she said eventually. "I haven't quite got my head round it. Please don't say anything to anyone. I want to keep it quiet for now." Just then her other telephone rang. Only one person used that line. Fighting to regain composure she motioned for Angela to field the incoming call.

"Good morning Chairman. No – it's Angela. Yes, fine thank you. Yes." Angela nodded. "Yes," another bob of her head. Certainly...." Another nod and another.

Carried away now, Angela's head bobbed with growing rapidity and she barely managed to prevent herself from slipping in the odd Okey-Cokey-Snooky-Pokey for good measure. The realisation unsettled her and she began speaking much too quickly, all the while signalling wildly for Hope to take the phone.

Conversation with the Chairman, no matter how brief, always made Angela nervous. Once when she bumped into him in the corridor she had anticipated his usual enquiry. Failing miserably she replied that she was quite well and thanked him for asking, only to realise he had merely informed her that it was raining again.

"Hope's here now. I'll put her on." Flustered, Angela clamped a hand over the receiver. "He's still talking and doesn't realise the call's breaking up. I can't make out what he's on about." Panic had set in, and willing a rescue bid she made a final attempt to extricate herself by thrusting the phone at Hope.

Hope played Kevin's itinerary through her mind. His train would be approaching Kings Cross. She took the phone from a grateful jelly and smiled at the familiar sound of his voice, and then at the person across the office reviving herself with coffee at the same time spilling some down her skirt.

Hope missed Kevin when he was away from the office. Some of the magic went out of her day with his absence. With her pencil poised, she awaited the instructions that would follow, but Kevin surprised her.

"Well – if it hadn't been for that MP's suicide you might just have made it to the front page and in front of one of the biggest mergers this country's ever seen! By the way – the shares are up by more than the analysts projected." There was early laughter in his voice as he went on, "I have to admit yours is a bonnier picture than that of Etherington and Shillens." Kevin glanced back at the news litter strewn across the table in the first-class railway compartment. "I acknowledge the somewhat objectionable Harry Nichols knows his stuff."

Hope laughed and then instantly wondered if that were wise. Was he displeased that her escapade had been positioned as though on a parity with the hotel merger? "That's something we'll never know," she ventured, uneasy about her ground.

He agreed then said, "Of course you've noticed their choice of wording? They've openly referred to you as the *n-e-w* Sally Lox Girl. You should be pleased." He did not wait for a response. "It means you can name your price. You've signed nothing. If they want you – and they clearly do – you can call the shots and name your price. But you can leave that to me. I'll make sure you do all right out of it."

Her troubled feelings of earlier changed to those of optimism. In her present circumstances any additional money would be useful; whatever she decided she would need finance; in any event she wanted nothing from David.

Eventually Kevin led her to business, and her pencil flew across her pad as she made a note of his precise instructions in the same shorthand outlines that had impressed her father aeons ago.

Kevin rang off. Realisation dawned and Hope became thoughtful. No matter how lucrative the photographic work, inevitably it would be short-lived, for if she decided to keep the baby she would not remain photographic material for very long. No matter how lovely the hair no one would want to look at someone the size of a whale.

After a day plagued by the telephone, almost to the point of tedium, Daphne's telephone dared to disturb the evening meal. Hope had almost finished and motioned for Daphne and Billy to remain seated. She went to the sideboard to answer the phone, and instantly her smile disappeared. "David!" Her husband's name formed a lump in her throat. She felt ill-prepared for this, their fist contact since their separation.

127

He had seen her picture in the paper and wished to congratulate her, though the crisp edge to his tone belied sarcasm. After the briefest pause he got quickly to the point of his call. "I was wondering whether you might make me a loan.... I've got my eye on a...."

Hope's mouth dropped open. She knew to her cost the type of thing that caught his eye: Fanny, and others like her. Unburdened by common sense his attributes did not include truthfulness. "No David. I'm not a banking service. If you want a loan see your Bank Manager."

The finality of her words put his back up and a surge of adrenaline fuelled an instant verbal attack as he began vying for position. During a spiteful onslaught he laboured the problems she had brought to the marriage, going on, "Mealtimes always had to be fitted in around your bloody schedule!" He accused her then of nourishing her own ego but in the next moment he swung to the other extreme and declared his willingness to forgive all that foolishness and to take her back. "But there'd have to be some changes. I couldn't go back to that same carry on."

What she did not know, and David did not volunteer, was that he had been fired two weeks ago for turning up drunk to the office once too often.

Hope could not believe what she was hearing. David was willing to forgive her! "You made a sham of our entire relationship. Thanks to you it was a complete waste of time! Clearly you put no value on it. You violated any trust or what was decent in our marriage. Your friend – I use the term loosely – was the complete and final betrayal! I shall be filing for a divorce." Her volley finished, Hope replaced the receiver.

Nonplussed, Billy looked to his mother when tears began to slide silently down their lodger's face. He remembered crying like that when his hamster died. But Hope did not have a hamster and he welcomed the suggestion that he should go upstairs to play on his computer.

To Hope's mind David's request for money divested him of any measure of decency.

To Daphne's mind he was capable of anything. She would put nothing past him, and she still thought him a bit too smarmy!

The aftershock of David's words provoked in Hope a feeling of guilt. Had she contributed to the failure of the marriage as implied, and had she really been on an ego trip, or was it nothing more than healthy ambition and a natural growth to accommodate life? She was no longer sure and tension formed in the base of her neck.

Daphne went to her. "All this will become a distant memory eventually and no longer matter."

"He was the one who wrecked things! He rejected me!" Hope sobbed. "And now he says he's willing to take me back." Slowly and painfully she started to weep. "I really loved him...." In silence she considered her aunt's marriage and how she had carefully measured her own against that unhappy union. She wondered whether she would ever again earn the right to love and be loved, and enjoy devotion. She doubted her ability to capture and nurture the formula long enough for it to evolve into something complete and enduring. In that frozen moment, as though glimpsing the future, she saw herself as an old woman, unloved and alone.

"And to think he even had the effrontery to ask you for money!" The acidic words cut into Hope's thoughts. "What is it?" Daphne had spotted something in her expression.

Quietly Hope confessed, "I'm going to need all the money I can get. I'm pregnant.... I only found out this morning. I've told no one except Angela. I wasn't even going to tell Bell yet. You see.... I was wondering whether to have an – whether to keep the baby." Her face changed then, and she looked straight at Daphne. "You may consider this a moment of insanity but I've only just realised how much I really want this baby." It was true. Somehow countering David's rejection of her as a wife had helped her to determine what was important.

Daphne thought for a moment before speaking. "It's not insanity. It's a mother's love. Let's leave the pots for now and go into the other room. There's something I'd like to tell you."

Once they were seated Daphne explained how she had considered having an abortion when she discovered she was expecting Billy. "John never wanted children you see. He wanted me to get rid but I convinced myself he'd change his mind when the baby arrived. He didn't and when Billy's condition became apparent he simply walked out one day and left us to get on with it." She confessed to feeling guilty at having considered an abortion, albeit momentarily, and for a long time wondering if Billy's condition were some kind of punishment for that brief lapse. "In any event Billy's my life and I wouldn't have him any other way. I love him just the way he is."

The story tore at Hope's heart and was at harsh odds with the one she had imagined of a young woman suddenly widowed and left to bring up her child on her own.

Hope was more determined than ever to keep her baby. The idea that an infant was developing inside her still seemed unreal, and yet she found herself wanting this child more desperately than she had ever wanted anything. The realisation put a different slant on things.

In that moment everything took on meaning – even her uncle's rape attempts, for without the resulting momentum she might never have moved away. She was glad she married David if only to gain this child. There was a pattern to life after all, though she doubted the sequence thus far would have delighted her father. Even so, her life was beginning to make sense and she resolved to speak to Isabel at the weekend.

Billy wandered in keen to show them the Christmas card he had made despite its being April. The presence of a purple dinosaur in the nativity scene produced two sets of raised eyebrows, and a puzzled frown from Billy who wondered if his original choice of orange might have been better.

Daphne caught Hope's eye. She asked purposefully, "Are you sure about your decision?" Pleased by the resolute bounce of her head Daphne turned to her son, "Billy love, what would you prefer.... for a baby girl or a baby boy to come to live with us?" Then put in quickly, "And don't say you'd prefer a horse or a donkey. That's not one of the options." A ripple of laughter flowed between mother and son until gently spilling over to Hope.

That night, as she fell asleep, Hope planned her child's future in much the same way as Frederick Thackeray had done for her many years before.

While Hope slept, the Director of Acquisitions & Mergers for Shillens International returned to the loneliness of his hotel bedroom and opened his newspaper. His eyes went straight to Hope's picture.

"The *orchid amongst the daisies*!" he whispered, smiling at the three-year-old memory and recalling how he had considered retracing his steps across the bridge in Mowlem to speak to her. He had seen her again when she had been summoned to Lester's Board Room during one of his attendances. Bolt upright in his chair he had been unable to take his eyes off her; her presence had siphoned his attention from the matter in hand. He noted every detail, particularly how she had grown up, which had been emphasised by the sophisticated styling of her hair. Little managed to deflect his attention from the job but this young woman had managed it twice.

It had not been until later that he discovered a significant gap in his notes. Smiling afresh, he recalled his sense of disappointment when he gleaned from Kevin Lester's introduction that she was married. He looked for her wedding ring now but the newspaper photograph was too grainy. Her husband was an exceptionally lucky man.

The next day Hope confided in her employer. Kevin listened in almost complete silence as she divulged her intention to file for a divorce. His sandy-coloured head dipped periodically until mention was made of her pregnancy and the decision not to seek financial support from David. Kevin stopped drawing a flower on his blotter; he always doodled when he was thinking. He stirred himself and after appraising his flower, or considering his words, he put forward a persuasive argument against the logic behind her thinking. He finished, "I'm not talking morally. I'm talking legally."

But Hope was having none of it and remained resolute; she wanted nothing from David Stratton.

"Okay – if you're sure that's the way you want to play it I'll have a word with the chap I mentioned." To save embarrassment he was putting her in touch with a legal chum, Charles Westbourne; it would cost her nothing. Charlie owed him a favour, several in fact. "There's one thing though and I'll not take NO for an answer. You're taking some leave, a minimum of two weeks. No arguments. In all the time you've been here you've only snatched odd days. You need a proper break." A smile gentled his tone, "Especially in your condition."

The suggestion was appealing. "I'd like that." The idea of a fortnight in Mowlem took shape in her mind, whilst a completely different picture formed in his.

Hope reverted back to business. "Which secretary should I liase with for the hand-over?" She knew without asking that he would not entertain agency staff.

"I'll have Angela."

Angela would be pleased! Hope could imagine her response.

"I like her spirit. Yes, I'll have your friend." He had watched the two of them together and noted their friendship. When Hope was stretched it was always Angela who volunteered help, never any of the others. The girl amused him. He was never quite sure what she would do next. "Yes – Angela will suit me nicely for two weeks."

Hope turned to leave.

"Before you go – I'm about to ring Charles.... about his new villa," the comment misleading, though nonetheless true. "Would it be in order to mention any of this?" His voice willed her to agree, which would greatly assist his plan. He waited whilst she considered this.

"Yes – why not? I know it probably sounds odd but in some ways Sir Charles has been a bit like a father to me. We both lost loved ones around the same time. Built on mutual support our friendship grew from there – but then of course you know all that." Her head inclined. "To be perfectly honest it might be easier if you prepare him, but do explain that I'm unable to speak to my aunt until the weekend. I need to do that face to face."

It was not difficult to anticipate Angela's response to the proposed secretarial cover. In the event her reaction was even stronger – extremely verbal and without a single mention of Okey-Cokey-Snooky-Pokey. Nevertheless she felt a swell of pride at being approached. But Angela was not daft; she knew that to be invited by the Chairman to do something was more of an instruction – even a *Royal Command* – and certainly non-negotiable. Despite her trepidation Angela was flattered to have been asked, but he still scared the hell out of her.

Chapter 17

The promise of new life brought Isabel the same froth of excitement as the day her brother agreed to come to live at Ivy Cottage. In her joy she took every conceivable opportunity to try to persuade Hope to move back home where she could look after her.

It would have been unkind of Hope to respond that she no longer had a home in Mowlem; and the idea of bringing up her child at Tarnville did not seem right, though the thought of doing so was appealing. Expressions of pleasure would steal some of the lines from Charles's face as he bounced a chubby infant on his knee; a sad void filled by the presence of a child, albeit not the one he sought.

Isabel's voice was laced with excitement when she told Hope that Charles wanted to see her. An indication of urgency took her straight to the library where she found Charles asleep in his favourite chair, his head on one side. Had her morning been different she might have crept away and returned later, but welcoming these first peaceful moments she slid into the winged chair opposite Charles, taking care not to awaken him. Absentmindedly, she observed a dust storm of powdery particles in the shaft of sunlight that illuminated the elderly face. Presently she felt a compulsion to reflect on the earlier part of her morning and she closed her eyes.

The day had commenced no differently from any other but it quickly became one that she was unlikely to forget. It all started in the little café area at the rear of the Post Office where she had arranged to meet Amy. The details were so clearly etched in her mind she was there again.... in the café enjoying Amy's company....

"But I don't feel pregnant."

Amy laughed at this. "Well apparently you are Miss Smarty-Pants – anyway I'm the nurse – a *State Registered Nurse*."

Hope spluttered on a mouthful of coffee. "You've qualified? You clever old thing! I bet Greg's pleased."

The face across the table took on a deadpan expression. "Perhaps a bit too much." Amy fiddled with the silk flower arrangement until the head of an anemone dropped off and had to be reattached. "Greg's so pleased he wants to put back the wedding to enable me, or so he says, to undertake more training in the field of midwifery. To be honest I think he's developed a case of cold feet. Unfortunately they didn't cover cold feet in my training. We did frost bite but that's a totally different thing." She attempted a smile. "He's probably realised just how near the wedding is and become frightened by the commitment. He's sort of distracted. You know – like he's somewhere else." Amy shook her head at the suggestion that his studies might be the cause. "No, I don't think so. He's over the worst and anyhow this is more recent. Anyway – though I've not told him yet, I've decided to stick with my original choice of nursing children. I may think about *midi* later but not yet. Right now all I want to do is apply to Braefield General for a position and get a little place with Greg. Ideally somewhere around here."

Hope watched the furrow deepen in Amy's brow. "Would you like me to have a word? We've been friends for a long time. He might open up to me. Maybe I could bring the conversation round by mentioning I've heard that Ivy Cottage is still available. By the way, it's to be sold rather than remain tied to the Estate. I can just see the two of you there."

It was the wrong time, with the baby coming and everything, but if she could have afforded it she would not have thought twice about putting in a bid herself. One day she would give seriously thought to acquiring a property, even if it were only a base for weekends and holidays – like Sir Charles had in Corfu. The comparison amused her, but if it were her own, even a tiny cottage would be just as special as any villa.

Gratitude showed in Amy's face. "I'd appreciate that, but you won't tell him I've discussed any of this with you? You know what men are like."

She certainly knew what men were like, but that was another subject entirely. Hope assured Amy of her utmost discretion.

The opportunity to speak to Gregory presented itself almost immediately, even before Hope had had time to formulate a plausible approach.

Arriving back at Tarnville she caught sight of the slightly stooped figure of Joseph Fearnley and one of the grounds-men engaged in conversation with Gregory at the far end of the stable block. The large, velvet head of Charles's hunter peered at her from over his stable door. Whilst waiting to catch Gregory on his own she went to stroke Tarkenta and breathe feelings of friendship into quivering nostrils. Another inquisitive face looked on from the adjacent stall and Hope spoke also to Illusion who whinnied her reply. The strident sound caught the attention of the men and a moment later Gregory broke away to join her.

The interview at Longdyke Farm had gone well, he told her. Expecting to hear more it surprised her when he dropped the subject and suggested a stroll through the grounds. She agreed; she had no reason not to, but that was before she knew what he had in mind.

After covering such matters as how blue the sky was, the unexpected mildness of the weather and other safe-ground fillers, Gregory grew serious. He asked how she was keeping before he steered the conversation round to the subject of the baby and Hope found herself answering his questions, which was not part of her plan.

"Do you intend keeping it – the baby?"

After a simple reply of Yes, she felt a compulsion to explain how important her infant had become.

He seemed satisfied. "What are your plans? Will you stay in Leeds or come back here? And what about your job – will you go on working?"

"So many questions Greg! Plans? I guess I'm still making them and as for Leeds – I can't say just yet. I'm not sure." All she knew was that she did not want to remain accessible to David. If it could be avoided she did not even want him to know that she was pregnant, though that would not be easy. When her condition became obvious it would be so easy for David to learn about it from former colleagues. "I suppose I'm not sure about anything yet – except that I want this baby." Her hand moved to rest protectively against her abdomen.

They meandered further until they reached the sunken rose garden, a favourite haunt of Lady Margaret when she was alive. The weak April sun had failed to remove the chill from the stone seating that encircled the sundial. Hope shivered and in the next moment Gregory's arm was round her shoulders.

"Cold?" She nodded. His eyes narrowed. "Have you thought about how you're going to manage on your own.... with a baby?"

Uncomfortable with his arm's continuing presence, the question shocked her. Surely he was not suggesting that she should put her child up for adoption – or worse. "Manage? I've thought about it though not in any great detail but I'm determined to succeed," like her father before her. Her fingers went instinctively to the smooth amber drop suspended on a narrow velvet ribbon round her neck. "And there's the photographic work. That's due to start up shortly."

Kevin Lester had gone through everything with the utmost care, and negotiated a hefty retainer from the Corporation. Additionally a meticulously worded agreement was now in place whereby she could withdraw at any time. He had even managed to persuade them to sign a Confidentiality Agreement whereby no mention would be made of her pregnancy. Furthering that, agreement had been reached that during her bulky months only her head and shoulders would be photographed. As the company was in the shampoo and beauty market and not the manufacture of baby milk formula they had been happy to conform, thereby awarding Hope the comfort knowledge she sought.

"It's important to prove to myself that I can do these things," she responded, returning to Gregory's query. She looked him straight in the eye in the same way she had when they were little and she intent on getting her own way, he always acquiescing, though not before giving the impression of carefully weighing up his decision.

But they were not little anymore, neither were their troubles, moreover he was not prepared to subscribe to any stubborn viewpoint as he had in yesteryears. Gregory adopted a gentle tone, which instantly reminded Hope of his concern following her father's death. "You needn't be on your own.... there's always me." The widening of her eyes did not attract his surprise. "I know that legally we couldn't marry yet, but later.... when your divorce is through."

Then she understood. Aghast, Hope realised that she was the reason for Gregory's so-called *cold feet*!

She turned on him fiercely. "I don't believe I'm hearing this! You – one of my best friends, engaged to be married to another of my best

136

friends – proposing marriage to me! Greg you must promise never to speak of this again," her voice emphatic. "I never want reminding of it. I don't intend mentioning this to Amy. In fact – this never happened!" With that verbal slap she sprang to her feet.

Gregory also got to his feet. "I've tried to love Amy but the fact is I love you. I've always loved you.... I always will."

His tone was one of deflation and she could see he was hurting. "Speak to Amy, Greg. You owe her that."

Fighting a clash of emotions, predominantly anger, she turned her back on Gregory and strode away from the nightmare into which she had stumbled, sad in the knowledge that things could never be the same between them again; for Amy's sake she must keep her distance in future.

Charles opened his eyes. Curious now to discover why she had been summoned, Hope pushed away the recollections of her morning. With a spontaneous smile her attention reverted to her elderly friend seated opposite her in the library.

"There you are!" Charles was suddenly attentive. "I'm sorry my dear. You caught me napping." He leaned forward conspiratorially, "When you reach my age you'll discover that dozing is only one of the little peculiarities attributable to old age – some less pardonable than others! Now then – I wanted to see you, didn't I?" He paused as though trying to remember why he had sent for her, and then began, "I understand Kevin insists you take a holiday....?" He inclined his head as though to encourage the nod that she obligingly gave. "Then you'll be needing this." His eyes never left her face as he handed her a document from the table beside him.

"It's a Passport application," she said, not understanding.

A warm smile preceded the gentle laughter that rumbled in his throat. "You're going to Corfu. You're going with your aunt and your friends Daphne and Billy. It's all arranged. My villa's all ready and waiting for you. The others are already on with their paperwork."

In the next moment Hope was kneeling beside him with his hands clasped in hers, her head against his chest. She fell to silence, which Charles knew blocked happy tears. Allowing her time to recover he kissed her silken head. She pulled away to meet his smile and he was more pleased than ever that he had had the foresight to purchase a villa.

The next two weeks were filled with holiday preparations and lengthy photographic sessions. The first photo-call took place in a studio one evening after work, to which Angela invited herself. Being her introduction to the camera Hope had welcomed her presence.

The shots were good but only good, Harry Nichols told her on the phone the next day. He said the natural quality of his model called for a natural setting, and he wanted to do it all over again in the Dales the following weekend.

Unaccustomed to rebuff, Hope's unwillingness astonished him. Upon learning her hesitation stemmed from a reluctance to break her routine of visiting an aunt in a place he had never heard of, the tiny village of Mowlem was found on the map, given due consideration, and chosen as the new location.

The activities on the riverbank caused more than a little intrigue amongst the villagers, many of whom crossed the fields to watch and claim kinship with the star of the proceedings. Charles had his own private ringside seat at his library window and derived pleasure from Hope's occasional wave.

Within minutes of the film crew's setting up the equipment, and screening-off an area where Hope would change outfits, to her horror one of the crew suggested she might be photographed on some stepping-stones he had discovered. Hope quickly strove to quell the idea; she expressed the opinion that they looked unsafe and consequently would not allow her to relax and display her hair in the way that they would wish. Harry reluctantly dismissed his colleague's idea whilst commenting that the stones looked perfectly safe to him. Compromising, he asked Hope to sit on the bank (with a Sainsbury's plastic bag beneath her to protect the fabric of her outfit) to incorporate the interest of the stones in the background.

When a member of the team handed Hope a posy of spring flowers she was reminded of the paintings her father had done of her mother, and years later of herself. Both pictures now hung in Isabel's room at Tarnville.

"Lick your lips and think some happy thoughts love!" Harry instructed.

"I'm doing that already," came the reply.

Dressed in a delicate shade of peach, Hope posed for each of the cameras indicated by Harry. "That's marvellous! Hold that expression – don't lose it."

The sound of cameras competed with the murmur of the river beside her. Before the team regrouped by the bridge and Hope went behind the screen to change, intrigued Harry asked, "What were you thinking just then? You had an expression I've not had the pleasure of seeing before".

She had been recalling a particular day more than 15 years ago. Drawing on the memory she told him about the two portraits her father had painted. Then, speaking about the one of herself, she explained, "I was five years old when he painted me in that spot." Smiling, she described her father's exasperated attempts to paint the movement of the breeze in her hair and how she had asked what colour he would paint the wind. Finally she admitted that her father had placed the stepping-stones in the river, and Harry nodded his understanding at her reluctance to use them.

After listening to the tale he begged permission to see her father's paintings.

The next day two photographs appeared side by side in the Press. One was of an oil painting painted by a father of his young daughter, the other a photograph of the daughter, now grown up, beside the same stepping-stones. The story line told how the father had placed a stone in the riverbed on the occasion of each of his daughter's birthdays with the promise that they would eventually lead her into her future. The indication from the remainder of the article was that Hope had been led, presumably by the stepping-stones, from an obscure village-life existence to the glitzy photographic world where everything was possible.

Though not unduly ruffled, in future Hope would insist that Kevin Lester cleared not only photographs but also any accompanying text before release for public consumption.

By the time Hope was due to leave for Corfu pictures of her were in evidence everywhere. Those of her leaning over the wooden bridge had begun to appear on billboards and in magazines, and even on the side of a bus, Billy told her with a smile almost connecting his ears. But the television commercial used the footage shot beside the stepping-stones.

Whilst checking in at the airport for the Corfu flight, Isabel noticed people, particularly one young man, openly admiring her niece. It was probably as a result of the advertisements but was just as likely to be due to Hope's presence. Isabel was used to looking at her but sometimes even she found it difficult not to catch her breath.

The holiday was over all too quickly and the friends agreed they would be sorry to leave Corfu. It had been a wonderful two weeks filled with laughter, floppy hats and sun lotions. Numerous postcards had been written and quite deliberately Hope had not sent one to Gregory but instead included his name on the one to Amy. She would never write individually to Gregory again.

The group would take back many happy memories, especially those of Charles's imposing villa where most evenings they relaxed on the first-floor veranda or one of the terraces surrounding the property. After watching the sun sink lazily into the sea, Daphne and Isabel had remained to chat or read, and Hope and Billy had wandered down the hill to the village where they perched on upturned barrels to share a pitcher of lemonade and watch the locals dance.

Hope was thinking about this now as the four of them sat together in an unassuming little bar they had discovered quite by chance. They were drinking beer. None of them liked beer but Hope's request for a jug of lemonade had lost something in the translation.

She looked about her. "I don't know what you think but I wish we'd found this place at the beginning of the holiday and not on our last day. There are few comforts, in fact it's quite shabby but in another sense it's perfectly lovely!" The place did something for Hope that very few places ever had; she almost choked on the emotion it evoked.

The others looked about them at the tumbled-down construction with its hotchpotch collection of plastic tables and chairs, few as white as intended and even fewer able to claim matching companions. The bar was little more than a shack tucked in at the end of a dirt track. They had stumbled upon it quite by chance after walking the length of a narrow, sun-baked path until it petered out, then squeezing through sun-scorched shrubbery rediscovered the thread of hard-trodden dirt that led them to the little haven jutting out almost into the sea itself.

Hope had no way of grasping the significance of this unimposing structure, or indeed the effect it would eventually have on the rest of her life. Despite her ignorance of what the years to come were already promising, inexplicably she sensed something about the place. Was it the gentle wash of the waves that were like a forgotten lullaby and now remembered, or was it the mere humbleness of the premises compared with the bright, music-filled bars frequented by holidaymakers? She did not know. She did not care. She only knew she wanted to stay there forever.

Chapter 18

Kevin Lester paced his office. He had not expected this and was unable to keep the surprise from his voice as he now asked, "Are you sure? It's a big decision and shouldn't be taken lightly." He came to an abrupt halt beside his desk and looked at his Personal Assistant. It never occurred to him when he packed Hope off on holiday that she would return to drop this bombshell. Had it been someone else he would have told them to go away and think it through again but this was Hope, who would certainly have deliberated lengthily on the consequences before reaching her decision.

Nevertheless he owed it to her, and indeed himself, to try to persuade her to reconsider. "Is there nothing I can say to make you change your mind?" Her head shook once more as it had to earlier questions. It was not her salary. He knew that. Recognising her worth he had paid her well right from the start.

Hope looked regretfully at her employer. She had been happy working for him. Kevin had gone out of his way to encourage her towards discovering her potential. If it had been down to pure choice she would not be handing in her notice, but she did not own the luxury of choice. If she stayed there was the risk that David would learn about her pregnancy, and she was not prepared to share her baby with a man capable of so much hurt. If she left now it would at least make some semblance of sense to colleagues, who would believe she had been tempted by Harry Nichols to enter the completely different world of flashbulbs and film, where people kissed the air and everyone's name was *D-a-r-l-i-n-g*.

"Is it really necessary for you to leave? It may be that your husband wouldn't want any involvement with the child. My view is that he's unlikely to show interest in the baby. He's shown precious little interest in his wife."

"Boxed in by circumstance I'm left with no choice. I simply daren't take that gamble. I'm not prepared to share my baby with him – not after everything he's done."

Kevin ceased his pacing and slid into the high-backed chair behind his desk, the action indicating a change of mood – reluctant submission – a rare state for the QC. Almost immediately his pen became engaged in drawing a flower on his blotter; the doodle grew in proportions and elaboration with the progression of their discussion.

He would continue to provide an effective buffer between Hope and the Sally Lox Corporation; it would cost her nothing. Hope cut him short. She could not permit that. He had done so much already. He responded simply, "It stands. It's not an offer and it's not negotiable." When she finally agreed but with the proviso that she paid for his services, he shook his head. "I wouldn't dream of it. It's not as though I can't afford it."

Coming from a profession where precisely worded statements were fundamental to its foundation Kevin cringed at his clumsiness. It sounded like a blatant flaunting of his wealth, which if anything was an embarrassment to him. When he bothered to think about it he could not deny he was inwardly proud of his success and the lifestyle it supported but sometimes he sensed his honest good fortune set him apart, and placed him firmly on the other side of the barrier others imagined between them. Even if he had not been in the favourable position he was, he would still have insisted on helping; somebody had to take care of her.

On the afternoon of her departure two weeks later – the early date agreed by mutual consent to conceal any telltale bulge – Hope's successor was named from the short list of candidates. Angela was to step into Hope's shoes, which pleased Hope but scared the hell out of Angela.

Over a finger buffet and drinks in the Board Room, a presentation was made of long-stemmed crystal wine glasses and flowers from Hope's colleagues. This had been preceded by a sensitive speech by Kevin, which left nobody in any doubt that he genuinely regretted her leaving. His gift was a beautiful antique clock, to represent the happy time they had spent working together.

Later when they were alone in his office he gave her a more personal gift, a beautiful trinket box carved from a single piece of seasoned yew in which she found a heavy gold chain to suspend her amber drop, which had become like a trademark for the S-L products.

At the close of business, Hope said her farewells and Angela walked with her to the lobby. "I'm going to miss you. Make sure you

143

keep in touch. I don't want to miss any of this little chap." She nodded discreetly towards Hope's waistline. "Won't be long before you're the size of a hot-air balloon."

Hope grimaced. "Stop that – comments like that I don't need! I might just go off the idea and wring the neck of that flippin' bird with the ridiculous long legs! I don't suppose there's any chance of my calling the whole thing off?"

"None at all kiddo – I just wish it were me. Get on with it and enjoy it!"

"Okey-Cokey-Snooky-Pokey – if you say so!" Hope mimicked before adding quietly, "Take good care of Kevin for me."

As acknowledged by Kevin Lester, Harry Nichols did have an undeniable skill in the field of photography. Harry's enjoyment of working with Hope showed in the material he produced and S-L climbed quickly to lead the UK's market place. A concentrated advertising campaign took the products overseas. The increased sales provided a further boost to Hope's resulting earning power, and her perception of the decision to leave Lester's no longer seemed the gamble it had done.

The ensuing months were filled with increased activities in the preparation for the baby, an increase in her bank balance and a noticeable increase in her happiness over the loss of her waistline.

Between photographic sessions – now only head and shoulder takes – Hope filled her days by helping out at Manstonleigh Day Centre where she was an instant hit with staff and patients alike. It was not long before the Chief Executive Officer noticed Hope's fastidious eye for detail and the new ideas that dripped from her as readily as they had at Lester Associates. Appreciating the value of her latest volunteer, Phyllis Wilkinson offered Hope a position on the staff. Whilst the post did not come near to nudging the salary she had previously enjoyed, the arrangement was sufficiently flexible to enable her to continue her photographic engagements, and helped to pass the days before the arrival of her baby.

After the birth she intended to step down from her current roles, seek good daytime care for her child, and return to full-time employment. However for the moment things could not be better and, as far as she was aware, she had succeeded in concealing her pregnancy from David and the general public. If that were not the case she would surely have picked up some hint from the fan mail she received, which even included a proposal of marriage from a lonely soldier in Ireland. Indeed, life could not be better.

Hope slumped wearily into the only comfortable chair in the Charity Shop at the rear of Manstonleigh Day Centre. When not required in the office she spent a good deal of time in the area set aside for fund raising.

"That's better!" she declared to the others. It felt good to take the weight off her feet. With the loss of her waistline it had become blatantly evident that the positioning of the shop fittings fell short of ideal. The lack of shelving necessitated storing stock beneath the rickety trestle tables that skirted the walls.

"Junior here...." Hope patted her abdomen, "doesn't take kindly to Mum squatting to rummage beneath tables."

An elderly volunteer sympathised, then went on at great length to describe how her *old Arthur* was just as problematic. Smiling expansively she chuckled, "M'problem wi' m'arthritic knees will continue, but yours'll sort itself out soon enough, though not afore turning into another'un," she cackled like a magpie intent on defending its territory. "Endless piles of washing. Demands for feeds all hours o'night. Rather you than me lass!" More laughter spluttered from creased lips as the woman remembered the demands of her three when they were young.

Toying with an idea, Hope merely smiled at the woman. She sat forward in the chair as she thought about a particular television programme. She rapidly took the thread of an idea through the initial planning stages and then without another word sped off in search of Phyllis Wilkinson. The others looked in the direction of the door that swung closed behind her.

"Problems with 'er waterworks I shouldn't wonder," said one. "I 'ad that."

Hope watched the pen wagging annoyingly in the CEO's hand whilst the woman listened to her suggestion.

Phyllis Wilkinson cleared her throat. "Tell me again.... it would cost us nothing you say?" The pen wagged with increasing rapidity as though to hasten Hope's reply.

Hope nodded. Mentally she crossed her fingers that she was right. "I believe that to be the case," she now said, providing herself with a safety net. "As I see it there's nothing to lose and at best you could have the shop area revamped with shelving and counters – just like a proper shop. And if a little café area were incorporated it would attract customers from the shopping centre."

Phyllis had seen the television programme under discussion, which undertook the refurbishment of worthwhile charity projects, and the frantic movement of the pen was replaced with thoughtful nodding of her head.

The staff and occupants of Manstonleigh had been riding on a high ever since the television company confirmed acceptance of the challenge to refurbish the Charity Shop. Everyone had pulled together to bring the project to completion. Local tradesmen, friends, and friends of friends, sprang from nowhere to lend a hand with plumbing, joinery and decorating skills – and to appear on television.

Hope on the other hand had kept her bulging waistline well clear of the television cameras and it was with an air of relief that she had found a legitimate excuse to leave the premises on this, the last day of filming. She sat beside her neighbour Jack in the van loaned to Manstonleigh for the purpose of taking the old fixtures and fittings for disposal at the tip.

Jack started up the engine. From what Daphne had told him he grasped that Hope's involvement in the project had been major. It seemed to him a shame she should elect to miss out on the official opening scheduled for later. Just then Billy appeared beside the cab. He banged his fist on the passenger's door to indicate that he wanted to accompany them to the rubbish dump but Jack knew it was because he wanted to be with Hope. She was good with Daph's son – always had time for the lad, keen to encourage his efforts.

"You'll miss all the fun Billy. Don't you want to stop and watch?" asked Hope.

Billy shook his head and she moved up to allow him to climb in beside her. The three rode off, each with their own silent thoughts.

Jack was pondering how the bonny lass beside him would manage on her own with a baby, but then reasoned she had Daph. Daph was a good woman, sensible like. She often popped over with a shepherd's pie, or warm scones if she had been baking. Hope, also deep in thought, wondered whether she were doing the right thing in denying her child its natural father. Billy on the other hand was thinking about the special cake that had been delivered to the Centre earlier in the day. It was covered in blue and white icing and was ever so lovely to look at. His mother told him that everyone was going to have a slice later. Nobody knew about it, except him. It was a secret – and he was good at keeping secrets.

It was quiet when they arrived at the tip. Theirs was the only vehicle on site. Jack opened the rear doors of the van and began to unload. He made sure that Hope did not lift anything heavy.

A loan tipper truck rattled its way down the long dirt track that led to the pit. It drew to a halt a short distance from them. It was not until a few minutes later that Hope noticed the lorry's high-sided container was reared in readiness to shed its load with Billy in its direct line of tipping. A tangle of wire held him ensnared by an ankle.

Hope waved and shouted for the driver to halt the cranking mechanism but he was not looking and her voice was drowned by the noise. She knew she had but seconds in which to act if she were to prevent Billy from being swept into the pit. With no time to think about her own safety or that of the child she carried, she ran as fast as she could, leaping over debris in her path with a new-found agility brought only to her pregnant form by the sudden surge of adrenaline.

Jack heard the commotion and emerged from the van just in time to see Hope hurl herself at Billy with such force she knocked him off balance and sent him and the offending coil of wire sideways and away from the path of the rubbish, which now spewed from the rear of the lorry.

Jack's legs were unable to grasp the frantic command transmitted by his brain. Transfixed, his breathing ceased when in the next moment he saw Hope caught by the avalanche and swept into the deep pit below.

Despite initial feelings of hostility Jack would remain eternally grateful that the other man's cab contained a phone to summon help.

The two men had barely managed to remove the refuse that had buried Hope when the paramedics arrived. Every moment of their frantic endeavours to reach her had been observed by Billy who wept above whilst trying to ignore the savage pain that throbbed in his leg.

Jack held his breath as he watched the medics feel for a pulse and check Hope's airways but his legs lost all strength when he was motioned to step back to allow them to stretcher her to the surface.

What they raised bore little resemblance to the bonny lass so full of positive energy who, filled with excitement, had laughed beside him not three-quarters' of an hour ago. He watched helplessly as they placed the lifeless bundle of dirty rags into the ambulance.

Totally beside herself, Daphne watched Hope writhing in semi-conscious agony on a hospital trolley.

Jack stood a pace behind, sick with frustration and feeling as guilty as hell. If he had insisted that the lass stayed back at the Centre none of this would have happened. He should never have let her accompany him. He didn't know what he had been thinking of. Yes he did. He enjoyed her company. She reminded him of his Liz, God rest her soul. He was aware then of Daphne's head on his shoulder. She was crying.

The doctor withdrew from the curtained hospital bay to confer with a colleague. Both men returned and spoke quickly to nursing staff. The first doctor turned then to whom he assumed were the parents.

"Your daughter's had a particularly nasty fall. Though the external injuries look bad they're mainly superficial. However she's sustained some internal injuries and we need to get some pictures of her head. It's her head we're most concerned about. Once we've done some checks we'll know better what we're dealing with. Is she up to date with her tetanus shots?"

Daphne had no idea. She shrugged, her expression one of hopelessness. "Will she be all right? The baby...." Daphne directed a prayer upwards, begging that Hope might be spared the tragedy she read in the doctor's eyes.

"She's being taken straight to theatre. We'll know more shortly but in the meantime the nurse here will take care of you." The doctor spared a moment to smile kindly at the couple he feared would not become grandparents today. "You know your son's leg is broken?"

Daphne did not trust herself to speak.

"You can see him now if you wish. Nurse, will you...." He indicated for the couple to be ushered from the area so he could turn his attention to the new life labouring in the swollen belly on the trolley.

"Hope.....Hope.....can you hear us? We're going to make you more comfortable.... need to ease you over." The senior nurse continued talking to her charge as she carried out the doctor's instructions. "We're just going to lift you." The nurse nodded to the team. "On the count of three.... one, two...."

Hope lay wrapped within herself. Save for the dragging sensation in her abdomen, everything seemed vague and strangely distant. She longed for the pain to stop. Quietly terrified, she knew the baby was coming and that it was too early. The ferocity of the pain went beyond what she had been led to expect, and held her imprisoned in the hibernation between consciousness and nothingness, but then unexpectedly she entered an enveloping darkness and she was falling again though this time more gently and into something warmly comforting.

"She's slipping," someone was saying. A fusion of urgent voices shouted from somewhere far off, but the words were irrelevant compared with the tranquillity awaiting her.

A moment later she let go and everything became silent until presently she detected the distant sound of a familiar baritone voice barely audible above the sound of the river splashing against her stepping-stones. She turned her head towards the hill to see her father. He was waving to her – it was Friday and in a moment she would be in his arms.

Chapter 19

News of the incident hit the media. Revelations that the popular photographic model had been pregnant and lost the infant as the result of a tragic accident attracted both newspaper and broadcast coverage alike and this was one time that Kevin Lester was unable to act as a buffer. Like everyone else he only learned of the tragedy via the media.

The reports began to permeate upon Daphne's abrupt departure from Manstonleigh's opening ceremony and provided the television programme with a new slant to the proceedings. Like a gem the victim – the instigator of the refurbishment – was none other than the person who had been plucked from the street to appear in the Sally Lox advertisements. Equally lively newspaper coverage was immediate.

Charles heard about it from his housekeeper who had rushed ashen-faced to find him after a telephone call from Daphne. Even before Joseph Fearnley deposited Isabel at the hospital there was already a magnificent floral tribute beside Hope's bed, which bore the message, "Get well soon, Charles".

Angela was the first at Lester Associates to learn of the tragedy, thereby gaining the unenviable task of breaking the news to others. She had been running an errand in the city when the ugly headline on the news placard leaped out at her – "Sally Lox Girl buried alive!" A gasp choked her lungs as she snatched up an early edition. Bemused by her friend's photograph, and with the pages crumpling in her grasp, Angela struggled to make sense of the accompanying article. It was not until the newsvendor barked annoyance that she realised she was walking off without paying. She tossed him a pound, which left him feeling awkward.

In less than an hour from her seeing the placard Angela and her Chairman arrived at the hospital with cards and flowers from well-wishers.

Unaccustomed to situations that were outside his control Kevin Lester strove to conceal his mental anguish. So thick was his emotion on arrival that he was stretched to the very edge when he took it upon himself to comfort those huddled together outside the room being prepared for Hope. Pleased at last to be doing something he teamed up with Jack to track down vending machines and they returned with bags of crisps and hot drinks that nobody wanted but politely accepted.

It was the first time that Isabel had met the man that Hope had spoken of with the type of admiration that comes only from earned respect. The torment in Kevin's eyes made him one of them though his appearance set him apart. His navy suit of discernible quality and deep expanse of crisp, white shirt-cuffs contrasted blatantly with the rest of them. Jack was filthy from clambering about in the tip and resembled his former coalmining days, whilst Daphne's dishevelled appearance told of her hasty departure, and Isabel had only just discovered the presence of a house-apron beneath her coat.

Kevin nursed a polystyrene cup of something barely resembling coffee. He was already considering the strategy for Hope's compensation claim. But there was plenty of time for that; the main thing was to get her right. He wondered whether she was aware that she had lost the baby. Abruptly, he halted the creation of a fancy edging round his cup with his thumbnail. The mockery of the situation struck him as he recalled how they had schemed together to conceal her pregnancy, even to the point of her resignation. Regardless of their endeavours Hope's secret was out and emblazoned in invidious detail across the media.

Kevin Lester shared the vigil into the evening. He took his turn to sit beside Hope's still form until eventually he acknowledged there was nothing he could do in the short term and took his leave. Angela declined the offer of a lift. She would stay she said but anticipating Kevin would have some last-minute instructions she accompanied him in his unhurried walk to the hospital exit.

Only last week the workaholic had surprised staff with the announcement that he was taking some unscheduled leave. Elaine was not oblivious to how hard her husband worked and this time had insisted on their taking up the invitation to join Charles in Corfu.

That morning Kevin had been looking forward to the trip but not now. Once outside he told Angela, hastily scribbling notes on the inside of a cigarette packet she had found, that she could consider herself a free agent during his absence. Furthermore she could tell the rest of them that he had said so. He suggested she might like to spend some time at the hospital. All he asked was that she exercised prudence when appointing an understudy to liaise with at the office. He admonished himself. The comment was unnecessary. Angela would carry this out to his complete satisfaction. He had been pleased with his choice for Hope's replacement. However, though he would never admit it, except possibly to his wife or Charles – Hope was irreplaceable.

That same evening Edric Colendon, the Director of Acquisitions & Mergers for Shillens International, flung his briefcase on to his hotel bed. The journey from Edinburgh to Leeds had left him jaded. He took himself to the bathroom to stand beneath the shower for a long time where he relied on the cool, invigorating water to strip away the day's tension and restore him to his former self. Only later, when running his electric razor over his face, did he allow himself to think about his flight home the following day.

Rarely did he find sufficient time to stay in his own place abroad and touch base with his family, and particularly since his new appointment with Shillens International. So seldom did he manage the trip that when he did his belongings felt foreign to his touch as though loaned to him by an unseen host for the duration of his visit.

Edric's nomadic lifestyle had been a requirement of his previous position and had continued with the new post. In some ways he felt as though it had always been like this, his living out of a suitcase, only returning to his permanent suite on the top floor of the Leeds Shillens each weekend to pick up a change of suits before setting off again. He no longer had a home base in the UK and even when he had, he had not thought of the rambling Tudor-style house in Kent as home.

Preferring not to dine alone in the hotel restaurant he rang for room service. His company status always ensuring prompt attention, a light meal of poached salmon arrived minutes later. If only staff would ease up and treat him more like one of the guests. His position in the hierarchy prohibited this but did not prevent his occasional longing for the luxury of obscurity. Instead of which he was set apart mostly to endure his evenings in isolation save for his constant companions: his laptop and a mountain of paperwork, which could be relied upon to absorb what remained of his waking hours until finally drained he sought rest between freshly laundered sheets.

Now, turning to his newspaper his eyes alighted on Hope's picture. The press had used the photograph of her beside the river in Mowlem where he had first seen her. His head shook slowly as his eyes skimmed the text. From habit he thumbed his way to the financial pages but this evening the share prices failed to capture his concentration and he returned to the greater suffering on the front page.

Half an hour later, having finished his meal and put his laptop on charge, Edric elected to take a stroll before grabbing a few hours sleep prior to his early morning flight.

His pace was leisurely. It was the first time he had permitted himself to slow down all day – all week. Using his easy stride like a metronome he incorporated his breathing into the pattern.

The city streets were quiet; they were resting in that state of limbo betwixt commerce and the nightlife scene. As he walked he thought about his family, particularly Memka and Luke, whom he did not see nearly often enough. Unplanned his footsteps brought him to a florist shop. Drawn by the window display he went closer. He shrugged. It would do no harm to send the girl in his newspaper some flowers. The decision brought a smile.

The florist watched the tall, handsome man at her window. She hoped he would make up his mind quickly. She should have put the *Closed* sign up half an hour ago.

Edric entered the low-ceilinged premises and navigated his way to the counter through an obstacle course of buckets crammed with blooms. An old memory came to him as emotive as the clash of fragrances vying for his attention. Dismissing any thoughts of roses or lilies he strode up to the woman who peered at him with tired eyes. He explained exactly what he wanted, after which her eyes looked noticeably less tired and widened perceptibly. The florist made a note of his precise request.

Hope's hospital room was fast becoming filled with flowers and the admixture of fragrances floated in the air conditioning. Elaborate displays and simple posies had been arriving regularly since the loss of her child; many from people she had never met yet felt affected by what had happened.

"Here, I'll take those." Angela took two more arrangements from a young nurse. "How nice." Angela was smiling. "This is from 'All your neighbours in Mowlem'. And this one...." she opened the little envelope, simply says, 'Like an orchid amongst the daisies. From a friend.'" Angela directed a mischievous smile towards Hope. The arrangement was different from the others in that it was less elaborate, yet at the same time it sheer simplicity made it exquisite.

Hope's head turned lethargically on her damp pillow to look in brief bewilderment at the rustic basket brimming over with white daisy-shaped flowers, in the centre of which nestled a perfect pale pink orchid.

The gift drew the attention of the others. Isabel turned to ask a question but Hope had already slipped back into a sleep of exhaustion. "I know she needs her rest," she whispered to Daphne, "but I can't help feeling fearful when she drifts off like that."

With her own first sight of Hope held fast in her memory, Daphne was grateful that Hope had been gowned and cleaned up before her aunt saw her. "She needs rest," the tone deliberately reassuring. "She's got a tough time ahead when realisation takes hold." Daphne prayed silently for the recovery of the young woman who, without a thought for herself or the child she was carrying, had saved her son from a disaster that did not bear thinking about.

With one leg almost entirely encased in pot and already annotated by the pens of nursing staff, Billy had been propelled away in a wheelchair by Jack to the restaurant in the next block where Billy thought they might find some cake for Hope. He was sure her sadness was due to their not getting back to Manstonleigh yesterday for a slice of the secret cake.

Angela offered to sit with Hope whilst the others took a break. At the first indication of their wavering she pushed Isabel and Daphne firmly towards the door, at the same time emphasising the need to keep up their strength. "Get a change of scenery. You need to stretch your legs. Get a coffee of something. I promise I won't leave her and you can do the same for me later." She watched whilst Isabel

154

somewhat reluctantly followed Daphne from the room. A night of catnapping in chairs showed in all their faces.

In the stretched days that followed, despondency was swift to execute an assault on the few remaining fragments of Hope's being. She wandered through the dark corridors of her mind where there was no promise of any happiness ever again. All the joy she had ever felt had been extinguishing. Dulled in spirit she shunned the appearance of visitors almost to the point of rudeness. Fervently she wished they would not come. Briefly, before it became too painful to contemplate, she reflected on the fact that only retrospection gave a cognitive depth of meaning to the only certainties in life – birth and death. They are remembered forever whilst the coming together of two bodies, the start of a whole new life, was unlikely to be remembered after the event.

In pained silence Hope clutched the crisp sheets to her and rolled away. She did not want to speak. She had nothing to say. She wanted to be on her own. She needed nobody.... she had nobody now.

It was a further week before David Stratton learned of his wife's accident and the existence of a baby. Hope's face stared up from the parcel of fish and chips on the counter. To enable him to focus his vision he turned the parcel round, then with an air of pride slapped the counter. He looked up at the familiar faces glazed with sweat behind the fat-fryers. "That's my w-wife they're on about," he slurred. "I'm m-married to her. That's.... her picture. A real beaut, don't y-you think?" The staff behind the counter glanced at the grease-stained picture of the Sally Lox Girl, just as quickly dismissing the customer's claim. They knew him well, and all his fancies; they had heard so many of them. Exchanging looks they willed him on to his next regular stop; the off-licence round the corner.

Hope's greatest fear had been that her husband would discover her pregnancy via television coverage of the refurbishment programme. Ironically there was no television in the shabby bed-sit he shared with another unemployed man. David was one of the last to learn of the accident and when he did he was too suffused with alcohol to take in the details. The next morning he neither recollected that he had been

155

about to become a father, nor anything relating to the tragedy that resulted in the loss of that unborn life.

Hope's disregard for her surroundings lessened as the days passed. Gradually the nursing staff grew in number and began to look familiar; once they had emerged from the faceless individual who had tugged her about and forced her to remain in the world that no longer contained her child.

The day eventually arrived when she was able to go home, but which home – Eastkirk or Tarnville? In the end she left it to them to decide. They would do that anyway. They could stick her wherever they liked. She no longer cared. She no longer had a child. Nothing now or in the future could ever matter again.

On her arrival at Tarnville, Hope went to stand at Isabel's apartment window. Her forlorn gaze swept to the boulders in the river below and her heart flipped at the sight. The poignant reminder of her father's love might have drawn tears had not her hospital pillows claimed them all.

Any pleasure derived from her return to Mowlem was short-lived, for soon afterwards Hope shrank into herself and refused to venture from Tarnville's solid walls.

Hope's depression continued until Charles took it upon himself to initiate the plan that was to be the start of drawing her back to those who cared. In secrecy he arranged for Billy to come to stay. Her words rehearsed, Daphne feigned an inability to accompany her son, and similarly Isabel too *had a lot on*, with the desired result that the entertaining of Billy fell to Hope.

With Billy's exuberance and constant wish to visit the stables Hope was forced to rally and Daphne was comforted to learn that the one whose life Hope may well have saved was in some small way helping to draw her back.

Today, walking in Tarnville's grounds in the sunshine, Hope resembled her former self. She was recovering.

In the year since her accident she and Charles had taken regular walks together. When she visited Daphne or attended photographic shoots Charles missed her company and his visits to the stables became lonely affairs. Even Tarkenta, stomping in his stall, sensed the break in routine.

Now, strolling with Charles in the comfortable silence enjoyed only by those close to each other, Hope became thoughtful and took stock of her emotions. Excitement and eagerness had remained her constant companions whilst awaited the birth of her baby. There was no doubt that the protection barriers she had carefully erected around her unborn child heightened those maternal feelings. Be that as it may, she had never held her baby, heard its cry or even known the colour of its eyes. How much worse it must be for the one whose stick tapped along beside her. Charles had raised two children to adulthood only to lose them both. Only now did she appreciate his loss.

She squeezed his arm. "It's taken a little time and the love of a good many friends but I'm mending – thanks to them all – not least you."

Charles opened his mouth as though to speak but closed it again. An odd expression filled his face.

"What is it?" In the expectation of a confession of pain, Hope broke her step.

Charles replaced the hand that had slid from his arm. "It's you. Though not visibly similar you painfully remind me of Christina."

Although he would be reluctant to admit it, Hope remained convinced that deep down he had become resigned to the fact that his daughter was aware of his search and so unforgiving were her feelings that she chose not to be found. She wondered if he would ever discover Christina's whereabouts, and whether she would meet her and if so whether he would live long enough to witness it. Stifling a sigh she patted the arm of the person who had become such an important part of her life.

That night Isabel heard her niece singing softly in the next bedroom and she took delight in telephoning Daphne to announce that Hope was finally recovering. That newfound happiness evaporated the next morning when Hope admitted to having languished too long in self-pity, and that it was time she got on with life.

After losing her baby Hope had been keenly selective about the photographic work she undertook, which was beginning to be reflected in her bank balance. Nevertheless, not wishing to go down the painful road of compensation, she had rejected Kevin's professional advice. She had seen the torment in the lorry driver's eyes when, disregarding his employer's advice, he brought flowers to her hospital bedside. Unable to speak and barely able to maintain eye contact he had simply held his gift towards her. She told him it had been an accident and that nobody was to blame.

As a starting point she planned to return to Manstonleigh. Whilst Isabel sensed that that was everything Daphne longed for, it was the last thing she wanted. She had hardly dared to think that Hope might decide to remain in Mowlem, perhaps seeking work locally, even at Tarnville. With the passing months Isabel had permitted herself to become optimistic but now knew she had deluded herself.

Later, when Isabel took Charles his nightcap, he commented on her preoccupation, and with misery in her voice she told him Hope's plans. After listening and indeed sharing her despondency he floated an idea. He had been thinking about returning to Corfu and saw no reason why she and her niece should not accompany him. In a relaxed atmosphere Hope could work out exactly what she wanted to do and if on her return she were still of the frame of mind to return to the city then at least she would be rested.

Hope had become as much a part of Tarnville as Charles, and Isabel was never happier than when she caught sight of her running up the staircase or sauntering through the grounds. Her niece had brought the house to life again but if Hope elected to go she would put forward no arguments. The spirit of youth needed more than the love of the older generation.

Charles's suggestion of a holiday struck Isabel as a good one; though she would not accompany them. It would not look right, she said, if his housekeeper joined the party, but she thanked him on Hope's behalf. It would indeed give Hope a boost before she returned to the bustle of the city, which now seemed inevitable.

Isabel would stay at Tarnville. She had more than enough to keep her occupied, and with some of her responsibilities away on a Greek island she would be able to spend more time with Peter Summerville. Since her niece's accident they had spent less time together. She missed him despite their regular telephone calls late at night and the letters in the clumsy style she had come to love. And she still had a lot to do for the annual supper dance that took place in the long barn, followed by singing round a bonfire well into the early hours for those with sufficient stamina to survive until then. Yes – she would stay at Tarnville.

"You can't be persuaded?"

Isabel shook her head. "I have more than enough to keep me here."

"Then perhaps I should extend the invitation to one of her friends. Billy would seem the obvious choice." Charles looked enquiringly at his housekeeper.

Instantly, she picked up on his reasoning. "I think that's an excellent idea. Hope wouldn't dream of turning down the invitation if it meant that Billy might lose out on a holiday. She loves that lad."

Charles made a steeple of his fingers. He tapped them gently to his lips and a look of deep satisfaction crept into his face as he nodded thoughtfully.

Chapter 20

Despite the early hour the airport was busy. Billy itched to be free to explore. Impatiently he nudged the suitcases towards the check-in desk. Two desks had been opened for the Corfu flight. The other queue was moving quicker. He shoved the luggage forward again with his foot as he had observed others doing, though he was more careful with the good leather case that belonged to Charles.

"That man's looking at you."

Hope had already turned before Billy's words registered, and it was with some embarrassment that she found herself smiling into a pair of brown eyes. With some difficulty she pulled her gaze back to Billy, who now chuckled openly.

"You've clicked!" He had been awaiting just such an opportunity to use the phrase overheard at his day centre. He was about to say it again but heeded the warning in Hope's eyes.

She shushed him. "Look, we'll miss our turn if we don't keep up." In an attempt to refocus his attention she made a show of shifting the three heavy cases another couple of feet.

Her face was well known and to some extent she had grown accustomed to people's interest though the scrutiny of the tall, dark-haired man in the next queue appeared more intense than most; moreover he looked familiar. His appearance channelled her thoughts towards her placing him in a commercial environment, concluding she had probably seen him on Lester's premises. Yet defying that logic another sense told her differently and that it was not in the setting of the business world that she had seen him. She racked her brain but could not place the owner of the mahogany-coloured eyes who continued to map her progress in the queue.

Charles watched the two of them, relieved of the luggage, making their way back through the airport crowd to where he was sitting with his walking stick grasped in both hands.

He had been faintly amused at Hope's insistence that he should take a seat whilst she saw to the luggage; amused and touched. She frequently displayed caring qualities, when all he wanted was to take

160

care of her. In a way he felt like the parent who wakes up one day to find the role of parent and child reversed to that of parent and carer.

Charles got to his feet. He offered his arm. "Come my dear. It's you who should be resting not me. I do too much of that these days."

He had not spoken above a dozen words to Frederick Thackeray, yet they had been aware of each other, and exchanged nods in Church. He was conscious of borrowing – indeed almost adopting – the child Frederick had loved. Now, converging with the herd migrating to the International Departures Lounge, he considered the young person beside him. His life would have been vastly different had she not appeared on his doorstep following Richard's death. He could not deny that the pleasure he savoured today should by rights have been Frederick's joy. If life had been fair it would not be his arm that Hope linked now. A feeling of guilt bowed his head. More times than enough he had witnessed the weekly reunion between Frederick and Hope. He felt he owed the man something in return for the joy that had entered his life and there and then vowed to take it upon himself to ensure that Hope refocused herself and began to live again.

Helda, a plump little woman with a perpetual smile, met them on their arrival at Villa Marchriard. With the express wish that Hope should not slide into domesticity, Charles had followed his usual practice of engaging a housekeeper for the duration of his visit, and specifically requested Helda whom he had had before and pleased him. Hope protested that she would have enjoyed cooking and doing whatever else needed doing.

He waived a hand. "I wouldn't hear of it. You.... and Billy here." he smiled at the teenager who beamed on hearing his name, "are here to enjoy yourselves, not to be tied to me or this place."

That evening the three friends enjoyed a delicious meal of hot, spicy lamb on the terrace, and over coffee they watched the sun blaze into the first of many spectacular evening displays – many of which Hope would enjoy from the terrace of another villa situated further along the coastline.

Hope appeared the next morning with an expression on her face that gave the impression of her being in love with the world; she looked every bit the child Charles remembered sitting patiently beside her stepping-stones. Dressed in a simple full-length, white crinkle-cotton dress with her hair cascading loosely down her back she echoed that memory. He greeted her from his seat on the veranda before cautioning Billy who leaned as far as he could over the balustrade to gain a better view of the villa he had been hearing about.

"We're going to see some donkeys," Billy announced, proud of his inside information. "You didn't know that did you?"

A chortle escaped Hope as she exchanged knowing looks with their host. "No – I certainly didn't. How wonderful, I adore donkeys!"

An hysterical childhood memory came to her of Gregory, Amy and her, around the age of nine, finding a bedraggled donkey in the lane. The forlorn look in those dark, long-lashed eyes had made her want to cry.

Even now she could not believe that she had done such a thing, and still shrank with embarrassment every time her aunt recounted the tale, which she did with unbelievable regularity. Without considering the consequences she had marshalled the others into persuading the rain-soaked donkey to negotiate the steps into Ivy Cottage. Once inside, Gregory was instructed to add more logs to the fire whilst she and Amy struggled to manipulate the miserable creature along the passage into the parlour and round the table to the fire. She could still recall the steam that rose from the animal and the stench as it began to dry out – not to mention the choice words exclaimed by Isabel on her return, or the look on her father's face when he read about it in the diary notes she shared with him later. The entire cottage was so full of steam her aunt returned home in the belief that she had left the kettle on the range. Memories – the bricks of childhood, the very foundation of life!

Hope shelved her recollections to pour enthusiasm into her voice. Wishing to help Billy to build some memories, she poked her head towards the teenager. "Donkeys – I just love them! Why don't you tell me all about them over breakfast."

During the meal she learned that Charles knew a nice couple on the brow of the hill. Billy emphasised the words in much the same way as Charles had but somehow managed to make the remark sound more like one of sarcasm, which prompted Charles to reaffirm that they really were pleasant people.

He took up the tale before Billy destroyed all credibility of his friends. "Tom and Jacqueline have a field beyond their garden where they keep three donkeys. I thought Billy might enjoy seeing them. They have two sons around your age Billy – Tony and Allan." He did not include mention of the other similarity, that Tony had learning difficulties. "Tony attends a Centre like yours Billy. He's learning all sorts of skills that will help him secure employment one day." The other son was very protective towards his younger brother, which had amused their parents when the boys were little but now provided a degree of comfort in knowing their most vulnerable child had a protector additional to themselves.

Billy was more excited about seeing the neighbours' donkeys than their offspring and re-entered the conversation exclaiming, "I bet you don't know the names of the donkeys." He studied Hope's face to see whether she did, and fell to laughter when she said she didn't. "It's Ella, Bonny and Walter," he giggled.

After breakfast Charles escorted them to the villa on the brow of the hill where they spent the remainder of the morning in the pleasant company of Charles's neighbours – who were indeed a nice couple – and three equally friendly though extremely inquisitive donkeys. Much to Billy's delight the three four-legged neighbours were allowed to leave the field and wander at will around the garden, with the occasional need to be guided away from the swimming pool.

Tom had read an expression in his wife's eyes and when Charles and Hope eventually made a move to leave he suggested that Billy might like to remain. "If it's all right with you we'd love to have him." He shared Jacqueline's pleasure at seeing how well the teenagers got on together. Their younger son had made several good friends in their previous neighbourhood further round the coastline and at his training Centre but so far he had made few near home since their recent move. "We're all going in the pool later...." Tom directed this last comment at Billy. "I'm sure we can find you some trunks."

Billy was delighted and ran to tell Tony whilst Allan, his father noticed, only had eyes for Hope – calf-love, intense and painfully obvious. Perhaps it was preferable she failed to notice the amorous eyes of the teenager who now stepped forward to shake her hand. The donkey handlers merely waved before chasing off on some further escapade or other.

When Hope suggested a walk Charles offered to accompany her as far as the village at the foot of the hill for late-morning coffee. He joked about that being as far as his walking stick could manage. Knowing he had access to both a car and a driver for the duration of the holiday Hope accepted he was electing to have an easy day in his second home, and did not press him further.

In the village Hope purchased four postcards, which she wrote whilst enjoying strong coffee and tiny cakes that looked scorched but tasted delicious. Albeit only their first day she managed to pen a few thoughtful lines, addressing cards to Isabel and Peter (her aunt would be pleased by her inclusion of her friend); Daphne and the staff at Manstonleigh (she would let Billy send one to his mother at home); Kevin Lester and staff; and Amy and Greg.

The frown in her brow was noticeable as she wrote the last card. Her friends were in the same state; engaged to be married but as yet with no firm date and she wondered whether Gregory would ever be man enough to call it off. Not wishing to dwell on a memory she preferred to forget, she scribbled her name at the bottom and handed the cards to Charles to post.

Charles left to make his way back to the villa. When he turned to wave Hope wondered whether she should catch him up to sit beside him on the terrace with a paperback, or perhaps her father's oil paints that Isabel had thoughtfully slipped into her packing, but decided reading and painting could come later in the holiday. She returned his wave and headed down to the sea.

Great rolls of sparking foam broke regularly on the beach to suck noisily at the shingle before jingling the fragments into another bright, jewel-coloured arrangement. The surf's steady theme was a joy in itself and had the effect of rejuvenating her in much the same way as Mowlem did after a spell away. She took the hard-baked track to the left and strode out with the playful tug of the breeze in her hair.

A group of children tormenting crabs from a rock pool, and an elderly couple walking a dog were the only people on the beach. Not long into her walk and despite a good breakfast, the pace and crisp sea air claimed a revival of her appetite. The few shops and bars were now behind her but then she recalled the little bar discovered on her previous visit.

The shrubbery was thicker than she remembered and had she not known of the unlikely existence of the premises beyond, like so many others who came this way, she might have believed she had reached a dead end. With care she eased the brittle growth to one side. Her passage disturbed a bird that had been resting there and its cry of outrage instantly alerted those at the tables of her approach.

She was just free of the entanglement when her eyes fell on the same handsome face that Billy had pointed out at the airport, and she felt awkward when she read surprise in his face. If she had noticed him before emerging from the shrubbery she would have retraced her steps and returned along the path unnoticed. As it was she was almost amongst the gathering and to take flight now would seem nothing less than juvenile.

Unlike her previous visit, most of the tables were occupied. Only two were free, both over by the wall with the sea just feet below. She went to the nearest from where she had an uninterrupted view of the hypnotic spectacle of the seascape of breakers. After a quick rummage through her bag for her purse she made her way across the area of crazed concrete to order a sandwich from the bar.

"I don't think you've heard a word I've been saying."

The dark-haired man shifted his gaze from the young woman entering the shack to the woman seated across from him. "I have heard every word. You think I should pop over to see the Collins family which has increased by one since my last visit, a boy this time – and two-year-old Marilyn is less than thrilled by his appearance on the scene."

Surprised he had any inkling of what she had been saying the woman glanced in the direction of his former gaze where she could just make out the trim, white-clad figure of a young woman in the gloom of the bar's interior.

The man swallowed down the remainder of his beer. "I think we'll have another," and without waiting for affirmation he rose to go inside.

"To eat sandwich…..do you have sandwich?" In desperation to make herself understood Hope had slipped into simplified English but the toothless face behind the bar displayed no understanding.

"Excuse me. Perhaps I may be of some assistance."

Hope turned towards the voice at her shoulder. The man from the airport was beside her.

"He doesn't do sandwiches but if you're hungry he does an excellent salad. It comes in a large bowl with chunks of crispy bread. You can have either cheese or tuna with it – that's it I'm afraid. The choice only marginally better than when buying one of Henry Ford's original cars – you can have any colour you like so long as it's black!" He was enthralled to see her lips part into the familiar smile of the advertisements, but now was just for him.

She thanked him. She chose cheese, which was conveyed to the old man who waited patiently for the decision to be made. The younger man watched Hope return to her table before ordering his own drinks.

The sun was high and Hope shifted her chair to shield her face. From this position she was able to study the man who had come to her assistance. Today he wore light-coloured slacks and a pale-pink, silk shirt. Even casually dressed he stood out from those seated in the full sun who sported brightly-coloured shorts and tee-shirts, which labelled them *tourist*. The greater number, the locals in dark attire, hugged the shadows. Discreetly she tried to see the face of the woman seated across from him but the shaft of shadow from her wide-brimmed hat concealed her features, though her voice was warm and full of love when she urged the man to take a photograph of one of the children with them. The child crouched by their table to feed a lone pigeon with crisps. The slightly older child, a girl, remained at the table. Suddenly there was a squeal of disappointment when the pigeon took flight and the moment was lost before being captured on film.

Just then Hope's meal arrived, a large soup bowl heaped high with every imaginable salad ingredient, topped with a generous mound of cubed cheese. She swung her attention away from the laughter to concentrate on her food. Every so often a wave splashed against the wall to deposit a cool spray on the hem of her dress.

She was not half way through her meal when disaster struck and a large wave crashed over the wall to take her and the occupants of two other tables by surprise. Those affected were totally engulfed and a commotion followed of excited shrieks and the abrasive scrape of chairs on concrete. Hope joined the activity. Nobody appeared to notice that the brown, lined faces in the shadows now bore curves of amusement.

Hope looked at her flooded salad bowl. Immeasurably self-conscious she did not know whether to laugh or cry but knew she would laugh about it later. Even before she began to sort out her emotions a single downward glance revealed that her previously crisp, white dress had become both limp and transparent, and now showed the detail of skimpy lace beneath. Almost at the point of realisation something long and silky was draped protectively around her and she spun round to look up into the face of the person who had come to her rescue earlier. The man from the airport was beside her again, a show of concern in his face.

"I saw the wave a moment too late to pull you clear. It happens like that sometimes. Other times it's as flat as a pancake. Do please come and join us and leave that puddle," he motioned towards the bowl awash with seawater.

A moment later Hope was seated between the man and his companion whose face she could now see. She liked what she saw. The woman was neither beautiful nor pretty; her nose was a shade too large to allow either acclamation but her smile displayed perfect teeth and opened up a pleasing face.

Still smiling the woman dug deeply into the large straw bag on the floor beside her. She handed Hope a towel. "You're not the only one to be caught out. We've all been victims. Those tables at the front are the ones to avoid when the sea is like it is today."

"I'll bear that in mind the next time I come," said Hope, grateful for the towel and the absence of cameras in the hands of professionals

167

intent on recording her predicament. It was exactly the sort of incident sought by those who were beginning to be found trailing her wake like excited chickens in pursuit of their mother for titbits.

"Are you here for long?" It was the man again.

"Two weeks.... I arrived yesterday." Hope wondered whether it was the woman's presence that prevented an admission of having seen her at the airport. She also noticed that his skin did not have the same sun-kissed glow as his companion's. From this and the fact he had been alone at the airport she surmised the woman lived here, unlike the one who continued to smile at her.

"Please – our apologies. In the confusion we've not introduced ourselves." It was his voice again, deep with the softness of velvet in the tone. "This is Claire and I'm Edric."

Laughing at the formality Hope shook his extended hand. "And I'm...."

"Hope Stratton.... the Sally Lox Girl," he finished, amused by the question that shot into the emerald green eyes he had first admired in Mowlem. "Your face is well known. And I was in Lester's Board Room when Lester introduced you to our team for the Shillens merger," he explained. The expression of intrigue on the other woman's face went unnoticed.

She had been right then. That was where she had seen him, at Lester's. Their conversation turned to the common ground of that meeting; the results of which she learned had had an important bearing on Edric's career. His brief monologue detailed how his career had hung in the balance during a lengthy standstill whilst the last conditions were debated.

Hope felt herself transported back to Lester's board room to take notes beside the Chairman and share the excitement and the anxiety. All at once a warm flush flooded her face with the recollection that she had sensed someone's watching her during the proceedings. It had been this man – the same person who had come to her aid in ordering her lunch and moments later to retain her dignity by wrapping her in a silk sarong.

After failing to charm the pigeon down from the roof the children returned to the table where Edric introduced them. "This young lady is Memka and the dirty one is Luke. This is.... Mrs Stratton."

Hope laughed at his introduction of the two beautiful, bronzed children who beamed at her. There was not much between their ages – around ten and 12 – the girl being the elder. "No.... please call me Hope."

Edric cringed. He half expected an exclamation from Luke that *Hope* was a funny name, but both children were listening to their mother's account of the identity of their new acquaintance. Claire reintroduced Hope as *the lady from the Sally Lox shampoo advertisements on television*. Within moments of learning that she was a star of the television screen – despite admitting she had never appeared in *Star Trek* – with the magical, manipulative powers possessed only by children, they managed to coax from her several amusing stories about incidents that had occurred during filming.

"You're very wet," observed Luke at the conclusion. "That's mummy's." He fingered the sarong.

"I am a bit but I expect I'll soon dry out." Several pairs of hands explored her personage to check this out.

"Are you on foot?" Hope nodded. "Then you must come back with us for a change of clothes." When she opened her mouth to protest Claire cut her short. "I insist.... you can't possibly walk back like that."

Chapter 21

Accompanying Edric and Claire for a change of clothes did seem to be the best solution to her predicament. The alternative, to walk back to Marchriard in a near-transparent dress, held no appeal.

Hope had thought the old man's bar accessible only on foot. Consequently she was surprised when her new acquaintances led her to where their car was parked at the rear, and decided the astonishment in Edric's eyes earlier was more likely to be due to her unconventional emergence from amongst the bushes than having seen her at the airport.

As soon as they arrived at the villa, large and elegantly furnished even by Marchriard's standards, Claire whisked Hope upstairs where she flung open wall-length, mirrored wardrobes. After showing her where everything was kept and inviting her to make herself at home, Claire went downstairs where her daughter was raking through magazines for a picture of their guest.

Hope reappeared a short while later wearing a stunning, floral shift. The bold design, a flood of vermilion and electric blue peony-shaped flowers, emphasised the paleness of her hair, which today more than ever resembled candle flames flickering down her back. The short length of the dress showed off her lower limbs to perfection.

Claire shared Edric's look of admiration. "That looks more stunning on you than it ever did on me!"

Hope liked the woman, a little older than herself. She was still debating Claire's age when Edric placed a cup of freshly percolated coffee on the rosewood table beside her. A split second later the children dragged him away. Thrilled by his presence they egged him into chasing them round the garden.

Hope turned back to her hostess. "It's so kind of you to have brought me back to tidy myself. I did look a mess."

"I only wish I could look as good. I don't even look like that when I'm done up!"

Hope politely dismissed the compliment. A shriek from one of the children drew her attention to the patio where Edric threw a rubber disk to the girl. The younger child leapt between the two until Edric turned to swing him high into the air and both children erupted into fits of giggles. Hope remembered her own delight when her father had done the same thing on his return home each Friday. Once, a strand of her hair had caught round his shirt button but the shaft of pain had been forgotten in the embrace. Carried along by the water-coloured memory she felt herself lifted high in the air, her short young legs kicking gleefully against her father's chest. But that had been in a previous life; a life when she had been happy and protected and the whole world shone beckoning to be explored.

The memory brought the return of an old familiar ache. Though stinging, these days she was able to go back and enjoy her treasured recollections.

Hope blinked hard. "It's nice when a father sets time aside to play with his children."

"Father? Oh no – Edric's not their father! That terrible task falls to my husband, Nicos. Edric and I are cousins. We – my husband Nicos, the children and I – are the only family he has. His parents died in a house fire when he was little. My parents took him in and we became like brother and sister."

Edric was not Claire's husband! Then sifting through the other snippets of information Hope compared Edric's loss with her own: her beloved father, and what she thought was a good marriage, and then finally her baby. All these stinging fragments lunged back as they did from time to time, unexpectedly and with as much ferocity as in their infancy. It took no more than a well-meaning word, the sight of a familiar object or even a remembered smell to spark off the torment. Even so she was learning that she did not hold the monopoly on grief; sorrow was not unique to her. Indeed her host for the fortnight had had more than a brush with sadness, and it seemed that Edric too concealed layers of sorrow beneath that cheerful countenance. Her landlady was right when she said that a person's yesterdays made them what they were today, though some people's yesterdays came perilously close to denying any promise of happiness for tomorrow, Hope realised.

Claire threw her a tease in much the same way as she might one of her children, "We're Edric's family but there is a *lady* in his life who means a great deal to him." Claire maintained eye contact as she finished, "Amber.... his dog! She's usually here with us but he took her back to his place earlier." Reaping the reward of laughter Claire nodded towards a cream-washed villa across the way. "He doesn't use it much. He spends most of his infrequent visits over here with us. I suggested once that he should let it off but I don't think he liked the idea of others using his things. He leads such a lonely life...." Her voice trailed off. "It wouldn't do for me, but he seems to cope though I wish he'd fly out more often – but it's his job you see."

Claire's eyes were on those in the garden and did not see renewed happiness creep back into Hope's face.

Returning to Claire's pleasing announcement Hope smiled. "I apologise for the error. I simply assumed that the two of you were married."

"We are – but not to each other." Claire turned back to her guest. "He was married. He's separated now – has been for a long while."

Hope sensed that Claire might have gone further into Edric's marital status had she not noticed his approach, but once he was within earshot she changed tack and spoke for the benefit of his hearing. "We don't see nearly enough of him, but enjoy his visits when he does fly in. He's wonderful with Memka and Luke, spoils them terribly. And they can twist him round their little fingers!" She threw Edric a wink at which he pulled a face.

In the last few minutes Hope's emotions had swung like a high-slung pendulum from the dizzy tip of pleasure at hearing Edric was not Claire's husband, only to swing back on a note of despair on learning he was married, but to another.

Edric came to where they were seated and her heart lurched in the same way that it had a moment earlier. Not understanding why she should feel like this about a near-total stranger, part of her wanted to give flight whilst another longed to remain and learn more about this man who was beginning to intrigue her. Yet still another part, the sensible part, was trying to remind and warn her that she was on holiday; under the magical spell of clear blue skies and warm summer sun everything and everyone took on the intrigue of being extraordinary.

Edric made an elaborate show of wiping his brow. "I don't know where they get their energy from in this heat."

"It's certainly not from me." Claire held out her hand for him to join them and he took a place on the matching cerise and green striped settee that faced them. Claire was speaking again and Hope attempted to give sensible answers in appropriate places whilst aware that Edric's eyes remained on her. Her tension lessened when Claire's son exploded into the room to stand in the middle of the silver-green carpet square. Luke was hungry and felt it important that they should know.

"Hollow legs. That's your trouble!" Edric turned to Hope. He shrugged and instantly enjoyed the bathe of one of her smiles.

With their eyes locked, they became slowly aware of Claire's voice drifting in from a distance.

"If you have anything now you'll not enjoy the barbecue this evening." A pleasing thought struck Claire. She pivoted back to Hope. "Would you like to stay and enjoy the barbecue with us later?" Her guest looked taken aback but she felt spurred on by her cousin's endorsement. Both children now were jumping up and down, squealing repeats of the invitation.

"It sounds very nice – but I really should be getting back." Flustered by the invitation and the emotions that had come from nowhere, which both surprised and perplexed her, Hope got hurriedly to her feet. "I'm.... I'm not here on my own and.... well.... I've already been out too long," her face was flushed, her explanation rushed. The intonation not her normal speaking voice, she imagined she sounded as nervous as she felt. "I really should be getting back. They'll be wondering what's happened to me," this delivered with a shade more confidence.

Claire did not give up easily. "Bring them with you. The more the merrier. I'm used to these two bringing back friends." Claire drew her children to her. "From habit I always prepare more than enough. Numbers don't count in this house. Bring them along. Please say you'll come." The children took up her efforts of persuasion.

Hope finally nodded when Edric added his own encouragement. "I'd love to but I'll have to check that the others haven't made plans." How she hoped that they had not.

Just then there was a shout of hello and Claire's husband appeared on the patio.

"Nic dear, this is Hope Stratton. Hope, my husband Nicos. Nicos works at the hospital. We never know quite when to expect him." Claire glanced at her watch. "This is unusual." There was a caring lilt in her voice meant only for her husband, as was the expression on her face. "Darling I've just been trying to persuade Hope and her friends to join our barbecue. I think I've nearly succeeded. See what you can do."

The thickset figure at the French windows was of a man in his early forties with a broad, warm smile and Hope liked him instantly. He greeted her like an old family friend adding, "Claire's pretty nifty in the cooking department, which I know to my cost!" He patted the area where his waistline used to be then squeezed his wife to him. "Claire's right. You must come along."

Half an hour later Hope was in the car beside Edric. She appeared bemused. He kept up an easy flow of conversation whilst keeping an eye out for potholes in the winding, coastal road.

During the afternoon he had managed to snatch opportunities to observe the person now seated beside him. The green eyes that first arrested his attention five years ago, today held a sadness that surely had not been present then. The Press had already alerted him to the cause of some of that sorrow but instinct told him that was the mere tip of the iceberg.

Lester's Chairman had introduced her as Mrs Hope Stratton but she no longer wore a wedding ring. The absence of a ring had been the first thing he noticed when ordering her lunch. Its omission pleased him albeit its absence told him she had had to endure long, lonely days and nights. He wondered how long ago that particular sequel had taken place – before or after losing her baby – and whether she were sufficiently over it to allow him to get to know her.

His curiosity heightened, he wanted to know everything there was to know about her, what delighted her and what inflamed her, though he could not imagine her ever succumbing to anger.

When they arrived at Marchriard. Edric walked round the car to open the passenger door. "You will come tonight won't you? I should be very disappointed if you didn't and so would the children." He laughed despite the honesty of his statement.

174

"I've got the telephone number Claire gave me." Hope tapped her handbag and reaffirmed her promise to ring as soon as she had spoken to the others.

With that she slipped through the wrought-iron gates under the surprised gaze of Charles who had watched the approach of the silver Mercedes from his bedroom veranda.

Charles was clearly pleased when Hope told him about her day, and voiced an opinion in support of their attendance at the barbecue. Labouring the point, Billy said he had never been to a barbecue.

"Well in that case I think we'd better go to this one!" laughed Hope. She took the piece of paper from her purse and went to dial the number.

It was not Edric who answered the phone, but she was nonetheless pleased to be speaking again to Claire. Then she heard his voice; it was like falling into soft folds of velvet. Edric had taken the phone and even though she could not see him she knew that he was smiling. He asked what time he should pick them up. Hope stumbled over her words of explanation that Charles's driver would drive them.

That evening it was Edric who stepped from the villa to greet them. The others, he explained, were round the back fanning the flames of a reluctant barbecue. His outstretched hand went to the elderly gentleman who walked with the aid of a stick, but his smile went to the lovely face at his side before courteously transferring to the bright-faced youth who accompanied them.

"I'm so pleased you could make it." Again the warm smile directed at Hope.

"Edric, I should like to introduce you to Sir Charles and Billy. Sir Charles is...."

"Your father – yes, I know." Edric looked warmly into the elderly man's face. "Sir Charles, you may recall we met a few years back when I sounded you out on behalf of my company on the availability of that grand house of yours. Tarn.... Tarnworth isn't it?"

"Tarnville," prompted Billy.

"Yes, of course – Tarnville," a smile instantly directed towards Billy.

Hope glanced uncomfortably between the two men. "Edric – Sir Charles and I aren't related, we're...."

"Just good friends, I think they call it," put in Charles, not at all displeased by the assumption. His head nodded perceptibly and his smile broadened, indicating no loss of ease on his part.

Edric's comment brought a flash of memory and Hope knew where she had first seen him and wondered whether he had any recollection but then decided he would have no reason to, and did not mention their almost colliding on the bridge in Mowlem.

It was noticeable that Edric regularly gravitated towards Hope after doing his rounds to check everyone's needs were being met by Nicos, busy in a thick fog of smoke.

Claire handed Charles a refill of brandy. "Once I've done the preparation I just let him get on with it. He seems to enjoy being splattered by the wretched thing. Give me my kitchen any day. I suppose it makes a relaxing change from his role at the hospital where every decision is vital."

"In this situation the nearest he gets to making an executive decision is deciding whether the chicken's done or on the verge of incineration!" Edric returned to Hope's side. "You know what they say.... if it's brown it's done.... if it's black it's....!"

Claire glanced at the three young people seated nearby with their plates piled high and was pleased when he did not complete his sentence.

Just then something cold and wet touched Hope's hand and made her flinch.

"It's all right. This is Amber, Edric's dog – the lady in his life I mentioned earlier." The large, brown bitch raised her head to sniff the air.

"She's lovely. She can smell the chicken."

"Or your perfume," suggested Edric. Amber was not the only one to notice it. Ever since her arrival he had longed to lean in closer to enjoy the fragrant aura floating around her.

"So you like Aromatics do you?" Hope ruffled Amber's fur and instantly the dog began to bark and dash about in a frenzy.

"Now you've done it. I do that – ruffle her fur – when I'm going to take her for a W-A-L-K." Edric laughed. "I don't know why I bother spelling it. I'm convinced the silly creature can spell. Inadvertently you've indicated a walk and believe me there'll be no getting out of it. She'll break into an exhibition of summersaults in a minute." Edric called Amber to heel. Amber took no notice and continued the antics of an oversized pup. Joining in with Hope's laughter he invited her to accompany him to return Amber to his place.

Enjoying their own private thoughts, Charles and Claire watched the handsome couple walk away with an exuberant blur of fur darting in front of them.

From the outside it was clear that Edric's villa was meticulously maintained. The cream walls and white balustrade looked freshly painted. The garden was more manicured than his cousin's and the introduction of delightful rockery areas set against a backdrop of shrubbery gave it a sculptured appearance. If the property itself shared a similarity with others in the area that was where it ended for when Hope stepped inside she was met with an unexpected elegance, far removed from that of the neglected bachelor dwelling she had expected.

Edric showed her into the living room; a lovely room where warm washes of deep cream and muted tones of blue formed the main décor with unexpected blushes of terracotta in the soft drapes at the windows, the cushions on the pale sofa and chairs, and the various large pots of lush green foliage. The furnishings were good quality, expensive. There was an undeniable statement of taste in the airy room, which she presently discovered opened on to a broad, red-bricked terrace that skirted the villa. Feminine touches, which Hope felt sure were Claire's, bound it all together, making it irresistibly inviting. Pretty sun-coloured blinds hung behind the drapes at the large windows on two elevations and several good-quality flower arrangements had their place on occasional tables, the latter draped in fine lace coverings. Hope could well understand why Edric had not taken kindly to the idea of renting out his villa.

Edric suggested a drink on the terrace before rejoining the others. He opened large, glazed doors and settled her on comfortable seating on the terrace before fetching glasses and a bottle of the wine Hope had favoured during the evening. The long-stemmed crystal glasses had never been out of their box before; there had been no previous occasion to warrant it.

Amber sniffed the air before giving a short strangled howl and flopping heavily beside Hope.

Edric stooped to stroke the chestnut mound by Hope's feet. "I keep wondering whether to let her have pups. I might one day. By the way, allow me to say that you – or your perfume – have made a hit. Whether you realise it or not you're being awarded a huge compliment. Only rarely does Amber leave my side when I'm in camp." He chinked his glass to hers. "Here's to you – and your perfume!"

"And here's to you – and your dog," added Hope, deliberately lightening the moment and allowing herself to breathe again. She sipped her wine. "She's lovely, though I don't recognise the breed."

"Rhodesian Ridgeback. Identifiable by the ridge of fur down the back that looks like an unruly parting. They're bred to hunt lions. She's pretty good at it too."

"Is she?"

"Well – I bet you've not seen many since you arrived!"

His humour had punctuated the brief, shining hours since their meeting. It had been a long time since she had laughed effortlessly. She admired his relaxed manner, which so promptly put her at ease. He was comfortable to be with and all she wanted was to prolong these happy moments.

Later, when the party began to break up, Edric walked Hope to the car. Claire and Nicos walked with Charles and Billy. Edric's pace slowed when they drew near the car. He told Hope how much he had enjoyed the evening.

"I was wondering whether the two of us might have dinner together tomorrow. Her hesitation stirred a wave of disappointment and he imagined her searching for an excuse, "Of course we could always make it another time – and it doesn't have to be for dinner." He'd even settle for morning coffee.

"Sorry.... you caught me unawares. It wasn't my intention to be rude it's just that I haven't socialised in such a long time. You took me by surprise, that's all." Detecting a veil of disappointment, unable to help herself, she nodded. "I should love to have dinner with you tomorrow evening."

He wondered what hampered her social life. Perhaps enlightenment would come tomorrow. Pleased by her acceptance he told her where he would take her – Maninner, set in the hills – his favourite restaurant. He had almost added in the entire world but that might have sounded as though he wanted to impress her, which he did, but not like that. It had been a long time since he had invited someone out; perhaps it had been too long and he was out of practice. Well, at worst, that would make two of them. There was something in her demeanour though, which was not quite hidden, that troubled him.

In the car Charles took Hope's hand. He patted it. Like a parent he had observed everything, particularly the attention awarded her by the young man he had already decided he liked. From the smiling face that turned in response to his touch it was evident that his companion was happy.

"A very enjoyable evening. A charming family." He patted her hand again.

"Yes."

"And you.... you seemed to be getting on well with Edric." He knew he was trespassing but took licence from their relationship. "I think my dear that we will be seeing quite a bit of that young man over the next two weeks."

She attempted to bury quiet laughter in his shoulder. "You miss nothing – absolutely nothing!"

Charles simply nodded. The passing years might be stealing some of the urgency from his step but did not dare intrude upon his mind. Defying his 77 years he felt as alert today as he had ever done. When he was with this girl, he had no age at all.

"What are you chuckling about?" He now asked.

"I'm laughing at you! As a matter of fact Edric asked me to have dinner with him tomorrow evening. I've accepted. You don't mind?"

"No! And if he hadn't asked you I'd have thought there was something seriously wrong with him. Anyway, Billy and I are going to be pretty busy ourselves tomorrow – aren't we Billy?" Billy nodded from the front seat. "We're going to fix up some fairy lights and later have a practice run with the barbecue ready for the following evening when I thought it would be nice to reciprocate by having our own party. And we could include Tom and Jacqueline and the boys if they're free."

Hope thought it a wonderful idea. Then his words sunk in. "What barbecue?"

"The one we're going to buy tomorrow," Charles replied without further qualification.

Hope had a mischievous mannerism, which was similar to that employed by his daughter before entering a tease to be shared between them. "The way you slant your eyes does so remind me of Christina. The look on your face just then stirred a very pleasant memory."

"I'm glad. I too confess to frequently seeking out memories of those I've lost. It doesn't take much, a mannerism is more than sufficient." Her hand exerted a squeeze in recognition of his hurt.

"Sir Charles is going to invite everyone to the barbecue and I'm going to ask Memka to come." Billy announced from the seat in front.

"Billy – have you clicked?" Hope could not resist the exchange. She winked at Charles and they leaned together, their laughter adding depth to the giggles coming from the front of the car.

Chapter 22

Punctual from habit, Edric Colendon arrived at Villa Marchriard at precisely the time he said he would. In point of fact he was early and had his driver park on the hill where for a while he watched some donkeys being groomed by two youths.

During those moments Hope, also ready ahead of time, went to join Charles and Billy on the veranda where a lively game of Monopoly was in progress. For a long moment she stood gazing over the balustrade on the pretext of admiring their afternoon's handiwork suspending lanterns amongst the trees.

Charles glanced up every so often to study her. These days he could read her like a book. Her manner was like that of an anxious child about to attend her first party but despite that looked wonderful. Two days in the sunshine had brought a healthy glow to her skin, which looked well with her choice of outfit, a full-length, cream crepe-de-chine dress with the matching jacket she carried in case it turned cool later.

When Edric's chauffeur-driven car turned in through the gates Hope went downstairs to greet him. Charles and Billy waved from the veranda when she reappeared in the sweep of the driveway below.

Charles felt every bit like a worried parent. He watched Edric present Hope with a corsage before settling her in the car. He stepped discretely from the balustrade as the car made a crunching noise on the gravel like the echo of his own appreciative applause. As it disappeared from view he could not help thinking how incredibly young they were but perhaps it was not they who were young but he who was getting old.

At Billy's eager prompt he returned to their game but his mind was more on Maninner Restaurant than Mayfair or Marylebone Station – and whether Fate had finally allowed Hope to throw a six.

Unaware of how soothing Hope found his voice, Edric told her about the restaurant where they were headed which being mid-week would be quiet. On route he asked his driver to pull over to allow them to observe the spectacle of a field pulsating rhythmically with the tiny beams of bright light emitted from thousands of fireflies in their dance of illumination amongst the long grass. Like a myriad of minute falling stars, Hope exclaimed, amazed by the strange phenomenon.

This would be only the third occasion that she had eaten in a proper restaurant, a fact she did not dare admit to this seemingly worldly person whom she imagined dined out regularly. She came from a background where there had been no grand dinners in fancy restaurants. The two occasions when she had accompanied Kevin Lester to business lunches, Faith Suppers at the Chapel, and the infrequent bar meals with David were the total sum of her experience of dining out.

Whilst she was dressing she had managed to convince herself that in the unfamiliar setting she would do or say something out of place. Upon which Edric would see her for what she was; a very ordinary young woman from a village-life background who by some quirk of fate had been allowed to slip through the door leading to the world beyond, albeit gaining status in her own right along the way. She was not from the same world as those Edric mixed with. He would likely find her lacking and unsophisticated.

Notwithstanding these reservations she considered the situation with some of the determination instilled in her by her father. She was going to a proper restaurant for a lovely meal in the company of an exceptional person. Edric may never contact her again but tonight was hers. The rest lay in the remit of tomorrow and it would be foolish to permit it to encroach upon the evening.

Swamped by indecision Hope suggested that Edric might order for both of them. She watched his brown eyes transfer to the novel-length menu before directing a question to the waiter at his side. The choice of wine she also left to him.

"What are you smiling at?" Edric returned their menus to the waiter.

"This place. You were right, it does have a friendly atmosphere."

Surprised to find such a grand establishment tucked away in the hills she looked about her, daring now to take in the details of the family-run concern, which had the reputation for being the best eating establishment for miles around. Hope would have voiced relief but that would be to admit to earlier reservations.

Soft Greek music played in the background and Edric informed her that there was live music at the weekends when the waiters pulled diners to the dance floor. He added that she would enjoy it.

Had that been a slip of the tongue or an intimation that he would bring her again? Her disquiet was already slipping away and she was smiling again. She could not help it. Edric conducted himself with such an easy, almost contagious confidence that she was instantly at ease. And Edric did not reach across to impale food on his fork from her plate as David had. As their meal progressed she forgot all about the earlier presence of butterflies. There had been few occasions when she had felt this happy and there was a sparkle in her eyes.

Edric studied her. "I don't know much about you – other than that you're the Sally Lox Girl," the comment only vaguely untrue. "But I fear you know even less about me." He paused to take a sip of wine and signal to their waiter for another bottle. "I should tell you something about myself, not least – that I'm married." He hated the need to speak the words. "It's something I should have told you before I invited you out." He watched but saw no negative reaction.

"I know. Claire told me."

"I see...." he nodded, "and a lot more besides, I shouldn't wonder."

His voice remained even. Nevertheless she wondered whether his cousin's disclosure had annoyed him. "She also told me about the other lady in your life – Amber." Instantly she saw gentle creasing around his eyes and knew no harm had been done.

"Did she tell you about Hilary – my wife?"

Hope shook her head. She believed she was about to be introduced to that period of his life, which he clearly regretted.

Almost reluctantly he began to unwind the story of how as a promising young executive he had found himself married in haste to the pampered daughter of the chairman of a rival hotel chain. He explained how his wife had gone through confidential papers in his briefcase, her actions resulting in a conflict of business interests and the consequent need to make a formal declaration to his Board.

His quiet monologue went on to describe how the unassuming house within the grasp of his salary bracket had not measured up to his wife's expectations and he had allowed himself to be persuaded to move into her commodious parental home to live with her father. Unable to think of it with any degree of affection he had never felt comfortable in the great rambling Tudor-style house in Kent.

Hope could not help feeling moved by the events relating to his entrapment and in her heart her tears mingled with his; to be hurt by one you love is to be deeply hurt indeed.

"Her parents divorced when Hilary was very young. She idolises her father – her *Dadda*. Nothing and nobody could ever approach the importance of Dadda – and certainly not me. It's a one-way thing. Sadly she can't see that. From what I gather Hilary was her father's trophy from the divorce. Her mother probably got the car and the dog." He grimaced as his tasteless humour. "I used to wonder if Hilary would have been a nicer person if her mother had brought her up. One day in a fit of temper she admitted that her only reason for marrying me was to acquire inside information from her father's rivals, and like I said, did that almost to my cost."

Edric's eyes lowered to scrutinise the stem of his wineglass. "In the early days she fooled even me. She applied the guise of the adoring wife and proved herself a capable hostess whilst at the same time engaging in commercial espionage and conducting a series of affairs. After my discovery of the former she threw discretion to the wind – perhaps an act of retaliation in wishing me to discover also her infidelity – and she invited one of her escorts along to a friend's party. I came across them together in the summer house."

He had no way of knowing that the one seated across from him had experienced the same level of betrayal and was able to appreciate his suffering.

"The marriage floundered on for another 18 months but in reality was over within the first year." His expression softened. "That probably sounds defeatist but I've never come across anyone with such a manipulative mind, and believe me I'm well accustomed to dealing with contrived board room tactics."

Hope imagined the discovery would have left him bruised and humiliated, and with a compulsion to award greater scrutiny to others thereafter.

"I'm known to my business associates as a hard-hitting, and if the circumstances warrant it, even a high-risk taker, but that's on the business front." He paused before confessing with abject honesty, "Notwithstanding all of that I suppose on a more personal front we just got on each other's nerves, and I came to realise my absence was appreciated more than my presence." He reached to top up her wine glass. "I abhor failure, particularly my own. Hilary wanted someone who was at home more, someone less compulsive and possibly not so...." he searched for the words.

"Wonderful and charming?" Hope suggested bravely. Colouring, she took a sip of wine.

It seemed an appropriate moment to mention her own divorce but despite his candid story, which shared surprising parallels, she could not summon the courage to tell him everything and said nothing about the horror of her finding David in bed with a prostitute. She still wondered whether she had been neglectful and consequently responsible in some way, added to which her companion's viewpoint on failure repeated in her ears: *I abhor failure, particularly my own.*

She sensed that Edric expected her to continue, as though he knew there was more. But her words ceased; she was not ready to speak of the child she had lost or how that and a failed marriage had impacted on her life.

Presently they went on to speak of lighter things and much laughter was heard from the candle-lit table in the corner. Hope's confidence grew as Edric put a series of questions to her, not probing, just friendly.

Eventually the conversation turned to her involvement with the Sally Lox Corporation. Edric laughed when he heard how she had been spotted by Harry Nichols and how the great Kevin Lester QC materialised at just the right moment to take control. Her skill in mimicry heightened his amusement and declared she had missed her way to becoming part of a variety act.

"Lester is a pretty amazing gent. My Chairman holds him in very high regard and there aren't many who measure up to...." Edric stopped abruptly. "I've just realised something. I was there that day. I'm surprised we didn't bump into each other." He leaned across to take her hand in his. "I don't seem to be able to avoid you – even if I wanted to – which I don't. I saw you for the first time on a bridge near Tarnville after I'd called on your friend. Then less than a couple of years later I couldn't believe my eyes when you walked into Lester's Board Room. And I know you came to Corfu last year." He had seen her at the airport when he had been chasing off somewhere. "You were with others. I believe Billy was amongst them."

Hope experienced a thrill that he remembered her. "Billy, yes plus Aunt Bell and my landlady Daphne," whom she admitted was really more of a friend.

"And your face has stared out at me from my newspaper and television screen ever since and recently it's your smile that greets my arrival at Kings Cross. When I get off the train I look to check they've not pasted an advertisement for dog food over you!"

She rolled her luminous green eyes at this. "It does seem that our paths keep crossing.... the airport the other day, and later at the little bar where I managed to take an impromptu bathe! Actually.... I remember seeing you in Mowlem but I'm surprised that you remember. It sticks out in my mind because I was used to seeing farm labourers, each wearing much the same shabby garments as the next. You were obviously a stranger. I'd never seen such fine clothes, not even at the Chapel socials." She also remembered the dark brown eyes that looked across at her now, but did not have the courage to say so.

"You almost knocked me off my feet, or rather swept me off my feet. I can remember turning to watch you climb the grassy bank on the other side. Your hair then was even longer. It floated after you as you strode up the daisy-covered embankment. I can remember thinking that you looked so out of place. You looked more like an exotic flower.... *like an orchid amongst the daisies*."

There was a gasp as Hope's hand shot to her mouth with the recollection of the wording on a small card.

Edric inclined his head. "Yes, I sent the flowers."

The arrival of an exquisite orchid, the centrepiece of a basket of daisy-shaped flowers, had intrigued her for days as she lay miserable and comfortless in her hospital bed.

"Something told me there was a story behind the message but couldn't fathom it." Then, for no reason she wanted to cry and he knew. This time both his hands were on hers.

Gaining strength from the gesture she continued, "Then you know that I lost a baby?"

He nodded and waited for her to go on.

"I didn't learn I was pregnant until after I'd left my husband."

She struggled to go on and he lowered his eyes to allow her to recover. She had permitted him to glimpse the cause for some of her sadness, and now fragmented sentences followed unchecked about her husband's betrayal.

"The prospect of a child awarded the promise that something good could come out of something bad. It brought some sense back into my life. After trying to disregard the obvious," she laughed, "my increasing waistline – events caught up to take over my entire life. I was terrified yet at the same time impatient to hold my baby.... but then I lost it." The tightening of his hands on hers gave her the strength to continue. "But I'm getting over it." She brightened. "This holiday is supposed to rest me before I take up the reins again. I need to work," her voice emphatic. She explained about her post at Manstonleigh that was being held open for her. "But eventually I intend to return to fulltime employment and pull out from S-L and Manstonleigh."

She had not realised how much she missed the flak and excitement generated in Lester's Board Room, until yesterday when he had related familiar tales. She had been happy at Lester's, happy and fulfilled and, unlike his cousin, she both understood and appreciated Edric's dedication and absorption.

"Fancy our being at the same meeting." she continued. "I was lucky to land that job. That was more to do with Sir Charles than anyone else. He instigated my introduction to Kevin."

Edric's face changed. "I owe you an apology don't I? I'm sorry if I caused any embarrassment yesterday. I simply assumed you were his daughter. I trust I caused no offence."

She assured him that none had been taken. "Actually, he is a bit like a father to me. I can tell him anything." With regards the latter, she realised she was beginning to feel similarly about Edric. "For all I've lived in the village since I was little we only became properly acquainted after my father's death. I was just 18. We struck up what I'm sure many would describe as an unlikely friendship. I'm immensely fond of him. He says we compliment each other. And I think I remind him a bit of his daughter." She explained how Christina had run off with a handy-man. When Edric showed signs of wishing to interrupt, she said quickly, "I don't want you to think me guilty of tittle-tattle. I'm not breaking any confidences. His search for Christina is common knowledge."

"No, I'm sure you're not. I was just going to say – snap! I was in Mowlem that day for a similar purpose. I came across Tarnville purely by chance when I was conducting some research of my own. My mother's people originated from the area and I was hoping to find out something of her background. Genealogy – it's the fashionable thing these days. I've tracked down my father's side, such as it is, but as for my mother I've only just started. It was only when entering my teens that I realised how sparse my knowledge was of my parents. So far I've not been very successful but to be honest I don't get much time."

Hope looked earnestly at him. "What – what was your mother's maiden name?" She hardly dare ask and willed him to say Lurdmayne – but if he did she would have to tell Sir Charles that his daughter was dead, killed in a fire.

"Wait for it...." he began. "It's.... *S-m-i-t-h*.... Maggie Smith. You'd never believe how many Smiths there are around Stillingford, though I did find details relating to one Margaret Ann Smith but she was born last century, which would make her around 140 when she had me!"

A mixture of disappointment and relief swept over her. It had been foolish but the coincidence had been too great not to enquire. If the search for someone with the unusual name of Lurdmayne were proving difficult, how much more so would it be for one with the name of Smith.

Hope slanted her eyes mischievously. "It could've been worse...."

"How?"

"Your mother could have originated from Wales and had the maiden name of Jones!"

More laughter. Their waiter smiled across at them.

Hope's recollections of a conversation with the heading of "What If" now presented itself. If his parents had not died in a house fire he might never have visited her village. If Edric had not shown an interest in genealogy would she ever have met him? And there, with a jumble of emotions, ended that particular sequence of thought.

Eventually Edric said, "Tell me something of yourself. I know so little."

She waved a hand dismissively. "There's little to tell."

"I don't believe you. Tell me something about your earlier years. Your childhood for instance – was it happy?"

Her eyes glazed with reminiscences of building tree houses, fishing for sticklebacks and picnicking in woodland, and within her first opening sentences he learned something of the vital role her father had played in her life, and the story behind the stepping-stones.

He ginned. "It's all right laughing that as a youngster you believed the stones would eventually lead you to Tarnville. If you think about it that's precisely what happened. I wonder what your father would have said if he'd known that one day you and your aunt would be living there."

She considered this for a moment. "He'd have taken it in his stride.... then laughed his socks off!"

"He sounds to have been a wonderful person."

"He was. He was always there for me. When he died I felt I couldn't live without him and when six months later I was still here I was almost surprised. I've never known anybody like him. He could convey displeasure with nothing more than a look, and believe me when he did that I knew I was out of line. He was a person with an unfailing regard for others and an aversion to any form of gossip. An admission of guilt would inevitably result in my being pressed for the facts. He was more interested in learning *why* rather than *what*. I once had to tell him about an incident involving a soaking wet donkey." There was a gleam of encouragement in Edric's eyes. "No, believe me, you don't want to know about it!" She shook her head, refusing to be drawn. "As I was saying.... after listening to my account, to my aunt's horror, he said he could appreciate the reasons behind my actions."

"He was totally unique and I still take comfort from the dream we shared, and I enjoy sitting by the river. It's a place where I can relax and allow the surroundings to soothe me. It's a place where I can be alone – a place where I can think and remember. Different from any other place on earth it's my little piece of heaven, infinitely lovely in its lush, green gentleness. Sometimes I imagine that in the next moment I'll hear my father's voice or catch sight of him on his way across the hill to meet me...."

Her voice faltered and to conceal the fragility of the moment she raised her glass to non-drinking lips before going on. "In the beginning I attempted to blank out what happened but in quiet, tranquil moments I award myself the luxury of drawing on my memories. Those deliciously happy years didn't prepare me for the sad ones that were to follow but thanks to him I still believe in dreams."

Chapter 23

The hypermarket bustled with activity. A handful of sombre-attired, olive skinned women milled around the fresh fish counter but mainly it was the holidaymaker in garish garb, pale skin glistening with sickly-smelling sun creams, who predominated the scene.

Edric wove through the throng with a trolley of foodstuffs for a picnic on the beach. Billy darted between the aisles in his search for items on their list and Hope had to curb his eagerness and remind him that smaller measures were adequate if they were to regain their appetite for the barbecue at Marchriard that evening.

Edric examined the contents of the trolley. "That seems to be everything."

"Except bread. Somehow we seem to have forgotten the bread! You go on. I'll meet you at the checkout." Hope left Edric and Billy with the trolley.

Hope found the bread section in the next aisle. Making her selection she dislodged part of the display and a pack of white baps tumbled into the pushchair of the young mother beside her.

During these moments Edric and Billy took it into their heads to help search for the bread and came across Hope just as she was breaking into an apology for her clumsiness.

Hope crouched low to retrieve the bread but once level with the cherub-like face her attention transferred to gently parted lips and the tiny fist that clenched a teething ring. Her hand went to touch downy hair, but then fell short to rest on the shawl. If her baby had lived it would have been about the same age. The memory closed her mind to everything else. Eventually the moment passed and she stood up. In a dry voice she apologised again, finishing, "Your baby is very beautiful.... I lost my baby."

The flat tone went undetected by the young mother who, adding to Hope's pain, replied in her best English, "You must keep good look on baby." She pointed meaningfully to her own dark eyes then towards the next aisle. "There is sweets.... you find baby with sweets. Mine other baby there. You look for baby there." Smiling brightly the woman moved away with her basket of groceries balanced on the hood of the buggy.

Billy stood silently by; the subtleties of the situation eluded him. But Edric had seen Hope sway seconds before squeezing her eyes shut. He put Billy in charge of the trolley and went to draw her into his arms.

It had been a jolt, one for which she had been unprepared. In her months of self-imposed exile she had not come into contact with any young children since her accident. The incident served as a reminder that beneath her sunny disposition dwelt a burden of sadness, emphasising she was more fragile than she had permitted others to know.

By the time Charles arrived at Edric's villa with Tom and Jacqueline and their sons in tow, the picnic food had been prepared and the episode forgotten. Comfortable chairs for the adults were taken to the beach through a gap in the shrubbery and large tartan rugs spread out for the youngsters. Claire's husband arrived towards the end of the picnic. He described himself as an hospital escapee in desperate need of sane company to which Edric retorted he was out of luck and jerked his head in the direction of five young people engaged in a boisterous game of handball with Amber barking noisily at their heels.

When the grownups retired to the shade of the garden Edric and Hope remained with the younger members. Charged by all the activity Amber was still acting like something demented and Edric suggested tiring her out with a walk along the shore. When the dog bounded back at his command she paused to sniff the air around Hope. Then, as was becoming her custom, Amber threw back her head to emit a long yodelling howl.

Howling had never formed part of her repertoire and Edric applied his own interpretation to the new talent. "It's that perfume of yours. I've had no control over her since she got her first whiff!"

They hunted for an arsenal of flat pebbles to fling ducks and drakes in the surf and Amber dissolved into a frenzied demonstration of impressive retrieval skills. After making their arms ache, and practically drowning the dog, they took it in turns to perform funny walks following in each other's footprints. When Edric trod in Hope's he whispered that he felt as though he had been treading in her footsteps for years.

They walked all the way to the little shabby bar that Hope had nicknamed the Old Man's Bar. There they pulled two tables together and Amber lapped noisily from a bowl of water whilst managing to dribble a quantity over the feet of a woman nearby. Amber settled in the shade beneath a chair and Edric rolled his eyes when she lifted her head from between outstretched paws to sniff the air.

"For a moment I thought she was about to give us another rendition in case we missed her last aria. I don't think I could stand an encore! There is one thing though. You'll never be able to sneak up on me without my trusty scout's sniffing you out!"

No sooner had five drinking straws begun to perform a symphony of rude noises at the bottom of five empty Coke bottles than the children exploded back into life and begged to return to the beach. Edric and Hope feigned exhaustion. They said they would watch from the table.

Edric swivelled his head. "He doesn't have many but when it's breezy like today the old guy doesn't put his brollies out. What little shade there is has already been taken. Are you all right here?"

He began to remove his shirt, his musculature a testament to regular workouts in Shillens's gymnasia. The warmth of his body was still in the fabric being draped around her shoulders and when his fingers inadvertently touched her skin Hope was startled by the intensity of the sensation.

"This will help to protect the back of your neck."

Over another drink they watched the young ones who with Amber's help had befriended some local children engaged in trying to fly a kite. Each appeared to understand the problem of its reluctance to become airborne and took a turn to gallop down the beach in a repetition of vain attempts to improve on previous efforts.

Edric's eyes narrowed. "That's something I always wanted as a child."

"What – a kite that won't fly?" This earned a jab to the region of her midriff.

Casual beachwear had been the uniform of the day and Hope looked well in navy shorts and sparkling white halter-top. She leaned back and cupped the back of her head in her hands. "This is the second most beautiful place on earth," she declared.

"Not the first?"

She shook her head and turned away. With glazed eyes she looked in memory at bright, sparkling water as it eddied round her stepping-stones. "But it's a good second," she said at last. She bent down to rummage in her bag. In the next moment she was lining him up in her lens and instructing him to say *c-h-e-e-s-e*. The camera changed hands and she felt eminently embarrassed when she became the subject matter.

"Now don't tell me you're camera shy – you who practically lives in front of the things!" Others looked on as Edric took a series of candid shots.

When he returned the camera she paced around photographing the area. "I'd like to have a go at painting this place when I get back," she explained as she resumed her seat. "It's a hobby of mine." The art materials her aunt had packed had not been opened and, like the paperbacks, she knew it unlikely that they would be.

Hope's eyes did a circuit of the suntrap. She took it all in: the sparkle of sea salt on the roof; the crazed concrete; and the nameless thread of life thriving in the walling where Edric rested his foot. No matter how many years went by she would always remember this moment; the Old Man's Bar would always hold a special significance. Even last year, a full year before they had claimed it as their special place, she had experienced an inexplicable affinity with it.

Though the excitement and stimulation of unpredictability invoked virtually opposite moods of nature, the seascape shared something with that other place: the most beautiful place on earth.

Charles was beginning to notice the frequency in which Hope spoke of their new friends, especially Edric. He liked the young man who displayed the body language of a confident person wise beyond his years. Pleasurable ideas had already begun to form. There he went again – wanting to take over where Frederick Thackeray left off!

Seated with Charles on the terrace Hope chattered on. She told him some of the things Edric had said that had made her smile and how his dog howled every time it saw her. She told him the strange story of

194

how their paths had crossed since their first encounter on the bridge in Mowlem; the day Edric had stumbled upon Tarnville.

"You say he was there researching his family tree.... on his mother's side?"

As soon as she heard the words Hope was filled with remorse. Like she, Charles was clutching at the same fragile straw. She could not bear to contemplate the hurt her stupid ramblings had caused, and she chased to answer unspoken questions.

"His mother's people originated from the area," she began. "But the surname's common and he's not got very far. *S-m-i-t-h – Maggie Smith*! I told him it could've been worse and she been from Wales with the name of...." But Charles was not listening. He had risen from his chair and walked a few paces from her. Shiny white knuckles grasped his stick as he gazed far into the distance, the depth of his emotions displayed in the droop of his shoulders.

Had it not been for this illustration of reticence she would have rushed to throw her arms around him and apologise for reminding him of his loss. She should have realised that if her mind had worked along those lines how much more likely would his.

Billy and Helda chose that moment to venture out to the terrace with trays of glasses and crockery for the barbecue later. There followed the noise of preparation, and the distraction eased the moment. If not an actual smile, a look of peace returned to the face of their gracious host though he disappeared inside soon afterwards, having spoken not a word.

Hope stared after him. She knew how a phrase, a smell – or in her case the sight of a sleeping child – could spark off a painful memory. In future she would be more mindful of Charles's feelings.

The barbecue was a great success. Claire had thought to bring along a collection of CDs, and when bright Greek music resounded through the garden the young people pulled the senior members to their feet. Pointing to his stick, Charles was the only one to escape. Billy's lack of co-ordination brought nothing to the sequence but his inability to master the steps did not detract from his enthusiasm and he applauded along with the rest when Edric persuaded Hope to her feet.

Hope raised her eyebrows at the others who had decided simultaneously to return to their seats. "Now that's not fair. I haven't got sufficient hang of this malarkey to warrant an audience!"

"Come on you two. Show us how it's done," called Nicos, holding his glass aloft.

With her head slightly to one side Claire nodded thoughtfully beside her husband. She glanced at Charles. He too was smiling.

Edric arranged Hope's arms at shoulder height before instructing her in the familiar wide-sweeping footwork. Soon they were moving in unison and for the duration of the folk dance no one else existed. At the conclusion the sudden crack of applause plummeted them back to the present with a start.

An expression on Charles's face intrigued Hope. He nodded thoughtfully as she resumed her seat beside him. "You remind me of your mother. Watching you just now you could have been her."

"I didn't know you knew her." Surprise sparkled in her voice before transferring to her eyes when she learned her parents had attended one of Tarnville's harvest supper dances where Faith had danced with his son Richard.

"It was a long time ago – before you were born, but you looked very much like your mother just now."

For the rest of the evening Hope remained conscious of elderly crepe eyes following her every movement and she glowed with the knowledge that she resembled the mother she had never known. She was immensely pleased that the resemblance had so stirred Charles's memory whereby she had learned of the likeness.

Despite the keenness of his observation Charles seemed troubled and appeared not to notice her smile. Then it dawned on her that she had done it again, only this time she had reminded him of the other child he had lost. He would be thinking about Richard – who had danced with her mother.

All too soon the lazy sun-filled days and tranquil evenings grew in number and brought the holiday towards a close. On the last evening Edric and Hope dined alone at Edric's villa. Together they prepared a simple meal of grilled fish and a selection of fresh vegetables and salad, which they enjoyed on the terrace whilst watching the sun blaze into its last display of magical splendour before their departure the next day. Filled with beach parties, barbecues and relaxing dinners it had been a marvellous two weeks.

Now, on Eric's terrace Hope ran her hands over her hips and expressed the expectation of having gained weight. "I've done nothing but eat for the whole fortnight! It's been a wonderful holiday. I've enjoyed every moment."

Edric reached for her hand. It was she who had made it wonderful. He wondered if she had any inkling of the effect she had on him. He drew her to him and when he nuzzled his face into her hair she brought her lips to his, instantly making him breathless. Despite her demonstrations of warmth something always made her pull away. She did this now but he had been ready and did not suffer the same anguish. Slipping from his arms Hope smoothed her hair and went to perch at the edge of a seat, the arrangement of her hemline suddenly of paramount importance.

She had told him of a friend's belief that yesterday's experiences made a person what they were today. He could not argue with that; indeed he need look no further than himself to appreciate the validity of that statement. Observing Hope now he wondered what had taken place in her past to bring about this marked change. He had no time for further contemplation; Hope was speaking – her choice of words the perfect gift.

"I'm going to miss you when we get back."

"And I'm going to miss you. But we'll have the weekends," he offered on a positive note.

The demands of his job took him away a great deal and prevented a regular presence during the week but he returned like clockwork to his hotel base in Leeds every weekend.

Hope beamed brightly back at him. "For the first time since my father's death I'll be able to look forward to Fridays again."

It had been established early on that this was no casual holiday romance – a dalliance, a mere distraction. They had enjoyed getting to know each other, though Hope had added little more about her marriage except to say that the unhappiness far outweighed the happy times. The comment prompted Edric to wonder whether it had been a single act or the combination of many that overshadowed whatever had been good in the marriage. More important – was she sufficiently over it to trust her feelings again?

He ran a hand affectionately along her forearm then without a word disappeared inside. He reappeared with the lace wrap he had surprised her with the previous day. He draped it round her.

"I've bought you a present too. It's to help you remember the holiday." She went to the sitting room to fetch the slim parcel she had been carrying on arrival.

Returning she explained, "It's not much but it's something you've always wanted."

With the removal of the tissue paper a boyish grin flooded Edric's face. "A kite! I wonder how Billy is fixed for giving me flying lessons." The grin changed to the smile he kept just for her and they slipped into each other's arms where they lingered until Hope broke the embrace. As though to compensate, she led him to an easy chair and settled on his lap.

Breathing in her fragrance Edric looked at the face resting against his shoulder. He was ridiculously happy; he was like an adolescent with an all-consuming crush; he was ecstatic when he was with this exemplary being. This was someone who enjoyed his company for who he was and had nothing to do with his position at Shillens. He was pleased by this perception for he had already decided that she belonged in his life.

Chapter 24

The grandfather clock in Tarnville's hall chimed the hour. As though doubting its reliability Isabel checked her watch. She glanced round the room. Satisfied that everything was ready for her employer's return she was about to go to speak to Cook when she caught the sound of car wheels crunching over gravel. Without a moment's hesitation she rushed to be the first to greet her employer and niece back from holiday.

Bewildered and with her smile slipping from her face Isabel halted amidst her descent of the steps. Charles looked weary; furthermore he was on his own. Joseph Fearnley was unloading luggage from the boot; Hope's baggage was not amongst it; apparently her niece had elected to stay over in Leeds. Isabel found it hard to conceal her disappointment but managed a wan smile as she went to relieve Charles of his hand luggage.

Perceiving her confusion Charles was quick to inform her that Hope was not far behind and in the company of a certain Edric Colendon, a Director of Shillens International.

Edric Colendon? Shillens? Then Isabel remembered Shillens was one of the companies Hope had had dealings with at Lester's. A bubble of intrigue nudged aside her former feelings. Who was this Edric and what was he to her niece? These and a hundred more questions occurred to Isabel whilst awaiting Hope's return.

When Charles had learned Edric was returning to his impersonal hotel suite in Leeds he invited him to Tarnville for the weekend. It occurred to him that Edric's presence might re-ignite the party atmosphere of the holiday.

Right from the start Charles had insisted that when Hope visited her aunt the two of them, plus their guests, should join him for dinner in the dining room. Isabel had only acquiesced when Charles emphasised he would welcome some company as dining alone had become too frequent an event. Isabel could not help wondering how many of Tarnville's Housekeepers had been invited to sit at the long table in the grand dining room. It seemed her employer was prepared to bend the rules in his declining years and extend boundaries laid down by his predecessors. This break in convention was not something she chose to advertise, though guessed folk knew. Staff talked. That was inevitable.

Before returning to Tarnville, Joseph Fearnley had dropped Billy at Manstonleigh and Edric and Hope at the Leeds Shillens Hotel for Edric to pick up fresh clothing and any messages that had been left for him.

Edric's position in the hierarchy was apparent from the moment Hope entered the hotel foyer on his arm where staff sprang to attention, abruptly ceasing all side-chat. The observation reminded her of when Kevin Lester had left his quarters to go amongst his staff. Edric seemed not to notice.

His personage today was far removed from the man she had come to know who had flung ducks and drakes like a champion and laughed and swum with bronzed children in the surf. The contrast came as a shock. Until this moment she had not consciously considered Edric's directorship title and now tried to imagine this same executive with his hair ruffled and a dog's leash taut in his hand.

The incongruous thought pattern dissipated when a young, female member of staff approached the person accompanying her Director to enquire whether she could get her anything – perhaps some coffee?

Catching Edric's almost imperceptible wink from the reception desk where he was making a call to his secretary, Hope spoke warmly to the young woman whose hand trembled slightly with the unexpected presence of her Board Member. She regretted the employee knew nothing of that other being; the wonderful, gentle person beneath the grand title.

Hope was introduced to Allison Ballard, Edric's secretary, a slim woman, approximately the same age as Edric. The secretary wore a well-cut pale grey suit. She wore it well. She extended her hand but allowed it to fall short whereby Hope was required to step forward. The significance of the slight movement did not miss Hope, who sensed the gesture had been deliberately moderated to state and underscore Allison's position, as opposed to hers – the lesser being accompanying her boss. The snub had been discrete and expertly directed at the only one to detect it.

200

Whilst waiting for Edric to finish issuing an instruction and for his car to be fuelled and brought to the front, Hope toyed with the idea that she was being oversensitive, but when she and Edric made their departure she caught an undisguised expression of total disregard, the indication being that Allison considered she could be safely dismissed as being unimportant.

The explanation for the snub did not hit Hope until after they left the motorway to weave along the narrow lanes near Mowlem. She was amazed she had not realised it earlier. Allison Ballard was in love with her boss and saw her as a threat! The knowledge made her uncomfortable, particularly as Edric had come up with an arrangement whereby Allie, as he referred to her, would be her contact should she ever need to track him down.

Despite this revelation the drive to Tarnville was pleasant. The dappled light from the September sun filtering through the trees obscured the faded countryside, now parched from the summer heat. But closer inspection identified that the trees were already turning and the unmistakable herald of the next season had begun. Hedgerows, now brittle, had been cut back and were almost transparent in places. In another few weeks this tiredness would give way to the leafy masterpiece waiting impatiently in the wings when there would follow an unruly clash of crimson and burnished copper and bright golden yellow – the true emblem of autumn – until that too became nudged aside by a less vibrant artwork waiting to take centre stage to project dark, leafless silhouettes against a colourless canvas.

Hope sat forward in her seat to drink in the surroundings of her childhood. Net curtains twitched at the tweak of inquisitive hands; the grandeur of the gleaming car had alerted villagers to the presence of a stranger in their midst and Hope shrank back with the desire to prolong these last moments of anonymity.

Tarnville came into view through the car window and Hope wondered what Isabel would think of Edric; Daphne had taken to him and she was anxious that Isabel should like him also.

Edric had anticipated the keen scrutiny of Hope's aunt. He was not disappointed. Curiosity and something resembling feline protection showed in the alert grey eyes that rarely left him during the grilling, which nevertheless was genial.

"You sound as though you've enjoyed yourselves," this directed at both of them. Isabel shifted her attention back to the handsome, dark-haired young man seated beside her niece. "I understand you're joining us for the weekend. You've picked a good one. It's the harvest supper dance tomorrow evening – always a merry affair. You'll enjoy it. I can vouch for the fact that there'll be plenty to eat." Her head was still spinning from all the preparations. Her attention transferred to Hope for almost the first time in the last half an hour. "Freddie and I loved it as kids. We used to hide in the barn loft with our pals to watch the festivities. The grownups pretended they didn't know we were there but now and then one would pass us bits to eat. Those were happy times." Her eyes glazed. "And I can remember the supper your parents attended before you arrived on the scene. My – how your mother could dance! She quite wore your Dad out and others had to take his place until they too dropped like flies to go to stand with Freddie laughing on the sidelines."

"Sir Charles told me. He said my mother danced with his son."

"That she did right enough pet and with Sir Charles himself as I recall."

"And with Sir Charles himself, you say? He omitted to mention that!"

"Well he did and we clapped him until our hands tingled. And then there was Master Richard – now he was one for a petty face, but he was just one of the many she wore out that night. I can see her now…..spinning and twirling, her little feet executing steps none of us had ever seen before."

"Bell," Hope said slowly, "Do I really resemble her as closely as he said?"

"Your mother? You do indeed – like a mirror no less. She was a very bonny creature." Isabel's eyes moved to include Edric. "My brother and his wife had been trying for a child for a long time but nothing seemed to be happening but then Faith fell pregnant. I've never seen such happiness." Her voice grew quiet with the recollection of how short-lived their joy had been. "Faith was a lovely person, thoughtful, nice temperament. She made my brother a good wife." Isabel angled her head. "I'd say you inherited your mother's beauty and spirit, and your father's intelligence and sense of humour. They didn't have much. They didn't need much. They had more in their short time together than most people have in a lifetime. Faith didn't want anything. Not an important man or a great fancy house. She just wanted her Freddie. In him she saw goodness and a sense of humour and someone she could talk and laugh with. They longed for a child though, and it seemed their prayers had been answered, but then tragically Faith died in childbirth."

Edric's eyes showed pain and Isabel could understand why her employer liked him enough to pay him the huge compliment of allocating Christina's room to him.

Isabel was beginning to pick up on the closeness of the young people who smiled at her in between beaming at each other. In all her years with Bert she had never shared anything approaching this adoration. But life changed. She had news she was bursting to share but there was more than enough happiness in Hope's life at the moment; her own news could wait until tomorrow. Isabel's fingers went to trace the gold chain concealed beneath the bodice of her housedress.

Edric detected Isabel's momentary lapse of concentration. "Some of the same qualities displayed by Faith have passed to her daughter. You'd have been pleased by the consideration shown by your niece towards young Billy and Sir Charles. Nothing is too much trouble for her. A rare gift in a person these days."

"And it doesn't rest with people. She's also kind to donkeys!"

"Oh Aunt Bell – No!"

Isabel shrugged as though understanding eluded her. "Why don't you go and put the kettle on while I tell Edric about Dolly the donkey – who got wet in the rain."

Edric's eyes widened. "Yes, why don't you?" he encouraged. "I was more than a little intrigued when you mentioned having had some sort of run-in with a donkey and it looks as though my curiosity is about to be satisfied."

There was something settling about the young man laughing with her niece; something indicating a suggestion if not a promise of permanence in their relationship, and Isabel was warming to the idea.

"Right then – Dolly the donkey. It had been raining heavily all day...." she began.

"Awh! I'm going to make the tea!" exclaimed Hope, rolling her eyes.

It seemed to Hope that the whole county had turned out for the Harvest Supper and as in previous years she marvelled at the great quantities of food laid out on the arrangement of trestle tables. She knew Isabel and the staff had been busy but only now could she appreciate the intensity of their labours. She blew a kiss across the sea of faces to her aunt at the far side of the courtyard but she was deep in conversation and did not see.

Isabel stood chatting with Peter Summerville, every now and then her hand going to feel the tiny bump beneath the fabric of her bodice where Peter's engagement ring hung safely on the gold chain that had belonged to his mother.

Hope's gaze moved on, alighting now and then to smile at friends. Gregory was standing apart over by the wall. He was watching her. It was the first time she had seen him since their row. She looked for Amy but before she had time to search the crowd for the familiar mop of dark curls a great cry of excitement went up from the villagers and the air was filled with cheering.

Charles, looking considerably younger than his years, arrived in their midst in a wagon drawn by Tarnville's two great shires, Bill and Ben. The gentle giants, the pride of the district, caused a stir of excitement whenever they put in an appearance. Joseph Fearnley had had them groomed to competition standards, their manes plaited with coloured silks, and an impressive array of rosettes attached to their halters. Joseph brought the magnificent animals to a halt before he hastened to help his employer down from the wagon.

Charles alighted to make a speech of welcome and offer heart-felt thanks for all the labours encountered during harvesting. Afterwards he was escorted to the adjacent field of prickly stubble where he was handed a pole to which burning sackcloth had been tied for him to light the bonfire. The fire was lit; the crowd exploded into thick applause, and once again the annual harvest celebration commenced.

"It's clear that Sir Charles is really fond of you." Edric had been unable to disregard the old man's gaze. "He's hardly taken his eyes off you." He laughed. "No doubt giving me the once-over, checking I match up to expectations!"

"Honestly Edric!" But Hope loved Edric's humour. She reached up to kiss his cheek. Instantly her eyes strayed to Charles who had seen and nodded. "Oh Edric you're right. He looks absolutely livid and clearly doesn't approve of your presence. Perhaps you should leave right away!"

She was laughing with him but her mind was on Charles's keen attention. Again and again she had seen that same look of distraction. How she wished she could venture into his tunnel of thought to discover the subject of that distraction.

The evening air was pleasant and Edric suggested a walk. They had not gone far when he noticed Hope had goose bumps. Accepting no excuses he went to fetch her jacket.

Edric was just gone from sight when Gregory stepped out from the shadows. This the first encounter since their exchange in the rose garden, the void between them was bridged with cool embarrassment.

"How are you?"

He had been drinking though was not drunk, at least not to the measure of her experience of Bert or David.

"I'm well thank you. And you?"

He nodded and tugged his hands free from his trouser pockets. He came forward, his arms going as though to embrace her but she stepped away, instantly despising herself for doing so.

"Sorry." His arms dropped away. "I knew I was beaten but would've been a fool not to let you know my feelings. Now I just want to say I'm sorry for the strain I put on our friendship. I want us to be friends and put all that other stuff behind us."

"We are friends. We always have been. Nothing could change that."

Hope recoiled when his arm shot towards her and his mouth moved as though to kiss her, but with his next words she realised her error and was suddenly filled with greater fear.

"Those are sparks. Sampson's barn's on fire!"

205

Grasping the enormity of the statement Hope turned to look in the direction of Gregory's extended arm. Her mouth dropped into a gape. "But how could....?"

"A courting couple – a spark from the bonfire carried on the wind – who knows?"

They ran as fast as they could towards the old barn where sparks rose in bright splutters from the roof like a shock of orange confetti swirling against the night sky.

Gregory began hurling bales of hay from the vicinity. "Alert the others. Get 'em down here fast. Call the brigade. I'll stay and shift these." Suddenly sober he called over his shoulder, "Be as quick as you can. Tell Joe it's taking hold!"

With the single scream of *F-i-r-e* Hope was practically consumed within a quicksand of running bodies surging towards the old barn to do whatever could be done.

The urgency of the situation prevented any explanation as she sped past Edric, carrying her jacket. She shouted for him to follow the others, and wondering at the horror in her face his pace quickened to fall in with the stampede flowing like lava towards the far field.

By the time Hope returned there was something sad hanging in the air and she had a premonition that something terrible had happened. On legs like jelly she fought her way through the crush until she saw the little group gathered around someone lying on the ground beside the burned out barn.

A woman's voice drifted to her hearing, "I daren't look. He fell through the rafters and landed on some sharp equipment. I think he's dead." Then responding to the question of another, "I believe it's Hope's friend."

Hope began to suffocate as the strangled shout of *E-d-r-i-c*! left her lips. No! Not Edric! Please God – not Edric! Please....

Faltering steps took her stumbling into the midst of the little gathering and there on the ground, blackened and hurting, lay her beloved friend of so many years – Gregory.

Amy was kneeling beside him. She had carefully covered his burns with the shirt one man had removed and handed to her but she was more concerned about Gregory's laboured breathing caused by the deep punctures in his back. With Hope's arrival she felt able to extricate herself from the role of professional nurse and step back to catch her breath, and weep. Edric received Amy into his arms, damp with nervous sweat, whilst Hope melted to her knees to whisper caring words to her friend.

Tired, singed eyelashes struggled open. The early trace of a smile twitched the corners of Gregory's mouth with the knowledge that Hope was there beside him but suffering resurfaced and his face twisted with the next spasm of pain. He drew her gentle words to him, allowing them to bring peace to his fiercely hot, taut face.

"I still love you. I always will," his words a mere whisper.

To prevent any further declarations drifting to the ears of others Hope pressed closer. "Yes – I know Greg. Hush now." Despite the heat in his blackened face she saw a single bulbous tear form in the corner of one eye. "And I've always loved you," she told him, adding silently, like the brother I never had. "Everything's going to be all right. You'll see." She urged him to stop trying to speak. "Close your eyes and rest a while. I'll be here when you wake."

Those were his words; the words he used one evening during her long struggle to come to terms with her father's death. She wondered if he remembered. When he closed his eyes Hope stood up to catch her breath.

Amy was on her knees again. She wanted to hold Gregory's hand but it was too badly damaged. Instead she laid her hand gently over his heart to let him know she was there.

With his eyes still shut he murmured, "I loved you from the first moment I saw you. I'll always love you."

Gregory never opened his eyes again. He died with all his neighbourhood friends around him, with the image of Hope's face before him and Amy's hand on his heart.

Gregory was gone! Unable to absorb the fact, Hope struggled from Edric's arms to stare in disbelief at her friend's still form. A surge of hysteria stole something from her in that dreadful moment of understanding. She seemed to lose everyone important to her: her mother, her father, her husband, even her unborn child – and now her friend. She looked up anxiously through her tears into the strained face of Charles and at Isabel, buried in Peter's embrace, and then into the caring face of her most recent love, Edric. The significance had been grasped, the lesson learned: to care too deeply is to run the risk of great hurt.

The innocent question put to Gregory some years back now framed itself in her mind – Where do you think we'll be in a few years from now? And once again she was relieved it was not in the scheme of things that one should know.

It was more than a week before Gregory's parents felt brave enough to go through their son's personal effects. When they did they discovered the bright, chatty letters Hope had written to their son were more obviously worn from frequent handling than those containing tender, caring endearments from his fiancée, but were sufficiently wise to keep this to themselves.

Chapter 25

Isabel forgot about her news and when she did remember, her engagement no longer seemed an appropriate thing to raise. In any event her forthcoming marriage was something she proposed to keep quiet until her employer's long-term plans became clear.

She owed much to Charles. Not only had he taken her niece under his wing, even securing her a job, he brought the two of them to the sanctuary of Tarnville. It was not in her nature to ignore this. If it had not been for Charles's disregard for convention their lives would have been immeasurably different.

It was no secret that Charles intended to settle in Corfu; it was only the timing that remained vague; the next episode depended on the success, or otherwise, of finding Christina. But maybe his advancing years would require the decision to be made sooner rather than later. Fortunately her fiancé understood her desire to ease her employer's declining years and she welcomed Peter's patience and absorption in the running of his farm. Until meeting her, his farm had been his life, if not his obsession, and he readily admitted to having more than enough to occupy him until the day she was free to become his wife and live at Broad Gates.

Six months after the fire, dream-like trances still stole Hope's attention and, like today, others watched her floating in and out of painful memories they did not share.

"Penny for them."

Daphne's caring tone drew Hope back from a warm spring day where she had been relaxing on a grassy mound, her ears pricked to the silvery tinkle of bells on Morris Dancers' gaiters and the bright chatter of friends. From all her memories of Gregory it was always this one that prevailed. It was with relief that she was tugged back now into the safety of her landlady's sitting room. A moment longer and she would have likely strayed beyond the glorious May Day sunshine into the ugly sequel that took place later to spoil her happiness, and forever after trespass upon her dreams, the expression in her uncle's face a lingering torment.

Hope sighed. "Oh – I was thinking how life's not always what we expect it to be. It's a bit like being lost and not knowing where we're headed. Sometimes it's a blessing that we don't." Pensive, she concluded, "And in some cases.... we don't even know where we've come from."

They had been discussing Edric's quest to discover something of his mother's early years, and Daphne assumed Hope referred to this now. "But he'll continue his search?"

But Hope's thoughts had moved on to the unwavering scrutiny of Charles and the questions his surveillance evoked. Her expression was one of profound confusion until her mind caught up. "Search? Oh – you mean Edric's search for his mother. Yes – I'm sure he will – though he doesn't gets much time with his job."

Despite his schedule, home or abroad, Edric made a point of ringing Hope every evening, often staying on the line an hour or more and sometimes, grabbing a moment between meetings, he would ring her at Manstonleigh to let her know he was thinking about her.

"As a matter of fact we're making enquiries this weekend when we go through to Tarnville." With a run of weekends spent in the glitzy bustle of the city, the promise of two days' quiet held some appeal, and Edric's keenness to discover something of his mother's origins presented an ideal opportunity to explore the villages around Mowlem. "I'm looking forward to it." It promised to be an idyllic two days, though her landlady's expression did not endorse this.

Daphne had welcomed Hope's decision to visit Tarnville less, and actively encouraged the idea of allowing the newly engaged couple some time alone. Having persuaded Edric to take advantage of her spare room in preference to spending weekends in the confines of his hotel suite, Daphne had come to enjoy her family weekends. A telephone line and fax machine had been installed for his ease of transition. The arrangement worked well, and Billy chatted to Edric in a way that he rarely did with others. This weekend would fall short in Daphne's eyes; she almost envied Isabel hers.

Isabel stood in the main hall, her arms outstretched. "Come here," she said, impatient to embrace them both.

"You.... and Edric here," Hope turned to beam at the one who had wrapped her in a borrowed sarong six months earlier, "Mowlem, Sir Charles and Tarnville – what more could a girl want!" She giggled like a schoolgirl within her aunt's tight embrace.

Edric looked on, displaying pleasure at the warmth of Isabel's greeting. Hope was learning to smile again. He had begun to wonder whether she would ever be able to return to Mowlem without being consumed by sadness. Their first visit after the fire had been crushing, memories of Gregory overshadowing all that they did. Feeling like an interloper he had floundered in his attempts to ease Hope's grief, and had been powerless to check her tears following Amy's announcement that she had decided to go into midwifery. That she should undertake this further training had been Gregory's wish, Amy said, her dark shining curls bobbing. Gregory's last words had been to tell her that he loved her. To Amy's mind, her further training in midwifery was as good a way as any to show that his love was steadfastly returned.

Hope had been inconsolable at this.

Now, Edric dropped their baggage to the floor as Hope vacated Isabel's arms and it was his turn.

Isabel's laughter rang out in the noble proportions of the hall. "What on earth's that jangling in your case Edric – the *Crown Jewels*?"

"Buttons," he explained, somewhat self-conscious at the admission to the unlikely inclusion amongst his packing. "Like I assume many women of her day, before discarding a garment my mother would cut off the buttons for use on others. Her box of buttons was one of the few things to survive the fire," he explained, instantly denying space to the memory scratching at his mind, and craving attention: the recollection of strong arms covered in glistening dark hair lowering him through a window to let him drop into the safe arms of another who waited far below.... and the exhaustion of disappointment when neither of his parents followed in response to his cries.

Attempting to disregard the ooze of sweat prickling his hairline he watched Isabel with her head aslant. "The practice probably isn't followed much now but in those days buttons were often handmade, some even hand-painted. I imagine many would stir the memory of a specific garment, in turn evoking the memory of some event." He

211

considered his words. There was a particular button that he thought of now, a symbol of one of his earliest memories: cuddled by his mother, a strand of her pretty fair hair touching his cheek as she nuzzled him fondly, nibbling his ear like a rabbit.

Isabel already knew the story of how Edric had lost his parents and was clearly affected by his admission. Then lightening the moment, for her own sake if not for the others, she chortled, "It's a good job you don't have to cart my collection of buttons around with you. You'd have a devil of a job!"

There and then in the middle of the hall Edric unzipped the soft leather case to take out a small metal box with an embossed design of lack-lustre tincture, the original enamel colourings having been lost forever; the stark evidence of the invasion of fire on his home – and his life.

It was the type of decorative tin that might contain favourite confectionery in a Christmas stocking. Childlike, Isabel removed the lid and explored the contents, the buttons spilling through her fingers, fluid and smooth, the sensation pleasurable. She admired the quality of some, the type that might be employed to create a feature rather than a mere fastening device. Few such buttons resided in her box.

Edric rummaged through the coloured disks until he found the one he sought. As though handling a precious stone he placed a mushroom-shaped button carefully in Isabel's palm. His eyes never left the navy button on which was painted a red rosebud. "I can remember sitting on my mother's lap, twiddling this button on her bodice. It's the earliest memory I have of her." His last was of her tear-stained face pressed against an almost opaque window, a smoke-streaked hand placed tightly across her mouth to silence her scream as she watched his father lower him carefully out of the small window through which only he could squeeze – then he dropped and never saw her again.

Isabel confessed to having memories in her box too: buttons from Hope's confirmation dress and the tiny ivory satin buttons from her own wedding gown.

Hope leaned between the two to extract a foreign body from amongst the buttons. Turning it over in her hands she examined the bare foot of a china ornament.

Edric became wistful. "It's always been there. Probably popped in for safe keeping until the piece could be repaired." He considered it briefly. The damaged ornament like everything else would have been lost in the fire. His mood lightened. "No – Isabel. These aren't the Crown jewels – they're my *family jewels*! Living out of a suitcase I can't take much personal stuff around with me but I always find a space in my packing for these."

How bizarre that the clashing elements of fire and water had irrevocably changed the lives of all three of them, Edric mused, reflecting on the tragic deaths of Hope's father and uncle by drowning and his parents in a house fire.

Just then the gentle tip-tap of a walking stick on the polished floor alerted them to Charles's presence. He had been there some time awaiting a pause in the conversation. He extended a warm welcome and reaffirmed their arrangement to have dinner together that evening.

Seated beside Edric at dinner Hope continued to wonder about the significance of Charles's continuing observation of her, but at that moment Clarice, whom Hope noticed had grown up considerably over the last few months, announced that there was a telephone call for Mr Colendon from a Miss Ballard.

When Edric returned to the dining room it was evident it had not been good news. Hope thought about his family in Corfu and reached for his hand. Briefly, he explained his father-in-law had suffered a heart attack and died, and his estranged wife sought assistance in making the necessary arrangements. In an apologetic tone he informed them that he would be curtailing his visit to leave for Kent in the morning.

That night Hope hardly slept. With his father-in-law and rival gone would the relationship between Edric and his wife be revived? Would the feelings he had once had for Hilary be rediscovered whereby they would be able to set aside past animosity?

The next morning in the driveway Hope placed a finger over Edric's lips to prevent any words of parting.

"Never say – *goodbye*." Stinging eyes stared up at him. "No matter what the circumstances, please never use that word."

Edric's nod signified his grasp that there had already been too many goodbyes in her life. In the comfort of Daphne's home she had permitted him to browse her journals. It was from those pages he had learned about her formative years and discovered those things about which she remained reluctant to speak.

One evening she noticed a quizzical expression enter his face with the discovery of ugly crosses gouged into several pages. Employing few words she explained the marks represented her father's death; her uncle's two attempts of rape; and the betrayal by her husband. Without needing to be told, Edric knew the fifth cross signified the date she lost her baby.

That same evening her entire life story poured forth like a surge of turbulent water bursting the unstable restraint of a dam fallen into disrepair, her only pause to wonder at her choice of words that seemed inadequate to convey the discovery of her husband in bed with a prostitute. Thereafter it had not been difficult for Edric to appreciate her consequent feelings of rejection or understand her withdrawal from his embraces. He had scooped her to him and told her he would allow no harm to come to her ever again. But that was not the antidote for a broken heart. Only time and a great deal of genuine love could provide that.

Now, Edric considered Hope, poised nervously beside his car to wave him off to Kent, but before he could say anything her next words surprised him.

"Even if you decide you no longer want to go on seeing me I never want to hear you say goodbye. I'd prefer you just to go without saying anything – not even offering an explanation."

"Sweetheart! I can't believe you just said that. Whatever reason could I have for not wanting to see you? To be honest I loathe our days of separation." He looked at her, the area around his eyes pleating with concern.

"Just promise you'll never say that word."

"I promise." Mystified, he drew her to him and held her close for the few moments she allowed. He smiled down at her. "You're a funny pudding! Why would I ever want to leave you?"

A lonely weekend stretched before Hope. She leaned over the bridge to gaze at the river, its surface torn by the assault of a brisk March wind. She turned to wave to Isabel at her window in the west wing before heading off towards the village.

Different curtains dressed the windows of Ivy Cottage. An elderly couple from Braefield lived there now. She knew no more than that. Had she still been considered a villager she would have known more, even down to which side their hair was parted. Perhaps she had become an outsider or perhaps more simply she had yet to catch up with current gossip.

These transient intrigues gave way to others, more poignant and pressing and each now jostled for attention. Once again she wondered what awaited Edric in Kent. Would Hilary seek a reconciliation of their marriage? Though she hated to admit it, Hilary *was* still his wife. Would Edric's caring nature allow her to assuage what had gone before, and conveniently forgetting past bitterness, carefully sweep the remains beneath a rug of falsehood?

It had promised to be such a wonderful weekend. They had planned to ask senior villagers whether they recalled someone with the name of Maggie Smith. But a telephone call had turned everything upside down with the result that she was alone.

Other uninvited thoughts also pressed in unchecked. Even now she was unable to get Richard Lurdmayne out of her mind – or more precisely the possibility of an entanglement between her mother and the then heir to Tarnville. If only Edric were here. If he were, there would be no room for these thoughts. Swept along by his humour she would be firmly settled in the arms of his personality, experiencing that unique, exquisite happiness that depended only upon his presence.

She had not purposely sought these feelings in which she delighted, though admitted now to being utterly lost to Edric, loving him with a passion whereby she felt no longer capable of cognitive thought. Lately she had had the sensation of being caught up in a current of such momentum she was alarmed by the passion it evoked. Even if she wished to fight against it she was already lost in a depth of helplessness. But now Edric was on his way to Kent – to be with Hilary.

With a determined effort Hope threw off all thoughts of Edric's wife and those of Richard Lurdmayne. She lengthened her stride.

Less than ten minutes later she was knocking on Hattie Middler's door and a moment after that seated with a cup of tea in one hand and in the other a slice of chocolate cake of such proportions it nearly filled her plate. The cake was not homemade Hope noticed; yet another sign that Hattie was slipping further from her former self.

Almost at once the old lady drew her visitor towards the gateway to her private world of confusion. "You'd better keep an eye on your animals if you've got any. Have you got any? I'm missing some. I seemed to have more cats when I got up. There're some funny folk knocking about. They're stealing all the cats. And the milk doesn't taste right. I don't know when they get in. I don't go out so they must come in when I'm asleep. You can't trust nobody. My other coat's gone. They'll have it." The anxious face gave way to smugness. "Serve 'em right if it doesn't fit!"

Hope was about to soothe her but Hattie's flight of illusory torment was already giving way to digressions.

"Are you warm enough? What day is it? Is it Sunday?"

"Saturday," supplied Hope with one eye on the old woman the other on the tortoiseshell cat poised ready to pounce on Bobby who dozed unsuspectingly with his silky head lolling in the hearth.

"And I thought it was Sunday. Are you warm enough?"

Hope ignored the repeat. "Hattie – you've lived in the village longer than most. Have you ever heard of a lady called Maggie Smith?"

"A.... lady?"

"She came from around these parts." Hope purposely kept her sentences short, a requirement of speaking with her mouth full, and in order not to confuse the old woman whose dementia had accelerated whereby she now required twice-daily assistance from a team of carers. "Yes, a lady called Maggie Smith."

Hattie returned to her tea as though withdrawing from the conversation through lack of interest, and Hope began to wish she had not made this her first call. She had just begun to think about cutting her visit short when a satisfied smile broadened behind the teacup.

"She could sing like an angel...."

216

With a sense of loss Hope wondered who Hattie was talking about now. She did not ask. The chances were the answer would be just as meaningless. She had just taken a bite of cake when Hattie finished her sentence.

"Maggie used to stop 'em dead!"

The delectable taste of chocolate was hastily swallowed. "*M-a-g-g-i-e Smith?*" An elderly head nodded on rounded shoulders. "Hattie – this is important. Where did you see this lady?"

"Lady? What lady are you on about?"

Conducting a conversation with Hattie could be hard work at the best of times but right now Hope felt like shaking her. "The lady called Maggie Smith – where did you see her?"

"Stillingford." Hattie's skeletal fingers played with the remains of her cake. Her eyes fixed on the resulting sticky mess she added, "Stillingford market. Maggie Smith always went to Stillingford market every Tuesday without fail."

This had to be the same woman. Hope was convinced of it but did not want to subject Edric to the same level of disappointment suffered by Sir Charles, but just as quickly she reasoned that the circumstances were different in that Edric was not seeking a living person.

Sensing she was on the verge of significance Hope went to sit at Hattie's feet on the peg hearth rug, which looked in need of a good shake. The Border collie obligingly moved up whilst Spice trustingly climbed on to her lap. Further questions bubbled from Hope's lips but flowed too fast and befuddled the elderly mind that struggled to comprehend.

Hattie's eyes lowered to study the collar on the cat purring on Hope's lap, then as though not recognising the collar began yanking at the blue elasticised band. "What day is it? Is it Sunday? Have you been busy? I s'pect you're tired. Will you have a nap this afternoon? I usually do. It'll be dark early tonight."

Hattie had passed through the gateway to that other world known only to her and Hope knew it useless to attempt to coax her back.

But perhaps on another day she would be able to accompany Hattie through the avenues of her mind and learn more about Maggie Smith, the lady from Stillingford – who sang like an angel!

Chapter 26

Isabel sent Hope to inform Charles that dinner was almost ready. Confident she knew where to find him Hope went straight to the library. The door was ajar. Charles was on the telephone. He appeared to be speaking to his friend and lawyer, Kevin Lester. Furthermore it seemed that she was the subject under discussion. Hope froze.

"Amazing I agree but there's no denying the strong resemblance." There was happiness in Charles's voice. "You're right Kevin and for the life of me I can't understand why it has taken me so long to realise." He paused to listen before responding, "Yes I am. Absolutely – though you must appreciate my joy is accompanied by sadness...." Charles swallowed his emotion before going on, "I regret it didn't dawn on me sooner, for like I said there was always something indefinable that craved my attention." Another pause, then, "I'm not sure. Possibly. I doubt my interest has gone unnoticed. I've seen bewilderment in Hope's eyes more than once – probably believing me deranged in my old age!" Short laughter then a longer pause, followed by, "Yes – truly amazing! I knew you'd be pleased. I still can't believe it's taken me so long to realise. The truth has been literally staring me in the face all this time! Yes – it is marvellous – now that I'm over the initial shock. I certainly hope so. That's right. Yes – your understanding is perfectly correct. So, there you have it – and the reason behind the changes I wish made to my Will."

An involuntary shudder ran the length of Hope's body. She had heard enough. Without even realising that she had done so, she knocked on the door. That hollow sound, ordinary in itself, reminded her of another: the knock on the door at Ivy Cottage on her 18th birthday, the prelude to news that would change the rest of her life. Why did she feel that history was repeating itself?

Despite his age Charles spun round with the agility of a dancer. On seeing Hope his expression softened. He gestured for her to approach. "Hope has joined me," his voice as warm as the smile that plumped his face. "No doubt come to tell me that dinner is ready." He acknowledged her nod of affirmation and then held the receiver towards her. "There's someone who would like a word with you. It's Kevin. He has something to tell you."

Panic stripped any remaining colour from Hope's face. A dry tongue explored the enamel of her teeth. She needed time to think and get things straight in her head but the moment did not afford that luxury. She knew what Kevin was going to tell her and even considered not taking the phone. She did not want to hear it – any of it – and certainly not like this; she needed time to prepare herself. Sir Charles was wrong. She was not Richard's child. Frederick Thackeray was her father! And Sir Charles should not be making changes to his Will. Instead of winding down the search he should be stepping up efforts to find his remaining child. She would be covered in shame if she became responsible for the cessation of that search and the transfer of his affections.

Survival reflexes kicked in and to steady herself Hope concentrated on her breathing, which no longer seemed an automatic process. Thoughts of what she had overhead would not leave her and her hand trembled as she took the telephone from Charles. "Hello Kevin."

Despite her turmoil Hope experienced joy on hearing the familiar voice. The well-articulated roundness of Kevin's words poignantly reminded her of the hours spent in his company whilst taking notes and for a few moments she revelled in the allure of the seductive world of commerce.

But now, suspended in silence, Hope listened to what her former boss had to say. It did not take long. At the conclusion she applied her playback style of which Kevin was reminded, "Three o'clock, your office on the 27th." She replaced the receiver.

Unaware of the confusion in which he had left Hope, Kevin Lester switched off the hands-free facility and returned his client's papers to their folder. He glanced at his watch. It was getting late. He swilled down the remaining finger of Scotch and replaced the glass on the low table where he had taken the call. His hand lingered with the recollection that Hope had introduced the piece to his room. She had been right, like she had about most things. She had an eye for detail. Very little missed her and he wondered whether she had picked up on what Charles was planning. Kevin had always hoped that things would turn out well for her. He took out his lighter, flicked it and lit a cigarette. If events continued on their present course it seemed likely that everything would eventually slip into place. A satisfied, smoke-filled sigh escaped him as he turned off the up-lighter and went to find his driver and prise him from his newspaper.

Hope was still grappling with emotions when Charles took her arm to escort her to the dining room. The subject of her parentage had not been broached, though she guessed that particular package would be delivered on the 27th. Instead she learned that her successor was leaving Lester's to marry her airman and take up residence in Henlow. Hope was invited, and Edric too if he could make it, to Angela's leaving party in the Board Room at the end of the month. Kevin particularly wanted to see her *as he had something to tell her*. Whatever it was evidently pleased him, for there had been a smile in his voice.

Hope adored Tarnville. She always had. She had loved the house right from her very first sighting at the age of five when she heard how the majestic stone structure had nurtured the surrounding area since the days when toil was punishing, the working day void of daylight and considerably longer, and blackened, weary bodies stomped along lanes crushed to the hardness of iron with the incessant passage of clogs. But the fact remained that she was a visitor at Tarnville. She should never be more than that. Christina, the rightful heir, was out there somewhere.

Charles sensed her musings. "It's regrettable that Edric's being called away has changed your plans for the weekend."

Gathering herself a little, Hope brightened her expression for this old man who apparently cared more deeply for her than she realised, and now applied his own logic for her quietness. There could be no admission of her eavesdropping, or a rejection of his generosity – not until after the 27th. After all, she might have got it wrong, though knew she had not.

They were about to take their places at the dining table with Isabel when Clarice, pink-faced and flustered, announced that there was a telephone call for Mrs Stratton from Mr Colendon. Charles threw Hope a look of I told you so. Dinner could be held back he told her and shooed her out of the door.

"Edric! I'm so pleased to hear your voice."

Was that anxiety or excitement that brought an unnatural pitch to her voice? "Sweetheart – it's good to hear you too. Everything all right?" a stupid question. Things were more likely to be normal at Tarnville than they were in Kent where things were very strange indeed.

Instead of being met by the deceased's daughter ravaged by grief he had been welcomed as though on a social visit. The sudden death of her father seemed not yet to have sunk in with Hilary. Treading as though through splintered glass he still waited for her loss to register and the flood barrier to rupture and release the flow of tears. Before he could ponder further, Hope's voice bubbled brightly over the distance between them.

"Everything's fine, but I miss you. I wish you were here and especially as I've uncovered news of your mother!" Proudly she led him through her conversation with Hattie, stepping round the bits about missing cats and coats and its getting dark early. "I know it's not much but I'm certain she was speaking about your mother."

When they eventually turned to the reason for his presence in Kent, Edric told her he would be taking a spell of leave to cover the funeral and preceding period. His next words sprang from that. "What do you say to our visiting Stillingford market this Tuesday? We could see whether anyone else remembers my mother." He knew it was a long shot but it presented an ideal excuse to break his uncomfortable stint in Kent. He quickly worked out that he could be back at Tarnville by Monday evening to spend the best part of three days with Hope before returning for the funeral and a meeting with the lawyers.

Hope was already counting the hours. There would be no problem in her taking time off from the Day Centre where her employment arrangements remained flexible, and she had no immediate photographic commitments.

Her involvement with the shampoo magnum had led to other things. Highly lucrative – Kevin Lester had made sure of that – often those further assignments came her way at short notice. She remained grateful to Phyllis Wilkinson for the accommodating nature of her post whereby she was able to slip in and out of her administrative role.

In recent months she had modelled bridal-wear, planted a tree, opened supermarkets and the like, and had a film shoot lined up for the following week when she was to do something spectacular wearing a well-known brand of jeans. Harry Nichols had yet to give her – and clear with Kevin – the finer detail of exactly what he meant by *spectacular* but she gathered it involved a stunt's person taking a tumble on her behalf down the escalator in a new shopping mall for her to emerge in the next frame looking distinctly ruffled, her shirt displaced and her hair for once in total disarray. The jeans however would appear as impeccable as they had before being introduced to the excitement on the escalator and inventive mind of Harry Nichols.

"It's a date!" confirmed Hope. "I'm sorry Edric – I don't wish to appear rude but Sir Charles is holding dinner for me and I ought to be getting back."

"Of course." He was about to say goodbye but remembered the promise extracted on his departure and said instead, "Take care my love. I'll rejoin you as soon as I can."

Happiness flooded her entire being but within the few seconds it took Edric to replace the receiver she heard an amiable voice informing him that his meal was ready. From the little she had learned about Hilary she was surprised by the pleasantness of the tone. Edric had been referred to as *my dear* and in that precise moment Hope forgot all about the telephone conversation she had overheard in the library, which was now of low priority.

Upon her return to the dining room Charles indicated they should take their seats, at the same time nodding to Clarice that she could begin serving.

Towards the end of the meal Charles prompted Hope to tell him about her day. "Tell me, did you bump into any of your friends?" He looked to his right in time to see the usual sparkle burst into Hope's face that so reminded him of Christina and yet still took him by surprise.

Hope relayed the events of her day, spotlighting the discovery that Hattie had known Maggie Smith. Isabel began asking questions but it was not until finishing their exchange that Hope noticed Charles had remained quiet. His eyes were on her, and like an explosion the memory of his telephone conversation with his lawyer returned in infinite detail.

She felt a compulsion to speak. "You're quiet," the words not casual but formed by a caring friend whose innermost feelings can be conveyed from within the framework of very few words. Charles apologised; he was *merely thinking*. Hope waited and was almost relieved when he did not elaborate. Suffering a loss of focus she remained astutely aware of the silent figure on her left as she listened to Isabel's suggestions for other possible lines of enquiry.

A commotion redirected the women's attention to the head of the table where Charles had upset his wineglass. Wine had saturated his place setting but mostly found its way to his person. Armed with her napkin, Isabel was instantly on her feet.

But Charles brushed her aside. It was unnecessary to make a fuss. Admitting to feeling tired he tossed his soiled napkin aside. Instead of going to change he would probably take the opportunity of having an early night, and excusing himself he left the room.

Isabel waited for the door to close behind him. "He's not been himself all day. I do hope he's not going down with something."

Hope knew that what her aunt had picked up on had nothing to do with his health.

After Isabel too turned in for the night Hope remained to gaze unseeingly out of the dining room windows. In daylight hours her gaze would have taken in the sunken rose garden where she had had her verbal exchange with Gregory, and when those memories too flooded back she decided the best escape was to follow the pattern of the others and retire to bed.

On the way to her room she heard a tapping noise coming from further along the corridor and drawing nearer detected that it was coming from Christina's bedroom. She paused at the door and strained to catch any hint of further sound. The noise started up again and then she knew. It was Charles. The regular tip-tap, staccato rhythm of his walking stick started again as he recommenced pacing up and down his daughter's room. Her hand went to grasp the bulbous doorknob but instantly fell away. Charles was beyond her reach. He was in the throws of letting Christina go in order to transfer his affections to another – the one he perceived to be his son's child. Guilt ridden Hope moved away.

Sleep did not come easily to her. Unbidden, jumbled pictures of her father, Gregory, and of a handsome couple who danced together, jostled for predominance. Hope plumped up her pillow. Her thoughts strayed to Edric with the accompanying realisation that she could not tell him about this latest development; at least not until details had been put to her officially. She plucked at the sheets, fervently wishing that none of this were happening and that she could go back to being Frederick Thackeray's daughter, an ordinary child from the village, with no hint of the possibility of her being Sir Charles Lurdmayne's granddaughter and consequently heir.

She slipped from her bed and sank to her knees. Choked by tears she concluded her prayers with a request that Frederick Thackeray – whether or not he were her real father – might be allowed to give her a sign to indicate whether Edric were the one to accompany her into whatever future the stepping-stones held in trust for her.

Chapter 27

Torn wisps of cloud marbled the bright March sky. The town of Stillingford spilled over with activity; it was market day. Hope and Edric had left the car in a side street and now amidst the bargain hunters they paused to take in the scene where canopies flapped in the wind and vendors chanted singsong details of the same wares that had changed hands there for more than a century. Almost anything from apples to zinc bathtubs could be purchased there, though the latter, no longer put to their original use, were now filled with early-flowering pansies, and in later months would overflow with busy-lizzies; having become much sought-after, the uninviting cold receptacles had found their way into cottage gardens.

"Now what?" asked Edric.

"Start asking around, I guess." Her actions less hesitant then her words, Hope tugged Edric towards the outer edge of the marketplace where a line of stalls hugged the wall like a legion of limpets.

The pattern of old repeating itself, some of the townspeople stopped what they were doing to focus on Hope. It had been like this ever since she was young and trailed the wake of the man who remained the foundation of her life. Having once alighted on her, eyes would linger to luxuriate in the depth of something rarely seen away from the large screen or covers of quality magazines, leaving the observer with a sense of overwhelming appreciation; a fact that went unnoticed by the subject, who displayed no comprehension at all of the spectacle she presented, and from which others took pleasure.

Yet, as Edric had already identified, Hope's real beauty lay not in her appearance but in the unfading loveliness of her inner self. It was her modesty and heart-warming comportment that had consolidated his first attraction. In addition to not being affected by her own person, she was one of few women who managed to attain a sense of normality in his company. In the past others had gushed on learning his position within the Shillens organisation where he had only to step outside an hotel to find a chauffeur-driven car at his disposal. Though this morning his attention was on other matters, his mother's early years in particular.

225

After a fruitless hour of trawling the marketplace Edric's eyes strayed to the low-roofed inn at the far end of the square where he suggested they might have lunch.

Hope's fingers went to part the curtain of hair that a sudden gust of wind had whipped across her face. Skilful fingers inserted three loose plaits before tossing her abundant mane neatly behind her. "You have all the best ideas," she grinned, her face upturned to receive Edric's kiss.

They breathed in the odour of wood smoke and stale cigarettes that clung to the fabrics of the interior and did not notice the woman who followed them into The Fleece Inn, the same establishment Frederick Thackeray had frequented many years previous. They ordered hot beef sandwiches with a bowl of chips to share. The woman, nervous in her movements, deliberately selected a seat nearby where the lighting was poor.

Edric stifled a yawn, the aftermath of a series of bad nights. "Well – so far nobody's even heard of Maggie Smith." He wiped his fingers on a serviette. "I didn't expect any great revelations. Nevertheless I had hoped that we might learn something." He leaned across the small round table that rocked on the uneven stone-flagged floor; his voice dissolved to a whisper. "It's usually the men who can't take their eyes off you – particularly Sir Charles." The warm smudge of pink in her cheeks amused him. "I do believe you're blushing!" His amusement dissipated when Hope did not smile quite so readily as she had when they first laughed together about the old man's observation.

He began again. "You seem to have the attention of the nice-looking woman in the shadows to my left. A friend of yours....?" Edric shifted his eyes towards the lone figure. "Smart dark outfit, somewhere in her mid- to late-fifties." He watched Hope glance matter-of-factly at the table over by the wall and then swiftly avert her eyes.

"She saw me looking and smiled!"

"Well smile back – it's only polite."

Before Hope's foot could locate a shin beneath the table the woman had come to stand hesitantly beside them.

"Please excuse my staring just now.... but is your name Hope Thackeray?"

Hope nodded. So that was it – the woman had picked up on her association with the S-L advertisements, or one of her other assignments.

However Edric noticed the woman used Hope's maiden name, not Stratton, thereby closing the door on that assumption. He prickled to alertness, whilst Hope waited in the expectation of the woman's search for a scrap of paper for the purpose of obtaining an autograph.

But there was no such movement from the woman who stood beside them in questioning uncertainty. The light that strayed grudgingly from a nearby window modified what seemed to be a birthmark or scarring along her jaw line, lessening its trespass but the smile that leapt to prominence softened its imprint almost to the point of eliminating its existence. Her intense gaze continued to concentrate on Hope.

"I was certain it was you the moment I set eyes on you. Even after all these years you're still just like your picture...." The woman's words ceased abruptly. "I'm sorry. This must seem rude.... I should explain. I first noticed you out there – enquiring about a friend of yours." With her eyes still fixed on Hope she jerked her head in the general direction of a window.

"You know something about my mother?" It was Edric. His seat scraped the uneven stone floor as he vacated it with the insistence that she should join them. He grabbed himself a stool from the next table, almost upturning another in the process.

"Your mother? No.....no, I'm sorry." The woman's eyes lingered on the disappointed face before transferring to his companion. "Hope," she said gently, "I knew your father." She waited for the words to sink in. "I was his landlady. Fred had rooms with me during the week."

Fred? A handful of close friends had called her father Freddie but mostly he had been known as Frederick. The abbreviated name indicated that this woman had been more than just his landlady; something else told her that it was all right and she should not mind. The woman was speaking again, but Hope remained dazed and those further words were slow to reach her hearing.

"I knew it was you the moment I saw you. Even though you've grown up you're exactly like your picture!"

It ensued that Christine, as the woman eventually introduced herself, owned one of Frederick Thackeray's oil paintings: a picture of Hope similar to the one in Isabel's possession, though produced later, born out by the inclusion of ten stepping-stones in the riverbed.

Only after waving goodbye to Christine from the prestigious car, that had looked so out of place all afternoon outside the row of humble cottages, did Hope begin to experience her first realisations of awareness.

Full of apology she turned to Edric. "I'm so sorry," she said quickly, her cheeks burning. "I can't believe we became so side-tracked we ended up discovering things about my father when we came here specifically to enquire about your mother. I'm really sorry – I seem to have monopolised the entire day."

"If you monopolise my entire life you'll hear no complaint." Edric took her hand until a bend in the road demanded the presence of both hands on the wheel.

Hope was quiet throughout the drive back to Tarnville and was grateful that Edric seemed to understand and made no attempt to enter her thoughts. Her mind was on the painting stowed in the boot, and like the incessant repetition of a dripping tap she kept going over all that she had learned that afternoon. The fact that hitherto she had known none of it was only now beginning to strike within her a cord of amazement.

That evening when Edric had retired for the night, Hope went to sit beside Isabel to revisit the subject of Christine, and the painting that now hung with the rest of Isabel's art collection, which in recent months had increased with those produced from holiday photographs; the one of The Old Man's Bar remained Edric's favourite.

"Yes, I knew about her," admitted Isabel. She took Hope's hand, her voice purposely filled with reassurance. She glanced up at the newly acquired painting. "It was nice of her to give it to you. I'm sure she treasured it." Then, "Freddie told me about her. I met her once, and again briefly at his funeral. It was clear he cared deeply about her and yes...." Isabel confessed, with the knowledge that her niece longed

228

to ask the question, "they lived together as man and wife though he told me once that no one could ever replace Faith."

Hope inclined her head slowly as she struggled to take this in, and once more felt herself spirited back to the neat little room where she had been startled to discover a framed photograph of her father. The sight of his twinkling eyes smiling at her from a stranger's sideboard had shocked her, and possessively her eyes had scanned the room for others.

"Bell – I hardly dare ask.... but were there any children?"

Isabel shook her head. "No pet, and Christine was a widow when Freddie took rooms with her." She longed to temper the blow. "You must realise something. Your mother had been gone a long time. Your father was a handsome man – with natural urges. You shouldn't judge him." She sighed. "I think in the early years he chose not to mention that other part of his life for fear it might cloud the images he helped you create of your mother. And as the years crept by I suppose it simply became easier not to tell you. You shouldn't look at it as some sort of secret purposely kept from you. I imagine he worried that you might feel pushed out. I believe it was that, and the enduring memory of your mother, that prevented him from remarrying. You see – Freddie and your mother had something special. You only had to see the two of them together to realise that. And you pet, came out of that special union."

But had she? If only she could be sure. Hope turned away on the pretext of studying the newest acquisition to Isabel's wall but could not see beyond the formation of her tears.

Hope and Edric planned to visit Hattie Middler the following weekend. Hope was sure that beneath the old woman's confusion lay further clues relating to Edric's mother. However those well-laid plans were scuttled immediately upon their arrival at Tarnville when Harry Nichols telephoned with details of a major film shoot for Hope. The finer points had already been laboriously gone through with Kevin Lester, he informed her, before disclosing the high-profile name of the magazine which was hosting the assignment.

Hope discussed the proposal with Edric who made no attempt to conceal his astonishment at the amount of money involved.

Edric wanted to drive Hope himself but she overcame his protests and persuaded him to see her safely on to the 20:35 train that Harry Nichols would join in Leeds. After watching the train depart Braefield station Edric returned to Tarnville with the prospect of spending a lonely weekend in much the same way as he now appreciated Hope had when he had been called away.

The following morning Charles invited Edric to join him on a tour of those areas of Tarnville that remained unfamiliar to him. In his role of assessing premises to determine their suitability for adoption into the Shillens chain Edric had developed a discerning eye and keen appreciation of fine properties. With an undeniable purity of design Tarnville was certainly a fine property and Charles's suggestion was like grain to the threshing floor.

He already leaned affectionately towards the sprawling, comfortable home of his host and welcomed this timely diversion, at the same time applauding the opportunity to explore more of the beautiful interior with its fine collection of paintings, handsome fireplaces and the like, and wander corridors that echoed with the whisper of unseen footsteps. His eyes swept detail after detail, room after room; the whole proclaiming, albeit mannerly, a certain stateliness within its unstudied grandeur where fine antiques and Victorian silver put in regular appearances throughout the rooms.

Throughout the morning Edric enthused with genuine appreciation and when he admired the Queen Anne bureau in the library he surprised Charles by his ability to detect the presence of a concealed drawer. After first seeking permission he removed one of the smaller drawers and then placing his hand beneath he caught the hollow container that dropped into his palm.

Amazed, Charles brought together his hands, clumsy with the unrelenting progression of arthritis. "Well I never! I'd forgotten all about its existence."

"My party piece." Edric said simply and afterwards admitted, "My cousin has a bureau just like it though not as grand. Claire's is a reproduction, but an exceptionally good one. You may recall it?"

A vague recollection of the piece did come to mind but before Charles had time to grasp the splinter of memory Edric was handing him something. A folded sheet of paper, yellowed with age, had been wedged into the base of the compartment.

The folds split in places as Charles unfurled the brittle paper to reveal a note written in ink now rusted in colour, which transported him to a scene that had taken place many years ago when, like a little bit of theatre, his daughter, defiant and shouting, had declared her feelings of love. The unfamiliar penned hand set out words that reciprocated that avowal and stirred recollections of those that had burdened his memory for a quarter of a century.

"PRIVATE & CONFIDENTIAL. Christina, I love you."

There was no signature but Charles was in no doubt as to the author of the declaration slipped to his daughter surreptitiously to avoid parental observation. He felt an obligation to explain. "It's a note to my daughter.... written a long time ago by the young man she ran off with."

Respecting his privacy Edric's eyes did not stray to the contents of the note as he retrieved it from limp fingers to return it to its hiding place, to be revisited during a more private moment.

Edric was surprised when Charles seemed rejuvenated by the discovery and drawn towards speaking about his daughter; surprised and pleased. Their conversation moved on to cover all manner or things from antique furniture and Charles's passion for horses, to the general running of the Estate. Edric was in his element and under Charles's directorship and keenness to introduce him to every corner of Tarnville he gleaned much during those pleasurable hours.

As they wandered through the rooms Edric's attention would be directed towards a particular painting or article with the enhancement of some fascinating background information or enthralling tale. He was even shown the chip in Christina's bedroom fireplace where she had hurled a toy in temper when her mother had tried to persuade her daughter out of her tantrum and into a dress not to her liking. This previously unknown willingness to speak about Christina was unexpected. It was as though a door had been opened that allowed his memories the freedom of the spoken word.

What had started out as a short, pleasurable exercise likely to last no more than a couple of hours ended up claiming the entire day.

Isabel came across them whilst going about her duties but they were so engrossed they barely noticed her. A short time later she joined in with Cook's belly laughter when, having already received a similar request for a buffet luncheon, they were asked for an evening buffet to be laid out in the same, informal room that led off from the main dining room.

When entertaining an intimate friend or associate it was not unusual for Charles to forgo formalities and elect to dine in one of the smaller rooms when he would favour a buffet whereby he and his guest could help themselves and eliminate the need for interruptions.

That same evening, Edric came to Isabel's sitting room.

"You look tired," said Isabel. "I think Sir Charles has worn you out – but it's a lovely old place isn't it?" Her true feelings evident in her voice, she tossed aside her book. A smile twitched across her face whilst awaiting the response that did not come. She tried to read his expression. "That was fatal," she chirped on. "Now I bet you're more convinced than ever that Tarnville would make a marvellous hotel."

"It would – but Tarnville isn't for sale."

Isabel relaxed her shoulders. She was about to say that the metamorphosis of Tarnville to that of an hotel should never have been considered, when the telephone rang. She took up the receiver only to suffer disappointment that it was not her niece. Her expression changed. She held the receiver from her. "It's for you. It's Hilary."

Disbelief, quickly followed by annoyance flickered across Edric's face. Irritated that his secretary had seen fit to give out the number he took the telephone from Isabel in time to catch a tumble of words seeking advice on the purchase of a new car.

Whilst inwardly convinced that a vehicle from the *Three-Series* would be more than adequate for his wife's needs, he answered questions put to him about the *Five-Series*, and t hen wishing to wind up the conversation he promised better particulars would follow from his Transport Manager. Hilary seemed satisfied with this and rang off leaving him to ponder the real reason for the call, for it certainly was not about the proposed purchase of a BMW.

Albeit the circumstances of his visit to Kent had been far from conducive he had informed Hilary of his intension to seek a divorce and she had promised to mull it over. He wondered whether that was the reason for the call but at the last moment she had decided against it and to leave it a while, giving one last show of having the upper hand and the ability to make him sweat a little longer.

The revival of his wish to apply for a divorce had presented itself as long ago as the latter part of his holiday in Corfu when he recognised that whether or not Hope might be persuaded to entrust herself entirely into his safekeeping it was she who held the key to his future happiness. Hope was the best reason he could think of for his wishing to be free of Hilary. Hilary would likely make a great song and dance about it, that was the very nature of Hilary, but he had no reason to believe that she would prove to be a real stumbling block, particularly as he held the Ace; maybe that was at the root of the call.

By now her solicitor would have pointed out the grey area brought about by Dadda's death, and no doubt she now wished the formalities had been finalised years ago. Certainly he wanted no portion whatsoever of Hilary's inheritance; the very idea would stick in his craw. Nevertheless he was able to guess the outline of the advice she would have been given.

Isabel looked questioningly at his unfathomable expression. Finally giving up she suggested a walk before they turned in for the night.

Edric's mood changed. He agreed that some fresh air would benefit them both.

They had only strolled as far as the copse beyond the stables when the weather closed in. Thunder reverberated above their heads, swiftly followed by splinters of lightning. The sudden downpour drenched Isabel and Edric. They ran for cover. In the relative safety of the courtyard Isabel, panting for breath, expressed relief that Hope had been called away and spared the ordeal. When Edric looked puzzled she explained that ever since her 18th birthday her niece had associated thunder with the storm that had contributed to her father's death.

Edric could identity with Hope's emotions; for him it would always be the repugnant smell of smoke.

Chapter 28

After the excitement of two film shoots the remainder of Hope's week verged on anticlimactic and for the first time her duties at Manstonleigh felt tedious and burdensome. Edric's telephone calls helped but only went a small way towards supplying a few happy moments to each long day.

Edric rang off. Hope stared at the telephone in Daphne's kitchen. Her expression of desolation brought a pause to Daphne's activity of unpacking her shopping for Billy to put away.

"Problem?"

"It's Edric. He's got to go back to Kent…..to tie up more loose ends…..he'll ring me," the brevity of her words underlining her despondency. Despite her resentment of their hours of separation Hope had become acclimatised, but the knowledge that Edric was returning to Kent – moreover to be with his wife – was a completely different scenario. She imagined Hilary to be stunningly beautiful, greatly accomplished and infinitely more worldly than she was, attributes which surely no man could fail to appreciate.

"Never mind. What's one weekend?"

Hope almost snapped when she informed Daphne that she had barely seen Edric in the past few weeks. The realisation challenged her former feelings of gratitude that Harry Nichols had taken the trouble to track her down and whisk her off on an elite assignment, though thoughts of the resultant cheque brought her emotions full circle. She remained astonished that anyone should pay that sort of money for a few moments in front of a camera. Her father would have thought the same. He would have laughed with that big, distinctive laugh of his and exclaimed that they were "proper daft and not reet in t'head!" – but at the same time he would have been immensely proud.

"Loose ends – from what I know of Edric that's probably putting it mildly. Particularly when you consider the size of the estate he's dealing with. But once it's finished you'll have his undivided attention and all the weekends you could possibly want." Daphne turned to wink somewhat obviously at Billy before reaching to nudge their crest-fallen companion. "What do you both say to a proper fish and chips supper from up the road? It's been ages since we did that. Then you...." Daphne broke off to prompt her son who was deliberating over a bulging, brown paper bag in his hand. "Tomatoes.... in the fridge love, that's right, in the salad tray at the bottom.... " Amending her look from one of patient encouragement she beamed back at Hope, "And then you young lady can tell us exactly what you got up to in the early hours of the other morning over in Lancashire on that blessed escalator!"

Billy squealed agreement and Hope allowed herself a miniature smile at Daphne's belief that fish and chips might compare favourably with a weekend with Edric.

"And as for Edric," Daphne went on, "you'll be seeing him at your friend's leaving party next week."

Hope had almost forgotten about that, but before her emotions quite achieved cheerfulness she suffered the return of a familiar queasiness in the pit of her stomach. She had yet to learn what Kevin Lester planned to tell her. Though now, adjusting to Daphne's mood, she chose to believe that with Angela's departure from the firm Kevin might have it in mind to extend an invitation to return to his workforce. Yes, of course, that would be it. She wondered why she had not thought of that before. For the moment she refused to believe that it might be anything else. She was not prepared to think along other lines – unless she had to.

She had intended saying nothing about the telephone conversation overheard at Tarnville but after much deliberation she had eventually come down on the side of confiding in Edric. Edric was practical; he was level headed; he had to be to cope with the demands of his job. He would be able to advise how to avoid offending her aged friend who had been there for her ever since her father died. With that, the same loop of confusion caught up with her once more and she succumbed to the treadmill of previous anguish.

True to his word and as regular as clockwork Edric rang Hope each evening, often surprising her with others in between. He made just such a call from his hotel room on the evening prior to Angela's leaving party and had only just hung up when the telephone rang. It was Hilary, having tracked his whereabouts to Scotland through his secretary. Without preamble she confirmed her agreement to a divorce. He knew she would – after the expected protracted silence designed to imply that either she was considering the matter in infinite detail or the matter was of such little importance it did not warrant immediate attention.

The instant she rang off Edric wanted to take Hope in his arms and give her the news but the closest he could get was the weak embrace of a telephone call.

Without first planning what he might say he dialled the number a second time but then decided it would be better to speak to Hope in person when he could see her face to face and read her mind. Now he was faced with offering an appropriate excuse for having rung twice within a matter of minutes.

Perceiving her surprise Edric stifled youthful joy. It was vital he did not divulge even the merest hint of his news; nothing must be allowed to detract from the announcement he would make tomorrow, the prelude to the question he longed to put to Hope.

"No – there's nothing wrong." Quite the opposite, he thought and now went on quickly, "I've been laid on my bed thinking – about you of course – and other things. You know I mentioned some time back that one day I might develop a side-line, set up a board of executives to run my own investment company, eventually diversifying into opening a property portfolio? I've been meaning to mention that I've already identified a good builder – one with no capital. His workmanship is sound – first class in fact. He has the building expertise whereas I would provide the financial backing. You'll agree that's a good combination. I got talking to him when I was in Kent." It had occurred to him to tell her at the time but his mind had been taken up with the preparation of his latest Board presentation. "I have to admit that the chance meeting has encouraged me to think more seriously about the feasibility of such a venture." In the classroom Edric had excelled at business studies and by the age of 17 he knew he wanted to be a businessman.

Hope made all the right noises but could not help wondering whether this might mean Edric's putting down roots, permanently or otherwise, in Kent, where he would be uncomfortably near Hilary, and she was not sorry when this particular line of conversation dried up.

Pushing her mind towards other concerns she said, "Actually Edric, I'm glad you rang back. There's something I need to talk to you about but I think it would be better to chat it through when I see you. I need your advice. I almost raised the subject the first time you rang but something in your voice told me your day had been difficult and had taken something out of you."

Deliberately controlling his voice he said, "And I've got something to tell you, but likewise it's not something you should be told over the phone." Sensing her curiosity reaching out to him over the distance he wondered how long he could keep the excitement from his voice. A boyish grin creased his face. He was already pondering whether Hope would prefer to choose her own engagement ring – for he was certain of her answer – or whether the occasion might be further enhanced with the production of a ring of his own choosing at the time of his proposal. A pleasant giggle caressed his hearing as Hope tried to prise further detail from him.

He concentrated on repressing his excitement and preventing it from exploding into a verbal confession. "No, I'm afraid I can't tell you now." Calmly, as though having undergone endless rehearsals to perfect this previously unknown bland tone he said emphatically, "It wouldn't be right. It's something I should tell you in person." Amazed at himself he drew his bottom lip between his teeth and almost had to clamp a hand across his mouth to prevent an escape of mirth. He had never felt so blissfully happy but then he had never been just one step away from the certain promise of a lifetime of happiness. Knowing he could not keep up this pretence he strove to wind up their conversation and assured her that he would explain everything when he saw her at Lester's the following day.

Finally allowing happiness to paint a grin on his face Edric replaced the receiver. He glanced at the travel clock beside the bed where he had lolled comfortably to make the call. If he went to the shopping mall in the basement he might just catch Henderson before he locked up for the night, and without further delay he sprang to his feet.

Five minutes later he was inside Nugget; had already sworn Henderson, the manager, to absolute secrecy, and had displayed in front of him some of the establishment's finest engagement rings.

Back in Leeds during those same minutes the smile had already slipped from Hope's face to make way for the thoughtful furrow that practically gave voice to her impassioned emotions.

Something was wrong. That much was certain. In the past she had been able to rely on the round cadence of Edric's voice to soothe her. He had a delicious, smiling voice – a complete contrast to the stilted monotoned inflection of a few moments ago. Additionally he had made no mention of Hilary in either call, or indeed anything about his progression with the *loose ends* he referred to earlier in the week. Intuitively she sensed that Hilary was behind the change. She considered ringing back but was in no mood to tease the number from Allison Ballard.

Despite an abhorrence to believe it, the reason for the change suddenly became clear: Edric was preparing to break off their relationship in order to return to his wife! As though to add further amplification to this burst of intuition she remembered learning that Hilary had rung him at Tarnville during her absence. At the time she had merely thought it odd that he made no mention of it himself. Now she knew why and with that realisation all the colour, excitement and promise drained from her to leave behind nothing but drabness and unimaginable boredom.

A newspaper was opened, the pages turned, the crossword considered. Concentration was impossible. Finally excusing herself she left Daphne and her son to watch television and retired to the privacy of her room to think and dream of what might have been, but now never would be if her conjecture were correct.

Later, when she was almost in the arms of sleep she was tugged back to wakefulness by the recollection of her prayer that Frederick Thackeray, whether or not he were her real father, might give her a sign to indicate whether Edric were the one to take her into whatever the future held in trust. There had been no sign. She no longer expected one. She rolled over to face the wall and count the flowers on the wallpaper.

With an exquisite diamond solitaire engagement ring nestling in its leather box in his jacket pocket Edric made his way back to his hotel room.

Only now did he realise how weary he was. It had been a tiring day. The mood of the afternoon's meeting had caused his agenda item to drag on longer than scheduled. In an attempt to ascertain the way the vote was likely to go he had glanced around the table during his presentation but the faces of his fellow Board Members showed little beyond their discomfort resulting from the air conditioning that was playing up again. The Leeds Shillens had experienced a similar problem and a note had been made in the broad margin of his agenda to check whether it was the same contractor or a mere coincidence.

In the end the vote had not come down entirely in his favour. Nevertheless his detailed proposal had not been thrown out completely and, as he told Samuel Shillens later, he was confident that after a little fine-tuning he would eventually obtain full Board approval. The expression in Samuel's eyes and slight nod of his greying head told Edric what he wanted to know; his elaborate scheme, which was unlikely to be surpassed and promised the continuance of a sound position for the Shillens organisation in the international market place, already had the Chairman's approval. All he had to do now was go back to the market researchers; revamp the presentation package; get more out of the planners....

Revitalised, Edric's thought pattern ran on. His own brainchild, it was a project he had worked hard on. He had kept late hours, and the detail on a *need-to-know-only* basis, coupling that with the signing of carefully worded secrecy clauses. It was something he believed in and only rarely had he allowed his mind to stray from the components of the scheme.

Despite the ongoing stimulus derived from the formula apparent for its success, surprisingly his thoughts now happily transferred to the bulge in his jacket pocket that represented something infinitely more important. He opened the small, leather box and for a long moment admired the fine diamond again before placing the box at the back of his room safe.

Minutes later, in the steamy atmosphere of his hotel bathroom, he slid into the welcoming warmth of deep, sudsy bath water. Warm, fragrant suds crept up over his torso to swirl elaborate patterns in the dark hair on his chest as he switched off and began to rehearse what he would say to Hope.

He allowed the warmth to ease away the tensions of his day until the enactment of tomorrow presented imagery on the methodical stage within his head. At the conclusion of a somewhat moving Act, when Hope responded with a resounding *Yes*, he wanted to be the first in the audience to rise to his feet and applaud wildly.

Reluctantly, Edric withdrew from his reverie. He had only just taken up the bar of *Imperial Leather* when his nostrils flared with the compulsive reflex caused by the obnoxious odour that for several minutes had been teasing his subconscious mind, daring his senses to face the declaration. He had hardly begun to lather the soap briskly in his hands when it hit him what he had smelt during the past minutes – *smoke*!

His eyes swept the ample proportions of the bathroom to the door behind him from beneath which long curls of pale, grey smoke were stealthily invading the room. A thick fog already obscured the far end of the sharp, Grecian-style gold and white décor. The nightmare that had haunted him since childhood had once again become reality – FIRE! The newest in the chain, the Edinburgh Shillens, was on fire!

Edric's mind began to race. The urgent need to place wet towels at the foot of the door brought him splashing to his feet but in his effort he slipped and fell backwards into the large corner-shaped bath. He fell awkwardly, his spine engaging cruelly with the elaborate tap arrangement, and a sickening pain shuddered the length of his body to stab the soles of his feet.

Irrationally his mind filled with an agenda item from a meeting some months back that highlighted the need to readdress the Group's current emergency drill; the wording conjured to his eyes plagued him.

Analysts had provided projected calculations for a normal, simple flow of people making an exit from a building, going on to show how those same figures might change with the introduction of elements such as panic, unknown layouts with unfamiliar exits and perhaps smoke inhalation. The findings, supported by two independent expert witnesses, held the attention of the entire body of the meeting. He and his colleagues had been shocked by the substantiating data that showed in the event of an emergency the likely expected sequence of activity would follow a pattern not unlike a script.

Despite a presence of danger, individuals, unable to alter their scripts, would continue to focus on their habitual work pattern whereby regular routes became locked into their usual routine, making it hard for them to break free and perhaps take a different path. Still more data proved that programmed, habitual routines and movements of staff would likely take employees like lemmings towards their normal points of exit with an almost disregard to other, safer escape routes. The recommendations had been unanimously accepted, amongst which the requirement for staff to switch tasks on a regular basis, thereby encouraging a change in their scripts to facilitate ease in deviating from their usual patterns of behaviour.

Had that recommendation been implemented? Whose responsibility had it been to ensure that it was? Were staff and guests at this moment progressing in a steady, swift passage to safety? *Was Hope with them?*

Edric's mind had become befuddled; all cognitive thought had left him. He began to cough painfully whilst lungs laboured to expand in his unbearably tight chest. More pain.... then nothing.

Edric felt himself being lifted up high to be squeezed painfully through a small window far above him through which only he could pass. The larger window directly below would not yield; layers of paint clumsily applied by the previous owner had sealed it fast forever. Strong arms began lowering him through the opening. Rigid with terror he peered back through the glazing, now partially opaque, at the beautiful tear-stained face of his mother who stood weeping behind his father. The choking smoke they had awoken to find filling their home had streaked her short, pale hair. His father continued to hold him painfully by his forearms for a few seconds longer – but then the moment was gone – and he felt himself falling, tearing his knees on the brickwork as he tumbled to the safety of cooler arms waiting far below. Then.....nothing.

Chapter 29

Hope entered Lester's impressive entrance hall and glanced about her. Her nervousness threw her off balance and she was reminded of childhood games when friends had dared each other to venture into the graveyard after dusk. Her unease rudely pointed out she no longer formed part of Kevin Lester's workforce and accordingly relinquished all previous feelings of belonging. Fortunately the emotion was short-lived and vanished altogether when her eyes fell on familiar faces gathered there.

A young man from the Conveyancing Department was the first to notice her arrival. He strode predatorily towards her, his little group observing his actions, overtly wishing they had taken the same initiative.

"I'm well thank you," Hope responded to the ginger-haired fellow's enquiry, whose smile danced in a polished face that did not look old enough to have discovered the daily chore of shaving. Something strayed across his freckled face that hinted at worldliness and did not sit comfortably with his youth. Enlightenment warned Hope from allowing him to steer her into deeper discussion when he made clumsy attempts to manipulate the conversation towards personal levels, her photographic work in particular. Her smile intact, she gave a single nod that managed to convey her disinclination to being drawn into a discussion about herself.

Since the camera's discovery of her she in turn had uncovered an element of the human race that made a practice of attaching themselves to stick like glue at functions. At best it could be amusing, at worst embarrassing, though this shiny-faced young man in a gush of youthful vanity was unlikely to prove problematic with his blatant efforts at seduction.

Her initial nervousness gone she was firmly back in control. Carefully stage-managing any gestures she might unwittingly display she took a measured step backwards and reclaimed her personal space. Though his name eluded her she recalled her husband had worked in the same office, and she wondered what her ex-colleagues knew about that part of her life, the part she had almost managed to forget, though not quite. Just then the shriek of a familiar voice rang out in the elevated marble interior.

"Hope!" Looking amazing in a dark-green, figure-hugging dress Angela flung herself into Hope's arms almost toppling the youth sideways with her propulsion. "I was worried you weren't going to make it!"

Hope drew back to focus on the beaming face. "Absolutely nothing would have prevented my coming." She leaned into the faithful arms of the friend who had been her rock throughout her troubled marriage. Hope put a high value on genuine friendship and cherished that of Angela. Without the need to declare it, each knew there was nothing one would not do for the other. Whilst she may have fallen short with regards some of her relationships, not least her uncle and husband, she had been dealt more than a fair hand of friends.

The carefully contrived moment eroded by the interruption, the young conveyancer shifted his weight to the other foot and moved off with a jaunty strut. Feigning indifference he headed back towards his little group to face inevitable witticism but noticing a solitary figure by the staircase he pivoted smarty to take himself smiling sweetly to the side of the slender new acquisition to the typing pool.

Angela looked enquiringly at Hope. "Edric not with you?"

"He's been in Scotland all week. He's flying down. In fact...." Hope glanced at her watch, "he should be landing about now." Despite a growing anxiety relating to the news Edric's had for her, a spontaneous cartwheel of excitement cavorted across her stomach.

"Just for me....?" teased Angela, "or could it be he's got a hot date with some other lucky chick?"

Hope's embrace tightened. "Mmm – something like that." She trusted she was still smiling.

Speeches and a presentation were given in the Board Room and Kevin Lester, skilled at speaking, gave an enlivened address heavily punctuated with humour, the style of which an eye opener for his newer recruits. Throughout this period Hope's eyes kept straying to the ornate clock – a gift from a grateful client – on the inlaid-cabinet over by the door, sensing that with each passing moment she came nearer to hearing that which apparently she could not be told on the telephone.

Edric's flight details were drawn from memory. He was overdue, even allowing for a delay and an extraordinary mass exodus of late-afternoon traffic further aggravated by those attempting to extend the weekend by any minutes they could cream off the working week. She could not help pondering the cause for the lateness of the slave to punctuality. Perhaps he had been met with an obstacle of delay when he dropped his bag off at the Leeds Shillens. Retaining the base for the storage of his things laid him open to the availability of staff and their related problems. Hope held that that availability was frequently abused, and was surprised Allison Ballard was not more conscientious in shielding him more effectively.

With the progression of the clock Hope grew concerned about Edric's non-appearance. Convinced that Hilary remained the common denominator she did not relish Edric's proclamation, yet she could not deny entertaining the same thrill she had always felt at the mere thought of seeing him. In spite of everything she longed to see him – even if it were to be for the last time.

The party began to break up. The Chairman watched as a giggle tugged Hope's attention to the corridor beyond the open door where the ginger-haired youth, now thick-headed from wine, leaned heavily on a girl who seemed to find him amusing.

"Not dashing off, I trust?" He had seen her glancing at her watch during the time it had taken him to snatch a word with the Company Secretary. "Not in a rush to get away are you?"

Instantly catching his infectious smile, Hope's face softened. She shook her head. "No – I was merely wondering what could have happened to Edric."

"The hotel business my dear. The tedious demands of commerce – nothing more exciting than that," said Kevin admiring the flattering escape of loose ringlets at her temples and the nape of her neck, which softened her upswept hairstyle. In a faultlessly fitting, tube of ecru silk Hope looked every inch the photographic model. "Edric is a very lucky man – but then I'm sure he knows that." Teasing now, he shook his head ruefully. "If I were 25 years younger...."

"You'd what…..?" she coaxed.

"I'd give that young man of yours a run for his money – that's what!"

There was more truth in his jest than he would ever admit and he was in good company. There had not been a man present that afternoon who, given the chance, had not wanted to gravitate to Hope's side, and indeed with some amusement he had observed several who managed to find sufficient excuse to do so, but it was clear where her loyalties lay and he had smiled at their efforts.

He knew Edric before the start of that relationship, in his commercial role and before joining the Board of Shillens International. It had been clear from the way the young executive had been regularly drafted to the front line during the time of negotiation that his sound business abilities had been recognised, and that he was in the process of being groomed for stardom. He liked Edric instantly, in the first instance admiring him as a businessman whose sound business sense far outweighed many of those more senior in years and experience. But primarily he liked him as a human being and nothing since had presented itself to change his mind; and Charles Lurdmayne had appeared gratified when he passed favourable comments about the young man known to be keeping company with their mutual friend.

Kevin beamed at Hope and wondered again whether she had any inkling of what Charles was doing, or indeed anything of the knock-on effects it would likely have, for she was certainly sufficiently astute. He sensed her attention upon him and returned to his previous raillery. "Yes, I would – I'd give Edric a run for his money any day!"

Hope joined in with his easy laughter. There was nothing uncomfortable or distasteful in his playful banter, though when he motioned for her to precede him in walking towards his office she grew anxious and regretted not having the strength of Edric's arm close by.

Seated on a settee in the Chairman's office Hope breathed deeply and prepared herself to hear about Charles's latest instruction to his lawyer; not least the story behind it.

Ever since her eavesdropping, her mind had worked overtime, exploring all possible angles, clutching at straws, seeking plausible explanations for what she had overheard. But never once did she envisage anything approaching that which Kevin eventually volunteered, and for the moment she simply stared at him, unsure whether the burn beneath her eyelids stemmed from happiness or sadness.

Her eyes unblinking, she repeated Kevin's words, "Retiring? You! I don't believe it!"

Shrugging good-humouredly he nodded his sandy-coloured head, which now that Hope considered it, displayed increasing evidence of white amongst the pale red.

"I've spoken to the Board – did that some time back – but the official announcement won't be made until next week so I'd appreciate your keeping it under wraps until then. Rather than hearing it from some other quarter I wanted to tell you myself." He hastened to explain that in order to keep himself amused he would be retaining a handful of clients, Sir Charles and she amongst them. Detecting the surface of a protest he waved a hand, effectively countering anything she might have said.

She explored this trait of polite stubbornness, and then the fact that despite having the majority of his staff assembled together, rather than steal anything from Angela's day, he had purposely chosen to leave the announcement of his own departure until the following week. That he had taken her into his confidence, even though she was no longer in his employ, only went to emphasise the continuance of their shared regard. Hope could not help admiring the integrity of this man.

"I still can't believe it."

"Well, it's true. I suppose I've even surprised myself. I've certainly surprised my wife. Poor Elaine.... " he shook his head, "I don't think she believed I'd actually go through with it!" He laughed. "I've told her she's going to have to get used to having me under her feet." He grinned at the thought.

"In between rounds of golf.... fishing.... and spending time with those grandchildren of yours." Hope nodded towards the clutch of photographs residing on the large antique desk, "plus all those trips abroad that you were always promising to take."

"You're right – I guess I'll not get under her feet much." Kevin detected a change creeping into her face. "You look puzzled."

246

"No – not really," she lied. She could not admit to her earlier fears of learning something she did not think she could handle about her parentage and consequent change to Charles's Will. "It's just that...." she searched for a plausible explanation and began again. "It simply never occurred to me that you might be ready to retire." She exhaled, satisfied with her contribution, at the same time wondering whether that was the totality of his news, or whether there was more to follow.

"Don't tell me you expected me to die at my desk!"

She surprised herself with a genuine laugh. "Certainly I did – with your barristerial boots on!"

The door opened just wide enough for Angela to poke her head in and glance enquiringly at Kevin who nodded at the disembodied face.

"Kevin's told you then?" Angela came in, even now aware that this would be one of the last times she would enter the renowned office of Kevin Lester QC, and she glanced about the room in the same way a vendor does on vacating his property.

"Yes – and I'm still stunned! But it's brilliant news. I'm really very pleased, even a little envious." Hope swivelled back to the man she had held in high regard ever since meeting him in the grand library at Tarnville and later that same day nervously taking notes from his well-articulated dictation. What a picture she must have presented wearing what she had managed to throw together before being bundled into a leaky boat to escape rising floodwater; a young person just free from childhood and barely come to terms with the skill of writing shorthand. What a great deal had happened since that opportune introduction of less than five years ago!

Feeling no urgency to return to the mundane paperwork on his desk, Kevin suggested that Angela's last duty might be to ring his executive team and invite them to his suite for a further drink and to ask the Chef to knock together a few nibbles.

Hope considered the Chef's interpretation of the Chairman's request and correctly predicted the heavily-ladened salvers that appeared a short while later. Kevin never changes, she thought – works hard, plays hard – he truly deserves his retirement and please God let it be long, healthy and happy.

Even after breaking his employ she still found Kevin immensely stimulating to be around. She recalled how the organisation seemed to lack something whenever he was away, and upon his return how it came alive again. Smiling to herself she thought that perhaps a version of the *Royal Standard* should be flown from the roof when the Chairman was in residence. With her head to one side she consider this man who was like Sir Charles in so many ways, fatherly and supportive, whilst in others vastly different and very much in the fast lane. Both men had in their own way played a major role in her young life, and which seemed likely to continue.

She watched Angela at the desk where she discretely turned papers over before extending the Chairman's invitation to his team. She was comfortable, at ease. It was hard to imagine now how horror-struck she had been when she learned she was to provide secretarial cover to the Chairman, and later when she was selected as his new PA. Fond of them both she was pleased the two had gone on to share something resembling that which she had considered herself privileged to enjoy.

Left with little choice Hope finally accepted that Edric was not coming. After receiving no further earth-shattering news from Kevin she took her leave in the early hours of the evening though not before promising Angela that she would wear a super-elaborate hat to her wedding.

Hope made her way across the reception area where newspapers lay folded on the desk, as they had always done, awaiting collection by the Chairman on his departure. The headline of one caught her eye and provided an explanation for Edric's non-arrival.

Silently her lips formed the words, "Inferno – Edinburgh Shillens – one dead." Her eyes chased to read more, and applying her technique for summarising business reports she carefully read the introductory and concluding paragraphs before skim-reading the rest. She refolded the newspaper and returned it to the custody of the new Receptionist who, grasping none of her facial expression, smiled pleasantly at the world in general and then at her newly applied nail polish.

Chapter 30

Daphne had just settled down to watch television with Billy when Hope arrived home. She turned in her seat, her smile transferring to the region of Hope's wake but then saw she was alone. "Edric not with you?"

"He didn't make it." For some reason she did not quite understand, Hope felt a compulsion to make Edric's excuses. "There's been a fire at the Edinburgh Shillens. Being in the area I imagine he got caught up in all that that entailed." It actually made sense now that she came to think about it.

Enlightenment showed in Daphne's expression. "It was on the news but had almost finished before I realised it was one of Edric's hotels."

Hope could not help smiling. In Daphne's view Edric practically ran the Shillens group single-handedly. She could be forgiven for thinking so, for the fax machine in his room was rarely redundant at the weekend.

"A person died but they didn't say whether it was a member of staff or a guest, only that the name was being withheld until the next of kin had been informed." Daphne's eyes lowered. "Someone's in for a lot of heartbreak."

Moved to silence Hope attempted to shut out her recollections of the news received on her 18th birthday. Dragging herself free she checked her watch. "Missed it – we'll have to catch the later news."

Billy glanced at Hope, then at his mother. "Who's kin?" he asked, his jaw stilled from chewing toffee just long enough to ask the question.

The late-night news did little more than duplicate what they already knew though it contained amateur film footage that corroborated the severity of the incident, showing black smoke billowing from bedrooms and an alarming display of urgent flames licking the sky. Almost in unison both women exclaimed it a miracle that more lives had not been lost. The report concluded on a note of speculation. It was thought that an air-ducting valve had fortuitously jammed and prevented a wider permeation of smoke and consequent greater loss of life.

Just then the telephone rang and Hope bounded from her seat in the certainty it would be Edric to apologise for not making it to Angela's party. Safe in the knowledge that he was unlikely to say anything on the telephone about a reconciliation with his wife, she grabbed the receiver urgently to her ear.

But it was Isabel; she wondered whether to expect her for the weekend. When Hope overcame her disappointment, she apologised for her oversight in not getting in touch.

"It's not a problem. When it got to this time I didn't think you'd be landing. Peter's here. He sends his regards. We've finished our meal. We're just having coffee."

Hope picked up something from her tone. "Lovely. I hope you have a wonderful evening," she said with sincerity. "It must be nice not having your usual gooseberries in tow!" When Isabel tried to regain a foothold in the conversation her efforts were suffocated beneath Hope's flow. "Yes – I know we're always welcome. You've made that abundantly clear but sometimes a little privacy is to be valued. Make the most of it – go mad – have another coffee!" A chuckle drifted to her ear. "Sir Charles not home then?" Hope asked, knowing that although encouraged to keep up her friendships, Isabel seldom invited people to Tarnville, but preferred to keep herself available should her employer need her.

"No. Honestly I can hardly keep tabs on him these days!"

Hope delighted in her merriment. There had been days when her aunt had rarely smiled let alone luxuriated in spontaneous laughter. "How d'you mean?"

"I don't know about being in his autumnal years – he's acting more like a youngster, dashing off here, visiting there, planning this and that."

Hope's grin transferred to her voice. "You make it sound as though he's started keeping late hours and found a liking for wild parties!"

"Heaven forbid! Though he's certainly found a new lease of life. I only wish I knew where he found it because I could certainly do with some! He's only been back a day and now he's shot off again with

250

Joseph Fearnley – Scotland this time. They're doing the rounds looking for a bull. According to Joe, poor old Samson's past it."

Charles's prize-winning Ayrshire bull had shown little interest in passing on his genes since he succumbed to sunstroke after eating a plant that made his skin susceptible to sunlight, and for a time Samson had to be confined to the seclusion of a darkened barn. After that the structure became known as Samson's barn, the same barn that not long ago had caught fire and claimed Gregory's life.

Isabel continued, "And, as you might expect, after that he's off back to Corfu. And I'll tell you something else, though you must promise to keep it to yourself," her tone dropped conspiratorially, "I think he's a bit taken by that Helda. You know, that nice woman he's always so particular about engaging out there. I think it's her that keeps writing to him. There's been a right flurry of letters arriving here from Corfu."

But all this went over Hope's head; she caught only the mention of Scotland. "Bell.... exactly where in Scotland is he staying?" A dreadful thought had occurred to her; her heart was leaping in her chest as she awaited the reply.

Isabel had seen the news and quickly put her mind at rest. "It's all right pet. He's nowhere near Edinburgh. In fact he won't even be up there yet. Terrible though that fire at the Shillens. That's the new one isn't it? It's been right bad. We watched it on the telly."

Breath returned to Hope's lungs and when Isabel went on to chat of other things she explained how Edric had not made it down to Leeds and she believed the fire to be the reason. "So I'm not sure what we're doing...." apart from a lot of talking – though she must guard against giving her aunt the slightest indication of any of that. "In fact I thought it was him ringing now."

"Y'talk about Peter and me not getting much time together. You two don't do much better! Him called away on the death of his dad-in-law, you landing that job, and then him having to trail all the way back to Kent the other week, and now...."

But Hope cut in, "Bell.... you know when I was up north with Harry.... and Edric's wife rang?"

"Yes....?"

"How did you find him?" Her aunt would consider it a strange question but it had to be asked. She wanted to invite comments on whether he appeared happier following the call, though dare not; to enquire would be to award credence to that which threatened to steal so much, whereas leaving it unsaid denied it realism, albeit only temporarily.

Isabel thought back. "He seemed tired, but Sir Charles was probably to blame for that. I think I told you he'd been given the grand tour. Why do you ask?"

Why? How could she answer that? Hope stumbled, "Hmm.... I thought so too.... just wondered what you thought," not her best effort at fielding a question, she conceded.

"Just a bit tired," Isabel said again. "I'spect that job of his doesn't help. And talking of jobs.... have you reached a decision yet?"

"I'm not taking it Bell. It's not for me." Harry had called her a fool and pointed out that Japan was where the real money was, adding almost sulkily that it was up to her and made no difference to him either way. But his manner had not matched the comment. She had never seen him so put out. With others yes but never with her, but he reverted to something approaching his former self when he saw her mind was made up. He even put his arms round her, and softening his rebuke called her a chump – his beautiful chump. "I don't want to live on something as transient as looks," Hope continued. "I don't want to get caught up in all that flaunting and posing. I prefer to merge into the background. My current undertaking is just enough to be fun. I can cope with that."

Isabel almost laughed. "No matter how hard you tried, merging into the background is one thing you'd never achieve. Dressed in sackcloth and with your hair cropped you'd still stand out in a crowd!" There was a little pause before she confessed in a voice catching on suppressed emotion, "I don't mind admitting that I'd have been worried out of my mind if you'd taken it."

An explosion overhead shattered Hope's sleep. For the moment disorientated she sat up in bed. She looked about her. Her bedroom was suddenly alive with precise colour and diminutive detail, and then just as quickly plunged back into colourless obscurity. A second clap of thunder brought clarity of understanding and Hope shot from beneath the bedcovers to squirm in a sweat of terror behind the door, almost entangling herself in the towelling robe hanging there.

No one had ever managed to assuage her arc of charged emotion brought on by thunderstorms. It was as though the channelled ferocity herded her insistently towards the boundary of recollection and from there down a twisting path through various lenses to stumble headlong upon those fearful, static images she desired to forget. Isabel had done her best to allay her fears, even pointing out that Hope made her entry to the world during a thunderstorm. But the desired implication was lost on her. The attempt failed to activate the inner protection mechanism and appreciation of the sheer ordinariness, and upon the next clatter she had wheeled on her aunt and shrieked that both her parents had died during thunderstorms – her mother whilst giving birth. Additionally, though now never mentioned, Hope still recalled the squall on the night that Bert had made his second attempt to rape her. Thunder and lightening would always herald disaster and snatch her up to hurl her headfirst into her own check list of emotions and some of her worst memories.

If Edric had been in his room across the landing she would have run to him. But he was no longer in her life. She was certain now that he had gone back to his wife. A rebellious rumbling sequence preceded the next deafening boom, which vibrated the very fabric of the house, the uninterrupted waves transferring to Hope's innermost frame. Her mind now engaged in terrorised gymnastics, great bulbous tears sprang to her eyes to slide down her cheeks. "Edric!" she sobbed.

Daphne found her slumped against the door with her knees drawn up to her chest. Her pale face iridescent with tears mingled with beads of sweat. Very gently she coaxed her into her arms where she held her close for several long moments before leading her downstairs where she made hot drinks.

"This'll put you right," Daphne said cheerfully, handing Hope a steaming mug of tea. She jerked her head towards the ceiling. "Nothing wakes Billy. That one could sleep through earthquakes!"

The beginnings of a smile softened the corners of Hope's mouth. Building on this Daphne made a bid to hold her in conversation until the worst of the storm had passed.

Tiredness eventually overcame them and in the silence of Daphne's front room Hope turned to pondering Edric's whereabouts and whether he was happy, or as miserable as she was, but those reflections became fragmented and skipped about making it impossible to concentrate. Then all at once her hand was hurting and she looked in bewilderment at the narrow twine wrapped around her fingers, themselves deathly white. Her eyes traced the length of twine to the colourful kite soaring high in the sky above her. Its tort string straining with every tug had cut off the circulation to her hand. She struggled to release the kite and free her fingers. When she looked again her gift to Edric was no longer airborne but had descended to the hard-baked path in front of her. Approaching the Old Man's Bar it disappeared and Edric stood in its place. Without a word he turned from her and began walking away, the gap between them widening with each easy stride.

Detecting the silken head slumped against her shoulder Daphne settled back into the sofa cushions and wondered again about Edric's non-appearance and the fact he had not telephoned, for there was certainly more plaguing this young person's mind than solely the consternation brought about by a thunderstorm.

Daphne would have been even more anxious had she known what the next few months would bring and the crucial role they would play in the formation of the remainder of Hope's life – and indeed her own.

Chapter 31

Hope was surprised when two months passed with still no word from Edric. Her despair had entered the painful process of acceptance, but at this very moment, perched on frayed upholstery at a desk, which too had seen better days, her mind for once was not on Edric.

She looked around uncertainly at her unfamiliar surroundings. Apart from the overweight woman on the front desk who directed her to the correct floor there had been no one to welcome her to the office whose clutter and shabbiness did nothing to alleviate her initial misgivings. An ugly bank of metal filing cabinets lined the opposite wall; the tops stacked high with warped, wire filing trays, their contents spilling to an untidy mess that looked as though something might be nesting there.

Not long ago she had considered herself privileged to enjoy the unparalleled accommodation and very latest equipment at Lester Associates but never more than at this precise moment. She questioned what the secretary was like for whom she was providing cover; first impressions did not boast of an organiser. Why on earth had she allowed Angela to persuade her to sign up with a secretarial bureau? She supposed she could still extricate herself; she could grab her handbag from beneath the desk and beat a hasty retreat to the railway station.

Just as she was weighing this up the shabby, paint-chipped door flew open. Buckling beneath the weight of a battered briefcase whose inadequate fastener flapped against scored hide, a man pitched into the office, almost losing grip of the newspaper and mess of papers pinned beneath his free arm. The smile he directed at Hope was broad and seemed to convey relief as well as welcome.

"You must be Miss Stratton from the agency. Excellent – good – good."

Bobbing her head rhythmically with his, Hope considered correcting him on her marital status but in the absence of a wedding ring any redress might prompt the expectancy of an explanation. "Good morning. Yes, I'm waiting for Vivian Dyson."

The man, defying gravity, stood a shade over six feet. The lack of a necktie gave the impression of his having just dragged himself from bed, which was true, but working late he had barely gained comfort from the bedcovers. He extended a hand towards her; a flurry of paperwork and the necktie he had been carrying slithered to the desk.

"I'm Viv. Welcome aboard." He was instantly amused by the surprise in the remarkable green eyes that met his, and if for no other reason than to add some light relief and decoration to his day he could be forgiven for hoping she might stay longer than the last one who had not even managed the day. "Busy day ahead. Lots to get through. Give me five minutes then pop through and we'll get started." Retrieving the tie he draped it round his neck and scooped up his papers. Moving on he kicked open the integral door marked Assistant Editor.

Hope continued to stare after him. So *t-h-a-t* was Vivian Dyson! The quickly-spoken man in no way resembled her preconception. Whereas one might have worn trousers this one definitely wore trousers, and she would have been blind not to notice he was good-looking, moreover handsome, though the memory of Edric permitted no place for the admiration of others.

Hope did as Vivian Dyson suggested. After allowing him five minutes – no doubt to glimpse his newspaper, which she had noticed was not the Barlayne Express but a competitor's – she went to receive her instructions for this, her first day working as a Temp for the Assistant Editor of the Barlayne Express Newspaper.

For the remainder of the morning she worked industriously on manuscripts pulled periodically from the battered briefcase. Though not essential, the ability to write shorthand had been touched on at her interview as being an advantage and she fervently hoped that after clearing the present deluge of scrawled notes she might be able to persuade this man, with the handwriting skills of a doctor, to dictate his further work.

A comforting familiarity resurfaced as though she had stumbled upon secretarial skills concealed beneath a veil of abandonment. Finding again her own brisk rhythm her fingers struck the keys with a reflex, fluid action, pausing only to note things on which to seek clarification: a person's name; their designation; how they fitted into the organisation; anything that might aid her effectiveness – if she were to stay, and that was by no means certain.

As though mesmerised by the steady sight-and-reflex action she began to drift and shortly found herself again in the long line of wedding guests waiting to congratulate Angela and Alex on their marriage.

She had heard nothing from Edric since his stilted telephone call on the evening prior to Angela's leaving party. Six weeks after that she attended Angela's wedding – on her own. Continuing to type at speed she allowed herself to return to the wedding reception that had taken place a little over a month ago....

Loneliness displayed itself openly in Hope's face; smiles no longer automatic were generated for the benefit of others. She had not wanted to attend the wedding on her own but had been unable to stay away.

Edging forward amongst the guests Hope was now only a matter of moments from having to explain why she was unaccompanied but her account would be brief. Relying on Angela's preoccupation she would avoid entering into detail.

Surrounded by strangers smiling and laughing together in exchanges of pleasantries Hope drew closer, her own first spontaneous smile in weeks almost taking her by surprise.

As she should have anticipated, Angela caught up with her at the very first opportunity and practically dragged her into one of the hotel bedrooms set aside for the wedding party.

"I can't take it in. I simply can't believe it – not you two! I expected you and Edric to be together always."

So had she, though did not confess it, but did admit to feelings of desolation. "I get up. I get washed and dressed but then what? I'm not a whole person anymore and when I close my eyes I see his face. There's no room in my life for anyone else. I've nobody now. Everyone should have someone. You have Alex.... Bell her adoring farmer." Hope's pain was obvious.

She had taken her aunt's open display of wearing Peter's ring as an indication of an imminent wedding. Yet, and despite the fact that Charles had made known his intention to take up residence in Corfu, Isabel's marriage was not scheduled to take place until the following year. By which time she expected the running of Tarnville to have passed to the capable though temporary hands of Joseph Fearnley and his wife.

Charles had laboured the point that Hope should visit him at Marchriard. She would, of course, though it would evoke painful memories of those first happy days with Edric. But perhaps with the forgiving distance of time, as with memories of her father, she might eventually be able to enjoy those moments again.

Nevertheless, like everyone else, she would be sorry to see Mowlem's figurehead take his final departure. The village would not be the same without Charles. News of his departure had unsettled tenants and a letter had been delivered to each household, explaining that contrary to rumour the Estate was not being broken up or sold, but would continue in much the same way as it had always done. This brought further speculation; many surmised that the daughter of the house had been traced, and an air of expectancy whispered through the neighbourhood. Whereas Hope knew differently, though was careful to keep her own counsel, not even sharing what she knew with her aunt.

As yet there had been no intimation from Charles of the directive to his lawyer and as his departure date drew near Hope's anxiety heightened in the anticipation of his doing so. But she was ready, for when he did she would politely but firmly decline the proposed inheritance. The only remaining problem was the wording. She had been working on that and it changed every time she thought about it. It was important it should not sound rehearsed, which would indicate prior knowledge of his intentions.

Aware of Angela's concerned face watching her, evoked a longing to share these things, but she decided against it and slipped into the lace-clad arms that opened to receive her.

"Anj – everything's changed. Nothing will ever be the same again. I don't think I'll ever get over Edric," that wonderful person whose path like an act of destiny had crossed her own so many times. "Despite its not working out, I shall always be thankful he came into my life – even though it was only for a short time." Her sad face lifted to confess, "I can't stop thinking about him. I don't even want to try. I can't function anymore. It's almost as though he *d-i-e-d*. Yes – it's just like that! I feel just like I did when my father died," her voice weakened with the assault of that ingrained horror. "I feel as though time has collapsed around me. I don't know what I've done to be cast adrift like this. Anj – I just want my life back – I want Edric back!"

Angela searched for the right thing to say then feebly enquired, "Have you tried ringing him? Perhaps if you...."

Hope shook her head.

"Why on earth not?"

Hope told her how she had begged Edric never to utter the word *goodbye*, and extracted a promise that if at any time he wished to end their relationship he would merely slip away with no final farewell.

At this Angela wanted to knock their heads together. She said that that was just about the daftest thing she had ever heard. But her tone softened as she suggested contacting Edric's secretary. "Have you spoken to *What's-er-name*? Perhaps if...."

"Allison? No I haven't." Hope cut in. If Allison Ballard did not already know, she did not want to give her the satisfaction of learning that things were over between she and Edric. "I never hit it off with her. Anyway I got the impression she had designs on him herself."

Something in the set of Hope's eyes and incline of her head indicated emotions that challenged her confidence, something that was unlikely to ever leave her, yet in another sense may well sustain her. There was something unforgiving that would give her the strength and determination she would need to carry on.

Angela put her face close to Hope's and saw the same level of withdrawal that followed the stillbirth of her baby when all her senses seemed to close down. "It seems to me that you've come to your own particular crossroads in life. I can't begin to imagine all of what you carry in your mind but what I suggest is that you make a fresh start." Angela embarked on a string of expressions of encouragement: "You can do it. You're strong. You're one of the strongest people I know. Maybe it's time to rethink your aims. I know you've always said you don't want to go the whole hog on this modelling thing – but why not? You're a natural. I'm still stunned by your decline to go to Japan! But then again I acknowledge that you're not one for sitting on a pedestal. I remember you once told me you were happier sitting on a three-legged stool milking next-door's goat! It occurred to me then that there must be more to living in the country than meets the eye."

Angela let out a delightful giggle. "And I still say I'm surprised they allow you to donate blood. I remain convinced that your veins yield nothing but river water."

"*River water?*"

"Yes. That village of yours is part of you, including its river. The contest between Japan and Mowlem never existed. The village would win every time and I've no doubt that it will win you back in the end."

At this Hope became thoughtful.

Angela continued, "Well if not modelling, do you remember saying you might go back into your old field and find something like your role at Lester's?"

"I've been looking but I've seen nothing. I'm unlikely to. Nothing could compare. You've been there. You know exactly what I'm talking about. Anyway – I've been out of it too long. I'd be rusty." Even after a short break Hope knew, her shorthand speed could drop by as much as ten words per minute.

"Rusty be damned! Do what you told me to do. Start taking the news from the television. I hadn't a cat in hell's chance of getting it but the attempt bumped up my shorthand speed. You say you haven't seen anything suitable – I bet you haven't considered temping. Did you know that's how I landed the job in Personnel? Temping gives you the opportunity to explore beyond that small portion you're allowed to see at the time of interview. You get the chance to feel whether a company is right for you. Furthermore if something permanent comes up you're there on the spot to make all the right noises. Like I said – I arrived at Lester's as a Temp. I liked what I saw and for some reason so did they. The rest is history."

Hope promised to think about it. She pulled a face. "Okey-Cokey-Snooky-Pokey, if you say so." Anyway – perhaps Angela was right. Perhaps it was time to pick up the pieces and move on.

"There's so much out there just waiting for you.... and you are going to agree to be a Godmother aren't you?"

"You're not – are you?" Hope's voice rose by an octave.

"Certainly not. There's only room for one in this dress!"

The dress, made for her in Israel, had been a gift from Hope.

Angela ran her hand across her waistline, neat and enviably flat. "But when we do get round to it, I want you to be it's Godmother.

Hope laughed. "*It?* What a rotten name for a baby! And does Alex know you're planning to turn his life upside down?" this spoken with a girlish grin. "I'll say this for you. You're certainly a planner! And yes – I should be delighted to be Godmother to any forthcoming new arrival – just so long as you promise to come up with a better name than It."

Hope went to check her mascara in the dressing table mirror. After a small adjustment she lifted her head in much the same way as she did for the camera. "Now I suggest we leave my troubles in here and go find that delicious new husband of yours."

A cup rattling in a saucer that did not match its mate was placed beside Hope. The noise snatched her from her rumination and deposited her abruptly back at the shabby desk in the Barlayne Express Newspaper office, and a month on from making her promise to Angela.

"Thought you might fancy a break."

Hope glanced up at the pleasant face of Vivian Dyson and thanked him for the coffee, a good measure of which was in the saucer.

"You can certainly churn it out," he said before drinking from his own cup. This one far outshone any of the others who had passed through his office, and not just with regards ability. It struck him as a pity that Hope Stratton sat on the other side of his door. "When you've finished that," he indicated the document on which she was working, "bring five copies to the News Room – noisiest room down the corridor – last door at the left. I'll be there for most of the day. And if you get through that little lot," laughing pleasantly he motioned to other scripts in the battered tray beside her, "you might take a look at that," he jerked his head towards the *rat's nest* on top of the filing cabinets. "See if you can lose that mess for me – but don't do too good a job and lose it altogether."

Whilst he valued a sound filing and retrieval system he had neither the time nor the patience to set out his requirements, the consequences of which had proved disastrous with the passage of time and string of Temps who had meandered through his office to leave their mark. "Just see what you can do," he grimaced, modifying his instruction,

261

feeling less confident about this task than those she had already performed for him.

A fleeting memory of one of his former assistants sprang to mind. Dressed as though she had been misdirected to some bohemian party she arrived late. Weighed down with costume jewellery she jangled everywhere she went. Able to smile about it now he recalled she lost an earring amongst the filing. It had taken most of the day to locate it, and she left deposits of chewing gum in his ashtray. He also recalled not being sorry when she departed to descend upon the next unsuspecting client.

Vivian's hand had barely reached the doorknob when the door swung open and a young, tousle-haired man came in. He had a round, boyish face, which made him look younger than he really was. There was a flash of annoyance in the eyes as he began to speak.

"Not coming to the briefing Viv? Got a better story or just...."

Vivian's gaze slid over the man's shoulder to Hope.

Sensing they were not alone the other man halted abruptly. Still with annoyance blazing in his face he turned and awarded Hope the full measure of his aggravation. His expression changed instantly.

Even with her hair coiled tightly behind her head Hope still managed to look as though she had just stepped off the front cover of *Vogue*. The suit did not help. The job had come up at short notice and as her business suits were now noticeably dated she had made her selection from her later, more exclusive wardrobe. Whilst the chestnut and grey striped suit was one of her more conservative outfits, even to the mildly discerning eye the exceptional lines and cloth gave more than a hint of a story beyond the reaches of the average workingwoman.

The round face swivelled back to Vivian Dyson. "All that.... and she can type as well!"

The young man left as abruptly as he had arrived but not before throwing Hope another glance.

As though reading her thoughts Vivian fed her with answers. "I'm sorry about that." With the intention of sparing her further rudeness, he had purposely not introduced her. When he was that way out their lead reporter could be all mouth and sarcasm. "That was Stewart Trimble – all wind and very little substance, as you'll find out." If you stay long enough, he mused, remaining hopeful that she might as she brought an air of efficiency to his office that had been missing since Sonia left to care for a terminally ill parent. Since then he had existed, sometimes barely, with the dubious help of a succession of Temps. "He's better for knowing. Trimble's a good reporter – has a nose for a story – lives for that all-important scoop. I doubt he dreams of anything else but given a free rein he'd land us in Court before you could shout *Hold the front page*! He gives the impression of being ruthless but he's not as tough as he makes out. I overruled him on the lead story last week and he's likely to froth about it for some time yet – probably until the day he leaves."

"Leaves?" she said, noticing that one of his eyes twitched though decided it unlikely to be a wink on such short acquaintance.

Vivian nodded. "Yes. He's working his statutory notice. He's only just tendered his resignation so we've another three months' flak." His voice cracked on a laugh. "Don't let him worry you though. He's – on the other bus – it's the men who should be worried. He admires the fairer sex but prefers the boys if you catch my drift."

Hope's fingers fumbled their way back to the keyboard.

Chapter 32

Captivated by the excitement of a newsgathering environment, Hope continued at the Barlayne Express Newspaper office. Initial impressions of clutter and chaos were quickly elbowed aside by the stimulation of being at the sharp end, assimilating news as it happened. The whole set-up was exciting and when Vivian Dyson offered her a permanent position she felt compelled to give it careful thought.

Vivian had watched her grow from feelings of uncertainty to sharing those of the indescribable thrill of the day-to-day challenges of news reporting. He had no idea what the bureau paid but convinced himself that the salary he was offering would entice Hope to join his team.

Hope weighed things carefully. Whilst the Barlayne offices were some distance from Leeds the train service had proved reliable. However if she entered full-time employment she would have to forfeit her involvement with the Sally Lox Corporation and her interest in Manstonleigh, and since Edric's unexplained disappearance she felt the need to hold on to all things familiar, which included her photographic work and Manstonleigh. Employed by a bureau she could work as and when she pleased, taking time off to accommodate those other commitments.

In the end she was left with no alternative but to reject Vivian's offer. It was solely the flexible nature of agency work that prompted her decline, she explained, and at the first hint of a query made it politely clear that she would not be drawn on the reasons.

Vivian could not have looked more concerned had he believed her to be battling with some form of illness.

Her evasiveness, Hope felt sure, would result in their parting company but Vivian surprised her by asking the bureau to allocate her to his office on an indefinite basis with provision for cover on those occasions when in-house resources were unable to cope with her absences. Hope could not have been more pleased, especially when steps were taken to top-up her salary from the bureau.

No two days were ever alike and Hope felt a buzz of anticipation on her arrival each morning. Reviews, scandals and disasters: they were all there competing with the pressure for space.

The image of Edric's face remained just one small particle of memory away, yet she had found something that stimulated and absorbed her mind as nothing had before, and for the most part suffocated the unruly meandering of her mind.

It had turned cool for the end of July. Wind accelerating round the corner tunnelled itself at Hope as she left the railway station. She glanced up at the sky that spoke to her of rain. Striking a brisk pace she headed for the Barlayne office block.

She was looking forward to her return after taking a break to make a new television commercial. The remainder of her week had been shared between Tarnville and Manstonleigh and it was whilst at the latter that an opportunity presented itself to divest herself of some of the trappings from her past.

The idea arose from something Billy said about wanting to learn to cook. Her suggestion to develop a self-contained flat in the little-used area at the side of the Day Centre was favourably received by Phyllis Wilkinson, who continued to bless the day that Hope had persuaded her to contact the television people on the refurbishment of the charity shop. This latest suggestion was for small groups to take it in turns to spend a day or two in the apartment to learn, and in some cases relearn, routine household tasks that would help to equip them for life beyond the protection of Manstonleigh.

An enthusiastic discussion had ensued amongst the staff from which it transpired that between them they had everything required to furnish the proposed flat. Hope, the main contributor, had been quick to offer every stick of her furniture stowed in Daphne's garage. There had been a time when the furnishings provided a feeling of security with the prospect of her acquiring a cottage for holidays and weekends, but filling it with reminders of her marriage would be to invite unwanted memories; better to let those memories go.

From this decision came another; she enquired of Kevin Lester what might be involved in reverting to her maiden name and he had the process in hand even before she replaced the phone.

These resolutions promoted feelings of contentment and freedom though did nothing to lessen the acute ache for a communication of some kind from Edric. Each evening on her arrival home she ran upstairs in the hope of finding a missive on the fax machine in the bedroom that once had been Edric's. She no longer expected to find one but still felt the need to check.

Edric had not kept much in the room and had never sent for the few things that remained. There was no personal trinket or photograph, just odd items of clothing. A couple of nice sweaters lay folded neatly in a drawer and a pair of slacks hung forlornly in the wardrobe with a pair of casual shoes stowed beneath. Not much to fill the gaping void he had left in her life.

The first splashes of rain startled Hope and she quickened her pace to reach the office before it started with vengeance. Rather than the incessant rumble of the city where pedestrians leaned into the elements without so much as an upwards glance at clouds with cotton wool edges turned to mother-of-pearl, subtly streaked with pink and mauve, she preferred the concentrated silence of the countryside where rain reflected sunlight and was considered pleasurable and looked upon as a blessing.

She strode past the lifts and headed for the stairs and her office on the first floor. There was a spring in her step. It felt good to be back and she was already wondering what the day might hold. This was her favourite time of the day when everything still lay in the obscure haze of anticipation and the working day had not yet slipped into gear.

Halfway down the corridor she peered round the Editor's door at his assistant, Helen, a young woman prone to plumpness and always on a diet, with short dark hair framing a milky complexion, and a passion for collecting teddy bears. She was opening the post when Hope enquired whether any problems had been encountered during her absence. Helen leaned back in her chair, her blouse gaping between the buttons, and told her about the Temp the bureau sent: a nice girl, a team player.

"And Viv's never a problem. Anyway – what about you? Did you enjoy the break?"

"It was good – caught up with friends – that sort of thing. I enjoyed it...." There was something in the widening of Helen's eyes and the way she asked the question that prickled Hope to alertness.

After a pause Helen's face creased with amusement until finally unable to hold it in check laughter exploded to circuit her office and rise to the strip-lit ceiling before bouncing off the walls covered with pictures and forward planners to the fax machine spilling missives to the linoleum floor, eventually escaping through the open door to tantalize to varying degrees the hearing of those making their way to the offices where QWERTY keys were already in action.

"Developing a liking for fluffy felines?" Helen managed through her laughter, her head aslant in anticipation of a reaction. "By the way," she teased, "that's got to be my all-time favourite!" Helen's eyes were bright with knowing whilst those trained on her failed to conceal their timid look of failure.

Hope looked away, her emotions demoted to the status of guilt. Her cover was blown. She had been dreaming an impossible dream. She exhaled. Apparently her colleague had seen the first showing of the new commercial, which exposed her as having other employment. She was reminded of the morning she arrived at Lester Associates to find her colleagues knew all about her overnight stardom with the Sally Lox Corporation; she wondered how many at the Barlayne Express knew about her other role. From her first day she had gone to great lengths to contrive a totally different image and keep herself as far removed as possible from the icon of the screen and printed page, and indeed until this moment thought she had succeeded.

Helen left her chair to circled round in front of Hope. "Don't look so flustered."

"How long have you known?"

"How long? Let's see – I'd say about five minutes after you arrived. Only kidding! I suppose it was around your second week. You see – you don't conform to the regular secretarial mould, not that you don't have the skills, you understand. I mean the way you're turned out – I mean just look at you – and how you carry yourself." She laughed again but pleasantly so. Don't worry – you don't look anything like your TV image."

The laughter was faintly reassuring. "That was my intention. Have you said anything?"

Helen was surprised by the plea in the green eyes. "To the others? No. As you never mentioned it I guessed you didn't want people to know. Anyway – working in this environment I've seen too much of that sort of thing. Once the cancerous invasion of privacy starts, the victim is denied any personal life from thereon." Her smile broadened. "There's one thing I have to say though – this latest commercial is a winner! I love it – you seated in the open-air café in front of that *Greek-god-of-a-man* you sense is watching you. It's clever filming. Clever and effective taking your close-up with your hair seemingly blowing in the wind, then zooming out to include the bough of a tree to reveal the stillness of your surroundings, only to zoom back in to catch your look of annoyance as you spin round to tackle the man you believe is messing with your hair but find he's gone and glimpse him walking up the hill. Ah – but then we see the real culprit – that adorable white Persian kitten turning summersaults in a frantic attempt to reach your hair ribbon – absolutely beautiful! But never mind the cat – did you get that guy's phone number?

True to her word Helen told no one and Hope continued to enjoy anonymity. However Stewart Trimble had his own suspicions about her recurring absences. His reporter-nose had led him to wonder whether she might be someone's mistress who dropped everything to accompany them on their travels. It seemed as likely an explanation as any. With secretarial skills far exceeding those expected of a Temp it was obvious that Hope had some specific reason for electing to work from an agency. Such employment would not pay much, which only left pliability.

Today was Stewart's last day with the Paper and apart from covering a fashion show later, he was kicking his heels, and chose to kick them sitting on Hope's desk.

"So, Hopeful – will you stay with old Viv?" He watched her returning files to the new pine cabinets at the other side of the room.

Her dislike of the nickname did not show and in any event it was an improvement on the first one – *Hopeless*. Vivian Dyson's timely arrival removed the need for a response.

The trill of the telephone took Stewart sprawling untidily across the desk to answer it, the caller's name instantly intriguing him. "It's for you Hopeful – Kevin Lester." He delayed placing the receiver in her eager hand. "Kevin Lester.... the big-time barrister?" he said, watching for affirmation, seeing only measured neutrality. He became thoughtful.

Kevin Lester explained that something had come up. Their mutual friend had asked him to join him in Corfu by the end of the week and he wanted Hope to know his whereabouts should she need him.

Hope expressed appreciation for this thoughtfulness then referring to Charles's forthcoming relocation said she regretted not being there to help Kevin, and added she was pleased that she and Charles had him as a friend. Her former employer let the compliment ride and she smiled at the predictable silence.

He went on to praise her on the new advertisement, admitting that whilst he had not yet caught it, his wife had, which had resulted in keen attempts to persuade him to buy a kitten in addition to the hair spray that apparently holds any hairstyle – even when under siege from livestock.

Meanwhile Stewart had positioned himself carefully with one ear keenly trained on Hope's telephone conversation and the other more vaguely on something Vivian was saying. He caught the words "Corfu by the end of the week" and was more convinced than ever about Hope's absences. Thinking fast he put a proposal to Vivian.

"Yes, if you're sure you'll look after her. And you're right. It would help her gain an understanding of the reporting field. Yes – yes by all means take her along." Vivian turned to Hope who had finished her call. "A break from routine will do you good. I'm letting Stewart take you to the fashion event this afternoon. It's probably more in your line anyway."

Breath barely stirred in Hope's lungs as she wondered whether there was something significant behind his choice of words. She watched him uncertainly.

"And if you feel comfortable with the idea you can try your hand at pulling a piece together." Impressed by her editing skills in knocking together some of the sloppy material the others produced he

269

wondered whether her flair extended beyond the ability to correct the work of others.

Hope had not realised that her fate was under discussion at the other side of the office and now suffered apprehension, until she brought to mind what Vivian had said about Stewart's being *on the other bus* and preferring the boys. Breathing more easily she allowed herself to wonder what it might be like to view a fashion show from the audience rather than the catwalk under a bombardment of flash bulbs.

The barrister's name and the mention of Corfu had whetted Stewart's reporting appetite. Seduced by his thoughts he made sure they left the office with sufficient time for him to take Hope to lunch.

The leading barrister, Kevin Lester QC, and Hopeful an item – an infamous love-triangle – juicy! Now that was a story he would like to run with – the high-flying barrister in a role reversal! The hundreds that that particular guy had brought to their knees in the courtrooms would delight in reading those columns, though the reputed legal skills and reputation of the man warned him he would be unwise to touch that particular story. Notwithstanding this, a steady flow of ideas for notable headlines tantalised his mind and for the brevity of a moment he even toyed with the idea of feeding the lead to one of the nationals. But if he did, what would he get out of it? – zilch!

He might not do anything with it but he would give it some rein, test the water and see whether there was something there worth uncovering. And if there were it would show him in a sound, principled light if he were able to arrive at his new employment with a scoop already researched and ready to run with.

Kevin Lester stood gazing sightlessly from his French windows. He had a burning desire to ring Hope back to amend his story and tell her the truth about his trip, for the arrangements he was being asked to put in place would affect her more than anyone. Although the circumstances of his task did not strictly bind him by client confidentiality he had given his word; he could say nothing and regretted there was no way open to him whereby he could alert Hope.

Chapter 33

With the sole purpose of impressing Hope, Stewart Trimble was particular in his choice of restaurant. Consequently he was somewhat putout when the Manager clearly knew her and greeted his underling warmly.

If asked, would she volunteer that her barrister friend had introduced her? Alternatively, had he merely uncover a spoilt bitch whose Daddy was in the habit of bringing her? A further thought: could Daddy be the proprietor of a competitor – perhaps even one of the nationals – and Hopeful have been sent out to feel her way around the bottom rungs of the ladder before being whisked away to the safely of the ivory tower at Daddy's place? Hell – his mind was doing somersaults! He needed a drink and he would make damned sure he got enough down Hopeful's neck to loosen her tongue.

The manager had taken it upon himself to show them to their table; the same table Hope had shared with Edric but now was forced to look across into the round, shiny face of the irritating man who insisted on calling her Hopeful. Clenching her hands in her lap she watched Stewart, bloated with pride, as he glanced about as though afraid of missing something.

It soon became clear what he had in mind. He was like a predatory cat prowling the perimeters of her life, forcing her to pick her way through an obstacle course of prying questions. Neither was it difficult to guess his strategy, for immediately upon stating that due to driving he could not drink any more he ordered yet more wine, and despite her protest another bottle was brought to the table.

Hope thought quickly. "Would you mind if I switch to brandy? Too much wine gives me a bad head." In actual fact she had barely had any. Taking her glass regularly to sealed lips, to Stewart's inattention she had given a convincing impression of keeping pace with his consumption.

Stewart motioned agreement.

Stifled by his incessant questions Hope felt a need to escape for a few moments. "Stewart, would you excuse me, please?" She removed her napkin from her lap.

"That's what drinking on a lunchtime does," he said coarsely, providing an offensive display of the partially-chewed contents of his mouth.

At the conclusion of the meal Stewart was beginning to feel the effect of the House Red. With the quantity of brandy Hope had tipped down her throat he wondered how she was feeling. It surprised him that she was still upright let alone maintaining the power of speech; his own skill in this regard was already proving unreliable. Slurred words were by now stumbling from a rubbery mouth that all too eagerly spilled his thoughts whilst he struggled to hold in check the numb thing that once had been his tongue.

Not only had the steady application of brandy seemingly left Hope unaffected, her secret, if she had one, remained intact; he had gleaned nothing new about her.

Barely concealing his irritation Stewart swayed through the diners ahead of Hope. Nearing the door Hope appeared to stumble. Instantly the Manager stepped forward to steady her.

"Thank you Max." Meaningful eyes sought his. "That – was perfect."

Lined eyes that rarely snatched enough sleep these days twinkled understanding. "Only pleased to help. You take care now." He watched her move to the door with the objectionable young man with whom she had arrived and wondered what had happened to her previous companion, Edric Colendon, who had eaten there regularly and now never did.

Intrigued, the wine waiter also watched. He had never been asked to serve a customer with measures of cold tea in place of brandy before. That would amuse the wife tonight – if she were still awake when he got home.

Hope further confounded Stewart at the fashion show where she appeared to know what she was about. He had expected her to follow his lead, instead of which he found himself trailing the wake of her swift shadow. She seemed to have a knack for getting up close in a way that he never had, the models conversing with her as though they knew her. He did not care – it was a lousy last assignment. He aimed the camera half-heartedly and took a picture. No notes were needed to support the piece he would fax through to the office later about a line of lanky lasses parading fashions in which nobody in their right mind would be seen dead. He glanced at the growing notes in Hope's pad. Let Hopeful make of it what she could. Disinterestedly he finished off the rest of the film and passed it across.

Having first-hand experience of the frantic brew of activities behind the scenes Hope had purposely waited until the interval before discreetly seeking out some of the mannequins she had worked with in the past. It amused them to discover her on the other side of the catwalk and each favoured her in preference to other members of the Press.

At the conclusion of the event something about Stewart's manner made her uncomfortable when he offered her a lift home, and she was quick to point out that it was well off his route. Eventually accepting a compromise he agreed to drop her off in the city centre from where she assured him she had a choice of public transport.

Stewart's hard acceleration and violent breaking made it an uncomfortable drive and right from the outset Hope longed for sight of the city. Rather than afford room for her anxiety to grow she turned her attention to the countryside flashing past the car window in all its mid-summer glory. She must have daydreamed for in the next moment they had left the main road and were bumping along a dirt track.

The handbrake was applied with a jerk. A flicker of amusement crossed Stewart's face.

"What would you say to going out with me from time to time Hopeful. I'm going to need someone on my arm at various functions." The new job would call for a lot of that and he was not convinced his partner Allan was ready for all of that. "You'd have a great time. I'd pay you – you know – to be seen with me."

She was appalled by his inference. "You'd what? You'd pay me! Just what do you think I am?" All restraint disappeared beneath a surge of anger that narrowed her lips and stole any pleasantness from her voice. "What do you take me for?"

"Exactly what you are. Now don't go getting all hysterical on me. Don't tell me you haven't taken money off a bloke before!" In one swift action he grabbed the hand that had moved to the door handle and pinned her back into the passenger seat.

The smell of garlic assailed her and bright spittle splashed her face as he continued arguing his case. She struggled to reach a coin from amongst those kept in the ashtray for parking. Locating a fifty-pence piece she scored it repeatedly across his knuckles until attaining freedom.

A moment later she was outside the car, had removed her slender-heeled shoes, and was running towards the safety of the main road. With no clear idea of what she should do next, and the rhythm of her heart pounding in her neck, she continued fleeing the car that would surely draw alongside at any moment.

The driver of a wagon approaching from the opposite direction caught an unattractive impression of the situation. Travelling too fast to stop he swung his vehicle at speed into a dirt track ahead, barely coming to a halt behind a parked car. After a bit of skilful manoeuvring he re-emerged to cruise beside the bonny lass who looked half scared to death.

Hope was tiring. Eventually she had to stop. Gentle coaxing persuaded her to glance up into the concerned face beneath a receding frizz of pale hair that peered down from the cab window.

Hope knew there was a particular question the man wanted to ask when, unable to form the words, he shifted to more comfortable ground and suggested she might feel safer in his cab.

Normally she would not have concurred but a swift glance at the car reversing up the farm track convinced her that the proposal was preferable to the probable alternative.

Daphne was astonished when Hope arrived home a short time later. "What on earth.... ? And I can smell fish!"

Dishevelled and looking as though she had been sleeping rough in a hedge bottom somewhere, Hope stood before her in the hall, her hair spilling untidily to the waist, both stockinged feet torn to shreds and bloodied, and with a suggestion of weeping in the eyes that despite all of this were framed by a face that was on the brink of laughter. Bob, Hope's unlikely knight-errant, had had her smiling through her tears from the point when he offered to go back to sort the geezer out!

"I'm okay, really I am, though for a few terrible moments I didn't think I was." Hope explained the reason for her appearance and arrival home in a fish wagon on route from Grimsby. "He gave me this." She held out the heavy parcel of fresh fish her self-appointed guardian had hastily put together in his newspaper before assisting her down from his cab. This bestowal of kindness was, Hope knew, an attempt to make amends for an element of the male species. She had no difficulty in accepting it in the spirit it had been given and thanked him again for her safe passage home.

After a long soak in the bath Hope worked on her coverage of the fashion show before using the fax machine in Edric's old room to send her submission to the desk where she knew Vivian Dyson would still be working.

Downstairs Daphne was amidst the preparation of her own version of the miracle involving loaves and fish: fried fish and chunks of homemade bread. And Billy was keen to show Hope his painting of two shire horses pulling a wagon at harvest time. She had given him the painting-by-numbers kit to remind him of one of the happiest days of his life when he had helped Joseph Fearnley and the grooms prepare Tarnville's two great horses for a ploughing competition. Billy's continuing fascination with horses was one of the reasons behind Hope's wish to secure her own base in or around Mowlem where she could have her extended family for short breaks and weekends.

Refusing any help in the kitchen Daphne suggested Hope might keep Billy company and assist with the painting.

Whether it was the smell of the linseed oil and paint or a distant memory of her father at his easel Hope did not know but she said, "I'm going to start painting again. I'd forgotten how much I used to enjoy it." And – perhaps the activity might go some way to dull her mind and cease its endless longing to discover whether she might after all be related to Charles as a result of a clandestine affair between her mother and his son.

275

Weighing just as heavy were questions relating to Edric. She longed to know what he was doing, where was he living – and with whom. Painting had helped her in the past when the concentration of fine brushwork gained her a short escape from the pain of her father's death; perhaps it would again – or was it now too late and the chain of despair and loneliness would never go away?

"I wonder whether Manstonleigh's charity shop could sell any paintings I produce."

The corners of Daphne's mouth curved with approval. "I'm sure they could, though you're not having this one back!" Appreciative eyes slanted up at the tranquil scene of Mowlem hanging above her mantelpiece. "That's not for sale at any price!"

Hope was amazed when it was her coverage of the fashion show that appeared in the Barlayne Express and not Stewart Trimble's. When she was shown the galley proofs and typeset plates she thought her colleagues were playing a joke but Vivian Dyson told her it was no joke. He had liked her choice of reporting angle.

After a well-written concise résumé she had switched to recounting such events from the viewpoint of the model, pointing out the pitfalls and struggle of some mannequins in the constant fight to retain a slender form. Into this was cleverly woven a worthy mention that the larger model, the shape more closely resembling the woman in the street, was now finding her niche. It had been exactly right for inclusion in the Women's Section.

Vivian had expected a good piece though not the powerful human elements skilfully incorporated in her coverage. He had been right in his assessment of her abilities. Furthermore he had discovered other attributes, the knowledge of which he chose not to share beyond his wife. The discovery had been made one evening when his wife's magazine slid from her lap to lay open at a full-page spread for Sally Lox hair products and he found himself gazing into his Assistant's face.

Only time would tell whether the camera would shortly be looking for a new subject – or alternatively the camera would win and he would be advertising for a new Assistant. Vivian was taking no bets.

A steady flow of assignments followed and in addition to learning to drive, Hope received proper training in the field of journalism, first in-house and later on a day-release and evening-class basis.

She continued to work hard, in her spare time painting, frequently from photographs taken in Corfu, and between these activities managed to curb the list of unspoken questions relating to her lineage, and to a lesser extent the ardent longing to know something – anything – about Edric. Sometimes though her thoughts did break through and then the counterweight of balance would drain the energy from her mental process.

Chapter 34

"The bride, Isabel (Bell) Patterson, formerly the housekeeper at Tarnville, was given away by her ex-employer and friend, Sir Charles Lurdmayne, who flew in from Corfu two days ago especially for the occasion...."

Charles read the newspaper article aloud to Hope draped youthfully over the back of his favourite chair in Tarnville's library, his silvery head nodding approval.

"Your father would have been pleased," he said at length. "Your aunt's marriage yesterday and not least this," he tapped the newspaper, "you a Press reporter – a journalist! There seems no limit to what you can accomplish."

The parental-like adulation directed at her maturing ability was so reminiscent of her father's over her first squiggles of shorthand that it almost hurt and Hope reached to place a kiss on Charles's cheek. "As I'm sure you're only too aware, there're loads of things at which I don't excel – though I'm hopeful that I'm about to improve one of them."

She did not explain the giggle that escaped her as she was reminded of the nickname a boyish-faced man had given her a year ago whilst introducing her to the field of journalism, the career that seemingly had been waiting for her.

"My total inability to knit anything without the unscheduled appearance of holes has always been an embarrassment. At school I barely progressed from knitting dishcloths to the dizzy excitement of producing a scarf! My friend Angela is expecting a baby and I've persuaded Bell to help me create something more suitable for a new arrival than dishcloths or scarves!"

She was looking forward to her role of Godmother but beneath her buoyant mood worried that nothing should go wrong with Angela's pregnancy. Time, she realised, was marching on – but that was good. She would never forget Edric and despite everything that Isabel and her friends told her, there would never be room in her heart for anyone else. Nevertheless over the last sixteen months her memories had become more manageable and less intrusive.

Smiling to herself she wondered whether Edric might see Isabel's wedding photograph in the paper, and if he did whether he would notice from the name at the conclusion of the article that she were the author. The Barlayne Express did not have as wide a coverage as some but did include Leeds and if Edric still retained a base at the Leeds Shillens....

It was better to suppress these thoughts. She returned to reading her piece under the headline of "Wedding Bells for Bell".

During the ceremony Hope had caught a brief glimpse of her father's landlady tucked in at the back of the church. Christine would have heard something about Isabel's marriage and attended out of curiosity or perhaps a sense of being linked to the family by her association with Frederick. The sighting made Hope regretful she had not keep in touch with the woman who had given her a painting and had meant so much to her father, but after Edric went she had not wanted to court anything that might stir the embers she fought hard to suffocate. She looked for Christine after the service to invite her back to the reception at Tarnville but she had already slipped away.

It had taken no more than the sighting of her father's common-law wife to stir the memory of one of her last days with Edric, when they had been endeavouring to discover more about his mother's early years. In parallel likeness, back at the reception Charles had been overly keen to pull her away from Hattie Middler, presumably in case Hattie began speaking about the Maggie Smith she remembered in the market square *who sang like an angel*, and the old woman's ramblings become too torturous for her to bear.

Contrary to Isabel, Charles never mentioned Edric; unwilling to engage in conversation about him it was as though he had lost the framework of forgiveness. In the early days his silence was easier to cope with than the multitude of questions falling from the lips of others; though not now. His silence was no longer helpful or indeed appropriate. No matter how painful the experience she should not neglect her memories of those heady, fun-filled days – for they were all she had left to sustain her.

But that was yesterday, when the swell of happiness had given her a sense of inner strength to cope with her loneliness. Today she was less confident and now hankered after that same strength.

In the knowledge that Charles would be taking his usual afternoon nap and Isabel and Peter were collecting together the last of Isabel's things, Hope slipped out of the house. There was something she had to do, and after everything that had happened now seemed the right time to do it.

Nervous beads of sweat prickled her hairline as she made her way towards the river along the stone-flagged path where moss had trespassed to make the cracks spongy to her tread. In her distraction she did not notice, nor appreciate the startling miniature flower arrangements sprouting eagerly from amongst other cracks. She threw one last look behind her before making for the bridge.

The river beneath the planking barely moved. She had learned to identify with its moods. Its pulse fluctuated between today's tranquillity and the raging torrent that on occasions threatened to overflow its banks when, like some marauding beast, it declared a threat to low-lying land and property alike. Able to identify with each, she loved all its characteristics, the placid and the unmerciful. She respected the river. In return it had rewarded her with comfort, nursed her through turbulent times and even, when at her lowest ebb, stimulated her towards action whereby she had taken life's bit firmly between her teeth.

Today the water was in languid mood. Had it been different she might have been less inclined to pursue her objective. She made her way along the opposite bank towards the spot where she had stood with her father on the occasion of each birthday to watch the placement of a further stone in the riverbed; and they unknowingly observed from Tarnville's library window.

Today the 18 stepping-stones stood proud of the shining surface. Another step took her to the water's edge and within a stride of the first stone, but then she hesitated.

Like a magnet the familiar structure on the far side claimed her attention like it had always done. Smiling to herself she reflected how it had not been until later that she came to understand her father had been speaking figuratively of her future. But had he? With recent learning she now dared to wonder if he had in fact been speaking literally. Could it be that her original childlike comprehension had been correct and that Tarnville was to be her future after all? What exactly had been Sir Charles's instruction to his lawyer? Could Richard Lurdmayne have been her real father?

The moment was lost beneath a squabble of magpies exploding from the lofty sycamore trees behind her. She glanced back at the stepping-stones. She would not walk across them today. Instinct told her the time was not yet right and that something was not yet in place.

Chapter 35

The following year Hope became the proud Godmother to William James.

Hope was sitting on the padded window seat that Angela had made from a length of floral fabric, which added a splash of colour to the cool blue and white colour scheme of her front room. Hope was aware of the new mother's scrutiny. "Afraid I might drop him?" She shifted her gaze back to the baby in her arms. "We wouldn't do that would we Willie-Jim? Your Mum's frowning," she whispered to the sleeping child, "but believe me, *Willie-Jim* is a great deal better than what she originally wanted to call you. *IT* wouldn't have suited you at all!"

Angela laughed. "Honestly you get worse! If I'm frowning its because I can't get over the change in you."

Hope's newly bobbed hair repositioned itself as she angled her head to look enquiringly at her friend who was reaching up to water the green plant suspended in a basket from the ceiling by the bookcase.

"And it's not just the new short hairstyle, which I might add suits you. It's you. You've...."

"Moved on?"

Angela nodded, wiping up a drip of water that had missed its target and landed on the television cabinet.

"You were right when you told me I'd reached the point where I needed to take charge of my life. It may not be exactly what I'd hoped for. Nevertheless I'm happy. Working at the Paper continues to excite me. I still look forward to going in each morning. I simply love it." She confessed to never expecting to find another position to compare so favourably with her role at Lester's.

The haircut had been a split-second decision and underlined the stance she had decided to take. The action was as clear a statement as she was able to make: she was finally finished with photography work and ready to leave behind all that it entailed.

Her decision saddened Harry Nichols who had enjoyed working with the poised, cool model. Many had paraded before his lens but Hope was one of the few who managed to maintain a detachment from all the pomposity attracted to the business.

On the other side of the coin, Vivian Dyson had been delighted and the following day he dragged Hope out to lunch to present her with a revised contract of employment, which put her in charge of the Women's Section.

"Is a career on its own enough for you....?"

Hope knew full well what lay behind Angela's question: was she over Edric? The answer was No, she would never be over Edric – though carefully scripted her reply, "I'm kept busy at the Paper, and of course there's my painting." She had been amazed by the success with which her untrained brush had been met. After buying her paintings from Manstonleigh the main purchaser, a woman in her mid-forties, had sought Hope out with a view to buying all that she could produce.

She knew the woman by sight. Some Sunday evenings she and Edric had strolled through Leeds, frequently ending up at the waterfront where there was a little shop whose window displayed all manner of interesting bric-a-brac. The shop was closed but they had caught sight of the woman busying herself behind the locked door. It had been their intention to explore the interior but they never had.

After agreeing the deal it struck Hope as strange that despite his absence Edric continued to cross her path as he had in the past, albeit this time in the modified form of the woman they had observed together.

"And there's something else...." Hope admitted slowly, "not only do I have my job on the Paper and my painting, but I'm doing a bit of writing – fiction. I say fiction though it's primarily based on my life's experiences. It's called *The Stepping-Stones*. I'm not far off finishing it but recently changed my mind about the ending. I'm struggling a bit with that, but I'm in no particular hurry."

Her daily journal, initially kept for her father's benefit, had eliminated the need to draft a plan. It was all there: a wealth of detail recording all the love, abuse and pain she had ever experienced. Those meticulous records depicted a variety of contrasting literary pictures, which swung like a pendulum from a backdrop of lush green countryside and quiet village life, to the noisy bustle of the city with its emphasis on shareholders, increased profit, high profiles, better media image, and where everyone spoke of diversifying and never fretted over harvesting.

"My friend an author! Why didn't you tell me?"

"Steady on. I'm hardly that! You're forgetting I'm a mere first-timer and my efforts may well remain in the cupboard gathering dust for evermore."

Angela admonished her. "And you never breathed a word! Don't you dare say I can't read it after this!"

"I promise you'll be the first to see it when it's finished." If it's ever finished, she added silently. It seemed unlikely with the happy conclusion gone from her life, presumably to return to his wife. Surely no man had ever been more loved than Edric. How could he have failed to interpret the message in her eyes?

Hope looked back at Angela. She nodded thoughtfully. "Yes.... I reckon the Paper, my painting and my scribbling are enough to keep me occupied – at least for the moment – and until I see what's round the next corner."

Their laughter disturbed the infant in Hope's arms, who now stirred and claimed their attention. Angela fell to thoughtfulness, recalling how Hope had been looking forward to motherhood.

"What're you thinking?"

The question caught Angela off guard. She improvised. "Nothing particular. Just – how things have changed and how we've both moved on whilst adapting to those changes. Who'd have thought when we met that a few years later we'd be sitting here – me with that little bundle of noise," she nodded towards her son, "and you a celebrated model turned newspaper reporter!"

A few years later.... Angela's words, cruelly similar to some of her own, were like an unwelcome guest rummaging through the drawers of her mind to reveal recollections of the innocent question put to Gregory during a May Day event at Tarnville: "Where do you think we all will be in a few years from now?" She now had the answer: Gregory dead, Amy bereaved, and she – a whole catalogue of tragedy and misfortune had since presented itself to plague her.

Angela studied her, seeing at once the brilliance of sadness in her eyes. These days Hope could look sad even when she was smiling and she wondered whether her friend had been brave enough in her writing whereby she would discover the cause within the pages of *The Stepping-Stones*.

"You've come through such a lot," she said, as though sharing the myriad of disturbing pictures crowding Hope's mind. "You've managed to put all of that behind you and now you're getting on with life."

"If you're referring to Edric, yes I suppose I am, though I have to say not from choice. I still love him. I always will." She was surprised how emphatic her words sounded; she had too readily laid bare her feelings. "The simple fact is he just didn't love me enough...." An uncomfortable silence followed. "Hey – don't let me go getting all maudlin! My life's good – and getting better all the time." She smiled down at her Godson whose mouth opened almost wide enough to swallow her.

"My only disappointment is that I missed a property that recently came up in Mowlem – Ivy Cottage – but I expect another will come up in time." Angela expressed understanding that the cottages formed part of the Estate. "Mostly they do but several have passed into private ownership, which I suppose could be viewed as a personal gift from Sir Charles to the community that's served his family well." Hope changed the subject, "Gosh – is that the time? Here take this tired little treasure. I need to ring the office and check my voice-mail to see whether I'm straight out on location tomorrow or starting in the office. Is it okay to use your phone? My mobile's on charge."

Angela opened her arms to receive her son, now yawning wide enough to swallow elephants. "Of course you can. You don't need to ask."

When Hope returned to the room a short while later, Angela noticed her changed mood and pale complexion. Her eyes widened to stay any quizzical comment from her husband who had joined her.

"Come – sit down. What is it?" Angela made room on the settee.

Hope stumbled into the gap beside her. "My next assignment...."

"Is it a tricky one?" Alex was interested and sat forward in his chair. He enjoyed her lively company and could not understand Angela's continuing concern. Hope had always struck him as a lovely, well-balanced young woman.

"That would be putting it mildly! Viv wants me to cover a Press briefing at the Leeds Shillens at nine o'clock tomorrow." The horror in Hope's face barely hinted at her true feelings. Katie, the secretary she shared, had left several messages on her voice mail. Most made her smile, others merely shrug but when she heard the last one she felt as though someone had torn the world from beneath her feet. "Nine tomorrow!" she repeated. She turned to Angela. "I can't do it – Edric will be there!"

"You don't know that – not for certain. Anyway I should think it unlikely that he would involve himself in a Press briefing."

Alex agreed. "He'll have his minions for that."

Hope shook her head. "You don't understand. He's bound to be there. It's to cover his brainchild. He was working on a totally unique idea for the hotel industry."

Katie's message had been sufficiently explicit for her to know it would be unlikely that Edric would miss the opportunity to address the Press in person. Without breaking confidentiality she explained how Edric had confided in her about an elaborate idea he was developing. She ended on a sigh. "For both our sakes I can't do it." Her tone implied self-doubt.

"Yes you can!" exclaimed Angela. "You've got to. When you've done this you'll finally be able to put Edric behind you and get on with your life."

Hope was not convinced that she wanted to put Edric behind her. A few moments ago they had been discussing the inroads she had achieved in getting her life back on track. Now she was less certain and suddenly felt exposed and vulnerable and was already working out the sum of the hours between now and when she would be forced to return to that other era; the part of her life in which she had hoped to remain forever but which had been snatched away from her.

Angela squeezed her hand. "You've invested so much in your future. Don't let this knock you off target. Believe me, it's right that you should do it. Look at me." she poked her head at Hope. "Wasn't I right when I suggested working as a Temp?"

Despite those words Angela felt uneasy. Everything had been going so well. This latest development could set Hope back – and if it did would she recover a further time?

Chapter 36

Even to the casual observer it was clear that something out of the ordinary was afoot. On discovering members of the Press armed with cameras, hotel guests had begun dawdling about the foyer in the anticipation of catching sight of a celebrity and entourage.

Hope was grateful for the presence of so many media bodies and associated paraphernalia. All night long she had imagined this moment, fearing she would be instantly recognised and Edric alerted. In the event her entrance to the Leeds Shillens, where not so long ago she had been a regular personage on the arm of one of its main Board Members, went unnoticed. Taking in the scene her eyes darted nervously around the entrance hall whose vastness today appeared shrunken by the gathering of so many journalists and guests. With no indication of when the former might be escorted to a conference room nervousness had painted a glaze across her upper lip. Just then a hand descended heavily on her shoulder and she wheeled in the expectation of seeing Edric.

"I thought it was you but wasn't sure from the back. The short hairdo still throws me." His head aslant, Harry Nichols stood before her flanked by two leather bags crammed full with camera equipment. "I still say it was sacrilege taking scissors to it. But it's done now." Remembering voluminous hair that spilled beyond her waist he managed a smile. "You covering the briefing for that Paper of yours?" She nodded, relief now softening her green eyes. "Me too. They approached me to take some shots for some literature they're putting out. Believe me – it's exciting stuff."

All puffed up and with a smirk of pride in his voice Harry explained he had been engaged as the official photographer in the matter and had received a privileged briefing the previous week with the opportunity to take aerial shots from the corporate helicopter, which he suggested would be deeply coveted by opposite numbers present today.

Hope joined in with the immodest rave reviews of this lovely man who at this moment resembled a peacock in spring strutting his path with aplomb.

There were several elements attached to this assignment that excited him, he went on, each in its own way a challenge to his photographic skills. Only rarely had he missed sleep over a job; this one, his tone implied, had been the exception. Bearing in mind the size of the organisation, if he came up with the goods, which he would he emphasised, it was not inconceivable that even larger doors might open up for him. Revelling in pleasure he pondered some more, unaware that the silent person beside him knew more about the project than anyone else present, himself included.

"So, flower, we find ourselves on the same side of the camera."

Hope returned his big smile though would prefer not to have bumped into anyone she knew. Harry would want to know how she was settling down in her new career and engaged in conversation would make it difficult to maintain a low profile. She had planned on being amongst the last to be led through, thereby securing seating nobody else wanted at the rear of the room but from where she would be able to observe Edric over a safe distance. Harry's next words removed any possibility of that.

"Stick with me petal. I've already sussed which door they'll take us through." He nodded towards a door beyond the Reception desk. "If we weave over there now we'll be amongst the first to go through and get the best seats."

It would have been futile to protest and in any event he was already steering her towards the door. At the point when she had begun to wonder whether she might tender the lame excuse of needing the ladies' room Harry nudged her almost rudely to the front just as the door opened and suddenly she was amongst the first to be herded into the corridor.

Harry was talking fast, giving her hints and tips but all she could think about was the urgent need to escape the ordeal that was now only moments away.

To her immense relief management invitees already filled the first four rows of seating: local councillors, shareholders and the like. Conversely her anxiety heightened when she noticed Samuel Shillens on the front row; the Chairman's presence would not summon one of *Edric's minions* to the fore as Alex had speculated. Now she was certain that Edric would chair the briefing, and not for the first time she wished she had had the nerve to ring in sick; accidentally mix up her appointments; even pay an unscheduled visit to the dentist; anything but this.

Harry pushed her into the row immediately behind the VIPs, brusquely urging her towards the middle when she made a show of settling in a seat at the side. "You've a lot to learn about camera angles, Sweetie. Whenever you can, always take it from the centre-front. Depending on your choice of lens, shooting from the side can land you with all sorts of problems when lining up straight vertical structures with the subject."

They sat down and Harry began sorting out his equipment. He did not like the lighting; there was too much of it he said. Whilst Harry muttered some more about the lighting and ferreted about in a bag for something, Hope experimented with her seating position.

The central position was not so bad. If she sat to one side she could obscure her vision of two of the three chairs on the risen dais. She could only pray that Edric would not elect to sit on the other; the only way she could removed that chair from her vision would be to slouch awkwardly to the other side and almost in Harry's lap – a position that would certainly draw attention to herself, if only from Harry. If Edric chose that seat she would just have to cross her fingers and trust that her bobbed hair and unlikely presence amongst the media might succeed in camouflaging her.

Feeling braver she looked around and recognised faces from previous assignments. Her breathing had barely returned to normal when her eyes fell on the round, boyish face of Stewart Trimble in the subservient position at the edge of the room several rows behind. His eyes were upon her though did not linger but continued to travel the room. His indifference left her wondering whether he were still smarting from her reaction to his outrageous suggestion or, and perhaps more likely, Vivian's rejection of his article in favour of hers or whether, as she hoped, her changed appearance prevented recognition.

With the arrival of three dark-clad figures she did not have time to ponder further. Under the pretext of retrieving something from the bag by her feet Hope shifted position. Harry frowned a question, which went unacknowledged as she made a show of training seemingly keen attention towards the front where, with relief, it was not Edric who took the chair she was unable to eclipse with someone's head. A man with ample proportions filled that seat. He had an exceptional head of almost white, crinkled hair that shone beneath the ceiling lighting that Harry had growled about earlier.

Edric was there; Hope sensed his presence and her heart leapt at the recollection of the smile that would be directed towards the audience.

Samuel Shillens had risen to his feet to introduce the panel on the dais. Those around Hope began scribbling furiously whilst her own pen remained strangled in her grasp.

". . . So, ladies, gentlemen – all that remains is for me to hand you over to the team. The Director of Acquisitions & Mergers will take you through the details of why you have been invited here today. After you've been provided with an understanding of this totally new and innovative concept – which others will undoubtedly seek to emulate – he will hand you over to his colleagues – the Directors of Finance, and of Resource Planning.... " he turned to nod to each, ". . . who will endeavour to take you through their field of remit. From what you are about to hear you will discover for yourselves that Shillens International is indeed in touch with the needs of the times! It gives me great pleasure to hand you over now to the Director of Acquisitions & Mergers."

Even before the Chairman resumed his seat Hope's eyes sought the sanctuary of the floor as she prepared to hear Edric's voice again.

Someone in the row behind muttered, "What a mouthful of a title. I trust their innovative concept that everyone will seek to emulate is not as long winded as the designation on this chap's business card!"

Instantly Hope prickled with protection and would have turned round to glare but Edric had begun speaking.

Upon hearing the very first syllables Hope felt her jaw slacken. It was not the expected round-toned, velvet-like voice of Edric that filled the expectant room but the voice of another. She pressed her lips firmly back together. Filled with consternation, under the distraction of flash bulbs she took the opportunity to squirm in her seat and gain a better view.

It was the silver-haired man who was speaking. There followed a moment of stunned innermost silence when it seemed to her that her entire being had been liquefied. Further confusion stumbled through her mind when she dared to lean the other way to steal a look at the other two Directors. Edric was not in attendance.

Understanding eluded her and deliberately went over the Chairman's introduction, satisfying herself that he had indeed used Edric's title. Could Edric have been promoted and his place been taken by this older man? Unlikely – apart from the positions of Deputy Chairman or Chairman there was no rung left on Edric's ladder. Agitated, her hand sought comfort from the smooth, amber drop suspended on its chain beneath her jacket.

The only explanation that made any sense was that Edric had left the organisation. Upon this Hope lost all concentration. She longed to know where he was and what he was doing. Likewise, no doubt he would be interested to learn she was now a journalist, and eminently surprised to hear she was covering his project.

All at once she recalled his wish one day to set up a board of executives to run his own currency and investment company, diversifying eventually into opening a property portfolio. He mentioned having identified a good builder. There could be no other answer. Edric had done it – he had struck out on his own! Other things began slipping into place, not least where he had met the builder. Now she was in no doubt that Edric had returned to Kent – to Hilary. Wistfully, she wondered whether they were making a go of it this time. Perhaps with Dadda out of the picture they stood a chance. She hoped so and in that precise moment knew she loved Edric enough to truly hope that he was happy – even if that happiness did not include her.

At the end of the briefing, having heard not a word or taken a single note, Hope was guided by Harry to where light refreshments and finger food had been laid out. She was not sorry when Harry evaporated and she spotted him moments later speaking to someone at the other side of the room.

She had been nervous about coming upon Edric but now felt cheated and tried to persuade herself that the feeling was absurd and it was better this way; better than having to play charades, chatting together as though mere friends, when with ears pricked in anticipation of endearments she would long to lean in close to breathe in the familiar fragrance of his skin. In the next moment her inner self rationalised that she could not leave it like this. Something deep within her core demanded confirmation that Edric was all right; that he was happy. Only then could she close that particular chapter and get on with her life.

As though on cue, Hope noticed Allison Ballard going about the task of handing out literature to support the briefing. Hope was toying with the idea of approaching her when a waitress appeared at her side.

"Mrs Stratton? May I get you something? Here – let me pass you a plate." The waitress swivelled to the pile of plates on the table. "I weren't sure it were you...." her words trailed off in the knowledge that if she were overheard she would be reprimanded for being overly familiar and not presenting the professional image she was sick of hearing about. She knew her Ps and Qs and when to keep her trap shut.

With one eye on her manager the waitress handed a crested plate to the woman she had always liked and was not all stuck-up and snooty like the rest of the Directors' womenfolk. Mrs Stratton was a right nice lady and loads better than the others, and she had always made a point of speaking to her, protecting her claim to being part of the human race. She had liked her right from her first day of working at the Shillens when she made a mess of serving her with coffee from an appliance that had been switched off. But Mrs Stratton said nothing – not so much as a muff – and even went so far as to thank her after draining the cup of lukewarm, muddy liquid.

The use of her discarded married name threw Hope momentarily. "Thank you Haley." She took the plate whilst looking warmly at the young waitress, who seemed pleased to be remembered by name; she used it again. "How are you Haley?" She would have asked after the sickly kitten she found her weeping about in the ladies' room except that it had probably died and to ask would open old wounds; and if it pulled through it would be fully grown by now, making her question irrelevant.

Being careful to keep her chatter from the keen, roving eyes of her manager, Haley spoke pleasantly for several moments, then with reluctance said, "I s'pose I oughta press on and hand these plates round." She hesitated, turning back. "We were right sorry to hear the sad news about Mr Colendon. We all miss him." It was true, the staff had liked him and the place had never been the same since. Several of her colleagues, herself included, had cried inconsolably when the news broke. She was about to recommence her duties but something in Hope's expression held her back.

"Haley – what do you mean? Tell me…..what sad news?"

The faint hysterical edge to her voice pulled further explanation from the young waitress in fits and starts. "The firm…..in Edinburgh . ….the fire at the Edinburgh Shillens."

There was a long drawn-out silence as though waiting for the world to start revolving again. Hope slumped forward to take support from the table.

Haley removed the plate to safety. "Mrs Stratton – let me take you outside."

Receiving no protest and mouthing to others that madam was finding it a little warm, the waitress led her from the room. In the corridor she watched Hope spill into an upholstered chair, her forehead shimmering with pinpricks of sweat. Haley said nothing until panic set in on seeing all colour drain from Hope's face. "Perhaps I should go fetch someone. Should I? Do you want someone?" She watched for affirmation. Mrs Stratton looked ever so queer. Perhaps she should shove her head between her legs or something....

Hesitantly, Haley performed the necessary function, Hope's head lolling forward on slackened shoulders. "Oh eck! Mrs Stratton wake up – wake up Mrs Stratton. Oh 'eck!" Haley glanced about for assistance but the corridor was deserted.

Lacking in self-awareness Hope studied the floor through closed eyelids. She must not open her eyes. If she did the tears would start and never stop. She began to rock until she eventually succeeded in blending the movement with the rhythm of the river splashing against the stones beside her. In a moment the river would rise up and flood the whole village. Gregory would try to persuade her into a boat but she would refuse and that would be the end of everything....

But consciousness prevailed.

All this time – and she had never known! How had it been possible to sit through a televised newscast and not realise that the person whose life had been lost had been Edric's? Behind closed eyelids Hope saw disturbing pictures of firemen engaged in a battle to control jagged flames striving to introduce an incongruous palette of neon to a dark horizon. Why had she not sensed something – felt something?

But she had! She remembered telling Angela how Edric's disappearance had left her feeling bereaved. Somehow she *had* known! Something deep inside her had warned of the tragedy but she had been too busy trying to fill her empty days to make sense of those feelings.

Suddenly she felt isolated. Her entire life had been a mockery. It might as well be over for there was nothing left to endure or enjoy. There could never be any more; it was finished. What had it had all been about?

Vague phrases uttered by the young waitress began to filter through her thoughts.

"I thought you knew. It were terrible. Everyone were right shocked. It made management put a whole lot of new fire-drill practices into place, I can tell you! And a man died." Haley watched Hope's face lift, her eyes widening as though to challenge her.

"You mean.... as well as Mr Colendon?" But Hope could see the girl did not comprehend and quickly rephrased her question. "Do you mean someone else as well as Mr Colendon died in the fire?"

"No! A man died yes, but it wasn't Mr Colendon. I don't know much about what happened but he didn't die! All I know is he was badly hurt and he never came back."

Edric had been badly hurt – but he was alive! Overwhelming joy swept away the risk of tears in Hope's impatience to learn more. "How badly was he hurt?" Something that went far deeper than relief had entered her voice. She was on her feet and already making sense of why Edric had gone from her life so abruptly: he had suffered burns, perhaps disfigurement, and had not wished to keep her bound to him by pity. Had he really no idea how deep her feelings ran and that nothing would have taken her from his side?

Despite the guest's visible distress Haley had derived an incongruous sense of pleasure from the past few minutes. Few displayed the same level of friendliness towards staff as this lady. Regretful at being unable to furnish these answers Haley shook her white-capped head. "That's all I know. I'm right sorry." Then, inspired, "You could ask his old secretary, Allison. She can be a right snotty-nosed bitch but she might...." Haley recoiled with the realisation of what she had said. "Awh – I'm right sorry. I didn't mean – well I did, but not like...."

Hope smiled in a way that said she understood.

"I mean she might know some more."

Hope had come to the same conclusion but thanked Haley warmly.

Back in the room Allison Ballard smiled pleasantly at Hope's approach and was already peeling off a sheet of typewritten detail from her pile of papers when recognition slipped into place. Momentarily bemused she glanced at the yellow badge on Hope's lapel that identified her as a member of the Press. This meagre claim to fame had the effect of retaining the smile a while longer. Allison had enjoyed the last hour or so liasing with the media, Board Members and guests. With an air of importance she had glided around looking every bit as though part of the higher echelons than that of the secretarial ranks, and Hope was fleetingly reminded of Marty.

Hope accepted a typed sheet without awarding it a glance before embarking on a line of questioning relating to the secretary's former boss.

The expression on Allison's face faded towards that of veiled indifference. "Edric? Injured? Yes – yes he was." She smiled over Hope's shoulder and pressed a paper into a hand that trespassed rudely between them. Her expression reverted back to one she felt more deserving of the woman standing before her. "He never came back."

"So I understand," commented Hope, eager to learn more. "Can you tell me anything else?" She hated having to put such vital questions to this woman whose eyes kept wandering the room in zigzag, butterfly fashion to alight now and then on someone considered more worthy of a display of her perfect teeth.

"He ended up in a wheelchair," Allison said eventually, her smile moving on to another.

"A wheelchair! Do you know anything else, like where....?"

"Look," Allison interjected, glancing meaningfully at the woman who was beginning to try her patience, "I'm sorry – but I have a job to do here." She nodded across Hope's vision to a man making his way towards her.

"Yes, yes. I appreciate that, but I must know. Please.... perhaps you have an address or something," Hope prompted hopefully.

"Afraid not." Another hand thrust between them to receive a sheet from the diminishing bundle; once more the orchestrated flash of teeth. "I believe he's living abroad – Greece or somewhere."

The conversation died away when Allison began chatting to another. Hope waited a few moments before applying her own interpretation to the averted stance; she would learn nothing more. Putting distance between herself and the woman who displayed an astounding lack of compassion she wandered away to sift through the meagre information gathered so far. Allison had mentioned Greece. Of course – Edric would have gone to his villa in Corfu! She must go to him. Nothing must prevent her. Her bright eyes urgently scanned the room for Harry Nichols.

Harry was clearly intrigued by Hope's request but told her she could leave it in his hands, adding that he owed her at least one special favour for the amount of work she had put his way.

Almost breaking into a run Hope hastened from the hubbub of noise to the seclusion of the corridor where she made three telephone calls in rapid succession, the first to Vivian Dyson to beg permission to take some immediate compassionate leave.

Picking up on her employer's concern she felt obliged to share her news with him. Grasping the picture, Vivian put forward no obstacle to prevent her immediate departure for Corfu and furthermore instructed her to keep her mobile switched on whilst her secretary rang round to check the availability of flights.

"Thank you Viv! Thanks for everything. Oh and before you go – I've arranged for first-class text and photographs of this Shillens thing to be delivered to you not later than two o'clock today. And Viv – I can promise that no one else will have better photographs or details!" This was no empty promise; Harry would not let her down.

Hope regretted not being able to contact her aunt but Isabel was touring Cornwall with Peter. Next she rang Daphne who became squeaky-voiced on hearing her news and began to cry, every now and then punctuating her sobs with exclamations that she had always known Edric would not have disappeared without good cause.

Finally she rang Angela who misinterpreted excitement for hysteria, and it took several minutes before Hope was able to convey anything meaningful. Angela's concluding remark made her chuckle; the last chapters of *The Stepping-Stones* were, she said, apparently writing themselves.

Hope wanted to ring the entire world but learned she did not have time when Katie rang back to say she had secured her a seat on a flight departing Leeds-Bradford that evening. Katie bade her a good trip, reminding her more than once not to forget her passport and from which desk to collect her flight tickets and currency.

Chapter 37

Hope stood like a statue a tableau across the road from Edric's villa. She could hardly breathe. Nothing had changed; the cream-washed structure was just as she remembered it and a surge of exquisite happiness brought a swim of emotional tears that she blinked rapidly away.

Despite this unprecedented joy tiny seeds of doubt managed to creep beneath the surface. What if Edric did not want to be found, or if his wife now lived with him? She had not thought of that. It might be that Hilary would open the door! Suddenly that which yesterday had seemed a sound plan now struck her as idiotic and rash. She should have rung Edric before flying out.

A door opened behind her and she turned to see a young woman shorter than herself with a tendency towards heaviness. She wore the uniform of a holiday representative and held a dish of food for the cat that now emerged from the shrubbery to execute a feline dance of affection round her thick ankles. The woman glanced up.

"Can I help you?" She came nearer, curious to discover what brought this stunning personage to her boyfriend's villa. Her hands tugged her uniform to neatness over free-flowing curves.

Hope was not oblivious to the spectacle she presented. Whilst her choice of outfit was not in essence dressy, neither was it the garment of someone out for a saunter round the supermarket, but she had wanted to look her best for Edric, and he had always liked her in this colour.

"I was about to call on a friend," she said, nodding to Edric's villa across the road. "I'm hoping it's not too early to pay a visit," a merry smile was directed at the woman.

"The old gentleman?" the holiday representative too now nodded towards the cream structure. "He's away at the moment. Won't be back until around the end of next week." She ceased abruptly with the realisation that she had already said too much. It did not do to tell strangers that a property was unattended.

Old gentleman? Hope's face burst into the beginnings of a smile. She supposed a person in a wheelchair would appear old to someone used to dealing with young, party-going holidaymakers. But the woman was speaking again.

"Or perhaps you mean the previous owner? I remember him vaguely – a good-looking man – had a dog that went everywhere with him. Do you mean Mr Colendon, the rather nice man in a wheelchair?"

Hope found herself nodding whilst questions sprang to lips suddenly rendered incapable of speech. The previous owner? Edric had moved! Her keenness to know more took her on unsteady legs through the gateway to stand before the woman. "You say Edric doesn't live there anymore? Do you know where he's gone?"

The woman was already shaking her head. "The new occupant might, but like I said he's away."

Despair had all but overtaken Hope when she remembered Edric's cousin. "Of course!" she said. "Claire and her family who live over there," she pointed, relief easing the return of a smile. "They'll know where he's living. I can't imagine why I...." But the woman's head was performing a repeat of the same sideways movement.

"Claire and Nicos Petrou? They're away too. Claire took the children out to join her husband. He's been lecturing or something abroad. I understand they've gone out to join him, I suppose to make a bit of a holiday of it."

The news narrowed Hope's smile. Why had she not telephoned before coming out? Why? Because she had the impulsiveness that rides tandem with idiocy, but mostly because she wanted to see Edric, not speak on the telephone when she would be unable to enjoy his smile or share an embrace. She hardly heard the words of apology as the woman made a move to go inside to prepare for work. With barely a smile Hope's hand raised in a weak gesture of a wave.

She threw one last look at the villa where Edric had once lived, and then aimlessly strolled away with no clear idea as to what to do. It was really stupid to jump on a plane without ringing first. Really stupid! Already acknowledging it a ridiculous idea, she wondered whether Charles Lurdmayne might know something, but if he had learned of Edric's presence on the island, furthermore in a wheelchair, he would have told her.

It suddenly occurred to her that Edric would have made arrangements for the redirection of his mail, and maybe if she made enquiries…..

She had just quickened her step when the scratch of a twig startled her to awareness. Without planning to do so she had taken the track leading to the Old Man's Bar, which she had photographed and painted many times and visited many more times with Edric. How strange and how uncanny, she thought, theorising it possibly spiritual, for had she not prayed for a sign to indicate whether Edric would share the rest of her life? Could finding herself on the curtilage of the Old Man's Bar be that sign, or was she merely being fanciful?

It might be that Edric still frequented their favourite haunt, for surely he would not have gone far from his family.

Hope beamed across the counter in the anticipation of gaining recognition, though none was apparent. Not unlike her first visit, in like manner she made little headway in making herself understood by the proprietor. Her frustration poignantly reminded her of the day that Edric came to her rescue. How she wished he would walk in now.

Walk! In all her distraction she had forgotten that Edric was no longer able to walk. She swayed with the thought of her wonderful, handsome friend held captive by a wheelchair but then in the next moment, inspired, began adding painstaking displays of mime to add emphasis to her questions, not caring whether her elaborate circular arm movements became a source of amusement to the locals habitually tucked into the shade.

She was delighted when the toothless grin widened behind the bar, and only recognised failure when a stubby-stemmed glass resembling the size and shape of a goldfish bowl was pushed towards her. Annoyed by her lack of communication skills she paid for the beer she did not want and rammed her purse back into her bag.

She carried the bulbous glass outside, automatically making for the table beside the low wall where from habit Edric had rested his foot. Scanning the ground her eyes carefully raked the detail of the sand-scattered concrete but detected no evidence of an inscription made by the tracery of narrow tyres that might indicate the recent passage of a wheelchair.

A wave at the height of its momentum detonated against the wall and sent a plume of salt-fragrant spray high in the air. The eruption startled her and in the next instance went weak with the memory of something long, cool and silky being draped around her person. It seemed an age since that first meeting.

That had been the first time they had spoken, though not the first time they had seen each other.

Both had expressed surprise at the frequency their paths had crossed, as though purposely throwing them together. Edric had declared it destiny, likening the recurrence to the predestined paths of the planets.

Their first encounter was on the bridge in Mowlem when each gained an impression of intrigue about the other. Did that count as a meeting? She supposed it did. Then in Lester's Board Room when she sensed someone's eyes on her. And, though they had not known it at the time, each attended the Press call in York for the hotel merger, when she had the fortuitous run-in with Harry Nichols; the prelude to her photographic career. She supposed the delivery of flowers to her sorrowful hospital bedside might also figure, and of course the smile from across a busy airport terminal.

They were meant to be together otherwise why had they found themselves on this repeating collision course? Convinced now that she had been right to come to Corfu she pushed all earlier doubts into the bin of forgetfulness.

Absorbed by memories she leaned back in her seat. The world with all its distraction and clamour for focus could remain outside the boundaries of this private, tranquil haven; suppressed and held back where it belonged. There was no room for any of it here in this exquisite cushion of peace where there was no sound save the comforting shush of waves breaking rhythmically below and a soft hum of chatter in the background.

People talked too much, seemingly unable to appreciate silence. She and Edric had the ability to convey mutual thoughts by a mere expression or the squeeze of a hand and had shared many peaceful moments.

Memories of the happy days spent in his company, when the world had made few demands on her, sprang up to paint masterpieces on the panoramic canvass of her mind before straying still further back to find those that formed the framework on which she had hung the fabric of her life.

She had never expected life to be fair. She grew up accepting the heartbreaks delivered to her door. There was little wonder that she was so furiously independent, for she had purposely stridden towards that goal, but was her cock-strut show of independence the result of past experiences, or only that small part she allowed others to see? What about those days when she had been forced to watch her aunt tied to an uncaring, brute of a husband because she had no means of escape? Was she *really* independent or merely determined to avoid that same path of entrapment?

Her eyes swept the tranquil scene before her, instantly losing herself in the iridescent blue where sky and sea competed for predominance over the other. The reflection from the surf hurt her eyes and she swung away to rest her gaze on the bar, which she now appraised.

Apart from a telephone line slung lazily through the branches of a tree and a sign written in Greek lettering above the doorway there were no obvious changes. In truth she would have resented the intrusion of modern-day living.

It was still early and only a handful of people occupied the tables today. She noted with satisfaction that it continued to be predominantly the Greek who supported the establishment; in the main the tourist had not yet spilled over into this place that abounded with so many precious memories.

Huddled in concentration in what meagre shade the building provided, a group of men frowned at playing cards. Others, silent but for the occasional click of worry beads weaving through their fingers, watched from behind slouched shoulders.

Hope looked at the occupants of other tables. A couple in the far corner and another close by caught her attention. The first couple: a young woman in her late teens or possibly early twenties appeared focused on her much older companion with shoulder-length, wispy grey hair and a vulgar clutter of gold chains of varying lengths beneath a shirt worn open to the waist. An embarrassing display of affection made Hope avert her eyes to the second couple where a spindly youth, not many years departed from grubby schoolboy knees, listened to an older woman whose unskilled application of eyebrow pencil gave the perpetual impression of an imminent question. Should she become alarmed it would be impossible to tell from those solid lines etched so unnaturally high. A shout of lipstick drew notice to the bold hyphen of thin, straight lips that accompanied the inquiring expression. Hope's attention was drawn to the tracery of veins that stood knotty and proud of the tired, crepe skin belonging to the hand, almost masculine in appearance and bedecked with gems, which strayed regularly to the young man.

She watched these two charades being played out in front of her. In some ways she was no different and even formed part of it for had she not feigned happiness when all the time her heart was breaking? What from their respective pasts had made these unknowns prepared to sacrifice themselves and accept their present state of mind and style of living? But perhaps her assumption was wrong and the elders relatives, parents or guardians. But she knew they were not and was glad she did not know the circumstances that had led these vulnerable young people to this. She could never be like that, manipulated, dependent.

Returning to her initial thought she supposed she did possess an eager intensity towards independence, which was undoubtedly the fruit of her past, and nurturing mind of her father, who despite her failure rate would nevertheless have expressed satisfaction. Like it or not, as Daphne would say, we are the result of all our yesterdays. *Yesterday* – she would give up all that she had achieved if she could return to those more richly rewarding days when Edric had shared her life.

If she could find him it would not matter that he could not walk. As for Edric – she could only guess at his feelings, though likely there was a clue in his abrupt disappearance and the fact that he had seemingly done everything he could to keep the detail of his accident from her. Was that the reason he had moved – in case she came looking for him?

The clashing elements of fire and water had irrevocably changed the lives of so many of them; one or both of those elements had touched them all. Isabel's life changed right from the day of Bert's drowning, though in many ways for the better, whilst others had not been so fortunate. Amy had never been the same since losing Gregory, and she herself had not escaped trauma, not least when the gentleness of water robbed her of the best father in the world. And the fearful element of fire had made no less than two separate bids to claim Edric's life!

A hoarse cough from one of the card players refocused her attention. The proprietor had come out and also glanced across. He stood at the entrance where for several moments he manipulated a string of worry beads with remarkable dexterity between knotty fingers. Somewhat regally he surveyed his domain then relaxed his short stature and began to wipe the mix-match of white plastic furniture with a level of care more worthy of highly-polished walnut.

By the time he reached Hope's table his smile had become a grin. He pointed with marked pride at the Greek lettering above the door. From this she deduced the sign was new and warranted notice. Obligingly she nodded her own endorsement of approval. Satisfied with her response he moved on, occasionally beaming back at her, and she wondered what he was thinking and whether he guessed the nervous intensity distilled from her descending loss of expectation. She suddenly felt immature and wished herself able to tap into the knowledge of his lifetime.

Her attention shifted to the beach where two young boys were playing and a man walked his dog. Every now and then the man leaned on his stick and spoke to the children. One child carried a kite, the other a section of the tail that had become detached. The man was helping them to fix it. The dog kept getting in the way.

In agonising remembrance, objects leapt from the scene to torment her. The kite: she and Edric had watched children with a kite, and for fun she bought him one; like a child he had delighted with the gift. The dog: over this distance it could be Edric's dog except Amber would be much older than the dog leaping in the surf like a tennis ball with frisky topspin.

Such emotional agony! How dare the man walk his dog on the beach today and those children bring their kite! She pressed her eyes shut against the pain. Tears born from frustration and the anticlimax of her morning worked their way through her lashes. She reached into her handbag for a handkerchief and immediately the air was overpoweringly fragrant. When she replaced her purse she must have displaced the top of her perfume bottle, for the wasted fragrance of *Aromatics* was all around her, permeating the air she breathed.

The discovery had hardly been made when she heard the beginnings of a familiar throaty sound. Faltering at first but then gaining clarity the noise grew more positive until suddenly raucous howling shattered the silence.

Hope's eyes shot towards the dog on the beach. Amber? But the strident sound did not come from there, though like everyone else the young dog's attention had been caught and even now was bounding towards the bar to investigate.

Within moments it had scrambled up the few steps until it stood leggy and panting in the middle of the crazed square of concrete. Like a growing child the young bitch, gawky and out of scale, had not yet grown into quickly maturing limbs. It yapped and crouched playfully as though stalking something in the bushes.

Then Hope saw her. She had been enjoying a snooze in the shade, a bowl of water beside her.

"Amber!"

Still outstretched, the older bitch threw back her head and howled again in response to a long-remembered fragrance. Amber struggled to her feet, her level of delight evident from the elaborate figure her tail etched in the air. The erratic movement, so charged with excitement, spread to her entire body. In a clear demonstration of pleasure, practically scraping her belly across the concrete, Amber snaked her way towards Hope.

A softer sound measuring somewhere between a throttled yodel and a cracked bark escaped the soft brown muzzle that pressed urgently into Hope's outstretched hand.

The reunion was a delight to those who watched. Hope's arms went to encircle the dog. Even the card players paused long enough to watch her being dragged from her seat and almost to the ground by Amber's exuberance. In an excited frenzy the younger dog darted back towards its master who was ascending the steps to retrieve her.

Hope was still wrapped within a mass of undulating brown fur when she sensed the silence. She lifted her face to look at the man over by the steps and at once her face lit up with incredulous delight.

Such sounds as there were became cloaked in silence and despite the brightness of the climbing sun now casting all but short shadows Hope detected nothing of her surroundings. She was aware only of an uprising of happiness in her soul; Edric stood not six metres away. Light-headed, she looked at him. Apart from the presence of a walking stick he had not changed a bit. She struggled to find sufficient saliva in her mouth to swallow.

"Edric!" She could not be certain whether her lips actually formed his name but the pleasurable sound reverberated through her head.

Chapter 38

Edric's expression varied between disbelief and adulation. His arms opened and in the next moment they were one; neither noticed the pink grin widening beneath the new door sign.

Taking her hand Edric led Hope the short distance to the relative privacy of the beach where after considering each other from arm's length they melted together, his mouth eagerly seeking hers and she yielding as she never had before. From habit Edric prepared himself for her usual withdrawal but it did not come and she remained secure in his embrace, responding with a passion he had never dared hope that she might.

They parted to draw in deep draughts of breath and exchange looks that revealed their innermost feelings. The next moments were filled with something not unlike an electric current flowing from one to the other. Each sensed they shared the sensation and the knowledge that no matter what great happiness presented itself in the future these particular moments would never be surpassed but would be committed to memory to be taken out and enjoyed in delicious, private moments yet to come.

Edric stepped back to adopt a stance of admiration, his hand going to explore her bobbed hair. "I like it. It suits you." He had known about it; there was little he did not know about her. "You're even more beautiful than I remember. You've never looked more lovely."

"Lovely!" Hope attempted a look of horror but found she had no power over her smiling face, which briefly emitted laughter before dissolving beneath the confession that yesterday she had misunderstood something that someone said and thought that he was dead. "But I'd got it all wrong and learned you were alive, and then without even making sure that you were in Corfu I caught the first flight out." She listened to herself. She was gabbling like a schoolgirl; in a moment she would be giggling uncontrollably.

"I was a fool to have stayed away so long." He ran his eyes over her, absorbing every detail, including those things that could not be seen but only sensed by the inner eye of one in love with the subject. Appreciating at last the exciting contours of realism Edric knew he had been too long with only the echo of memories for company. "It's important that you should know the only reason I stayed away is because I love you. It's important you should know that. The truth is I couldn't bear you to feel obligated to share all that was facing me in my struggle towards recovery."

He hesitated. His explanation was out of sequence with events. "I take it your presence here is not just another of those strange coincidences, and that you know about the accident – the fire?" He watched her nod. His own head slumped forward. "You weren't supposed to find out – at least not yet. I don't know how much you know but after the accident I was hospitalised, first in Edinburgh then Nicos flew me out here where I remained under the care of his team for more months than I care to remember." His tone turned to one of gratitude. "Specialising in the spinal cord Claire's husband took a personal interest in my case and wouldn't allow me to give up. Not even for a moment. He became nothing less than a tyrant!"

He finished on a laugh whilst silently probing the reaches of his mind to verify the existence of those days when Nicos seemed graced with the ability to delve beneath the inconsistent attitude of his patient and determine the manner to be adopted. Some days he was as quietly caring as a new mother, whilst on others he would not think twice about delivering a stinging contradiction, at the same time knowing it would likely lead to confrontation.

"But Nicos never allowed the angry spit to become personal, though would frequently conclude a examination with the sighing, monotone remark, 'I can't do it without you Edric. Help me damn you – I can only achieve what you want me to achieve!' Unlike my own, his belief never wavered – or if it did he never let on. On one of my more despondent days he tossed the remark that he was wasting his time and was not convinced I really wanted back the use of my legs." Deep lines now creased his brow. "Believe me – with everything that had happened that was like the last straw. I offer no defence. I couldn't take any more and at that moment I almost hated him. Hated everything – and life in particular! Without knowing that I'd done it, I'd prised myself free from my chair – I think to lunge at him, though we never came to blows because Nicos and his team were already applauding those long-awaited steps."

Edric returned his attention to the one whose face had never strayed from his thoughts. "I was in a wheelchair for a time." He saw real hurt in her eyes. "Actually I was lucky. No, honestly I was. I was extremely lucky. I was fortunate to be taking a bath at the time of the fire. It was the bath water that went a long way towards saving me." His smile brightened as he chuckled, "Though it didn't save me from gaining a startling new hairstyle – and one not nearly as smart as yours. In fact I got the matching set. My eyebrows didn't escape a singeing. I looked a right sight!"

Hope sympathised. He kissed her hand. His tone grew serious. "In my haste to get to my feet I slipped and fell fracturing my spine. I was told the injury was unstable and that I might never regain the full use of my legs." He countered Hope's gasp with a tap of his walking stick. "But as you can see, despite this prop, I'm getting there, though admit that's more down to Nicos than my own endeavours." He became thoughtful. "I've come to appreciate why Claire affectionately refers to her husband as the *backbone of Corfu*."

Delighted shouts rang out a short distance from them and they turned in time to see two young boys wave briefly at the man who had helped to mend a kite. Edric called back words of encouragement in fluent Greek, then in a whisper meant only for Hope's hearing, confessed, "A mere adjustment – not, I admit, an engineering feat."

The boys galloped down the beach with their kite, finally airborne, tugging high above them. Watching their antics Hope and Edric leaned together in a bubble of laughter and not for the first time Hope sensed that children were important to Edric; the realisation pleased her.

"You really should have contacted me. If only I'd known.... but then I suppose if I'd not been so busy erecting barriers around an unhappy clash of idealism and my own damned self-respect it might have dawned on me that there was more to your disappearance than my pride allowed me to imagine." She leaned in closer. "I thought you'd taken me at my word. You know.... never to say goodbye. I thought you'd gone back to Hilary." She was suddenly speaking the words that described her worst nightmare. She had been a fool. Instead of looking for the reason behind his absence she had taken to wallowing in self-pity, believing herself discarded like a worn out

309

possession that was no longer loved, when all the time Edric had had need of her.

"Hilary? Now I know you're crazy! You numbskull – Hilary was never in the equation! Come here. Doesn't this tell you anything?" He kissed her then with all the feeling he had been saving up during the long months of separation.

"If there'd been any chance of that inane scenario I'd have told you – if only for the entertainment value!" In silence he studied her face and saw that it had indeed been a real concern, and now felt guilty for the elation he had savoured immediately prior to his accident.

He confessed some of this now. "Strangely enough, I heard from Hilary on the night of the fire when she rang to confirm her agreement to a divorce. I didn't tell you that I'd been actively seeking one, which was just as well because she went on to play a cat-and-mouse game, dragging it out beyond belief. I rang you straight away but at the last moment decided it was something I'd prefer to tell you in person." He swung his upturned walking stick at a pebble, his aim hurling it into the lively froth of a breaker to be pounced on instantly by the younger dog. "I can't tell you how hard it was to keep the excitement from my voice. Amongst other trivia I believe I ended up telling you instead about Andrew, the builder I'd met. Incidentally, he and I did end up in business together. We're small and although I suppose I'm more what you'd call a *sleeping partner*, the venture's been sufficiently challenging to keep my mind occupied. We're in new construction, mainly domestic," he paused to whack another pebble, "but we have some commercial jobs on the books. And, on a completely separate front, I continue to hold a healthy interest in Shillens International. The Board elected to retain my services as a consultant on the project I told you about."

Early indications were good. He envisaged his idea going much further and believed it destined to meet with huge success when the remaining hotels were brought on line and the next stage was introduced. The foreseeable future looked bright – and in more ways than one.

"I'm fascinated. I can hardly keep up! There've been changes in my life too, including a change of career. I now work for a newspaper...."

"The Barlayne Express. Old news I'm afraid – excuse the pun. And now you're responsible for the Women's Section. You see – there's not much I don't know about you." He watched surprise spring to her face, quickly followed by what he recognised as the prelude to further revelation.

"But I doubt you know anything about my last assignment, where I heard about your accident. I was despatched to the Leeds Shillens to cover the briefing for that same initiative you now mention."

It was Edric's turn to look astonished whilst she squirmed with something approaching childish pride.

"Amazing! Another of those phenomenal coincidences that continue to draw us together like a magnet."

Silently, she agreed. The pull between them was as strong as the hold Mowlem had on her, where the echo of the river pulsated in the background, comforting and gentle and totally harmonised with her soul.

Edric continued. "And there's me thinking I knew everything about you." He pulled her into his arms, conscious of her heart beating against his.

She raised her face to look at him. "I thought about your telephone call and each time attached the same speculation that your odd tone foretold bad news – the worst – your return to Hilary. I'll never trust my own judgement again."

"On that hellish night I was relaxing in the bath, going over how to tell you about my divorce." He decided not yet to enlighten her about his preoccupation in choosing an engagement ring half an hour before that.

"So much misunderstanding!" Her thoughts swung from inaccurate speculation to the reality of events. "It must have been dreadful, especially not knowing whether you would regain the use of your legs. I can't imagine how that must have felt."

"But not only did I have to face that prospect, there was also the probability that I'd lose you." He placed a finger over lips that were quick to form a protest. "I admit my choice, not yours." He did not at once remove his finger but kept it there to reinforce his point. "I obtained promises that no one would breathe a word about my accident but would allow me to make up my own mind as to whether I would contact you again." Further protest was silenced with a shake of his head. "There was no way I was going to allow you to share your future with someone in a wheelchair."

He did not see the brightening effect those words had on her, but went on to supply details relating to the fire: "A valve stuck in the air ducting. If it hadn't the incident would have been far worse, with almost certainly a greater loss of life. That must have been the first time the Board had reason to be grateful for the installation of defective equipment. It was the malfunction that localised the effects of the real killer – smoke!"

This released a rush of emotion like she experienced upon hearing words spoken by a young waitress when her seat of passion had been indescribable, and now under the clarity of Edric's gaze she attempted to explain something of those feelings.

When she had finished he felt swamped with guilt. "Don't look so sad. That's past. It's gone." He took her chin and tilted her face to his. "Can I ever be forgiven?"

She raised her eyes to enjoy once more the impulsive, humorous grin that was as infectious as ever.

Like the salt-tinged freshness skimming off the sea, relief swept over them to blow away all the cobwebs of anxiety. Nothing in the world could ever be more vital than this moment. This was real.

"I think I could forgive you anything," she said at last, throwing him one of her looks that never failed to make him smile. "But I'm disappointed you didn't take into consideration my feelings for you." Her eyes sparkled with emotion and the illumination of love.

Edric blinked hard. "But once the miracle happened and I was able to hurl that blasted wheelchair aside my perception changed and I knew I was coming back for you. But first I had to get back to being the person I was before the accident. I set myself aims leading towards that end, not least banishing forever the jerky movements that more resembled some animated character from a kid's cartoon! Then it became just as important to eliminate the stoop and to walk without aids: each achievement bringing me nearer to the day I would walk back into your life – and without the encumbrance of wheels or sticks."

He smiled down at her. "It was meant to be like this. Even Amber knew it. She's a bit arthritic now aren't you girl? Not like this daft offspring of yours." The pup looked up at him. "By the way this giddy thing is Topaz."

Hearing her name the dog wagged her tail and then bounded off down the beach to bark at nothing and chase something that only she could see. Lacking her interest Amber gazed after her. Not long from sleep she yawned noisily, which drew Edric's hand to fondle her silky head.

"Thank heaven her sense of smell has not deteriorated otherwise your presence might have gone undetected." He stooped to pat the dog whose ribcage sounded hollow beneath the hearty slaps of affection. "I remember saying you'd never be able to creep up on me with this trusty scout around!"

Hope giggled. "Her sense of smell would have to have been almost nonexistent not to detect the extravagance of perfume emitted from my bag."

Edric looked intent. He grew silent. There were things she should know but coming upon her like this he was unprepared. Nevertheless she had to be told. He wondered where to begin.

Weighing the traits of human nature that Hope most valued against those that she did not he was loath to imagine how she might react, particularly when she discovered the consequences. She had been used to making her own decisions in life and from this grew a fear that when these things were made known the knowledge might put a different slant on things and create an unbridgeable distance between them. The outcome was not something he felt able to predict with any degree of precision. If only she were not so self-sufficient, not her own person. Yet were not those some of the qualities that set her apart and which he most admired?

Taking a deep breath he studied her eyes, trusting and loving and, if it were possible, even greener than he remembered.

"Hope...." he began tentatively, "do you remember how Charles used to watch you – practically following your every move?" Then more brightly, "And how we laughed about it?" He knew the smile had slipped from his face to make way for a look of misgiving, but it was outside his control.

There followed a moment of awkward silence when each felt the compulsion to fill the void with words

Hope was the first to speak. "Yes...." She paused whilst attempting a laugh, at the same time striving to push away the unwelcome surface of anguish relating to her parentage. The subject had hung over her for a long time like an oppressive rain-bearing cloud with the power to wash away the very foundation of her existence – but she did not want to acknowledge any of that now – not today.

"There are things you should know." Edric's eyes shifted nervously to search the thin boundary where the brightness of the sky became one with the dazzle of the sea.

Hope did not wait to hear more and pressed her lips to his.

Upon pulling apart, unaware her action had been designed to halt his further words, he continued as though there had been no interruption. "A lot has happened since I last saw you."

Hope noticed his eyes no longer complimented his expression; an involuntary shudder accompanied the observation.

"And there are things you should know.... things that will have an affect on the rest of our lives."

He was watching Topaz and Amber investigating a dead crab and did not see Hope's alarm.

"But there's someone who's better able to tell you about it – and it's more their place to tell you than mine." He held out his hand to indicate they should leave the beach. "Come, I'll take you to see Charles.....Charles Lurdmayne. I think I can promise you an interesting reception."

The title had been dropped and her old friend referred to simply as Charles; Hope sensed that there was something deeply significant in this.

Chapter 39

Right from the start Charles had demonstrated an ability to embrace Hope from across a room. He did this now as he gazed in astonishment at her in the entrance hall at Marchriard. Hope beamed back from beside Edric, her face like that of a child exploring the intriguing contents of a lumpy Christmas stocking. Before Charles could find his voice she had bounded across the hall and spilled into his arms.

Though he had maintained a dignified silence, never once referring to Edric's unexplained withdrawal from her life, she had always sensed that Charles understood, indeed appreciated and even shared some of her desolation. His suggestion now that they should move to the comfort of the sitting room, to talk, struck her as irresistibly suggestive; what gripped her was a sense that something had shifted; something had changed.

What followed left her suffused in bewilderment, like something incomplete coming to her in a dream. But she was not dreaming. Apparently Christina Lurdmayne was *d-e-a-d*!

Oddly Charles's smile remained intact as he offered up this confession and Hope left the settee to go to kneel beside his chair and offer comfort. He patted the hand that affectionately squeezed his arm. His daughter's death had been revealed to him some time back; he was getting used to it, he said.

Skilled at harmonising to his mood Hope picked up on an air of expectancy – of there being more to follow, and instantly grew apprehensive that he might be about to speak of her parentage, and not least the consequent change made to his Will.

Even with Christina's departure from the world she could not permit herself to remain a beneficiary. It would not be right, yet she sensed the time for that particular scope of explanation was upon her; the regular throb in her chest quickened to a nervous thump and moved to the region of her neck.

More than adequately equipped she had made her own way in life and she considered herself fortunate. In the main, life had been generous; she neither needed nor wanted anything from her elderly friend. With all that had already happened today she was not ready to deal with this further conundrum. She fervently hoped Charles would not choose this moment to make his announcement. Mentally crossing her fingers she set her shoulders and swallowed hard and then quite deliberately switched her thoughts from her own concerns to those of Charles. Striving not to appear probing she asked how he had learned of his daughter's death. He would get round to that later, he told her.

Growing more curious by the minute, she returned to her place beside Edric to listen to what Charles had to say.

In a moment of silence Charles considered the young people seated across from him. Momentarily sidetracked he commented that Edric's eyes were bright again, not dead as they had been since the accident. He detected a burst of questions rising to Hope's lips, which seemed suddenly incapable of forming anything beyond a gape.

After a faltering start Charles began again. "It proved to be a long struggle towards recovery and one in which I shared in good measure. It was difficult to honour my promise and say nothing to you my dear, especially when I could see how Edric's disappearance robbed you of your innermost sparkle." He looked thoughtful for a moment. "I almost strayed into making a disclosure that day in the library when we shared the newspaper coverage of your aunt's marriage. For months I had been impatient for Edric to return to the UK to explain everything." He looked at Edric. "But he steadfastly refused – said he wasn't ready." A look of reproach remained fixed on Edric for several more moments.

"But let's leave that for the moment. My dear – do you by any chance recall the bureau in Edric's cousin's home?" A small gesture of his hands implied it was of no consequence whether she did and he hastened on. "At the time I must have been distracted – probably talking – and it wasn't until later, when amidst admiring my bureau at Tarnville Edric commented on its startling resemblance to Claire's, that I remembered it. I became intrigued. Albeit the two cabinets were fashioned from different woods they remained sister pieces. It nattered me and set me thinking."

Easing old, arthritic limbs to greater comfort Charles shifted his position before continuing. "I considered various possibilities but kept coming back to one. The most likely scenario was that the handyman employed to carry out some restoration work had prepared a detailed drawing of my Queen Anne bureau with a view to reproducing it. Apparently he did, with the piece finding its way into Claire's possession. You see...." he said slowly, "after thinking long and hard about it I could not deny that the man's workmanship had been superior to that which one might expect of someone engaged to carry out routine repair work. In fact he was extremely skilled. Anyway – taking all this onboard it became evident that the person my daughter ran off with was more of a fine cabinet-maker than an odd-job man. Perhaps the fellow had fallen on hard times, taking on whatever work he could find." His hands made a gesture of vagueness.

Grasping the silver top of his walking stick Charles leaned forward. "Vague, but nevertheless that was the first evidence I'd uncovered with regards my daughter's whereabouts." His silver-grey head bobbed on his shoulders. "In my excitement I dropped Claire and her husband a line to enquire how they came by their bureau. Claire wrote back – " A delightful chuckle preceded his next comment. "In fact we had quite an exchange of letters going on at one point. I dare say that staff probably thought I had a lady friend in Corfu!" Isabel's action of handing him the letters had been accompanied by a quizzical expression. "Anyway – the bureau. I learned that Claire's piece had been given to her parents as a wedding present."

For the moment ignoring Hope's obvious confusion he moved swiftly on. "And then, of course, there was the thing that really sealed my understanding. You'll remember the occasion you were called away, leaving Edric at Tarnville?" An unexpected swell of emotion entered his voice and his eyes appealed to Edric. "Perhaps you should take up the story."

With the significance of the explanation thus far still eluding her, Hope transferred her attention from Charles's emotion-filled eyes to the younger, similarly affected eyes beside her.

"Knowing my interest in fine properties," began Edric, "Charles offered me a conducted tour of Tarnville. As you can imagine I needed no persuasion. It was during our tour that we came across a china doll in one of the bedrooms."

Feeling at last that she had stumbled on to familiar ground Hope nodded. She knew the doll to which he referred; she had picked it up

317

when she stayed at Tarnville during the flood. "That would be Christina's doll."

Nodding, Edric paused to assemble the order of facts. "Then there was my mother's box of buttons. You remember.... my *family jewels* from which you extracted a small china foot. I'd always regarded it as just another item in the box, part of a broken ornament awaiting the repair that never happened. It was not until Charles put the doll in my hands and allowed me to discover the damage for myself that I realised exactly what had been residing in the safety of my mother's box all these years. Charles even showed me the chip in the bedroom fireplace where his daughter had hurled the doll in a fit of temper and broke the foot."

Hope's eyes widened with amazement. "How extraordinary! Where on earth do you think your mother....?"

"It's even more extraordinary than that," put in Charles re-entering the conversation, his voice normal again. "I won't ask whether you were aware of my staring because I caught your look of intrigue but having nothing concrete to go on I couldn't say anything. All I had was an inexplicable feeling – a sort of vague memory that annoyingly eluded me and didn't allow me to pull it to the front of my mind."

He could see that Hope was struggling to find a link between the discovery of his daughter's death, a Queen Anne bureau that bore a remarkable resemblance to another here in Corfu, and a broken doll in a bedroom back at Tarnville. But before she could find her voice he moved the story on apace.

"It wasn't until I came upon Edric showing your aunt the contents of his mother's box of buttons, and saw the doll's foot for myself, that I really knew for certain." At this a look of warmth was directed at Edric and then at Hope, and then almost with an air of drama he said, "I don't think I mentioned that Claire's letter went on to explain that not only was her bureau a magnificent wedding present for her parents – it had been made specially for them, by her uncle – her father's brother."

Acknowledging the silent words on Hope's lips Charles nodded. "Yes, that's right – it was Edric's father who made Claire's bureau. So there you have it. The so-called handyman my daughter ran off with was Edric's father. Edric is Christina's son – my grandson."

Charles exchanged expressions of affection with the handsome young man across from him whose hand every now and then reassuringly squeezed the one that had perceptibly tightened in his.

"However, as you will appreciate, this miraculous discovery brought a shock of great sadness because attached to the revelation was the undeniable fact that my daughter was dead." His voice became tight, totally unlike his own. "Because as we all know, both of Edric's parents perished in the house fire from which only Edric, a mere toddler, barely escaped with his own life to be brought up by his father's people."

After permitting a barely decent pause Hope was unable to prevent the exclamation, "Edric – your grandson! That can't be.... can it?" But in the next moment the full implication of the disclosure hit her mercilessly.

Like the first rays of sunshine straying through a chink in the curtains the future had only just sparkled into reality; now it was about to be snuffed out and the light from that particular window of opportunity become extinguished forever.

Turbulently conscious of the implications, a wave of nausea rose up to expand her fear. In a vain attempt to stay any further words she held Charles's eyes with hers. What if in the next breath he went on to make the further revelation that he had discovered the existence of a second grandchild? Where would that leave Edric and herself!

Desperate to keep a thread of concept intact she turned to frown at Edric. "But your mother's name was Maggie Smith," her voice desperate, uncomfortably urgent.

It was Charles who responded. "Partially correct. That was the name by which Christina chose to be known. I think I told you that when I didn't approve of her proposed marriage she put it to me that my parental view might have been different had our surname been anything but the old family name of Lurdmayne. When she was very young, unknown to either her mother or myself, she regularly went by the name of Maggie Smith. Even you my dear," Charles tapped the air with a singular movement of his stick, "provided me with information on that particular point when one evening here in Corfu you mentioned the name of Edric's mother. I tried dismissing it as nothing more than a coincidence. After all the name Maggie Smith is little

319

different from, say, Ann Brown, and doesn't fall into the remit of being at all unusual. But some time later you spoke about research you'd undertaken on Edric's behalf in an attempt to turn up information relating to his mother's background. During dinner you announced that Hattie Middler remembered a 'Maggie Smith who sang like an angel in the market square'. I knew then that none of it was coincidence. You see…..I knew that that *singing angel* was a very young Christina Lurdmayne!"

This was not a fragmented vision but a statement of reality and Hope's sudden intake of breath was plainly audible as she recalled the evening to which Charles referred and how he had spilt his wine and out of character retired early only to be heard later pacing the floor of his daughter's bedroom.

"Did you know that for a time Hattie was employed at Tarnville as the children's Nanny?" Hope shook her head. "She would take them on outings and it was during their weekly visit to Stillingford market that Christina donned the make-believe image of another and adopted the name of her favourite doll...."

"*Maggie Smith*," supplied Hope.

"The same," he concurred. "When I discovered my daughter had been making an exhibition of herself in the market square I did away with Hattie's services." A veil of remorse removed any sparkle from his eyes; even now believing his actions had been partially if not primarily to blame for the old woman's state of mind.

There was little wonder, Hope now appreciated, that the untimely death of Charles's remaining child, Richard, had affected Hattie so badly. Vague, disturbing recollections of her elderly neighbour's ramblings flooded back to bedevil her – 'He's gone too now'.

Hope struggled to assimilate all that she been told. Her head performed the slightest of movements to indicate a growing grasp of understanding, but all at once a further display of bafflement entered her face.

"But I distinctly recall hearing that Christina had dark hair whereas Edric's mother was blond," her tone defiant and unyielding. She stared back at Charles. "In fact – you've always said I remind you of your daughter but with regards colouring we were more like negatives of each other – one dark, the other fair….." She stopped abruptly.

What was she saying? If she were not mindful careless referrals to family resemblances might lead her aged friend to make the disclosure she most feared!

She snatched her attention from Charles to search Edric's face. "And you told me that the last memory you had of your mother was looking back at her through the window your father was lowering you from." She fought to remember his precise words. "You said something about how the smoke stained her hair.... Yes – I remember now. You said the smoke had streaked her *p-a-l-e* hair."

Whilst wondering at the hitherto unheard accusatory edge to her voice Edric inclined his head in agreement. "Claire has since mentioned remembering her beautiful dark-haired Aunt Maggie, but like you, my mother cut her hair and for some reason, choice or perhaps to further conceal her identity, changed the colour. I was too young to remember such detail." His voice exposed the smile that had begun to tease the corners of his mouth. "Later, when we returned to the library, Charles showed me some photographs, in particular an envelope of holiday snaps of his wife and children – a pretty, dark-haired girl and a young boy." He turned to Charles. "I can still see your expression when you told me the girl was my mother aged around nine."

Hope found all of this entrancing but not at all reassuring yet could not help joining in with the exchange of smiles.

Charles chose now to share his own recollections of that day and told how after the discovery of the doll he had persuaded Edric back to the library where he suggested he should make himself comfortable. Charles told how no words could convey how during the detonation of silence that followed he almost wept as he watched Edric's fluid stride take him to one of the leather chairs whilst he struggled to retain a steady hand to pour them both a stiff drink.

He held the crystal balloon towards Edric, all the while delighting in the same expression of concentration borrowed from Christina. It had been necessary to pause in order to catch his breath and absorb the magnitude of what he was about to divulge.

On concluding his disclosure he embraced Edric affectionately before pulling back to lose himself in the same brown eyes that had once looked out from his daughter's face. They had spent the next hour pouring over more photographs.

"So there you have it. I'm delighted to be able to claim Edric as my grandson."

Charles considered the display of shock that lingered in Hope's face. Appreciating that for the last hour he had been picking away at her previous assumptions he fell silent to allow her time to recover. He had not covered it all but he could see she had more than enough to be going on with.

He struggled from his chair. "I'm sure there are things you two will want to talk about. You've a lot of catching up to do. If you'll excuse me there are things I want to do but I'll see you both later. I'll be in my old room if you want me," this directed at Edric. Charles tapped his way towards the door.

Somewhat relieved by this unexpected reprieve Hope relaxed a little, then with the closing of the door said, "His old room?"

"Charles and I swapped villas. He's moved into my villa across from Claire and Nicos and I live here. He says the hill is too steep for him now and Marchriard too large but we so enjoy each other's company that I insist he comes to stay for long periods." All at once a grin of pride plumped Edric's cheeks to a youthful roundness. "I can't tell you how pleased I am to be able to refer to our mutual friend as my – *grandfather*."

How would he feel when his grandfather progressed to telling him of the existence of another grandchild, Hope wondered. Her whole world seemed bound towards destruction, though somehow she managed a calm, albeit abridged, reply. "I see.... so he's the old man at your villa."

Edric looked enquiringly at her.

"Oh – nothing, just another piece of the jigsaw."

There were so many and apparently Charles held the last piece: the piece that would complete, and in so doing, spoil the whole picture!

Edric went on, "After the accident I contacted him from my hospital bed in Edinburgh. He said nothing to anyone and came immediately. He came, as I recall, under the guise of looking for a new bull. I swore him to absolute secrecy where you were concerned, though that's shortening the story somewhat because he argued for days on that score."

Edric left his seat and went to the bookcase in the alcove by the window where he selected a leather-bound volume. With an air of intrigue he suggested she might like to look at the album with embossed Greek lettering on its maroon tooled-leather cover that he now placed on her lap. "I think you may find this interesting."

Sensing his eyes upon her Hope opened the album where, dumfounded, she found a record of practically every event of her career. Pages cut from magazines, together with original glossy photographs, obtained she knew not how, lay cheek by jowl to cram the pages. She had not realised she had taken part in so many commercial shoots. And at the point when her photographic work ceased there followed a flurry of newspaper clippings of stories she had covered for the Barlayne Express, and also every headline from the Women's pages since taking up Editorship for the Section. A regular annotation of carefully penned notes in the margin alerted her to the existence of another folder where the full articles could be found. Agape, she turned to Edric.

"You see!" he said, displaying a boyish grin, ". . . there's very little I don't know about you."

Perhaps there is something, she thought with deepening regret.

Unaware of her disquiet he tapped the album. "This was a way of keeping you close. Charles helped to keep me up to speed and even arranged for me to receive copies of your newspaper. And those...." he caught her startled expression when she reached the back-most pages filled with studio-quality photographs of all the oil paintings she had ever produced and sold, "again with his help, I acquired not only those but proudly own the originals as well though apart from a particular one of the Old Man's Bar I don't keep them here." He smiled fondly at her, then admitted, "I've got a nice place back in your neck of the woods. I keep the paintings there. It only seemed right that they should reside in the village where their originator grew up." He took her hand in his. "You were right about Mowlem. It is the best place in the world. It was my intention to return to you and then surprise you with news of the property, but I've gone and spoilt it all by telling

323

you. But seeing your surprise over the photographs I simply couldn't stop myself."

Amazement opened up her face. "It was you! You bought my paintings – I thought they were selling rather well! And it was you who bought Ivy Cottage!" She drew her bottom lip between her teeth. "I tried putting in an offer for it myself only to be told it had already gone." The words tumbled free. "I was bitterly disappointed, though not any more!" She wondered how she would have felt if the agent had thought to divulge the name of the buyer.

Despite earlier anxieties she burst forth into a monologue of descriptive stories associated with Ivy Cottage, many finely tuned to her father. There were so many it would have been virtually impossible to still her flow. She spoke quickly in the desperate attempt to fill every gap of her mind and prevent the surface of other thoughts, which if acknowledged would destroy her newfound happiness forever.

"It's nice hearing you chattering on. I've missed that."

Some of the tales were new, others he had heard before but were equally entertaining the second time around. When she did finally surface for air he suggested they might collect her things from her hotel and settle her in at Marchriard.

"And shouldn't you make some phone calls to let people know where you are? Or perhaps we should shut out the world for at least the remainder of today. What do you think?"

To ignore the world for the rest of today sounded like luxury but could they do that? Did they retain the right to claim today as being theirs? Then not wanting to waste a moment of the little time that remained to them she readily agreed. "You're right. There are people I should ring." At the very least she owed a call to Vivian Dyson for allowing her the freedom to come to Corfu; and by her reckoning her aunt would be back from holiday the following day; and she would ring Daphne in the evening, ensuring that she would be free to talk and put the string of questions she would want to ask. "And Angela – you remember Angela?" Edric rolled his eyes and she laughed. "I must give her a ring too."

Poor Angela would be having kittens waiting for news of the *last chapters*, which sorrowfully, Hope now realised, would remain unwritten. Unable to commit to paper the devastating conclusion that would shortly fall from the mouth of Charles her incomplete manuscript would be placed in a drawer somewhere and forgotten about – together with the rest of her life.

Yet she could not help smiling in response to Edric's bubble of enthusiasm and in that moment determined that she would smile, laugh and enjoy every moment of this, their last day together as a couple.

She slanted her eyes mischievously and endorsed his suggestion. "But not today. I'll not ring anyone today!" She was surprised by the return of brightness in her voice.

"That's settled then. The vote's unanimous. No contact with the outside world until tomorrow, apart from a call I wish to make. I want to book a table for dinner tonight."

He left her supposedly looking through the album whilst he went to make the reservation, but as she turned the pages she was thinking about the last piece of the jigsaw – which was held by their grandfather.

Chapter 40

Hope's intrigue could not have been more apparent when Giorgio, Edric's driver, swung the large Mercedes away from the hills behind Marchriard. Delighting in her childlike display of puzzlement Edric refused to enlighten her about their destination and joined her in laughter when the car eventually turned into the pothole-infested dirt track behind the Old Man's Bar.

"I thought we'd dine here this evening," his head deliberately averted from Giorgio, his voice tinged with mirth. "It may not be in the same league as Maninner Restaurant with regards sumptuous interior but not even Maninner's can compete with this superb, God-given setting. Though I admit that's not my main reason for electing to eat here. I chose here because this is where we met.

This open confession of love heightened her earlier misgivings and Hope wondered whether it might have been more prudent to enlighten him about his grandfather's notion before allowing things to progress this far but if she had, so flimsy was the slender thread of fate that in all probability this evening would not be happening at all. Accordingly it struck her as imperative that the next hours should be perfect and nothing permitted to mar their quality; after all, memories would be all she would have left to sustain her throughout the rest of her life; after tonight there would be no more cosy dinners for two and certainly no more private, loving moments.

Remarkably this erosive stab of realisation did not find a foothold but dissipated upon her stepping from the car to find herself bathed in unexpected candlelight. Her blaze of delight complemented the myriad of candle flames flickering on the tables in an earnest endeavour to illuminate the darkening seascape beyond. Some candles struggled to retain a flame in the soft, evening breeze skimming across the mix-match of tables whose shabbiness was lost in the kindness of the angelic glow.

Her tread became suddenly muffled and she glanced down to discover red carpeting beneath her feet. Notwithstanding its frayed edge and the fact it had seen better days its presence was as meaningful as a 30-foot length of pure wool Axminster outside a Shillens hotel.

"Edric, how perfectly lovely!"

Edric's face showed satisfaction.

The old man came out to greet them. He was wearing what Hope guessed was his best, if not his only suit. He nodded politely before exchanging effusive pleasantries with Edric who went to embrace him.

On breaking the embrace Edric drew Hope to him. "Sweetheart, I don't think you've ever been properly introduced. Hope, I'd like to introduce you to Yiannis, a good friend of mine."

The familiar, short-stature proportions of the proprietor stepped forward to take her hand heartily in his clumsy grasp. He bobbed his head theatrically before breaking into a flow of Greek, and despite understanding not a word she was left in no doubt as to the sentiments of his greeting.

"Yian – you've made a wonderful job of it – absolute perfection! Sorry if it's been a rush."

The only word Hope understood from the outpouring of Greek was the shortened name of their host but it was clear from the widening of the toothless smile that Edric was praising the efforts of the man who a moment later disappeared inside on a mission to cater to their every whim.

Wrapped in the protection of a whisper Edric explained that having no dependency on tourism the bar did not normally open in the evening but Yiannis had agreed to open up tonight to provide a special dinner to celebrate their reunion. Hope was enthralled.

Sunset was not far away and the girdle of fairy lights that had been hastily strung around the eaves and through the lower branches of trees lent the scene a magical quality. Keen to absorb every detail she gazed about her like an excited child.

Appraising bright green eyes swept the scene until finally coming to rest on the sign above the doorway to which her attention had been drawn earlier. There was now a strange familiarity about the Greek symbols.

"If I'm not mistaken that same illustration of Greek lettering appeared on the front of the album you showed me." Her vision returned to Edric. "What does it mean?"

He failed to stifle his amusement and his next breath exploded laughter into the quiet evening. "I really must compliment you on your powers of observation. It's pronounced E-l-p-i-d-a. It means….H-o-p-e." He shrugged pleasantly and creased an eye at her. "You always said you wished this place could stay the same and not get caught up in all the bright lights and blaring music of commercialism. The only way I could ensure that it didn't was to buy it for you."

Hope attempted to speak but nothing meaningful emerged from the lips that he now traced with a finger. Yiannis chose this moment to reappear with menus and an ice bucket containing champagne, the latter his own contribution to the evening.

Champagne fused together with joy and gladness to tease Hope's emotions as she watched Yiannis disappear inside to co-ordinate his wife and sister, who every now and then furtively peered out under cover of the dark interior of the bar to glimpse the happy couple holding hands across the table.

Now almost totally cloaked in darkness the fading tranquil seascape held Hope's attention but after a few moments she focused on Edric. "There's something that continues to bother me."

"About my being Charles's grandson?" His eyes widened to urge continuance.

She gave a nod, the resolute movement a statement in itself. "It's Kevin Lester.... You see I know how he operates and I can't believe he didn't manage to turn up facts relating to your birth, or indeed Christina's – sorry, I mean *your mother's* death. His first line of enquiry would have been to check just such records, and surely…."

"Yes – and of course you're right." Edric leaned back in his seat, the plastic, cooled by the evening air, creaking a protest at his movement. He began slowly. "He knew exactly who I was right from the start." He paused to formulate his next words. "But based on his friendship with Charles...." he grinned broadly, "my grandfather – which you should appreciate had been formed as far back as the equally solid friendship of their respective fathers – Kevin deliberately kept his findings to himself." Edric lifted a hand to stay her challenge. "Yes – yes, I know, and I take your point, but let me finish. He did eventually tell Charles that both my birth and my mother's death a few years later had come to his knowledge some considerable time ago – though I imagine he was particular in choosing his moment and when there was a stiff drink to hand!"

A hint of amusement still lingered in his face as he silenced the further exclamation that such action was not in keeping with Kevin's character. "No, Hope. Forgive me, but you're wrong. Think about it. Think about that special, enduring friendship. I'd say it was very much *in* character. Out of genuine friendship – in fact in much the same way as Kevin did with you – he refused payment for any of the dealings he undertook for Charles."

"That would indeed be a generous gesture."

"Especially when you consider the size of the estate. In your case what you enjoyed could be more aptly categorised as new friendship, whereas those two...."

"Have been friends all their lives."

"Exactly, and Kevin has since explained that acting in the capacity of '*friend*'….." a quick gesture of index fingers indicated the presence of quotation marks, "he felt justified in carrying out this particular element of Charles's business without feeling bound by the tight constraints of his profession."

He looked intently at her. "As Charles was not strictly his client – remember he accepted no fee – I suppose your former employer felt comfortable in deciding exactly what and how much information he should impart. It's obvious that he did only what he considered to be in Charles's best interests. Not least you should appreciate that Charles's search for his daughter went on for many years – a stress factor in itself. Added to that he's had to endure the loss of his wife, and later his son. And – which neither of us knew about and I've only recently found out – he's had several small strokes." He threw Hope a warning look. "Though you mustn't mention that I've told you." Edric thought about a recent stroke victim known to him. "It's such a gentle word for something that's frequently anything but gentle in nature."

His voice softened as though speaking to a child. "As we're somewhat younger I suppose we've yet to gain the same perspective of life." He squeezed her hand, "All these things were well known to Kevin. He knows Charles inside out – understands exactly what makes him tick. He would know better than anyone how important it was for him to find his daughter. After losing his wife and son I imagine finding Christina became something of an obsession. Consider what it would have been like if Kevin had removed the prospect of ever finding her."

An expression of doubt edged its way into Hope's face.

He went on, "I'm sure Kevin wrestled with his conscience but the bond of friendship won and by the very nature of the man he would have been scrupulously careful about what he divulged." He finished wistfully, "I imagine it must have been difficult to appear enthusiastic at the point when he was urged to engage the help of the Press, and more so when he had to dismiss the fraudulent response of the woman who responded as a result. Whilst knowing with absolute certainty that she was not whom she claimed to be, he could not afford to sound too certain that she was not the one Charles sought."

Edric took a moment to refill their glasses. "No – in my opinion his actions are to be admired. What Kevin did was carried out under the banner of true friendship." He raised his glass. "To friendship – especially ours."

He returned the flute to the table, his hand abandoning the glass in favour of her hand. "But I fear we're getting off the main subject." Meaningfully he exerted pressure on her hand. "I brought you here because I couldn't think of a better place to ask you to marry me." Loving brown eyes looked into hers as he now asked, "Hope darling, will you do me the very great honour of agreeing to become my wife?" Smiling he added, "I think it's time we put an end to all the dizzy, criss-crossing of paths and began to walk the same one together."

With a disquieting sense of unease he noticed his words had the effect of diluting the colour of her eyes; those same eyes that had captivated him ever since seeing them displayed like perfect jewels in the face of an 18-year-old. "I'll do everything I can to make you happy," he went on, searching the face that had grown unexpectedly serious. He waited for the words to sink in and for her face to light up. "And who knows.... play your cards right and I might even let you have a go with that kite you got me." But still her face remained unsmiling and any further words dried unspoken to choke his throat.

Hope attempted to soften her expression but her lips remained set and unsmiling. Extreme feelings of sorrow and regret moved in to take control and pilot her every movement. Had he been the Edric of some months back and not Charles's grandson she would have welcomed his proposal but how could she marry him now when within hours Sir Charles would announce that Richard Lurdmayne had been her father – and consequently she and Edric closely related? A burn of tears swelled behind her eyelids.

"Edric, I'm truly sorry – but I can't marry you."

She saw him flinch at the finality of her words. Angry that fate should serve up this unpalatable collation of circumstance, about which she could do nothing, she rose abruptly from the table, the rasp of plastic on concrete in tune with her emotions. She went to stand in silence over by the wall where the thirsty lick of the sea sucked in timeless, regular rhythm at the smooth stonework below. Only now that she was on her feet did she realise that she was trembling, and she stood for several moments swaying and willing strength to return to her legs. She wished she were a thousand miles away and that none of this were happening.

Comprehension failing him and unable to give voice to his frustration, Edric went to stand a pace behind her, his hands going to sit comfortably at her waist. Eventually he whispered towards her ear, "It's okay. I'm not going anywhere. I intend pursuing you relentlessly.... or at least until you catch me."

This further attempt at humour also failed and all that Hope heard was the declaration of raw hurt in his voice. Her face remained pained. She shared that hurt and could not speak.

"Something's wrong. Something's changed. I got it wrong. I had the crazy idea we'd be able to pick up where we left off." But for his anxiety he would have been embarrassed by the misery that broke his voice.

Hope turned. She could not fail to notice his look of hopelessness. "Edric...." she said gently, "things are different now. I learned today that you're Sir Charles's grandson...." She detected confusion in his eyes but mostly saw hurt, which rendered her incapable of preventing the confession that now escaped her lips. "I always thought I knew the meaning of love...." She realised now that what she had felt for David was infatuation and something very young and immature. "Only now do I know what love really is – it's what I feel for you. When it happens you have no control over your life from then on. It's both wonderful and painful and takes over completely, but with everything that I now know.... I regret it no longer makes sense."

Edric threw her one of the smiles he kept solely for her. "L-o-v-e – isn't supposed to make sense."

"Edric.... how can I begin to explain the fear I've been living with, and how newly-gained knowledge impacts on us?"

In that singular outburst the decision had been made and now there was no turning back; she would have to tell him everything.

She began tentatively. "Whilst I myself can't bring myself to accept what I'm going to tell you.... what matters is that Sir Charles does."

Without further pause she began her explanation, sharing with Edric her dismay concerning the identity of her natural father and feeding him with recollections of the telephone conversation overheard between Charles and Kevin Lester. To add further substance to her rationalisation she progressed to linking her fears back to the time of Charles's unwavering observation and, as though believing her point proven, finished, "And remember how we both commented on how he followed my every movement? Edric.... it's my belief that your grandfather thinks I'm his son's child – Richard's child."

There – the words were finally free from her lips, though noticed that the look of shock she had anticipated did not at once appear in Edric's face. Instead she caught what she perceived to be a fleeting shaft of amusement in his features.

"Yes, I remember only too well how his attention never strayed." Edric slipped an arm around her and with his free hand tilted her face to his. "But I've since learned that he wasn't looking at you at all but at me! In fact he apologised in case I considered him ill mannered. He even expressed concern about your interpretation. You see, your awareness had been noticed."

Hope stared back at him.

"It seems he began wondering about me more or less straight after being introduced. Despite it's being a muddle he found himself unable to think about much else. He's since come to suppose that he picked up on some family likeness. Seemingly he couldn't help being drawn towards studying me and later believed his subconscious had been caught by the remarkable likeness I apparently have to my mother. Seeing those features in the male face of a stranger I imagine the similarity was not immediately apparent. Nevertheless something kept tugging his attention back, making it difficult to look away. You'll remember he said as much this afternoon."

He chuckled now. "So you can cancel any thoughts you might have about being part of the Lurdmayne line. It wasn't you he was watching. It was me!" He ran his fingers tantalisingly down the length of her arm where fine hairs instantly sprang proud of pores. "I wasn't going to tell you this, but Charles knows I intend popping the question this evening. I hope you don't mind but in the light of what you've just said surely you'll be pleased to learn he wished me luck. In fact he told me not to go back until extracting the answer he and I both want to hear!" Edric took her by the shoulders and held her from him. "Now – he'd hardly say that if there were any substance to your suspicions would he?"

She supposed not, and as though a curtain had been drawn away to acknowledge the urgency of sunlight waiting beyond the barrier of flimsy fabric a flood of understanding spilled into place to present her with some semblance of clarity. Appreciation of the truth slowly dawned on her. Seemingly Charles's attention had not been trained on her but on the person constantly at her side. Furthermore the telephone conversation she overheard had not related to her at all. Certainly she had heard her name mentioned but out of context and now appreciated it had been Edric who had had star billing in the conversation.

Like early morning mist all former misgivings evaporated. There was not, and never had been, a question mark hanging over her parentage. She had always been and always would be Frederick Thackeray's child! Bubbling with joy she joined Edric in laughter. A few yards behind them three curious faces appeared in the doorway.

Slipping back into his arms Hope said it was as though she had had to tread through all the recent unhappy months just to live for this precise moment.

Upon this Edric expressed regret that she had had to endure so much unhappiness. "If I'd followed my instincts and retraced my steps that day on the bridge I could have saved you from all that."

She merely smiled. "But apparently that's not the scheme of things. I believe it was necessary for me to go through all the events of these past years in order to get to this one moment. Daphne told me I would gain strength from it all and even become a better person as a result. I don't know about that, but I do think she's right when she says it's the experiences of yesterday that make us what we are today."

"I'm sure she is. Just as I know I'm right in saying that we're right for each other."

"My father once told me never to lose sight of what was, what is, and what will be. At the time I didn't grasp what he meant but I've come to realise that when all seems lost the perfect outcome remains safely wrapped in that intriguing package labelled '*Not to be opened until tomorrow*'. There's a definite pattern to life, though we have choices and it remains our responsibility to build our lives brick by brick. It certainly helps to start with a good foundation. In that respect I was lucky." She reached up to press smiling lips to his. "I believe I've just stolen a peek into that special package meant for tomorrow!" She liked what she saw. Then too overcome to speak further she leaned into the safety of his arms.

Edric whispered declarations of love into the pale, silky hair blowing against his face. "If I had the ability," he said, recalling an entry in one of her early journals, "I'd like to capture this moment on canvass: this place, the expression in your eyes – and the wind blowing in your hair."

Could this be the sign she had been waiting for? Overwhelmed she looked at Edric studying her with his head on one side. In the next moment the years rolled away to reveal cherished recollections of the day her father had painted her portrait beside her stepping-stones.

Carried on the gentle memory, barely audibly she asked, "What colour would you paint the wind?"

"Whatever colour you wanted it to be." Humour rounded his features. He tutted softly. "But once again we've strayed from the main item on tonight's agenda. Hope, will you marry me – and come to live at Tarnville?" He knew his grandfather had been on the verge of telling her about having handed over the house and associated estate, and now he was pleased it had been left for him to tell her.

Hope jerked her head back to look at him. "Tarnville? I thought you said you'd acquired Ivy Cottage!"

"You reached that conclusion all on your own," he laughed. "I couldn't get a word in to put you right."

Hope's arms fell from around his neck. Her eyes flashed. Edric held his breath.

"Edric! A moment ago I was coming to terms with the fact that you're Sir Charles's grandson. Now I learn I should be thinking of you more in terms of being his heir. What would people think? They know nothing of what's happened. They wouldn't accept me. Not married to the heir of Tarnville!"

"This is precisely the reaction I feared," he said quietly.

She sought no clarification but continued from where she had finished. "They'd come to the conclusion I'd married you for all the wrong reasons – you know the sort of thing. I'm sure you don't need me to spell it out. I couldn't bear that. I just.... I just wish you...." Her sentence faded behind the insistent smile that pushed its way into her face.

"So, I'll take that as a *Y-e-s* then? he countered. You'll agree to make this career change to manage a household, an estate and me – though not necessarily in that order?"

His inference brought a warm flush to her face. Her career had always represented something outside the normal parameters of a mere salary cheque each month. More recently it had given back some of her lost vitality and kept her mind off other things but what was being suggested far outweighed the importance of any career.

Her head nodded and a moment later a glaze of happy tears sparkled in eyes made huge by what was being proposed: a future with the person she loved.

"*Y-e-s*," she murmured, surprised she retained the ability to speak.

Never before had her eyes been so extraordinarily green. He would remember forever the expression in her face.

Grinning now he said, "You think I don't know what swung it? You can't kid me. You can't wait to get your hands on my kite!"

Chapter 41

With so much happening and not least a wedding to arrange, Hope rang Vivian Dyson for a deferment of her return and to sound him out on the possibility of ending her employment contract.

Ever the effective newsman Vivian had the ability to read between the lines of explanation. Hearing that Hope had found Edric, and was shortly to marry, he knew he was in danger of losing the valued employee he had observed strenuously climbing to elevate herself from secretarial rank to middle management. Though his concern did not rest there; there was also the Paper's circulation figures to consider and quite deliberately, whilst Hope was amid voicing appreciation of his kindness, he leapt in without so much as a note of an overture to avow the public would enjoy reading an account of her story.

He had been surprised how long it had taken Readers (to his mind always with a capital R) to make the link between the Editor of the Women's Section and the photographic model, though having finally done so Hope's mailbag had grown to match that of those she would consider more deserving of celebrity status.

Vivian was quick to appreciate that Hope's tandem plea presented a useful handle. If he wished to retain Hope it paid to be amenable to the request for an extension of leave. Calling in a few favours he could, at least in the short term, cover her absence. To end her contract was an entirely different issue and far more problematic.

Nevertheless the requests gave clout to his bargaining power; they afforded leeway to make a proposal of his own and he put it to Hope that in addition to a continuance of absence he would agree to release her from her current contract – on the proviso she consented to the serialisation of her life story.

Even without knowing the detail it felt right to him and was undeterred by the pause at the other end of the telephone line. Dating back to his cub reporting days Vivian prided himself on having a nose for a story. Furthermore he knew he had an advantage; Hope felt indebted to him and that was always a good jumping-off point.

Her request to end her contract was met head on. Without drawing breath Vivian put his case, winding up with a resolution that fulfilled the needs of both of them, which she would appreciate if she would take the time to step from cloud nine to cloud eight-and-a-half long enough to consider his proposal, he told her.

The compromise came in two parts clearly marked *Parts One* and *Two*. As well as the first part, the serialisation of her story, he wanted her to continue overseeing the Women's Section after her marriage, from Tarnville if necessary; and – silently marked *Part Two (a)* – to undertake some ad-hoc journalism.

The usual all-embracing clause of "*as and when required*" gained no mention, though its presence was detected.

The bid to retain her services caught Hope wrong footed, yet during the ensuing silence permitted herself to explore her perception of the dual role of new wife, and correspondent with editorial responsibilities.

During these moments Vivian had been careful not to break her thought pattern but instead courted the silence in much the same way as he might in the interview situation when such tactics were employed to draw further, particularly unscripted, comment from the candidate.

Hope found Vivian's proposition more than a little tempting. She was accustomed to working under pressure and actually derived enjoyment from working to tight time restrains, the reward of which a satisfying feeling of self-worth.

And with regards the suggested serialisation of her story – why not? In that she held the advantage. She had bought herself some time simply by not divulging that apart from the final paragraphs and proofing, the story was complete and all the real spadework done. All that remained was the preparation of something succinct and suitable for a six-to-eight weeks' serialisation piece. Albeit she harboured scepticism that the general public viewed her with such high interest she was able to appreciate how a shortened version of "*The Stepping-Stones*" might fit comfortably within the configuration of the weekend editions when the Paper *was* bulked up and her glossy pullout-section added.

After inviting a candid verbalisation of the previously unmentioned *Part Two (a)*, and tweaking it in her favour, Hope had been happy, even a little flattered, to accept Vivian's terms and afterwards Edric said she possessed skills equal to his counterparts engaged in clever Board Room tactics.

With those arrangements in place the concluding days of August saw the return of Hope and Edric to England to prepare for their marriage, and now driving towards Mowlem Edric caught Hope admiring the ring he had placed on her finger the night of his proposal. The winding lane required concentration but he managed to steal a second glance.

"I wanted to buy something as beautiful as you but that was the best I could come up with."

Hope was too preoccupied to pick up on the compliment, he noticed; she would be contemplating the kind of homecoming she would receive from villagers. She, like he, would be aware of the movement of curtains and the inquisitive expressions drawn to cottage windows by the trespass of an unfamiliar car upon the territory. Repudiating the distance separating his proposal in Corfu and their arrival in England, news of their forthcoming marriage would have filtered along the remarkable village grapevine system ahead of their arrival. Hope would be aware of this; he on the other hand chose to steer clear of the phenomenon.

"You're home darling, in the place you love most in the world – Mowlem."

A glow of happiness lit up Hope's face and when his statement was followed by a mild curse she broke into a ripple of laughter at the same time bracing herself in the passenger seat as Edric, grateful for power-assisted steering, threw the car round an unexpected corner. His assertion that Mowlem had never had an encounter with the Town and Country Planning Department brought more laughter, especially when he declared the hairpin bend had no apparent reason for being there other than the whim of some deranged road-maker with an overly generous budget for road surfacing materials. Edric's humour acted like a dose of magnesium in settling the spasm in her stomach and she settled back to enjoy the remainder of the drive.

She had not expected to approach Tarnville from this side of the river. It would mean making a long detour further on but this would be Edric's contribution to her homecoming. He would consider it

338

fundamental to her happiness that she be allowed to familiarise herself with her original beginnings before taking her on to Tarnville where, until her marriage, she would have her aunt's former suite in the west wing.

As though sharing those deliberations Edric commented, "There's a reason for bringing you this way. You'll see why in a minute."

His tone was reassuring and she relaxed back into the plump, pale-coloured upholstery that gave out a distinctive smell of new leather.

In pace with the familiar scenery sliding past the car window the years peeled away and Hope could see herself as a child picking flowers in the hedgerows and a few years later careering down the lane in a splintery orange box mounted on a set of old pram wheels. She and the dubious conveyance had negotiated the tight bend somewhat less successfully than Edric, and abruptly parted company, both ending up in the ditch, she painfully winded beneath the cart. Moments later, grazed and her hair ribbon askew, she had been wailing on Hattie Middler's doorstep in the certain knowledge of gaining sympathy, a sticking plaster, and the secret remedy for repairing a dented ego: a generous slice of whatever Hattie had been baking that morning. Such a long time ago, she mused, and then moving on considered the events that had steered her towards this day and her return to the village with her fiancé.

With a deep sigh she turned to Edric. "I've just one regret."

"Only one!" he teased. Then caring, "And that is....?"

"Daphne and Billy." She sighed again. "With all the wonderful things that have happened that probably strikes you as absurd, but I love them both dearly and I'm going to miss not seeing them on a daily basis." She was pleased to note his nod of understanding.

"I'm sure you won't lose touch."

No, but it would not be the same. She would miss that wonderful, caring woman and her son's bubble of friendship. Billy would soon be 19. It was difficult to appreciate that time was also moving on for Daphne's son who by some quirk of fate remained locked within the mental age of ten. But she would be able to invite them to stay for weekends and holidays. Billy would love that. He still talked about the time he helped Joseph Fearnley to prepare Bill and Ben for the shire horse trials.

"Out you get. We need to do the rest on foot." Edric saw from Hope's sudden start that he had dragged her from reverie.

He brought the car to a standstill just beyond Ivy Cottage where the footpath to the river began. He glanced up and down the deserted lane. "It should be all right here. I'll come back for it later." Despite this measured judgement his mind was not solely on the safety of the gleaming mass of new metal, now peppered with a rust-coloured residue from the dusty lanes. "Sweetheart, there's something you still need to do." He looked pointedly at her.

Comprehension finally moved up a gear. Hope bit her lip. "To walk across my stepping-stones."

"Yes. I think it's time."

Without further exchange they strolled across the fields and Hope was amazed that after only three bewilderingly happy weeks' absence there was already evidence of a lessening of green in the intricately worked tapestries of the hedgerows. A rudely urgent encroachment of warm, golden tones was already present and vibrant in the colourful mosaic. It was like viewing the ever-changing scene through a kaleidoscope, occasionally nudging the barrel until it snatched the next display of even more remarkable loveliness. Losing much of its elaboration the arrival of a new season was less sophisticated in the city where, if one were not specifically watching, it could easily be missed. In the countryside it was different. Here the spectacle could consign Monet's refined, meticulous portrayal of the complexities of natural light to the forgetful blur of thick enfolding shadow.

The echo of the river claimed and tantalised their hearing even before their eyes alighted on the bright surface, broken only by the boulders placed in the riverbed annually by Frederick Thackeray.

At the water's edge the familiar spectacle on the far side stole Hope's breath and only now did she fully grasp what lay ahead. She stood enchanted; Tarnville, a landmark in the area, within whose shadow she had grown up, was shortly to become her home!

Smiling, Edric nodded towards the house. Hope followed his line of vision. Charles who had taken a flight two days earlier to ensure that all was in readiness for their homecoming was at the window, just as he had been on her first visit. It seemed a lifetime ago since she presented herself at Tarnville but before she had time to grasp the full memory of that fortuitous day which changed her life in so many ways she saw others huddled behind Charles.

"Bell and Peter! And I don't believe it.... Daphne and Billy!" Hope exclaimed, her face instantly infused with excitement. "What're they doing here?" Her head swivelled to Edric for explanation.

"Bell and her husband wanted to witness this long-awaited occasion. So did Daphne and Billy. By the way," Edric said almost casually, "I'm more than a little delighted to tell you that Daphne has agreed to join us at Tarnville as our Housekeeper – and Billy simply can't wait to struggle into a pair of wellingtons and get to grips with the stables."

"Edric! Tell me I'm not dreaming. Tell me it's true."

"It's perfectly true. Daphne still has to work her notice at the Centre, but she'll be free to join us after our marriage."

Hope's voice broke on her retort, "You think of everything – absolutely everything. But when on earth did you arrange all this?"

"Straight after you rang them with our news," he offered simply, making no mention of scheming with Charles to keep her from earshot whilst he made the telephone calls.

After more smiling and waving, Edric nodded meaningfully towards the stepping-stones. "Are you ready?" He glimpsed the emotion he had anticipated. "This is something you need to do on your own," he said gently, "but I'll meet you at the other side." His smile was reassuring. "And after this I promise we'll do everything together." He gave her an encouraging hug before going to the bridge.

Hope's gaze returned to the river, which had the same effervescent brilliance about it as it always had under the spotlight of a late-August sun, the glinting turbulence around the boulders in its path more spectacular than the sparkle of a thousand diamond rings. Hope cast a final glance at those at the library window before gingerly extending her foot towards the first stone.

Finally, and some eight years later than planned, Frederick Thackeray's daughter began to cross the river by way of her stepping-stones, each taking her nearer to the future he had promised.

As her foot reached for the third stone a glorious sensation of peace came over Hope, accompanied by the realisation that she was going home – to Tarnville and the powerful presence of her future husband.

She should quell her excitement or else risk losing her footing. Though it was evident that no recent rain had fallen in the hills to swell the depth and even if she did slip she would come to no real harm – unlike her father on the eve of her 18th birthday. She must not think of that! She should replace the stopper firmly on the bottle containing that particular memory otherwise it would escape to fill her mind and she would indeed lose her balance.

With the illustration of her father's love symbolised forever in granite beneath her feet Hope knew she owed this first crossing to his memory and with care stepped from one stone to the next, unaware that someone who cared greatly about her safety had had Joseph Fearnley wade out the evening before to scrub each surface to roughness with a wire brush.

Hope was about half way across when she heard the well-remembered baritone voice drifting to her hearing in the embrace of the late-summer breeze. Instantly alert, her eyes glistening, she turned intuitively towards the hill to smile at the exquisite memory.

"*Dad*!" Though her arms remained motionless she felt them circling above her head as they had always done at the first sight of her father on his way home each Friday evening. At last – without a shadow of doubt – the sign for which she had prayed! She squeezed her eyes shut to hold in the precious moment. "Thank you Dad," she whispered, the declaration of love heavy in her voice. "Thank you for seeing me safely into the future you promised."

Edric and the others followed the direction of her gaze, their breathing only returning to normal when she turned back to cover the remaining stones and take Edric's extended hand.

As she stepped from granite to the soft, green embankment Edric heard her murmur, "Dad – our dream goes on," and knew that Hope had finally passed out of her past and into her future.

Epilogue

One year later Sir Charles Lurdmayne raised his glass to those congregated in Tarnville's drawing room. "Hope, Edric – all of you gathered here today," he glanced warmly round at the familiar faces, "I should like to present a toast – a very special toast." He paused to permit the gathering to cease their chatter and focus their attention. "To Charity Christina Faith." As they were apt to do, his eyes strayed to Hope who had never looked happier. "May your child be blessed with good health and happiness all the days of her life."

"Charity Christina Faith," the others responded in unison.

Hardly able to contain her joy, Isabel had cradled the baby in her arms since arriving back from the christening but now pressed the infant towards Charles.

"Your grandchild, Sir Charles," she said and then, embarrassed, immediately corrected herself, "I mean your *g-r-e-a-t-grandchild*."

You were perfectly right the first time, he wanted to tell her, but glimpsing the exquisite happiness in the face of the new mother knew he must maintain his silence.

Visibly moved he gazed down at the baby. In the momentary quietness he confessed in words barely claiming more than a whisper, "Our beloved children give back more than a thousand-fold of anything we contribute." Bead-bright eyes looked back from the tiny face in the crook of his arm and in that moment Charles was forced to acknowledge that past actions had finally caught up, though miraculously not to plague but to bring him the undeserved certainty of great happiness.

He painstakingly rearranged the delicate lace shawl before holding the child out for all to see. "I can think of nothing better than the echoes of growing happiness and boisterous childhood activities to bring Tarnville back to life!" Once again there would be the sound of laughter and running feet on the stairs and landings, and imploring demands for games of hide-and-seek and bedtime stories. Then, speaking directly to Hope, "May this child have the sunny disposition of her beautiful mother," whose arms at last would no longer ache to hold the precious contents of the shawls of others.

Charles's attention remained on Hope seated some distance from him, her expression one of total fulfilment. He had been painfully aware of her resigned acceptance, the disciplined mind behind her beautiful face, and how she took up the requisite manner and even the body language after loosing her first child and similarly, if not more so, after becoming separated from Edric. Though now her happiness, complete and obvious for all to see, hovered on the brink of tears.

Laughing at his remark Hope blew him a kiss. The gesture, suggesting something beyond that of gratitude, startled Charles and dragged a restriction to his lungs. Would she do that if she could read his innermost thoughts?

In the belief it might amuse him, Edric had confided Hope's fearfulness that Richard had been her father. How near she had come to stumbling on the truth! Would Hope still blow him a kiss if she knew who she really was? Would her reaction be the same if she knew that she was h-i-s child, his third child – his other daughter whom for the sake of her happiness and the reputation of her mother he had been powerless to acknowledge as being his own?

Unable to prevent himself Charles revisited his memory of that auspicious day when the child fate had ordained he should watch growing up from a distance had from her own choice come knocking on his door. He had been unable to believe his good fortune when Faith Thackeray's child – his child – had chosen to enter his life.

> "Children's children are a crown to the aged,
> and parents are the pride
> of their children."

Proverbs 17:6